ALTER ALTER

ALTER
ALTER

by

Toti O'Brien

ELYSSAR PRESS

REDLANDS, CA

Printed in the United States of America

First Printing, 2023
ISBN 979-8-9853686-8-0

Elyssar Press
175 Bellevue Ave
Redlands, CA 92373

www.ElyssarPress.com

Cover Illustration by Toti O'Brien
Cover design by Stephanie Aoun Bou Karam
Book design and production by Stephanie Aoun Bou Karam

TABLE OF CONTENTS

ACKNOWLEDGMENTS

part 1

CASSANDRA

Cassandra

You looked fine when you left the bus, aiming at the marble bench tucked in a corner of the noisiest, busiest square of our town. Wasn't the place magical, in spite of the rumpus? Oh my, filled with ancient ruins, columns, arches, spilling out a beam of eternity… a blade, sharp, insinuating.

But past glory didn't impress you. You were born there. You had sipped it with milk. While the rest—the traffic, the crowd—took its toll. And those buses, so loaded you didn't miss room, you missed oxygen. So sticky, you'd peel off your skin. Was it why you rushed to the door? You needed air, you would later say.

You did not reach the bench. Too far. You sat on a nearby wall, emanating white coolness and a promise of rest, like an island peering out of your sudden vertigo. That was it, correct, Sandra? A whirlpool of pain sucked you inwards, cut your legs, squeezed your chest. Hurt, though, wasn't in your muscles or viscera. Where was it? Not sure. But you needed something firm to grab on… the bus wouldn't do. And you starved for a swig or two of breathing air, nothing much, a prison cell would suffice. Only, you couldn't be smashed among hips and elbows. Not for the next hour.

That's the time you spent sitting, while the afternoon

morphed into night, bringing a change in colors—darker shades, imperceptibly soothing. Then you simply stood up, took the next bus, went home.

What happened during those sixty minutes? You guessed it but you couldn't name it. Of course, you recognized it. It was not there for the first time. And you knew it wasn't yours by the intensity, so thick it almost detached itself, as it happens when you apply excess paint over something. There's a point when the medium no longer sticks to the surface, and it takes a life of its own.

Now you were the surface and that thing imposed on you, pushed you like a hand pressed against your throat. But it also felt alien, extraneous. "It's not mine, please take it away," you murmured. No one heard you. You looked normal, Cassandra, plain, neutral. And the thing passed, leaving no trace.

As soon as you sat at the dinner table, they told you. Grandma had died. Thousands of miles away while you sat on stone, unaware. Well, of course. Those things require perfect ignorance or they just can't occur. Grandma, right. Slowly, her agony had leaked through your cells in a rated version, like an echo, a reflection of sorts.

Still, she had reached you. She had pulled you off the bus, sat you down as if for a sacred function, a wake. You were named after her. Is it why? You didn't especially love her. You had seen little of her, didn't have a deep, strong…

None of it matters, Sandra, in these kinds of designs. You should have known by then. Caring, fondness aren't the point. It's not love traveling through the ether, scattering time and space, winning over gravity and matter. Not the love we believe we feel.

She had nailed you to the wall, as white as the grave she was about to rejoin. If you'd wish for me to tell you what for, what she had to pass down, I can. But there is no need, sweetie. You will find out.

There will be other deaths, Cassandra. Always far away, at a distance. You will lose your mind, turn in circles like a caged animal. You'll pretend not to know what's going on until you'll be tired of pretending. Over time you'll learn how to stop your frenzy a tad sooner, sit, breathe, whisper your mantra: "Please, take it away."

A bit later, the phone will ring. A week later, the mail will reach you and you'll check the date, the hour, the minute, to discover the unfailing coincidence.

You will wonder about what they'll want, those random deceased of yours. Not the dearest, the closest… love isn't the deal, we said. You will find out, no worry.

How you'll miss it, when there'll be no more virtual agonies left, no more calls from the trespassing zone. Then, the real gloom will begin.

Of course, this isn't all. There are words, written, spoken. There are objects, the scariest.

Like those earrings you stole, for instance, and then you never wore. You… You were on a bus, correct? Once again. On your own, you were touring the Black Forest in order to see the wildlife, the large raptors you adored. Eagles. Hawks. Dark. Huge. And the tall trees. Castles. Medieval towns. Mighty peaks.

At one stop, an Alpine resort, you ambled through the gift shop while waiting for the bus to refuel. Among edelweiss and beer steins, you saw those plastic trinkets… there, a pair of ear-clips—boy and girl in hiking gears, pretty boots, felt hats, cheerful smiles. You took them in your hand and looked for a clerk, but none was in sight. Now the bus was boarding. Nervously, you gazed around. Then you closed your fist.

You did not wear them once, didn't even know why you picked them, as they fit neither your age nor your style. You had to have them, that's all. You stored them in the safest fold of your wallet and you looked at them, often. They reassured you. They grounded you, so to speak, though they were gaily climbing, one foot up, stick in hand.

One day, you were climbing as well. His stairs. Some stairs leading to one of the apartments where he randomly abided, where you randomly met him. Now and then.

Unhappy as unhappy can be. Younger than he was. Way more stupid… Forgive me, Cassandra.

Unhappy, because you were in love and you couldn't end it, while he wasn't and never would be. In your dumbness you understood that much. Still, you climbed those and many other stairs, whenever, wherever, just to gather whatever crumbs he had to spare.

And you called it love, so let me repeat. There's a fundamental confusion you need to clarify. Yes, love is involved in what tripped you on those steps. But another quality of it, can't you see?

You were going up the wooden stairs, so typical of our capital town—the ancient matrix, playing lives on its grid— when you suddenly stopped, petrified. Watch! Your earrings! Another step and you'd trample them. You got mad at yourself. Can't I look after my stuff? Why do I carry things I should keep safe, at home? See? I drop them, I wreck them, I lose them.

Contrite, cautious, you reached down to rescue

your toys. Too late. The girl's foot was broken. The left one.
Strange! You had fractured yours many times. It was your
Achilles' tendon, your weakness. You stood still, dumbstruck
for a second, then you opened your purse to hide your treasure,
broken and all. And you stopped dead, again. Your earrings
were in your wallet. Those you had found were doubles, a mock
pair, an echo, a reflection.

No, they weren't sold in every supermarket in town.
You had seen a pair only, in a forlorn, remote little village.
They had struck you because of their extreme oddity, sheer
uniqueness. Now they had produced aliases, jujus, kachina
dolls—but with a mutation, an injured foot, yours. Your blood
slowed its flow, wearily staggering through your veins. You were
suddenly afraid to reach the next landing, ring at his door. After
all, the girl was hurt while the boy… what could it possibly
mean?

You tell me, Cassandra.

Other things will multiply, split, appear, vanish. You'll
get used to it. Let it pass. Do not talk about it, no need. Nothing
shows. You look average, plain. Sometimes a bit lost.

Incantation

When did it start? Oh, boy. Retrospectively, the last few months melt in a blur, perhaps because of the weather. Summer temperatures unusually lasting, bleeding into fall, must have dimmed her awareness of the passing season.

She, believe it or not, has missed Halloween. On a Tuesday, and she has worked until late. Then she has played the piano and lost track of time, finally crashing on the couch with a book. Meanwhile, unusual outside animation has peered through. She has thought of a party nearby, lots of guests arriving, departing. Quite surprising on a weekday, and yet not a problem. She has barely registered the noise.

But the next day her brain has connected the dots. "It's November, already," she has sighed. Right! And yesterday was… She has missed it for the first time.

She must have spotted the thing around Halloween. Nothing strange. The house is full of spiders. They are harmless and she lets them live. They are elegant, too. She loves the fluid motion of their nimble legs, like fingers at work on a keyboard. In the shower, she casually observes a few specimens, quiet, intent at their dance. She doesn't bother removing them.

But this one, perched high in a corner, looks weird.

Funny shape, made of segments. Wait, isn't it normal? She remembers from her school days: cephalothorax and abdomen. Spiders' bodies articulate in the center. Then why didn't she, ever… This guy must be bigger than usual. Yes, much bigger.

She has chanced upon a huge mega-spider, and a slight shiver goes down her spine. "Should I worry? Is it poisonous?" Then her apprehension dissolves. It must be innocuous. Only, an extra large size.

It grows every day. Every shower. To be honest, sometimes it looks larger and sometimes it doesn't. Monday morning it does, and her agitation resumes. "Will it stop?" The day after, the thing appears to have shrunken. She starts doubting her own objectivity. She'd need something… a term of comparison.

Here! Another spider shows up. This new one is average. An oblong shape, that's all. No waistline, no upper and lower body are discernable. This guy perfectly represents the category. It is pale, a gray shade.

While the giant is shiny, pitch black. Once or twice, she has seen it capture its prey. Strange behavior… if she ever studied it in class, she remembers nothing. First, the prey (little fly? Small bug, inconspicuous, like a speck of dust) is immobilized in place, paralyzed through the spires of a quasi-invisible web. Then, its hunter comes close and performs a trick that looks frantic—perhaps due to the number of limbs at work, overlapping like fingers racing through octaves in a mad, rapturous crescendo.

Yes, the predator paws its prey nimbly, skillfully, like a potter throwing a vase, a cook stuffing some bird, a very quick knitter. Or a prestidigitator playing magic, the audience mute, mesmerized. The whole scene, suspended in space and in time, both precipitous and infinitely slow, has a trance-like quality. She is charmed. A bit scared, as well.

Now the prey, wrapped in a tight cocoon (ah! that's what the hocus-pocus was for) looks like a protuberance, like a loose outgrowth of the hunter, which has come even closer. Will it glue the victim to itself, then devour it? And how?

She doesn't see it happen. Not for lack of curiosity, but she needs to get dressed. Analyzing the feeding habits of spiders is not today's plan. Or tomorrow's. She is wasting her time.

Later, though, she can't avoid noticing that her mate has swollen, like the snake that gobbled an elephant in one of her children's books. Did it gulp its booty altogether? Without breaking it down? Must have.

Then, it goes back to normal. Approximately. Back to normal, she thinks.

She is witnessing the prey-catching, prey-petting more often. Maybe, a kind of lent ended and a feasting season began. She is dazzled by the motions. The creature seems to have more limbs than it should. Is she counting sixteen? Paired, like for a double-stringed guitar? Wait, are the spiders two? Why didn't she guess it? Joined, attached. Perhaps making love. Wouldn't it be something? She should get her glasses. A step stool?

Please! She needs to get dressed. She is late.

It is only one spider. It has shrunk to size once again. As it stays still, one morning, she carefully numbers its legs. They are eight. Their fast movements give an illusion of quantity, just an optical lure. When they fumble the unfortunate

captive, they have a dizzying effect on her nerves. There is
a slight obscenity in what looks like erotic foreplay to the
incumbent merging, the mysterious communion she has never
managed to watch.

But, of course, the beast doesn't know that a curious
eye violates its privacy. Shielded by the magic circle it wrought, it
safely dwells in its universe, a small galaxy attracting new satellites,
following unavoidable gravity laws.

She has noticed that it frequently bends at the waistline,
hanging loosely at the bottom of its master web. Doubled over,
it draws a letter V in the air, coarsely traced in black. V for
victory, its favorite pose. It looks ominous.

Truly, such a big creature (will the anomalous
growth ever stop? should she worry?) shouldn't hang in her
shower. Right, she never cared for an insect-free bathroom,
but proportions do matter. This thing is so bold, it becomes
invasive. Sharing quarters is now inconvenient. Embarrassing.
Obviously, she should dispose of the intruder. What
is she waiting for? Get rid of the spider. Only this one, correct,
which seems to own the place, bossy, uncaring of limits.
Indecent, that is. "I will chase it," she mutters while she grabs
her bathrobe. Then, another thought tickles her—she should
get a stool and her glasses. She should look at the monster for
once, really close. How ridiculous. Go. Go. Get dressed.
"I must kill it," she intones every morning. But she
vaguely feels it isn't time yet. First, she'd like… Can't she admit
she is enthralled? Why are things spooky so charming, you can't
help another good look before parting? Why are monsters so
attractive you can't let them go?
Not attractive, no. Intriguing. She must…

There is something about the weather, this year. Summer temperatures bleeding into fall—did she read it somewhere? Was it a month ago? There is something. Stuck. Trapped, or else… She won't miss Thanksgiving. That is merely impossible. Almost turkey time, right? Oh, those birds flooding the supermarket, tightly shrouded in white, swaddled like newborns of bygone eras… No, not babies. They are corpses. She will not miss Thanksgiving, alas. And yet, will the weather…

Until, suddenly, a chill kisses her back inside the darn shower. God, isn't this pleasant? She nervously opens the faucet, craving, yes, the sweet comfort of hot water. Is this shiver from cold? Correct. Cold, cold, cold! Foam is lathering on her skin like a shawl of snow. Looking at her goose-bumped limbs, she hugs herself strong and tight, uncaring of what might still hover above her. Winter will chase the spider, she is sure. It will put it to sleep, like a princess pricked by a spindle.

Cold has come at last, like a parcel that was retained at customs for no reason, no reason at all, then finally released. It will cast a spell on the spider. A long-postponed spell.

Spell

Our talk briskly interrupted…

Almost. Isn't there an aura, a slight anticipation to those fits? Did I miss it? No, but it was precipitous. I couldn't truly see margins, say when normality ceased, quiet was shattered… I mean when "before" (the thing you promptly start missing) fell apart and "after" began, irrevocable.

You turned towards the wall, your voice tapering down at mid-sentence, and I knew. It's a matter of vibrations, of waves. Nothing esoteric, no. Electrical. Something so concrete you could transfer it onto a graph, measure it with numbers. No doubt, an extraneous pulse had started shaking you, infiltrating your own, altering your substance, also affecting me with a surge of emergency reactions. Danger. Danger. Danger.

You were bracing yourself against something I couldn't see, but it seemed to rapidly invade each one of your cells. Your whole body tensed up, almost compressed itself, getting smaller, wirier. Your thin, slender body now a fist, as if someone had hit you in the stomach, or you had sucked in your middle to skip the blow. As your guts sank in, your pelvis tilted forwards. Your feet moved apart, knees bent, head down, arms extended, open palms fending off… what? I had no clue. And you might have been also in the dark, busy fighting the unknown. Who cared

 Cassandra

for definitions, anyway? Evil can do without them. We should annihilate it, in fact, before it self-explains.

Then what happened? Why in hell did I think I could help? Why was I so confident? Without a second thought, I hooked my arms into yours, armpits locking armpits. I tried to weigh you down—for the thing to be unable to lift you, drag you away. I leaned against you like a lid, like a shield, for the thing you were facing to meet the dull obstacle of my back, opaque, ignorant. I must have naively assumed if no frontal surface, no tender vital organs were at reach, neither yours nor mine, evil would have no chance. It would have to retreat, after blowing as much of its fiery breath as it wished. Let it hiss and sigh. We would stand it. Our backs would be stones. Mountain ridges. Smooth, impervious, ice-covered slopes.

Why did I feel invincible? The thing was after *you*, was it, therefore… But how could I be sure it wouldn't shift targets and attack me instead? I apparently deemed that our interlocked posture would protect me as well. Oh, the irresponsible optimist. The arrogant daredevil, incurable.

Truth is, my courage wasn't original. Only a derivation. You inspired me and I rose to the occasion. Solidarity spontaneously bloomed. See, it's your determination, dear heart, that made me strong. You, so small, yet fiercely claiming your tiny, tiny self.

As I breathed, letting air fall into my calves, gather into my heels like lead, nail me to the ground… As my own breathing steeled me, I felt calm, almost drowsy. I couldn't sense the storm you perceived—only a sort of residue, a side or rather an aftereffect, as if I were present and absent, with you and elsewhere, somehow misaligned in space and in time. Wait.

Had the opposite occurred? Had you slipped away? Forward?
Backward?

Did it matter? I could feel, I said, something. A strange
dizziness, my ears ringing, roaring, my skull faintly expanding
with the slight rarefaction that comes with altitude. But my
increasing alertness was inversely proportional to yours, as your
muscles slowly began to release. Imperceptibly, you slumped
over me, your mass softer and heavier. So to speak. You
weighed nothing. And yet, you were so strong.

I let you drive home without comments. We both
feigned serenity.

I had witnessed a couple of crises before, but they were
so light and so brief I had wondered, afterwards, if I had just
imagined them. I had asked nothing. You had not volunteered
explanations.

This fit had seemed so violent that I was urged to act,
and yet neither of us felt a need for verbal acknowledgment.
No, we weren't embarrassed. On the contrary, a mute
agreement lingered in the air. Shush. Move on. Maybe, I secretly
hoped a time for clarification would come. But wasn't my wish
sheer curiosity? I should drop it, then.

From my window, I watched you enter your car, start
the engine, take off. I kept looking until you turned the corner.
What a miniature perfect warrior.

During the night, I felt weird. Perhaps lonely. I awoke
before dawn, turned the lamp on and then off, again. As I tried
to resume sleep, a nightmare assailed me. The thing—whatever
had come by earlier—loomed over my head. Did it want *me*?
Well, I wasn't scared. I grabbed some of my rage (always carried
a load close at hand) and threw a fistful its way, like a bunch

of mud. Now I felt a real urge to speak. "I'll kill you," I said
spitefully. In my sleep, again and again: "I'll kill you, I'll kill
you," until morning broke.

*

I see you in black and white. There's no trace of colors.
Don't know when, don't know why they have dimmed out.
You are in a room with low seats, pillows, carpets, one of those
kind-of-nurseries for the old and insane, ill and vulnerable,
meant to be cozy and just horrifying instead. Impersonal,
meaningless, soulless. A true blueprint of hell. You sit on a
small chair or maybe on a pile of cushions, and you have a toy
in your right hand. You have grabbed it out of despair, to hold
on to something, get anchored. You are shaking the toy and
yourself with the rocking motion we (all) resume when in deep
discomfort, lullabying our bodies as amniotic waters used to.
    The toy that you have found, I see, is a tambourine.
A mistake. It shouldn't be here. Those cute rattles of metal it
sports have sharp margins. Also, fingers can be trapped inside
the slits of the frame. Momentarily, though, the thing seems
to soothe you. To amuse you, perhaps. You are lifting it high,
unconsciously mimicking childhood partying or dancing. I
can't bear it, when time plays its tricks on you. It becomes a
whirlpool, a maelstrom. An abyss. Twists you. Swallows you up.
    Time has betrayed you more than it did others. You
seem to have lived so long, and so much in vain.
    As I reach the exit door, you stretch your right arm. Is
it a goodbye? Maybe it isn't. You hold up the tambourine as if
it were the moon… and the moon is your mirror. I can tell by
your gaze, as blank as the disk you are watching, yet imbued

with a shade of panic, regret.

Wait, wait. I can't leave you in such anguish, in the company of a piece of dead skin. I am better than a musical instrument and have filed, at this point, all of my cutting edges.

I rush towards you, ease the toy out of your fist, hug you tight, sit you on my knees, comfort you and then sing you to sleep. That is when I realize the absence of colors. Shouldn't it have alerted me? Rung a bell? I am reminded we are in the same room, but there is a separation in time. You have moved faster than me. I have sluggishly followed. Or was I delayed. Maybe, it is the other way around. Maybe I have fled and left you behind. Mea culpa.

There is a gap in time. It is small, but it opens an unsurpassable chasm and I am sucked away. Or you are, and I lose my balance, my arms clumsily extended, my palms groping emptiness. I tilt forwards. My knees meet the ground.

Incubus and Your Lips

Incubus came, as usual, during an afternoon nap. In the night I hadn't had enough rest. Still, I shouldn't have… Right. But tiredness numbed me, and I imprudently fell asleep on the couch.

As it was inevitable (can't doze off at weird hours, for short times, just can't) a mess happened with my REM, which seeped rather disastrously into the aura of my wake. Therefore, partially conscious, quite aware of my surroundings and self, I had to fight ghosts that normally remain sealed in the domain of dreams.

Not for me, sadly. I suffer from a mental disorder called "hypnagogic state." It has been described for centuries, but its causes are still unknown and it is incurable. One gets used to it, I guess, as I did.

Incubus is the king of this shady region, which he single-handedly rules. I say "he" because after years of gender fluctuations he picked up a definite male identity, and he stuck with it. He is unkind by nature. He is also predictable.

I heard him enter the room by the front door, noisily and with violent intentions, as always. But this time I decided to put fear aside. I was semi-blind, paralyzed, as the syndrome implies, so I did the only thing I could do. Wait for him.

Without fear, which was quite surprising. I waited as I would have for a lover.

I don't know what caused me to take the plunge, reverse roles, attempt something so antithetic to my prime impulse. It just happens, sometimes. We get saturated. We hit the bottom and then we bounce upward. The world tilts. We cartwheel, ta-da! Sort of miracles, prodigies that we can't summon at will. They only occur by themselves.

To the point. He came to lie beside me as it was his habit, but rather than shrugging away I sort of welcomed him. I even managed to shift my unresponsive limbs in order to niche against him. I tried hard as I could to hone my weakened senses, grab at least flashes of what he looked like. In his presence, alas, all is awfully blurred.

Semi-blind, I told you. Still. I caught glimpses. He was neither ugly nor handsome. Neither old nor young. "Average" is an accurate way to describe him. I had grasped the concept before, in spite of my dulled awareness. My conclusion, the most truthful depiction I could provide for the unnamed, the impossible, had always been the same.

He is common. Mediocre and banal. Undefined, like those identikits of alleged criminals only based on faint memories, sketched a zillion times to finally resemble no one. Or else everyone. Right. He looks like, feels like everyone or no one. Hair? Light brown, dark blond, hazel. Eyes? The same. Face? A kind of round square. Built? Robust but not fat. Tall? A bit more than me, I think. Nothing noticeable.

I know. From such a description, common sense would conclude he doesn't exist. Certainly, such vagueness suggests he's a fruit of my imagination. That he admittedly is. I have hypnagogia. Incubus is a hallucination of mine. A real one.

And that is the point that common sense (which namely shares Incubus' plainness) may not grasp… real hallucinations exist. Quite a bit, just enough to scare the hell out of you. Unless you decide, one day, that you have had it.

As I did, correct, when I started to make love to the monster sprung out of my mind to come crush my chest, make my muscles spasm. I decided he might as well offer something else. Why not? Though, of course, I couldn't find anything pleasant about him, I decided to bend in his favor, be unconditionally appreciative. Enjoy.

Now, here's the thing. I am reporting it because I'm sure it is meaningful. As soon as we touched, he started talking, speaking what to me was an incomprehensible tongue, mostly mumbling to himself in a bizarre monologue. But he exceptionally pronounced English words to which I listened carefully, as I sensed they were attempts to be urbane, to communicate. Nothing of the kind had happened before. His response to my sympathetic attitude, then, was surely positive, better than I had even hoped.

We made love. See, I knew he'd go for my body first thing, no escape, and he'd make a mess of it. So, I guessed, unequivocally orienting the meeting—the collision—sex-wise might be my best chance. Why did this simple truth take so long to emerge? Years, decades… With the impoverished means at my disposition (my reduced sensorimotor capacities), I bravely took the lead. I was strengthened by my despair, determined, furious. And we had a well-paced, strong, intense intercourse.

I went for his dick with no courtesy, no hesitation. For sure, this is what I mostly recall—getting hold of that part of him, the most concrete, most tangible. I remember his dick in my hand, my mouth, my vagina. I believe I could see it… No doubt, I could feel it. I'm not saying that it was spectacular. Not even remarkable. If I should define his sexual organ, I could only say "average." And you're not surprised.

Did it matter? Course not. His dick fucked me hard and I got an orgasm. Well, an average one I suppose, but decent, straightforward. Then, an orgasm is an orgasm, and it ultimately awoke me. Which means that, though I found myself on the couch where I knew I was, aware of what had just occurred, now I could see with clarity. I could move at my wish and Incubus, finally, had dissolved.

I was well, for once, relaxed because of my recent pleasure. Maybe I needed it. For sure it was welcomed. It was the first time that a crisis had been good for something, brought me something else than panic and helpless cramps. The first time that I was able to use it at my sheer advantage. Quite a victory, I thought.

I flashed back to the sex I just had. Did I like it, besides the quick dopamine discharge? A few molecules still trickled down my spine. Maybe another minute or two of peaceful waves would seep through my limbs.

Did I like it? I couldn't quite answer. I knew why I had wanted sex. It had been my way to divert attack. As an immobilized victim, I had scarce alternatives. Mine had been a raw, impulsive act of defense, with successful results. Is it called good sex? I guess it was average. Was I satisfied? Something seemed missing, but I couldn't pinpoint it.

Did you say it is obvious? Did you say the point is that Incubus "wasn't real"? Well, he was while we fucked. He gave me a real orgasm. That must be worth something. Would I like to do this again? No.

The night after, I dreamed of you. It happens. It's rare. I have known you for a long time. In fact, about the same time that I've known my Incubus.

Truly, Incubus first appeared shortly after I met you, after I fell in love and we dated and it didn't work. I remember that I left town for a week, trying to put you off my mind. I went to a beach town up North, a shore with cold wind and strong tides. While I slept in a nondescript single bed, the unknown, weird thing struck me, drenching me with terror and sweat. Then, I called it "the hands," because I just perceived deadly fingers trying to choke me, to kill me. I said nothing about it, and I didn't learn what the phenomenon was until much, much later. It took me even longer to adapt, make it viable.

As I said, I rarely dream about you. But, each time, the dream is peculiar and leaves me… It is like an omen, a prophecy. Only, saying nothing that will happen or should. And still meaningful, like a sign. Like a plant that never blooms, and then suddenly… Like a lunar eclipse. Rather, a solar one.

Eclipse? Oh my! Vision, in case. Apparition. Your presence is so vivid, detailed, it invades my cells and then lingers. But you're not a hallucination, no way. You're a dream from which I neatly, suddenly awake and reality is sharp, distinct, other. There is no blurred zone.

They are complex, my dreams with you inside. Long travels and frightening crowds, strange adventures, time stilling itself or else fleeing, endless waits and mad rushes. An incredible depth of feelings, so intricate that I can't unscramble them, or maybe I don't want to. They are too enmeshed in all strata of my soul and body. They comprehend innocence, hope and youth as well as disenchantment, resignation, despair. They are thick, these feelings that come as your escort. They sum up all my life, perhaps more. More than I can describe, just what I can handle. Perhaps.

Please, don't get me wrong. I like them.

Those dreams… they are coherent. Among them, I mean. Do you see the similarities? The rich texture, elaborate scripts, plus the ending, which is regularly and unmistakably a failed beginning. The beginning of something that the dream's end interrupts, then the next dream resumes or else restarts from zero, to get still no further than the embryonic stage where the action, alas, aborts.

True, the storylines vary, especially because our acquaintance spans over a lifetime. We have gone through many things and we have changed. The dreams mirror such an evolving landscape. But in summary the script could be simplified, unified as follows: dreams of you invariably end on your lips. On the very surface of them, with no pressure, certainly with no tongue involved.

On your lips where, I guess, I put mine although it happens casually, I'd say. Spontaneously, unconsciously. It is often or always a goodbye kiss we're exchanging. There could be an intention of sex, but I'll never know.

I will never know. I doubt I'll ever get hold of your dick in dreams, as I grabbed my Incubus' penis. There's not enough substance. No rage and no hunger. There's no room for strategy or plans, revenge or reward. No threat, no battle, no winner. There is no reality, no, not even the scrap that hallucinations provide.

Dreams of you are the epitome of the impossible, of the longing that can't be fulfilled, the incurable nostalgia for things that were not, but we absurdly, pathetically think could have been. And we don't let go. Dreams of you celebrate the intangible.

And still, it isn't true. See, I can perfectly describe the feel of your lips, both tenuous and burning, delicate and yet deep. Ethereal. Indelible. I'd sure give my kingdom for that simple touch, if I had one.

I would give anything for another dream of your lips.

Do not ask if I'd like for you to come back. Be my guest.

Annunciation

Sleep paralysis strikes at dawn, like an earthquake. I sit up in bed and that's as far as I go, my limbs and my senses seized by an alien force I can't oppose, no matter how hard I try. Frantically, my brain spits orders. Stand up. Open your eyes. Look. Speak. Scream. Usually, my body follows directions. When I am awake, I mean. Also in dreams, more or less. Sleep paralysis cruelly severs neuron from muscle. It is painful. Exhausting.

Sleep paralysis feels like someone hitting, pushing, slapping, shoving me around. I understand no one is here, but the intrusion is so thick, so palpable, instinct begs my reaction. There's an enemy, it says, yet more dangerous as it can't be identified. Fight or flee, instinct insists. I can't manage either. This is one of those instances when you have to find a third way, an unheard-of solution. At least try.

Today it's biting me like a pack of wild beasts… the campfire extinct while I slumbered, I didn't hear them come. Now I feel their warm breath on my neck, the raspy touch of a tongue, a paw landing on me. Gee, how many! In the dark, everything is called legion. I am tossed around like a toy ball, a puppet, by this thing I know doesn't exist, yet is proving me wrong.

My brain wants me to speak. It sends words to my mouth. Like a wounded trooper crawling uphill, soiled flag in hand, I wish to carry on but my tongue, palate, larynx do not comply. Until a sudden thought gives me supernatural powers, causing my phonating organs to obey without further ado.

"Are you a ghost?" I sigh. I can't recognize my voice, twisted, undecipherable. Darn! The enemy will not understand. Let's try again. This must be clarified, for god's sake. "Are you a ghost?" I need to know. I must, but…

Now a terror, one more, makes me shiver. I am speaking in English. What are the chances… The idiom I mindlessly picked seems unsuitable. Arbitrary. Peripheral. Should I have spoken Sanskrit? Ancient Greek? Latin? Hebrew? Something more dignified, universal. Esperanto?

Wait! An answer is whispered close by. Very soft, quasi inaudible, yet unmistakable. Not a noise. An utterance. "Yep," the thing has just said. I'm on the right track, then! See, language isn't a problem. A ghost, like a god (do they belong together?) must be able to understand across languages. Above particularities, I hope.

Feverishly, my brain figures out the next question. Quick! This is an emergency! Mouthing a new sentence, I swear, costs me an arm and a leg. And the sound of it, boy! How can the thing guess? "Are you mean?" I am finally able to say. My tongue is a whale stuck on sand. There's a pause, then a neat, clear answer. "No." Do ghosts lie? They don't. I would like to ask some more, but my mouth is full of lead and the effort to articulate superhuman.

Look! My fingers seem to recover some strength. Slowly, I take my ghost's hands. Do I? I have grabbed something beside and something behind me, like in Varsovienne position. The thing—I should not call it so, since it has admitted personality—the ghost is around, below, above, inside me… We coincide. I can't truly make out my own edges as long as I am hit, shoved, tossed, pushed to and fro.

At least, I've learned that no meanness is meant. I am less scared, more trustful. This was destined to be, like a perfect storm. I believe the ghost is no more responsible for this incident than I am.

I hold his hands. His? That is how I feel, and feeling is all I have at the moment. I am feeling his hands, boldly, intensely. Lovingly… what do I have to lose? Lovingly. Would you object? On what basis? Lovingly, and then rather pleasantly. At each blow against my cheek, my back or my chest, causing me to lose balance and vacillate, I squeeze him with a pulse, a secret sign of complicity—as if saying, "here it comes, darling, let's dance." We swing to the right, to the left, with the agility of two drunks on a ship in the midst of a terrible gale. But I am starting to like it. Something is going on, something good, between the ghost and me.

Then it stops, as abruptly as it started. Just routine, that's how sleep paralysis works. She has left my body. She? Correct. Now I can see her. My eyes have recovered functionality. Gee, I love the sense of sight. How have I missed it, for the last minutes-that-felt-like-eternity. A blue shine surrounds her, overwhelming, electric, so bright that I'm afraid to go blind again. The blue coils up in ovals, tall medallions festooned with small puffy clouds, like vapor, like foam. They arise from my bed, from my body. Slightly askew, they overlap and spiral, reaching for the sky. I mean the ceiling.

She is encased in one of those rings like an ivory miniature on a cameo. Her slim torso and limbs are brushing the frame, spilling out a bit, as if she intended to escape. Leisurely, without haste, ascending, I'm sure she will disappear as all visions do. Saints, virgins…

She is no virgin. I can tell by the look on her face. Young enough, but she knows it all. Slightly blasé. Quite pretty, with long curled black hair. She isn't me, though we look kind of alike. She isn't me, alas. She is going. Lord! I need to know more about her before she dissolves into ether. I have an itch, a feeling, an urge that I can't explain.

She is young, also antique. Wait, kind of old-fashioned, I mean. She must have been a famous artist's model, I'm sure, long ago. Now what? She can't just vanish. I should, must… Here! My mouth spits two words, "You? Are?"

"Sylvia." I'm awed, for some reason, and I feel compelled to say more. "Plath?" How stupid is this? She isn't Plath. She doesn't look like her at all. But I wanted to keep her around for another second, so I exhaled whatever first came to mind. She is shaking her head with a strange expression, both annoyed and sad. Meaning, "Of course, not. How could I?" Or else, "Really, don't you know who I am?"

She melts into the blue, which also starts fading.

I am awake, and totally wasted as expected. Sleep paralysis leaves you in a state of extreme prostration. If I close my eyes, I see crates, neatly aligned, filled with tons of blueberries. I remember blueberry fields, a nice sight, and yet incomparable with the splendid cobalt ellipses of a minute ago.

Well, they are gone. I need to get up. As I reach for the

alarm clock on my bed stand, as I grab it and watch it, I freeze. It has changed shape, has it? It is flattened, hinged, opens up like a book. And I missed my waking hour. I'm terribly late.

Wait. I am still hallucinating. Sleep paralysis does it. Aftershocks, that's all. Courage, courage. Sit up, turn around, touch your feet against cold, sobering tiles. The alarm clock is its usual self and I am on time.

But I rush to the computer and look for Sylvia, any Sylvia. Her face still so vivid… I bet she's close, still. We have just danced. We have held hands. Did a Sylvia die? Last night? Last-night-long-time-ago? Who is Sylvia? Perhaps that's a fake identity. Did she lie? I believed ghosts didn't. Will she come back? I feel I was her last station. Maybe, this is what her expression meant—her disappointed lassitude, while she smudged herself into smoke.

My limbs ache. I am an empty shell, my body a sheer vacancy of flesh and bone.

Bon voyage, my soul.

 Cassandra

Apocalypse

The night when the world ended, I thought I was sleepless. The day had been especially torrid and darkness, alas, didn't bring relief. Truly, I must have dozed off intermittently, as the voice of the police took me by surprise.

They were booming away from their choppers. With all the windows open, I could hear them as if they were shouting in my face. I was used to it. In summertime they came often. Fires broke out. Houses, offices, stores deserted for vacations attracted seasonal burglars. Ordinary people were prone to random attacks of madness, due to the high temperatures.

In a daze, I waded into the kitchen, where I noticed something strange—besides the officers yelling. A glare. I looked up. The ceiling seemed taller. As I probed the wall for the light switch, I stopped, realizing I didn't need turning it on. A cold, eerie luminosity peered from above. Somehow, the roof had become… transparent? I held my breath.

I didn't. On the contrary, I started to hyperoxygenate, getting dizzier by the minute. I could see through, could I? Pure and simple. Through opaque, solid matter, walls, tiles. They had not vanished. Their appearance hadn't changed, except they no longer blocked my vision. Everything had become… what, porous?

Not entirely. I mean things were somehow veiled, indistinct. But I saw the helicopters, no doubt. Three of them, lowering in rapid succession, almost level with my roof, my sheer, my inexistent-although-still-existent roof. Wait. Now, how was it possible? They were painted a gaudy turquoise, almost festive. What was that? Were they real or was a movie being filmed? Was it some kind of advertising?

Stop, please. What was wrong with me? Why would the color of the darn things matter under such absurd circumstances? Hadn't all parameters of reality shifted? I mean, of perception. Hadn't I stepped into a sort of mirage? Stop. Listen, would I?

I could hear their words so clearly, I said, they seemed etched in stone, so near they seemed intimate, confidential, notwithstanding their volume and in spite of the fact they were uttered by a sheriff or such.

"Alert! Someone in the house is in pain. Someone is in danger. We have detected a persistent lament. Someone needs immediate attention. We are going to search the house. Someone might need to be flown to the nearest hospital. Alert!"

I rushed towards the guest bedroom, separated from the kitchen by a small den. Only a few steps away, but another prodigy delayed me, hindering my impetus. For sure, things were happening or had happened with matter. Now it was getting denser, I thought. But I was too hurried, too anxious for a full, correct understanding. Maybe, time was dilating instead. Briefly…

It wasn't brief. On the contrary. Slowly, against huge resistance, as if the air had solidified into a deadly cobweb, I tried to proceed, my body stretched forward, arms swimming in a desperate crawl. But my feet, firmly attached to the floor, held me back.

Meanwhile, I scorched my lungs with screams, "Arthur! Arthur! Arthur!," as I called my young bro who must be in trouble, no doubt. He must have overdosed, my nightmare, my permanent fear, jesus christ, call the cops. Well, no need. Thank god, they were already here.

Then I came to my senses. I recalled my brother had passed, clean and sober, in his mature age. He had moved from the guest room, the house, many decades before. He was dead anyway. So what was… I had slipped into a wrinkle of time. Retrograded. Regressed.

Meanwhile, the air surrounding me had loosened. Truly, I didn't know what had happened, but I crashed headlong against the door, which swung open, and momentum made me fall on my knees. Right on the bedside rug, soft enough. My hands met the mattress, grabbing it for support. I rested my head upon it, exhausted.

The odor sneaked through my nostrils, thin, subtle. A faint scent of moisture and dust, both brittle and damp, full of contradictions. A smell of enclosure and past, both cozy and unsettling. Darkness here was perfectly dense. I could not see through walls. As a matter of fact, I saw nothing, my face niched, indented, buried into the bed. Then a hand touched mine.

Two hands. Not affectionately. Reassuring, that's all. Gently, but with a kind of remoteness. Very calming, especially since I had recognized them. By the size, exceedingly small, the shape, strangely conical, the long nails. Most of all, the skin texture, which for each of us is unique, unmistakable, as fingerprints prove.

"Elsie," I sighed. "Elsie, Elsie…" A compulsion, a commandment made it clear I should repeat each word thrice. No voice answered. I couldn't hear breathing. The hands replied, though, palms against my palms, fingers interlacing, vivid, sensitive. And yet something was odd in their placidness, their cool, their lack of urgency.

Then I recalled my sis lived across the planet, could travel no more and we had not seen each other, in fact…

Then I was back in the kitchen, standing still by the table, blinking at the glare, aggravated by the hovering presence of the police, yet feigning indifference. My stare vacuously paused on a vase of withered marigolds, parsed with blue myositis so small…

I considered a glass of water. The fridge was behind me. I should turn, but it seemed vital for me to hold the edge of the table, and my head ached for stillness.

My head ached because the cops were deafening me, as they kept hammering their warning like a broken record.

My son! An old ulcer pain stabbed my stomach. Was I finally awake? I had recovered the present tense. Present! Present! Once more, I rushed towards the guest bedroom that indeed was my son's room, and my son must be in trouble, and I had missed it. I had missed him, stuck in past confusion and sibling revivals.

My son! His room, movies, music, posters, clothes, old

 Cassandra

bikes, engine parts, random electronics, half smoked cigarettes, childhood toys, lost wallets, torn backpacks, leather jackets and charms, bongs and pocket knives, neckties and nail clippers.

I walked into the now-familiar space, lit by the mild, sweet, natural blush of dawn, and I murmured his name three times as per superior orders.

But I wasn't looking for him, well knowing he was gone—a grown-up living on his own. I just hadn't finished emptying the nest, having had other fish to fry. No urge, the task could be postponed. Good for me! My lack of alacrity in tidying the house and clearing my son's possessions had turned to my advantage, because now I curled onto the bed, surrounded by the most delightful of messes—an encyclopedia of life in its wondrous minutia, the most futile, the dearest. A festival of remembrance.

I was looking at nothing. Things came to my eyes at their pace, dancing graciously. I even managed, perhaps, another fragment of sleep.

The voice of the police awoke me. I could hear the words neatly, perfectly, spat like balls of stone from the mouth of a cannon, blown like poisoned arrows, thrown at me like grenades.

"Someone in the house is in serious pain. Someone needs to be succored. We are coming!" Were they? Why hadn't they yet? Clearly, they were fake. A projection. Advertising. A trick. A portent, or miracle, or mystery. Unsolved. Unsolvable.

And I shouldn't care, because it meant nothing. No action needed to be taken. Not even a lesson was there to be learned. I should go back to my own bed and get proper rest. Why had I fretted so much? Why had I allowed for my consciousness to be turned into a spoiled mayonnaise?

No one in the house needed help. No one was in pain, as I should have known from the start. Such an instance was utterly impossible, because no one besides me was in the house. No one at all.

part 2

HELL

THE ACCOMPANIST

So he is what I'll be left with, I guess. Humanly, I mean. What I will remember.

I smile. Letting go is such hard stuff, truly.

Kind of disappointing. I mean, him. You would expect more, how should I put it, dramatic? Philosophical? Priestly? Regal? That's it. Authoritative. While he is… transitory. He reminds me of a postman. A cab driver… well, they can be more interesting. A concierge, although they dress nicely and it counts. Were he neatly liveried, this all would feel different. Less trivial.

Why didn't they think of it? How come no one, ever…

Clearly, nothing was mentioned in the job description. He assumed he could don whatever he liked. Somehow, though, his casual outfit stabs me with longing as a uniform, I am sure, would not. Is it better, worse? See, his clothing nonchalance evokes faintly lit mornings, undone, untidy bedrooms. Messy drawers. Bunched up underwear. Mismatched colors. Smell of already worn, still wearable. Dailiness, what I will miss the most.

This is really too hard. Relax, if you can.

He wears skinny black pants, too sporty, too… juvenile? Checkered polo shirt… I dislike patterns, but I find this one kind of cute. A light woolen sweater, unneeded and

Hell

ineffably beige. A loose button hangs at the very tip of its
thread. Did he notice? Did he let it dangle on purpose, to give
me this urge to sew it back?

Then the nylon blazer, so sad, oozing a melancholy
other jackets don't have, a sense of… dejection. All those
zippered pockets, asymmetrical, random—I wonder what lurks
inside them. He wears sneakers…

*Now, stop. Don't go into detail. Not so photographically, so
didactically. It's useless. It is painful, indeed.*

His cologne. I mean aftershave. Sharp. His skin too
bare, and thick-grained. Do I wish he hadn't shaved? His
graying hair was once reddish. I guess. He bites hard the cuticles
of his nails. Long, thin fingers and sweaty palms. Can tell
without touching.

And how does he look without clothes? Suddenly,
I want to know. In the shower? Bathtub, maybe. I picture a
snapshot of flesh, foam coated, soon submerged. He is too
thin, with a tinge of forlornness. Like his zippered blazer, he is
shapeless, wrinkled, sagging.

How old? Forty-five. They are all forty-five. They
don't age. They come aged, in a way, ripened to the point, and
then they stay still—in a manner of speaking—until they are
replaced. I ask myself how long they last at the job, if they ever
quit on their own, who selects them, based on what, how much
they get paid. Wages must be low, or he would dress better. Buy
higher priced cologne. Aftershave… though, this one is just
fine.

He did not wake me up. He thought he would, the
sneak! Well, it's another manner of speaking. The poor guy
doesn't care, just goes by the rules. They always come before

dawn, to catch you supposedly unprepared. Talk of an early start. Does he go to sleep with the chickens? Not a life. Does he curl up in bed with a drink, TV on, daylight still peering through the curtains? Or else he doesn't sleep. Only catnaps. Does he sleep naked?

Forgive me. I can't help it. I wish I had slept naked last night, but I didn't. Why? Didn't I know?

I suspected. This is why he found me ready on the sofa with my crimson coat, ankle-length, which looks velvet but isn't. It has complicated buttons, like flowers, made of carved bakelite. At two a.m. I feverishly packed a suitcase, a few essentials and something to read. I kept it on my knees as I sat, until it felt heavy. See? My thighs had grown numb, and my mind had cooled as I waited… I knew luggage would be of no use, only burdening me along the way. So I kicked it under the sofa, where it bumped against something hard.

I remembered the gun. It was loaded. I kneeled, fished it out, then I went to sit on the armchair nearest to the front door. The gun was in my lap. Slowly, I aimed at the knob. A bit higher. I sat still, enjoying the feel of my chest smoothly going up and down, my breath calmer and calmer.

At five minutes to four I laid the gun on the table. I checked my make-up in the mirror. The tall dahlias on the mantelpiece needed grooming, water had to be changed. I postponed. I saw his silhouette through the stained glass, and did not let him ring. Worrying about the neighbors? Not really.

We have walked on the waterfront side by side, hands in pockets like in a movie of the Forties. I just followed, uncaring of where to. On the contrary, trying to be disoriented, to lose track of the path. Hard to do—I know this town inside

Hell

out. And I love the waterfront in particular. He must have been informed.

No one was around. We kept going, and he led me straight to the harbor. Cruel of him. The smells and the saltiness grabbed at me, scratched my throat like an itch, like a taste of blood. Boy, I wanted to say something, maybe cry. But I didn't. Ships were docked, massive shapes, dark against the lightening sky. I looked at them, mesmerized. The thing scraping me inside became sharper. I felt like running away.

He hailed a cab, pushed me in before I realized it. As he actually touched my body, I was startled… didn't think he would, he should have. It seemed inappropriate. Unfair. I squeezed on my side of the back seat. He sat quietly on his own. A glass pane severed us from the driver. In the enclosed space, the tang of his aftershave overwhelmed me. I thought I would be sick. I rolled down the window and I stared outside. We had left town, heading to the airport, I guessed.

*

They have barely opened. I see personnel wandering to place, climbing behind the desks. Lights turn on in the bar, I smell coffee and it gives me a kind of headache, like a pressure behind my eyes.

He comes close. Almost whispers, "Sit down." I am shocked. I didn't think he would, he should talk. And his voice, in spite of his looks… Wait. Two words? So short they count for one? Jesus, they are hitting me like a punch in the chest.

I had given up, you see? Speech, communication. I was getting comfortable, cradling into a bubble of silence. In the cab, watching the empty roads, I had started cocooning. Butterfly back to chrysalis, if you see what I mean.

Now he has broken the spell. "Sit down," he exhales, the accent obviously falling on "down." I feel as if he had put his hands on my shoulders and then lowered me, with a gentle push, on a sofa, on a bed… Wake up. Stubbornly, I shake my head and lean stiffly against a metal rail. Tears I don't want him to see are clouding my eyes. I just shut them. My headache swells like an incipient storm.

He's at the check-in desk. Of course, he will take care of formalities. They (the airline employees) are perfectly attired, pimped, beribboned like Swiss guards escorting the Pope. In contrast, his informal dress again looks incongruous, slightly offensive.

This has been poorly planned. In bad taste, to say the least. I wonder how no one ever…

Here he comes, after a long confabulation during which I had the pleasure of watching his nape, noticing a small balding patch. Tender. Or pathetic. How long has he been forty something? How old will he be, all of a sudden, once freed, when they'll give him his dues and send him packing? By the way, where does he live? I mean on which…

He has grabbed my elbow from behind and below, his fist an iron clasp. Without further words, he guides me through lengthy corridors, past a number of double doors. I start feeling cold. Invisible drafts pierce me like laser beams. No doubt, we are still in the airport, but I'm finally disoriented as I've wished to be. Only, it doesn't feel good. I am scared. It is physical, a shortness of breath, a weakness under my waist, as if urgently needing the bathroom, though I don't really… Signs are spare. The word "exit," the most frequent.

We have passed security. Turnstiles popped out of nowhere. An officer slept, his cap lowered over his face. With no luggage, no papers, we have just passed security, have we? He still holds my arm, maneuvering me like a puppet.

Then a burst of hilarity strikes me, very hard to contain. I start giggling. I am shaking all over and I cannot stop. He stays cool. No reaction. My brain stays cool as well, as if watching the scene from above, as if floating, or else splattered over the unreachable ceiling. "This must be a standard script," I think. "He must see this often. He's ready." Can you imagine how many crack up, how many go bonkers? He hasn't let my arm go, though my whole body is rattling. He has expertly loosened his grip, still maintaining a fluid yet firm contact.
Like a ballroom dancer.
The epiphany takes me by surprise, briskly ending my hysterics. Like a ballroom dancer, exactly. Stranger by definition. Passer-by. Whoever that is. Unpredictable. Often someone you'd never choose to be around, and still, for a while, you are intimate. You team up for the ride. Tightly linked and finely tuned. Looking as if you're enjoying it. Enjoying it. "Shall we dance," I want to say. Should I rest my left hand on his shoulder? He is too tall, or else I've already started shrinking.
I am looking him straight in the eyes for the first time, and he doesn't divert his gaze. But I see nothing meaningful, nothing responding. He returns my stare, that's all. He's not scared. He knows what he's doing. This must happen each time. Routine, only.

I move back and away. He doesn't stop me. I must look my normal self again. Quietly, I crouch on the floor and take off my shoes. I leave them on the side, lined up, two small soldiers. Barefoot, I take a step forward like a drunk, like a lost duckling, then resume our previous direction. He walks right behind me. I can hear him step very softly. I said he wears sneakers.

The aisle ends against a wall. A bench is bolted to the pavement. Without need for instructions, I stop. I wish now he would repeat what he has said in the main hall, with the same intonation. Please. This time I won't shake my head. We have arrived.

I have. I sit on the bench, my eyes riveted to the front of my coat. To the fabric, yes, precious yet sober. Dignified. Regal, that is why I chose it. I observe one of the bakelite buttons, spiraling like a conch shell between my thighs. I keep focusing, acutely aware of its sable shine lapped by a bloody ocean of red. I unflinchingly stare at my coat, red, yet more screaming while the rest gets paler and paler.

Hell

It's the three of us on the hill, simply aligned. Truth is, I
am in the wrong place, on the other side of the tree interposed,
alas, between the house and me. In this platitude (added to
an equally impractical linearity) I don't see a way to reach the
house, which of course would be my natural destination. Once
inside, I could change position, at least sit without further ado.
Sitting would allow me to take my head in my hands and ponder
the facts, which have started to escape my control. Actually, they
have totally escaped, since when I don't know.

Anyway, I should reach the house that is mine, for me
I mean, while the tree is just a challenge, an obstacle, something
put there to make my life difficult. Life? Not sure… although,
since I'm able to jot these reflections, considerations, even
plans, I should still consider myself alive. Well, of course. Only,
in a kind of interim situation, where reality clues are slightly
confused. That's all.

I can't reach the house and, see, that is a problem. I
cannot, because—as I was saying— we are flat. And lined up,
like printed characters on a page, and I've landed in the wrong
place for some reason, on the other side of the tree. Lacking
a third dimension makes it hard, or impossible, to bypass this

thing separating me from my objective. Unless… well, as you have figured by now (from your somehow comfortable outside perspective), there's a move and a move only I could venture to try.

I should plant my left foot (the one closer to the tree) as steadily as possible, nail it onto the ground (if such a term applies to the thin line defining this bleak, bare hilltop)… Plant my foot, I was saying, and fling my body across with all the strength I've got. Open up like a window, rotate on my hinge, overcome the freaking vegetation to be slammed in front of the house, facing the little door.

God knows if the door will open or if, very likely, it's affected by the general platitude. God? I don't know, I really don't. Then, where to would it open? I haven't thought that far. Because, look, before reaching the door I'll have to lunge forward (I will, promise) into uncharted territory. I mean into the void. I know it's there. I can perceive absence. That is why I am stuck. There's no path, no stairs, no trail, no slope, nothing. Just a void… will it allow my passage? How does emptiness hold? Does it give in? I have no clue. Also, I have no other choice.

Here we go.

*

I have fallen. No doubt. I was running like mad and I lost my balance. I have tripped, and then met the sidewalk. Did I land on my hands as instinct commands? Something suggests I didn't. Did I roll on the side, bunched up like a fetus? I fear it didn't happen. I brutally collapsed… I was terror-stricken. Those four Danes were following me, barking like hell, believe me. What had triggered their fury, I don't know. Did I provoke it? Not sure. I don't usually fear dogs, but those were something else. Where did they come from? A gate? A front door? I hadn't noticed them until they were behind me and (mistakenly, I know) I started accelerating. Wrong reaction. Oh, well. My, they were huge like horses, like cows, with their cartoonish look, black and white… yet not funny.

I must have hit the pavement very hard. Then what did they do? I'm still here. They didn't devour me. I don't feel any pain. Was I bitten? I don't… Truly, I don't feel a thing but I'm here, I told you. I'm telling you, I'm here. Maybe they ran me over, couldn't stop their momentum.

Was it me they were after? Now that I think about it, maybe I was in the way. Sure, I was in the way… they only had to bypass me. And I let them. I flattened myself on the ground, pancake-wise, and then I lost consciousness.

*

Hell is a bunch of dome-shaped little hills. Kind of primitive breasts, without the sensuality. Trust me, so freaking dry.

The good thing about it, if any, is equality. There is nothing besides an infinity of quasi-identical hills, dome shaped, each with a little house plus a little… something. I should say person, human. Only, it sounds inappropriate.

The tree? Disregard it. We got rid of the tree. It was a purgatorial feature, a residual, a kind of mirage. Trees have been disposed of, due to their lack of relevance. All that is left are hilltops, houses, and us—those prickly, aching bundles of consciousness.

Have you heard of lost souls? Well, the expression applies, though it sounds a bit folkish, a bit melodramatic in this purified context. Still, it kind of matches reality. There's a bunch of lost souls in hell. I am one.

Oh god (god?), let me revise the paragraph I just finished. Did I say reality? Yes. Yes, it works. Purified? Works as well. This is real… purified. Rarefied, though there are legions of us. I mean, you couldn't picture how many. No, you couldn't, and yet we are so orderly put, neatly separated, that no sense of crowd is conveyed. Humans, hills and houses are countless. But there is nothing else. All the rest is gone.

Demons? Please. The only thing reminiscent of popular myth is this crater shape. I mean, the hilltops surround a concavity, lining its sides like the niches of a necropolis. Like the steps of an amphitheater. With a Coliseum feeling. A beehive quality. Rather, an artichoke look. Onion, maybe? Something overlapping. Concentric. Maybe a spiral, a maelstrom. A gigantic conch shell…

Doesn't matter. The overall shape, the general perspective doesn't matter. We are these dots on the sides, this pixilation… this is what we are and what counts.

There's no demon around. There is us, which is a kind of comfort, do you agree? I mean, not being alone, knowing nothing occurred to me that didn't to a few zillions of others. Others, I never thought this word could contain so much tenderness. I never relished it as I am now. What occurred to me occurred to… But what happened to me? I haven't straightened it up, not yet. Will I ever? It starts mattering less and less. Actually, it doesn't matter already.

*

We have fallen. I have fallen on the side. The other side of him, probably… I've lost track, and probably consciousness. I have briefly come to in the ambulance. I was lying down, and I saw the ceiling. The light hurt me. The sound of the traffic outside was confusing, consuming. Nausea soon overwhelmed me. I must have fainted again.

At the emergency room they didn't let me see him. They said they could not. On arrival people were divided by gender, then couldn't be mixed up. That seemed kind of absurd, but I hadn't the strength to debate it. I was flat on my back, nailed down by a terrible pain, and I couldn't sit up, not even turn on my side. Gee, I could move neither my head nor my neck. Tears gathered in my eyes and made them burn, but I couldn't cry, which truly…

There were lights over me, like inside the ambulance. They irritated my eyes, so I tried keeping them shut. But sometimes I had to look, to know what they were doing… they just came and went, came and went. The pain was unbearable. And, no, I couldn't move, I kept telling them. They x-rayed both of my shoulders. After a long time, many hours, they said they found no fracture. Shoulders? Something was wrong with my back, not my shoulders. Something was wrong with my spine, and pain was just killing me.

All right, they said. Then, they couldn't discharge me. They'll do more tests tomorrow.

I thought I should ask about him again, though I was

growing indifferent. I was kind of forgetting—about him,
I mean. I only felt exhaustion, those tears burning my eyes,
and a wish for darkness, and pain. They rolled the cot where
I lay, covered by a paper-thin flannel sheet, through a long icy
corridor. I started shivering, but I didn't mind.

In the aisle where they pushed me, lights were finally
faint. A tall window, huge, uncurtained, was right in front of
me. From my supine station I could see lampposts, passing cars,
buildings across the street. I could hear the traffic, relentless,
though it must have been night. What time was it?

I heard a few women's voices. Old women, I thought,
but I couldn't turn, so I couldn't be sure. And I didn't care
anyway, until they got louder. On and off, a scream pierced my
timpani, made me shiver and shake. I didn't want to hear people
screaming. But I was at the hospital, right?

Then a whine began, a lament, shrill, persistent. That
burned more than the light did. I just couldn't bear it. Could
someone, please, do something? For that woman, yes, could
someone stop her? By herself, she would not. I knew she
would moan all night, her pitch rising now and then to gather
attention. Well, she already had mine, as I couldn't keep her
noise in the background. Jeez, I would go crazy. My hand
sought a bell, perhaps hanging from the metal cot I was on?
The wall? Nothing, I found nothing and couldn't turn. Then I
must have slept.

*

There's a lamp, and there is a cop. I don't know where
I am. I just see this guy, hear his voice and the voice of invisible
others. They speak softly among themselves, then he shouts,

"About the third passenger?" He is talking to me. I'm still half asleep. I don't answer. He keeps hammering the same question. Other voices join in. The phrase is repeated and repeated, until suddenly it breaks the surface, somehow, until I understand... the words, not their meaning.

What is it?

"The third passenger..." I stutter with effort, "there is no third passenger." "There was," they reply, and I gather something weird in their tone, a hint of irony, suppressed laughter perhaps? "No, no." I am shaking my head... that means I can move! Can I? "Think again. Are you sure? What happened to the third passenger?" I insist, as firmly as I can, "There was no third passenger." Now the cop comes close, his bulging eyes shining less than an inch from mine. He stares at me, threatening. He shouts, "And your dog? What about your dog?"

I am scared. I had forgotten about my dog. Where did my dog go?

I'm awake now. Dawn breaks beyond the large window. The night wailers have fallen asleep. I'm awake at the break of dawn. But why do they say so? Dawn doesn't break a thing. I haven't seen anything this gentle, this delicate.

*

Hell has welcomed me without welcome, I mean without formalities. I was given no handbook, of course, and there's no one to ask. No one seems to be in charge, that is what I mean. The lack of directions, info, agenda, news, plans, manifestos, is striking. On the other end, all is so self-explanatory, it gets boring.

It is supposed to. Boredom is one of the punishments, I guess. For which sin? No idea. Maybe those we haven't committed, but it's pure speculation. There's no rule, because all has been previously organized in order to limit variables. Nothing must be enforced… we have no means to behave unlawfully. We have no means to behave at all.

Each of us is stuck on a little hump, see, side by side with a ridiculous hut that doesn't have windows, only a small closed door and a pointed roof. Such a simplified silhouette, you'd think a small child had drawn it. But no. No, because it is perfect, as if machine-made. That's the chill of it…

They aren't truly identical. Yes, the houses. How so? Where can variation lie? Boy, you got a point. I don't know where variation resides, but listen to me. They aren't identical. About us? Well, we aren't identical, of course. We are us, though no better identified. We are others… I can feel, can perceive the otherness. As I said, it reassures me. We are shadows, I mean kind of shadowy. We can move around, a bit, laterally. At least, I think so. At least, I think. Do I have proof of others thinking? Well…

Well, it is a matter of faith. I have faith. I have faith and it's very strong. Does it sound ridiculous? Faith in what, you ask. It doesn't matter. Not here.

*

It wasn't my dog. It was his. It rode in the front, niched in his lap, between his torso and the handles, the leash loosely tucked against his palm. The dog was used to riding and never moved, never attempted to run. It was a good dog.

Now, where is it? It must be ambling loose in a part of

town I don't know. We were crossing it, right? But going where? Darn if I can remember. I couldn't find my way around that neighborhood, especially on foot. Will the dog? Will it make it home? That would be a miracle. If not, will it go astray? Will they catch it?

By the way, where is *he*? Did they let him go? Was he hurt? I cannot remember, but now I need to know. I must ask them again. Will they tell me?

Will the dog be capable of retracing its path? Will it get completely lost? I don't know, but I have faith.

Sins I haven't committed… I know what I'm punished for. I don't need anybody to explain about hell, or why I am in it.

It was time to turn the page but I haven't turned it, that's all. That's how it happens. You should turn the page, move on and move over, but you are stuck. You can't get yourself to start your freaking act, the one thing you have to perform, the one sentence you have to say. Such as, I am gone. Keep the dog if you like.

You postpone and postpone and don't do it. You cannot turn the page. Then, the book slams shut.

Now I know we were bound to a party, up the hill. A friend of his hosted it. Birthday party. But we never got there. Talk about a celebration, and now I'm stuck in hell.

*

Dawn has finished breaking… Its cute little show is over. A soft, feeble light spreads across the sky. The town is waking up, but nobody moves on the cots, not yet. I don't see a soul around, so to speak.

Let me explain what I've done for the last half hour. I have rolled myself onto my side. That took fifteen minutes. Actually, I'm approximating. I have no way to tell time. All feels like eternity, yes. I am pulling from my hips, trying to lift my torso and eventually sit up, but it seems impossible. I can't tell you the pain… let's leave it at that. I am pulling from my hips with an otherworldly effort. Who knew I could be so brave… I am not brave, in fact. I just want to get the hell out of here. Out of here, before nurses show up and moaners awake.

*

Then the party comes back to mind. I mean, we were there. On the hillside, a villa surrounded by vineyards. Wealthy people, I think… my recollection is vague. Was I feeling uncomfortable? I should not have been there. Not then. Not with him, perhaps.

Not at all, but there I was, was I, among the merry crowd. I knew no one besides him. As soon as we took off our coats, we asked for the toilets, and we swallowed those pills.

It was truly a strange villa, grand and labyrinthine. Tables were lined against the wall in a long, narrow dining room, a bit like a church nave. They were loaded with food, but I only noticed the fruit bowls. Salad bowls, kind of, but footed, reminiscent of some old-fashioned painting. Filled with pyramids of caramelized fruit, they looked like giant sculptures. Folks greedily grabbed at those brownish trophies, stole large chunks and devoured them, making ecstatic faces. I wondered what the things tasted like. They were mesmerizing, but I didn't touch them.

Hell

The stuff we had gulped down was strong, and I wasn't hungry. I was thirsty. Meanwhile, I had lost sight of him. Someone else was with me.

We were climbing stairs, small, turning round and round. My head was also turning. I was dizzy. My left palm dragged against the wall, kind of pushing it. My right hand held the rail and a glass of wine. I managed both. Climbing was kind of hard, but I really wanted to make it. To the top, I mean. My company, I'm pretty sure, was ahead. Then he turned back, encouraging me. Must have.

I was holding my glass of Burgundy when I landed myself on the roof. Fresh air did me good.

Music rose from the garden… well, from acres of park completed with woods and copses. Music was very loud and I liked it. The guy grabbed me at some point, and we danced. I started laughing, my eyes glued to the glass I held up high, like a flag. Yes! We danced on the roof, which was kind of flat… it sloped toward the center, in fact. I pulled toward the center… or else gravity did. We turned, hugging and dancing, pulling toward the center. I held my glass very high, very tight. It shone in the twilight and it made me laugh. Made me happy.

Then, a strange thing occurred. Then I was in the glass. I was in the glass. There must have been a window on the roof. What's that called? How large? It was round, transparent. Concave, like a reversed dome. Not sure, but almost.

I was in the glass. We danced on the window. I looked up at the darkening sky. No moon that I remember. I looked down. I could see the room with the tables, all those sweet, nibbled, maimed pyramids. I saw people under my feet. We kept spinning and swinging.

Then we crashed.

*

I have been able to stand. I am not walking, only dragging my feet, soles flat on the ground to minimize shaking. Something between my hips and my back is disjointed, and it's screaming out loud. I should scream out loud, but first I need to reach the front door. There… I stick to the wall, I hold on to it, push against it. I have found my purse next to the cot, right beside my shoes. Intact, yes. I am carrying my purse and my shoes. I only need to get to the door, hoping no one will stop me. Then I will keep walking, that's all. I am sure I will find my way. Home, I mean. Home.

Inferno

The three of them, and stairs.

Mostly stairs. I could say I hate them but I won't, because I am meek and because it isn't their fault. They are what they are… stairs. Don't do it on purpose. I mean, wearing me down.

Up and down, three stories. Or four if I count ground level, where I namely sleep. Well, I do, in small installments. They feed every two hours, like babies, so I take hour-long naps. Then, believe it or not, my commute eats the rest of my breaks. Yes, it takes me forever, forever, to roam those freaking ramps.

If a hare and a turtle race, who wins? No one, brother. I can tell because I AM the turtle. The round trip is sixty minutes, no kidding, up and down these darn steps.

Half an hour goes by before I reach the bottom, carrying three bowls of soup with two hands. On a tray, correct. Still, I'd need a third paw to steady myself, palm against the retaining wall. I don't have it, and therefore I hesitate, hesitate, one foot grasping the ground (the rock of which these steps are made) like a suction cup while the other one braves the void in search of the next landing, where it will stick itself with the same devotion, I swear. But there is a gap, you see, right in the middle, the awful moment when a side of me is left without foundation, airborne…

How I wish I could creep seated on my butt, simply sliding, thump, thump, wearing a pair of thick lederhosen. Yes! Bavarian attire for Oktoberfest… In such garb I could impudently drag my keister on stone, at least for a while. And, of course, on the tray there would be beer steins, foaming…

STOP!

Sorry… Inadvertently I have raised my voice. You didn't hear me. You can't.

What is in the bowls?

Not sure. It comes packaged.

Mid-size cardboard boxes, unlabeled but with a strip covering, I'd say, a third of the outside? A green band, a dark forest shade… Kind of a soothing tint but also a bit dusty, bit sad. It's a logo of sorts. It signifies something, I mean, other than just "box" or just "food." The green band, yes, conveys a sense of design.

I mean plan. As if someone out there still had one. Someone does, of course, because things arrive. They are delivered with perfect punctuality, and we never run out. Only, I think that the green is fading, but it could be my impression. The effect of repetition. Seeing these over and over creates a sort of addition, I guess. Habit, yes…

No, I don't keep them. The old boxes? Imagine. Could you picture the pile at this point? I slit them on the side, following written instructions. First I flatten and fold them, then I lay them outside. They are retrieved when new ones are brought. They are recycled.

Isn't everything?

I can't tell if the green has faded. Maybe I'm just afraid

Hell

that it might, one day. Do I have to look ahead, though? Tell the future? Come on. I have enough to do with these freaking stairs.

Do not get me wrong. I am not tired. My legs are. My feet, scared, hesitating.

They look kind of alike. Familiar. To me? Well, of course, but familiar wouldn't be the right word. Should I say monotonous?

They look similar to each other, I meant, in spite of the gap, the big hiatus… How can I describe it? Let's see. It isn't spatial. I told you what's between them. A mere ramp of stairs, pretty long and for me a total Odyssey, but that is because of my legs. My age, right. Anyway, a single flight divides them, as for neighbors in an apartment building. Distance isn't really the point.

And time isn't either, though they arrived at different moments, correct. They were all here when I was appointed. Yes, I got the whole formation. They wouldn't have hired me full-time, I'm sure, for an incomplete hive. How do I know they have different rates of seniority? Well, it's evident. They pile up, bottom to top, like newspaper. Obvious, is it? They superimpose. Also, once they are in, they age in distinctive fashion… You can sense, appreciate long tenure. Trust me. It leaves traces. The more they sediment, so to speak, the more they become… ritual.

Still, the chasm that sets them apart (though I'd swear they look fairly kin) is not age-related as it isn't the effect of living apart, like three timid bachelors, minding their own business. What is it about? Wait. I guess I had never seen anyone just so…

LONELY, that's what digs the gap, yes. Not a kind of

lonely you'd know. This is something else. Sorry! Unwillingly
I've raised my voice and it was… shoot, this is hilarious. It came
out like a croak.

I AM NOT LONELY. Perhaps bored. Well, these steps
keep me busy, don't they? Night and day, around the clock.
I know sooner or later I'll collapse face forward, splash in a
muddy pool dotted with china shards, like islands, like sinking
boats…

What is in the bowls?

I told you. No, I didn't. It is powdered and it comes in
satchels. Plain, no brand, logo, nothing. Bit depressing. That's
why the green of the boxes, you understand, becomes kind
of crucial. A barrier, I mean, against total nondescript… the
satchels, so neat.

No ingredient list. Of course, each the same weight,
the identical quantity. Color? Rust or brown. The shade slightly
changes, which makes it more… natural. Rust like… cinnamon?
Turmeric? Saffron. Smell extremely faint but peculiar. I disliked
it at first. Sort of in-between. Herbal, earthy, but slightly
medicinal. Chemical. Artificial, I mean.

Didn't I say natural? Yes, the color. The smell, sort of
mixed. As if disinfected? Preservatives added. Taste? Do I eat
the stuff?

I
DON'T

Lose my balance. All-splattered on gravel, waking up
with cheeks soaked in a soupy mess, slowly spreading, drawing
a geography of rivers, ponds, lakes and seas among pebbles.

Shards of china. Remains of the bowls, way too fragile…

They are old style. Tall, thick-lipped and ribbed on the outside, which is cute, pleasant to the touch. I hold the tray, not the bowls, correct. Except for when I handle them to my tenants.

Off-white, patterned blue. Not like those Dutch fineries you are thinking about. Lighter blue. How can I describe it? More kitchen-y. A bit different for each bowl (so I know which is whose).

I have nailed it!

Listen up. Here is one thing I know about the chasm, the ravine, the abysm between these folks. Their eyes don't look alike. His (I'm talking about the first floor inhabitant, counting downwards of course) are brown. Those of the second one are muddy, color of latte, because BLUE has started slipping in and diluting them. The eyes of the third chap are blue.

Not like those Dutch porcelains you can see on museum shelves. Not this tame azure, either, decorating the bowls. It's a watery blue, polluted and dirty. Artificial? Remote, yet not airy. Deep, without any texture. Deep, because it is buried.

They keep busy. That is why they feed every two hours. See, they never stop what they are doing, which is…

Wait. I have nailed it. This is where the difference lies. The unbridgeable fracture is… Wait.

Down there (level three counting from the top, three underground, at the very bottom) he is fixing a cabinet. En plein air, outside. There's no inside. Outside is where they dwell. It's sufficiently enclosed. Couldn't be more intimate.

He is wearing belted black pants. A bit overdressed?

Just his style. Never casual. But simple. He has a button-down shirt, no tie, frayed collar and cuffs. And who cares? He has rolled up his sleeves anyway. Ding! A pair of cufflinks has fallen on gravel. Oval shape, silver finely filigreed. He has stared at them for a second, then has diverted his eyes.

Since, he has focused on his task, repairing the old cabinet that keeps falling apart. Oh my, those thin boards are rotten and hardware is missing. He has gathered bolts, screws, nails, washers, hinges of many sizes on a leaf, now totally crumpled, and meticulously keeps those bits in good order. He has a couple of tools, for sure insufficient, but he has developed incredible skills with an overgrown, deadly sharp, extra tough fingernail.

Once, the cabinet must have been exquisitely wrought. I understand why he'd be so reluctant to part with it, let it rot, decompose.

All right, it isn't a cabinet. It's a miniature desk with shelves and compartments, yes, cabinet-like but a desk, with a secret drawer that pops out on command. He sticks his long, threadlike, meager finger into a narrow slit, to reach a hidden button. He is skin and bones, the chap of floor three. Still, the slit is small for his hand… The desk must have been custom-made, for a child. That's why the hardware is so tiny, the wood so thinly cut, everything so ethereal.

He insists until he reaches the button, I think, with his overgrown fingernail. The spring doesn't work well. He fiddles and wiggles. When the secret drawer appears, lined in purple felt, he adjusts it with unbelievable patience, filing here and there, maybe lubricating with… Resin? Wax? Perhaps honey, or saliva. Or tears.

Should three hares and a turtle decide to race, who would win?

No one.

See, the hares are utterly volatile. Easily distracted, they leave on a vacation and that becomes permanent. They expatriate and then they expatriate again. We haven't heard about those hares ever since.

But the turtle has her own plight. She sits on a ramp of stairs as we speak, eyes half-closed, all wrinkles and frowns, gingerly brushing the lip of three china bowls with one of her paws, trying to play a twinkly tune. No sound comes out, not that we can hear.

On the second floor… call it limbo as, upwardly or downwardly speaking, it is straight in the middle, stuck, secured on both sides and what-could-be-worse?

On the second floor, the hazel-eyed tenant (irises color of café-crème) perches on a very tall stool while reading a book.

Well, he fakes it. His eyes, most of the time, leave the page and stare at the horizon ahead. There is no horizon. Or a very limited one.

The book cover is green, but not the green of the boxes. A frank color… I wonder how it stays strong and fresh. Bold, garish, a color of Christmas, of flag. Does the lad appreciate it? I know he touches it often. Not the color… the cover, and his fingertips must feel some pleasure. Maybe his fingertips carry some meaning to his brain. Does he have one?

He does have a head, same shape as that of the others. I have said they look kin. Salt-and pepper hair and a beard, for the limbo guy.

Does he have a brain, though? His eyes keep wandering

off. Maybe his mind is unplugged, so to speak. Something is uncannily still in his posture, too eerily absorbed, too quiet. He has lost weight, although I'm sure he gulps the feed that I bring him. I don't deem him capable of…

Here's the thing. I am misjudging him. I am misrepresenting him, applying against him an unfair bias. And why? I have turned sad, and sad makes me bitter. Bitter makes me mean.

The truth is, he is reading. Not only. Now and then he extracts from his pocket a pencil (he is wearing a slightly old-fashioned jacket, beige or tan, still presentable). Slowly, mindfully… Yes, he has brains… Slowly, he clicks the back of the pencil to push the lead out. I don't know where he keeps his supplies or how substantial they are, but he sure treats his tool with infinite reverence, beautiful to behold.

He takes notes on the margins, I guess. Perhaps between lines. He writes with intent and parsimony. Discontinuously. Preciously. When he lifts his eyes from the page and he looks nowhere, what does he actually see? I believe he follows his thoughts like insects, butterflies, bees, mimicking their sinuous, curvy arabesques.

He keeps at his studious task night and day. Quietly, I said. Are thoughts mute? Are written lines silent?

Here, they are.

Once, I have tasted the feed.

Shouldn't have. It was forbidden, indeed.

I am supplied with a distinct forage that comes in another box, smaller, less rectangular. To be sure, marked with a band of red all around, like a skirt. A weird kind of red, as if the brown cardboard had seeped through, making it murky and dull.

Obviously, much less feed is needed for me. I am one and I take a meal per day. It is plenty. My stuff comes in plain white satchels as well, but the contents vary. I can tell the taste of different mixes. I recognize peas, lentils, beats, carrots and so forth.

Once, I have opened one of the "other" packets. With anxiety. I have imagined they might, they must be counted. I mean, there could be a form of control, of verification… I have feared I'd be caught and my imprudence would cost me my job. But I couldn't help it.

Taste? None, and yet addictive. Indelible.

I am sure the baggies are numbered.

Now the turtle curls on her side.

I know turtles don't. They only have two stances. Either they are on all four, or they have fallen belly-up and are frantically shaking their paws. They can also retire in their quarters, stonifying themselves. I know all there is to know about turtles.

Now the turtle dreams of a newly-sprouted lettuce, of its freshness. She remembers the passage of seasons. She remembers dew.

Why in hell did she embark on this freaking race?

On the first floor, going down, is the last arrived.

Don't get me wrong… he isn't recent. But I've said time isn't the matter. He is dark-eyed, his head shaved. On his left arm an anchor is tattooed.

(If I fall… when I fall… I will sooner or later… shards of bowls will peer among mud like islands or boats. I can't wait to lay my face in such tiny landscape, get lost in such distorted perspective… diorama… dollhouse. Need a change of scenery, I guess.)

He is cooking on a campfire, safely enclosed by rocks. Did he build the ring of stones? Perhaps. Like the others, he is evanescent. But muscular, and he moves with ease.

Not much. Move. Mostly, he stirs whatever is simmering inside the humongous pot-that-looks-like-a-cauldron. It could be a potion, that's true. He might be an alchemist.

He isn't. I know what he is making. I can smell oregano and capers. The acidity of tomatoes cuts the stagnant air like a blade. More than all, I smell fish. I smell octopus. Does it have a distinctive smell?

I smell octopus.

Mostly, he stirs, yet not in the mindless fashion of who is taking care of some routine supper. That is why I mentioned alchemy! He mixes, I'd say, with a kind of majesty, as if the result of his efforts held infinite value… matter of life and death, so to speak.

No, in fact. As if the meal he's hatching were a gift, a most special present for someone who were about to come.

Is about to come, but is late.

He has ingredients. I mean spices. Dabs, zests, immaterial iotas he pinches between his fingers. He adds sprinkles based on… smell? Well, he never tastes… Doesn't possess a spoon, of course. He stirs with a branch, elongated and smooth. Keeps his spices on leaves, like old number three does with nuts and bolts. I have no idea of when the fish, crustacean or mollusk got into the crock. It must have been there from the start.

How invincibly occupied is the lad with this long, slow simmering! I could say I see passion. I won't.

When I mete out his bowl, he halts momentarily, a vague smile on his lips. They are all kind, meek, armless. He stops stirring, pulls the branch out of the pot, leans on it as if it were a cane, gulps his ration. Who is he cooking for? Does he know that nobody is coming? That the hive is full and the trinity complete? That I, guardian, nurse, dealer, am his only visitor?

The hive's full and the trinity complete. Folks, this is ETERNITY.

Does he know?

Eternity

They all ripened at once. She saw them at teatime,
as she lay in the shade for rest (just a moment, a burst of
exhaustion, that's all) and looked up from her supine station.
Otherwise, she couldn't have spotted them… the outer
branches of the tree completely hid them, husking them under
a green curtain of leaves.

They looked ugly. Ill-assorted. Tinted in a variety of
hues that didn't go together, lemon yellow, ocher, red, orange,
rust. About the same size, but misshaped. Most of them
irregular, as if someone had deformed them on purpose, hitting
them with a fist.

They were multitude, unpleasantly crowded, bunched
up, not properly clustered. They sure didn't look appetizing, but,
honestly, what else did in the whole freaking place?

One thing was clear, though. They were ripe. Harvest
time, right?

She postponed a little, waiting for the coolness of
twilight. Then she looked for some climbing prop. There!
She saw a leather stool not too far. As she went to grab it, she
noticed it was a large python, very nicely coiled.

Perched on top of her improvised ladder, she

stretched, arms extended. The apples were still unreachable. She remembered she had a pair of high-heels in her bungalow, six inches or so, à la Marilyn. That would do. She kicked off her sandals and, barefoot, grass tenderly tickling her soles, she went for her party shoes.

As she made it back to the orchard, the snake hadn't budged. Although… look, somehow it had shifted, spiraling in narrower and taller fashion. Damn! Then, the heels-rescuing trip had been pointless. In addition, hopping onto the stool now would be more difficult. Should she switch to her sandals again? Too much trouble. She inhaled, held her breath, grabbed a low branch for balance and hoisted herself aboard.

In the heights she felt a bit dizzy, lightheaded… She suspected her support might not be exactly reliable. Was it moving again? Very possibly. Well, she wouldn't fall. She only needed…

Hurray! The fruit was within reach! Only, she hadn't carried a basket, a bucket… Should she just drop the things? In spite of their warped looks, they seemed callous, infrangible. And she knew firsthand, so to speak, how soft the grass was.

Her arm stopped in midair and she froze, struck by a distracting thought. Boy, she had no panties on. That was solely her business, and not very infrequent. But she wasn't usually climbing on pythons, was she? Calm. Stay calm. No one was in view, why bother? Still, a nasty sense of exposure perturbed her. Perhaps, vulnerability.

Hurry, then. She grabbed a pome, twisted its stem. It came off so easily that she teetered, having applied more energy than needed. If she shook the branches, no doubt, everything would fall.

Then she saw the small people. Round-headed, same crew cut for all, the same shade of copper. They wore rough brown tunics, like those of monks. She couldn't be sure of their gender.

Their necks craned, they stared up with kind, innocent mugs, large and imploring eyes. What did they want? Jeez, they must be drooling with hunger. She should shake those branches without further ado, send upon the bunch a bountiful rain. Wait! Wouldn't they be injured, hurt? The apples seemed so compact, so dense… like hail… like grenades…

The small folks looked up, mesmerized. Now she felt endangered. Some of them must have had a peek at her bottom side and noticed the nakedness. Maybe that was what they drooled for, truly.

If such was the case, shouldn't she have caught at least a sneer or a murmur, a sigh or a giggle… But no. They were dying of hunger, those puppies. So weak, they could not make a sound. Quick! She should toss the apples. They'd surely catch them. No, they wouldn't be hurt. She started shaking the branches, her eyes riveted to the canopy of green, fearing to lose her balance if she kept shifting her focus.

Oh, my. Weren't those thumps ominous? Suddenly, out of the blue, she recalled the girl and the stoning… those large pellets the villagers had lavished upon the lassie of small virtue. Once seen, you could never forget the damn show. Again, she regretted her careless garb.

Please! Tempted as she was, she shouldn't look down. Neither to make sure no one had been harmed nor to check if her privacy was still such. She should not, period! Her stance seemed increasingly precarious. Her head turned. She felt faint. Perhaps she should eat. Perhaps she should just leave her treacherous spacecraft, alight, step on land.

As if reading her mind, smoothly, slowly, the snake began to uncoil. She held her breath and stood still, fingers holding to the frailest of twigs until the last moment, wishing to close her eyes but staring right front instead, empty guts cartwheeling as if she were riding a lift down the Empire State Building.

No one was there to welcome her on arrival. The apple-eaters must have beaten a mute and hasty retreat. Did she scare them? Did they take her for some kind of deity? A sorceress?

She had omitted to pick a fruit when landing had started. Now she hopelessly prodded the grass, hunting for an apple. She knew she'd find none. All had been greedily consumed, core and seeds included.

Eve unfastened the thin, intricate straps of her party shoes, hooked them around her pinkie and then gingerly strolled toward her cabin. Party shoes… she loved them so much. Sequins had just started to peel off. Otherwise, the pair had been indestructible. Same as she, correct? True, this acrobatic routine, the hidden nakedness, the slight chill each time, as if she were about to catch a bad cold… The flashback, oh-so-brief, the road, dust and stones. Wasn't it all taking a bit of a toll?

It was nothing. She had managed, had she? Forever. She'd manage again.

Afterward, the acute, unbearable starving. She had never tasted… gone… they didn't look good… still… mismatched, hard like rocks… but the starving…

She recalled she had planned something for dinner. In

her bungalow. At peace. Something, you know, something very simple.

Tell the Devil

Nothing wrong with the basement.

A bit cold. Dampness must have soaked the walls. They are chilly, almost wet.

A bit dark, like a dungeon. That is fine. Twilight suits me even during the day. It is soothing.

The iron gate makes noise as it slides. Oil would fix it, of course. I'll take care of it in due time. For now, I push it as little as possible and then I squeeze in, like a lizard. I have grown skinny and that has its modest advantages.

I moved in a month ago, give or take. I'm still making myself at home.

Today I am cleaning a corner by the front gate, where weird stuff is piled. Mostly garbage, but who knows? Perhaps some antiques, some curios… I have just started to sort things out very carefully, rag in hand. Dust rises in clouds.

That's when Fred's head pops in, framed by thick iron bars, jutting like a medieval gargoyle. Absorbed, wrapped in half-shadow, I haven't seen him arrive. Or heard. I was lost to the world, truly, as only when he shouts in my face I realize a drone in the background, a crescendo of voices, the din of an approaching crowd.

What is this? Political rally? Procession? Pious icon transported among chants and flowers, or a bunch of school kids let loose on a field trip? Maybe a wedding poured out of the main cathedral. Or a funeral, on the grand side. Well, who cares? In a minute I'll vanish into my cave and ignore whatever commotion goes by.

Could it be an emergency? A fire, accident, theft, bank robbery? I would be equally indifferent. Let me slip back, make myself invisible, shy away, seek abode.

"The Minotaur! Coming!"

Fred is yelling. His cheeks are bright pink, his voice breathy. He has run, I understand, to give me the news. His eyes shine with enthusiasm, but my face must look dumb like a tortilla. I stare at him, blankly… until something lights up.

"The Minotaur?" Got it… The two of us have shared a desk in sixth grade. Still kids, nearing teenage. At least I was timidly poking it, just as now I brush these relics, you see? With the very tip of my fingers. When the prof started us on Greek myths, I fell dead on for the man-bull. Why? Mere boredom, pal. First, I filled my notepad with sketches of horned devilish dudes. Then I carved the decrepit wood of my desk with a declaration, "Minotaur I Love You." It took hours of labor, mute and cautious, a large book pushed on top of my diggings whenever required. Fred observed my exploit in its making, witnessing its painstaking monotony. I am sure my elaborate calligraphy (pretty letters, all curves, mellifluous with longing) kept him quite entertained.

This flashback takes seconds. Enough to shake off my inward mood, my mild, armless gloom. Now I want to go out, see what's happening. Keys? They must be in my purse, which I have the habit of losing. I just drop it in the weirdest spots, then usually find it by smell. By its odor, correct. I have had it for ages… Bought in Hungary. Transylvania, yes, sir. A satchel of leather, still exuding a pungent redolence of horses. Manure, to be exact.

Keys! I need them in order to unfasten the gate and let myself out. Shoot! Fred has picked the lock! In a blink, not sure with which fancy tool right out of his pocket. Needle? Safety pin? Darn fool. I feel frightened. Exposed. In front of a crowd! Now everybody can tell how… But no one is looking.

All eyes are pointed toward the street, meaning the lane of asphalt that surrounds the plaza in its whole. A wide ring. An oval, perhaps. The lane separates the sidewalk from the paved area in the center, a pedestrian oasis punctuated with fountains and benches, potted trees and flowerbeds. The crowd gathers on either side, enclosing the lane like a tunnel. Like a river flanked by thick human walls. I spot a variety of people, some tense and some casual, some amused or excited, some annoyed, impatient, in wait.

"Here! The Minotaur! Coming!" Fred barks as if he were announcing the passage of a comet, the advent of a prophet. Still the same, never changed… the trickster, the old ruffian.

Here it comes, the fabulous beast, running around the plaza. What is this masquerade? Cheap tourist pleaser, for sure. Courtesy of the municipal board right before the elections. The Holiday season approaches. You'd expect reindeer and a sled, would you? Not in this warm weather, so uncannily meek. And it doesn't matter. Anything would do for distraction.

It peers around the bend. It gets closer, running this strange race as madly as if it were carrying some urgent, crucial news. Wait! I'm getting confused. I am mixing two words, am I? Minotaur and Marathon. Do they go together? Not sure.

Look! The creature zooms in. I feel queasier than expected. Eagerly, I spy at the lower part of its body, hungry for monstrosity, for some secret revealed. How is a Minotaur made? Half-man and half-animal? That must be the Centaur. Are they the same thing? Truly, I… My handful of notions is all awfully mixed up.

But where does the beast start? Waistline? Navel? Hips? What is the divide between skin and hide? A rough seam? A scar? See, I crave those places where one thing begins and one… Wait… Wait… The whole lower body thing might be wrong. Head, perhaps? Tail?

I know, of course. Whatever is coming is merely a man in disguise, an actor, a fake. And still curiosity is tickling me, a morbid residual, I'm sure, of my former crush. Please! What runs up the lane is a fake, an actor. I should now restore him, in fact, to his proper pronoun.

What a bluff! Just as I was saying. The lad is disappointingly normal. Have a close look at myths, and they fall apart… All is smoke, pretend, lure. Though the man, I admit, runs in a fashion that requires some weird skills. How can he keep his balance? His chest is so tilted forward that his hips drag behind, so to speak, his legs almost disappearing in a thick cloud of dust. And his head, grotesquely inflated by a huge mane of black curls (clearly, a wig), must weigh…

As he nears, I spot a banal handsomeness on his features, a hint of blond showing between his forehead and his

Hell

sable postiche. What a fraud!

He has stopped. At my door? In front of the gate.
What. Is. Going. On.

Things begin to make sense. Fred knows him, all right.
They are shaking hands, are they? I should have imagined it.
Fred is the impresario, the manager. He must have dug up some
pre-election job for the town administration. A short, seasonal
gig, I am sure. He must be in charge of casting attractions,
stunts, extras that he plucks from his pool of street fair,
burlesque, circus people, you name it. All colleagues from his
prestidigitator old days.

Fred is pointing at me, making hasty introductions.
What now? No, I can't believe it! He is picking my lock for the
second time, bluntly ignoring the fact I had clicked it in place
as soon… He just doesn't mind, as if my place (mine, yes) were
part of his whole damn theater. But it isn't, and I had carefully
bolted the gate as I stepped out, to ensure…

I am about to protest, but something cuts me short…
a chill on his face I hadn't noticed before. Maybe he has
changed, has he? There is a shade of mockery, there's a taint of
mischievousness in his gaze, as if he were demonstrating the
frailty of my defenses on purpose, pointing at my exposure,
indeed. Slyly equating the openness of my home to the
cheapness of my virtue. Is he capable of such innuendo?

Apparently. He is gone before I know, leaving Minotaur
on the premises. I mean inside my cave. He has delivered the
man-bull (the fake, the impersonator) at my door as if I were
the warrior's repose. The reward. Did the guy travel from far
for this brilliant stunt? Am I meant to be the accommodation
Fred included in the deal but failed to provide? Lodging chez

l'habitant? Dinner, breakfast? I should not be surprised.

I am annoyed at the moment. Truly enraged. This intruder, this stranger into my cloister bothers me quite a bit. Who's this guy? I have barely looked at his face.

Now, his expression… intentions, I mean. What did Fred suggest, hint at, promise? Oh well, his intentions seem clear to me, but he looks kind. He looks armless, perhaps talkable to. I should try to explain.

He looks common. So common. As if made of plastic, of rubber. A toy soldier, an action figure of sorts. Looks insensitive. Oh, not in a bad way… He is armless, I'm sure. Still, I fear I won't be able to manage a complex conversation, to explain this is a mistake, get him to understand… Let him know this is an abuse, at least an imposition, and I'm not a professional paid by his agent to round up his check. I am not going to entertain the entertainer.

Neither am I this freak… this lonely spinster who had a mad crush on him (I mean on his character) since teenage, as the other (pimp, ruffian) might have implied. How can I…

Such an aura of naïve expectation on the face of this sweaty cowboy. Can I bail out? By Jove, I must.

He has produced a small business card by way of introduction. In reply, I stutter, "I'm… A…" Not Ariadne, please. What would he know about it? What do I? My mythological notions are faint snapshots from remote school days. Damn that thing I etched on my desk, complete with a signature (I know, I didn't mention it yet). "Minotaur I Love You," plus "Ariadne," right below. The entire class got to see my masterwork in a matter of days. The laughter! The smirks!

The addenda carved in by whoever used the same desk during the afternoon shift… the huge, erect penis mimicking the giant member of horses. Horses? Dicks, dicks, dicks… they kept reproducing themselves. Jesus Christ!

Satan. By then, I didn't mind. I suspect I even found the whole thing exciting, titillating. I did not feel ashamed. On the contrary, I guess I felt proud. But the memory has grown indigestible after years spent in sobering solitude. Especially here, in this hermitage where I have found at last some kind of tranquility. Until this very moment.

I wish I had been more secretive. Wish I had forwarded my address to no one at all. Not to Frederick. But how could I have abandoned him? He still gets in trouble, of course. City life never fit him. He gets crushed like a straw, like a seed munched by sharp parrot beaks. He gets swallowed and thrown up again. In and out of jail for petty crimes. Always broke or in debt and never repentant. Bound to the next mess with fresh enthusiasm, sickening to behold, pathetic at that. He hasn't changed. Back then, in the village, he could keep afloat, so to speak. Here he sinks but doesn't realize it.

Why am I loyal to him? Why do I care?

I shouldn't. Don't want to. Can't afford it. That's why I chose the basement, this uncharted, un-neighbored cloister. To get out of the way, to be left alone. I am busy. Doing what? That's the very point. Doing what is nobody's business. I am dehydrating in spite of the dampness, drying up, withering. Crumbling, and my dust protects me. Just kidding. Folks, I am recapitulating (enough said?) and I want to do it at my leisure. I care for nobody right now. Can't afford it. Well, except for Fred.

And what should I do with this bloke? Surreal,

isn't it, how he's expecting my favors. Favors? They are due. Truly, I mean, honest, this has been negotiated, no doubt. He exchanged this small in-kind bonus for a discounted fare, assuming that he was paid at all.

Why did Fred pick me? What did he recall of the old times? The bars? The pole dancing? When we first arrived in town? Does he know how many years have gone by? He has stopped the passing of time. He is a trickster, I know. But I'm crumbling. I don't think… Should seek a diversion. Entertain him in some other way.

He looks slightly annoyed, a tinge. His hand out, he waits. For my card? I don't have one. He waits for my reply. I haven't finished my sentence. I have left it suspended. My face has gone blank, as I spaced away. Sorry. "I am A… Anorexic." That will do. "Just another freak, like you, brother," I wish I could add. "Beg your pardon." I don't say it, of course. This last part I omit. Beware, woman.

What does he imagine he is? Does he think "attraction" means "attractive"? Does he take himself for an athlete? A hero? A star? Satan forbid. Get out of here, please. I want nothing shiny in this hole. This sanctum. This coffin.

"I am the Anorexic." It's done. I smile, vaguely aware of my teeth, which must look impressive. Long, my gums have receded. Unstained… I haven't drunk or smoked a thing since eternity. Well, my teeth. I feel feral right now. Look at me, Quixote! Have a peep, play x-ray with this velvet gown, assess this waistline as thin as that of an hourglass. My waistline is choking me. Look.

I know, I didn't mention it. I am wearing an obsolete costume from our (Fred's and mine) Renaissance Fairs. The

gown used to be crimson. It turned violet and rust, in patches.
More blue, there. More brown where sweat has corroded it. I
never got rid of this thing, for some obscure reason, as I never
dropped Fred. A similar pattern of perfectly idiotic affection.
As it falls apart, it gets more familiar, more darling. See? It has
layers. They turn out quite handy when you lose your own flesh.
Then you pile strata of fabric upon your bone structure, and
they anchor you. They keep you warm. Besides, velvet is sweet
to the touch, the more as it wears, losing hair like an aging lone
wolf.

I have zoned out again. What prompted this flight into
wildness? What do wolves have to do… The beast, here, of
course! The mythical creature. I have lost him. Or not. I have
only spaced out for a second, though it seemed longer.

I was saying. Well, in my imagination I was saying
to Quixote, "Look down. Gage. Picture the minimal frame
sheathed in this pompous corset, hidden within the hoops of
this immense crinoline. Can't you see how inconsistent this
whole business is? Can't you weight it and then, figuratively
speaking, hold it within your palm, toss it into the air like a
juggling ball? That's me. You have been cheated."

He has no time for looking and he doesn't care. This
man-bull, I see, is pooped. He barely stands. Looks drunk,
though he doesn't smell like it. He hasn't pronounced a word,
just held out his business card. Does he speak our language?
One moment… he looks doped. Drugged by fatigue only?
Perhaps.

He is longing, I am sure, for a bed, a mattress, a sofa. A
hammock would do, as long as some lay is on the menu. I mean
lie, as in lie down. I should feed him as well. A drink seems

more urgent, in fact. I am sure that he's parched. Forget alcohol, dude. I have none.

Milk! I have none. I can't have things white. Eat or drink, never, none. There's no explanation, besides, they spoil my constitution. Yes, kidding. There is no explanation. I stick to things brownish or green. In this clay pot, here? Bean broth reinforced with cloves, mandrake roots and a pinch of saffron. I have heated and reheated it on top of the porcelain stove. It only gets better. It can last a whole week. A refrigerator? Nonsense. This place is a giant fridge, don't you see?

I used to be afraid of lighting the porcelain stove, back at home. Was I four? Still three. Father yelled at me. He did not say bad words. Didn't call me names. Nothing of the sort… it would have been laborious and he didn't have time. He just yelled, "Do it! Do it!" and the pitch of his voice went up. But that scared the hell out of me. I looked at the stove, three steps from my small self. Three steps, there, in the corner where stoves usually stand. Sit. Squat. Immobile and haunting. Big-mouthed and toothless. Big-mouthed, its jaw a deep pool of dark. Secretive and gossiping. Mean. Its tongue an evil thing, red, alive, alien, awful.

Was I burned at some point? I do not recall. Did Mom say, "do not play with fire" before she was gone? Quite improbable. And I would have been too young for remembering. I stood, petrified, a match in my right, the box in my left, my hands split by a thin gap I didn't dare closing, my feet screwed to the floor. Dad shouted, "Four years old and she can't light the stove!" Then he took the matches away. His shrug of distaste mortified me, but I was relieved, relieved…

Grandpa squealed from across the room, his wheelchair

exiled in the most remote, coldest corner... he must have been freezing. "She's still three," he sneered. He meant, sure, that Father could not even count. Grandpa was Mother's father and he didn't like Dad. He laughed.

Fred giggled as well from the table where he idled at length, pretending to tend to his homework. Three years my senior, already in first grade, and entirely exempted from house chores. Dear Fred, my older brother. Oh, I caught up with him fast in school. Dumb ass... Meanwhile, he was giggling.

Why didn't I say it before? That the guy's my sibling? I don't mention it, as a general rule. Doesn't really matter.

I only have this broth, or else water. Here's a bowl. For you! Yes, the Minotaur. We are back, forget about my brother. He is gone, anyway. He has dumped the burden on me.

I have poured a full bowl for my guest. He has accepted with a courteous nod. He stands still. I gave him no spoon and no napkin. I don't have any bread. He asks for nothing. He's touching the bowl with his lips. He is taking a sip.

I have poured a bowl for myself. I guess I could use one. I am holding it up, hesitating. I am getting distracted, all right. I cast down my eyes and think of his nakedness. Well, I should. It's going to be my very business, just a minute from now. I think of his penis... it is going to be inside my mouth just minutes from now, necessarily. My mouth, first. I'll need to bide time. My vagina is crumbling, I am sure.

I am thirsty now, fiercely so. My mouth is, but not for this broth. Truly, his dick is the thing I'd like to suck on. Why so suddenly? A penis, no matter whose. I wonder what his cum tastes like, with anticipation. I don't know what took hold of me. Abruptly. This frenzy. Don't ask.

I think of his sperm with delight, but then I'm struck cold. I recall that I can't. Can't swallow, not even a drop. It is white. Not even just taste and then spit? Can't. It would taint me. White. Banned. Would spoil… Never mind.

"How are your feet doing?" About a footbath? Good thought. It distracts me. Has to. I'm banishing this sudden lust, its horrifying grip, humiliating.

I will wash his feet to bide time. As per contract… a bodily service of sorts. With some chance he might be contented, who knows? Should I get down on my knees? Assume such a subdued, slavish pose? Isn't it too exposed, too vulnerable? And suggestive as well. Shut up, you fake prude.

"Aren't your feet killing you?" No… He shakes his head. He is dismissing that part of his body as if unimportant, in spite of the fact he has circled the ominous square at an insane speed. For how many times? He has lifted more dust than a plague, a locust invasion or a bursting volcano would have. His feet must be bleeding. But he doesn't care.

I am desperate for a detour. Restless, I walk to the gate. A large flier is stuck among bars… It must have been there since this morning, certainly announcing the event, but I hadn't seen it. As I show it to him, I point at the calendar listing sites (towns and beaches, hamlets, winter resorts) where he will repeat his performance. Sometimes, twice a day. What a tour! Good for Fred. Each place is duly numbered, forty-four, forty-five… Then it lands on me, "How many parallels do you still have to go?"

"Meridians," he says. That's the first word he has spoken. A slight accent. Faint smile. A fugitive spark in his eyes.

Perhaps he is less dumb…

"Parallels," I insist. Then it lands on me he must be the Sun. Not in person. I mean his role, his character. I am saying that the Minotaur is the Sun. Right? Perhaps not. But I am up to something. I am getting somewhere. He is making this tour… The plaza is an oval. He rotates around an ellipsis. He does… he did orbit around me. Correct? I am the Earth, then. Our meeting is destined. I think so. Perhaps we belong.

Wait. I got it all wrong. Reminiscences of my poor school days keep emerging. If he is the one orbiting, he is the Earth. I am the Sun.

Course not. I am darkness itself. But there's no alternative… He turns, he is the planet. I must be the fixed point, the star. Dark? Undergoing a kind of eclipse. Lengthy hibernation. Sun? Star? What am I thinking? I know. I'm thinking of cards, tricks, Tarot readings, of course fake. As in… Fred. Who is Fred in this scheme? The Moon, obviously, half-faced, full of disguises. He has already vanished, right? We have been left alone, M-Monster and I.

Dusk has fallen outside. Short days. Winter is near. Is Fred going to pick him up soon? The Monster. How long was his break? Will they drive off tonight? Let me check the schedule.

As I turn and reach for the flier, he is dashing for the closest flat surface. There, he sits on a stool, lays his muscular arms on the table, rests his head on top of his wrists, limp like a bag of 'tatoes. Has he already fallen asleep? I just can't believe it. Narcoleptic? Poor sweet forlorn dude. How much does he get paid? I come near him. I am holding my breath, not so much in fear of awakening him… I am wary of his smell. At close range he must stink like a beast of burden.

No, indeed. He gives out a mix of the same stable odor that my purse exudes (my small leather purse, yes) and the wafts of some aftershave. Not bad, not at all. Should I let him be? Sneak away to the niche behind the stove, where I keep my bed? Undone and untidy, shielded by a curtain the color of sour, rotten grapes. You guessed right… it is the same velvet of the gown I'm wearing. I have cut a drape into the cloak, for which I cared little. I have hung it up there. It seals me, it cushions my dreams.

Can I nap? This business has tired me.

I cannot. Take a closer look. The dude's wig has slipped sideways and it's about to fall. Hope it won't. But I see… the paleness that I took for blond hair, against the black mane, is just skin. Is he thin on top? Bald entirely? I don't care. I don't.

Am I sliding my arm around his torso? Did I wrap his forearm (so limp) tightly around my neck? Am I trying to drag him across the concrete floor (damn hard under our soles) all the way to the alcove? Yes. This guy has to lie down, no question.

Surprise! He isn't that heavy, after all. These big muscles must be made of foam. What is he? A hologram? I can move him!

He's walking on his own, that's why… but in gentle fashion. He is letting me lead as if he were a child. A toddler. He just shuffles along quietly, quietly, carefully matching my step, meek, obedient. Still. His upper body is relaxed, all slack, and yet I can support it. My stomach is tensed like a fist, my chest a bunch of wire. I am strong and I'm proving it.

Only, not for too long. Thank heavens, my free hand's

already groping the curtain. I am pulling it while my eyes seek the mattress, a thin mat on the floor, as far as the sea bottom. Take it easy. I kneel, slowly, as I steel myself head to toe, afraid to lose balance, tip over. Here. We. Go.

He is kneeling as well, concertedly, docile. From now on, the thing is a breeze. I just squeeze away with a twist, shedding his large frame like an armor. He unfolds like a rag doll. Le voilà horizontal, all dressed up on top of my blankets. I can't help a closer look. Curiosity… Once again, the thought of his penis gets hold of me, abrupt. His thing, hidden within shiny trousers, obscured by a long cotton blouse ruffled at the wrists.

Wait. A memory has struck me. Aren't these frocks… did I see these garments before? Weren't those, perhaps, Fred's Renaissance… Did Fred lend…

His penis. Can't take it off my… I must move. I am busy. Not thirsty. Or I am, but I must feed the stove, correct? For this fellow's sake, or he will be sick in the morning. Here's my broth. I haven't touched it. Warm it up, stir it au passage. It will be my nightcap. I'll sip it at

ease, at the table, conveniently sat on my stool.

Wait a minute. I need to do something else. That man lies on top of my blankets, and there is no way they'll switch places. Will the stove be enough… This isn't my business, but I am concerned all the same. Here's a shawl, a shroud of brocade, thick like grief and heavy like stone, the color of rust. Made out of a costume, correct. I am spreading it over the creature. I make sure he sleeps tucked and cozy, this wandering planet of mine.

I will wait until morning, awake.

So Long Lucy Fair

He leaned over, unlocked the passenger door, pushed it open. I hesitated, then slipped in without further thinking. The seat was too reclined. I clumsily fumbled around for a lever. He might have smiled, kind of. I remember his upper lip, pearled with sweat.

I remember his upper lip, purplish. I looked at him, sure, a few glances, my gaze otherwise glued to the landscape that rushed in, slamming into my face through the windshield, dizzying me for good. He didn't turn my way, not even, I think, when I first got in. He was watching the road and he'd better do it, because we were speeding like mad.

It was dawn. No one was on the streets besides his racing, fuming, fiery Testarossa. Was it his? Well… And it was yellow. I had never seen one that color. I had never seen one of any color, in fact. Sticking to the road as if on suckers and yet sliding avalanche-like, the Ferrari gulped our downtown, swallowing streets, alleys, squares, plazas. Lacy palaces and fountains, bell towers and churches. Churches and bell towers again, peeking after each turn, waiting at each corner, hovering above us and then seemingly falling on us… but we had already dashed elsewhere.

How could he think of riding those medieval streets, this labyrinthine topography, in a bolide launched at ninety per hour? He knew how. He must have done it a lot, maybe as an anti hangover routine, in order to sober up.

I had not. Soon I turned on my side, cheek pressed against leather, eyes shut. "I am sick," I said. Although… I wasn't, truly. Let's give it another shot. The sun now shone in my face, a large incandescent disk, scarlet, gorgeous. I took a deep, deep breath before closing shop. Time for a serious nap.

I woke up, and things had entirely changed. First of all, I was freezing. "Could we turn off the air conditioning, please?" He laughed a high-pitched giggle, almost fake. The AC wasn't turned on. I rephrased, "Could we get the heat going?" "I am not sure." He chuckled again, this time gently. I sighed, and then looked for something to throw over my back. Sweater, t-shirt, shawl? A towel would do.

So far I hadn't paid attention to my clothes. I was in my nightgown and it didn't matter, of course. I often lingered in such attire all day long. Hey… it was just a loose dress with thin shoulder straps. Pretty, and covered with lace. Only, way too light.

The surrounding landscape was pale and monotonous. Mostly gray, in spite of the flashy sunrise, it stretched by the sides of the highway on which we rode so smoothly, so linearly, it felt motionless. That mock stillness gave me vertigo as well, of a different kind. "Where are we?" I exhaled. "Europe," he said matter of fact. "Where the hell?" I wished to add.

I relaxed instead. Before slumbering once more, I took a good look at him. Truly, several ones, but he didn't notice or mind. He was pointy. Small chin and French nose. Meaning a bit thin, bit protruding. His lips, inconspicuous, had a tinge of purplish, I said. Small ears. Little facial hair but lustrous black curls, sticking tight to his skull as if for a Roman statue.

His body, slouched into the driver's seat, sort of melted with it. He wore faded blue jeans, white shirt, leather jacket, battered cowboy boots. Quite banal… unnoticeable. And I wasn't noticing him. Only cataloging, for the sake of it. Only chronicling.

When I awoke, we were stopped in a rest area. A pine forest abutted the parking lot and then widely spread. No village in view.

He was not in the car. Did he walk to the shop to get cigarettes, a sandwich, a drink? Should I do the same? I felt ravenous. How long had I gone without eating? I was cold, still. I should get some wrap-around sort of thing.

Could I leave the car unattended? Should I lock it? Oh, please. I should leave the car just as I had entered it. Unconcerned, unconscious. None of my business. The air was crisp outside and I shivered, but the scent of pines suddenly reached my nostrils. I took a deep breath. It was wonderful.

First I heard the sound (the noise?), then I saw him. Oh god! In a picnic area near the woods, crowded with snacking families, the smartass had set up his number, butchering tunes on an unfortunate violin while shaking his meager hips like a rock star.

I got nervous. Police would come any minute. Our trip would be interrupted. There would be some kind of annoyance. Should I run, avoid trouble altogether? Good question. Only, where should I go on foot, among forests and highways, in the very middle of Europe?

Maybe I was over worrying. He looked perfectly at ease, I realized as soon as I got closer. On the pavement I saw his instrument case, all covered with stickers and lined with faded velvet, once (I thought) the color of peacock feathers. It was full of coins… various metals, copper, brass, silver, gold. Currency of many different countries, I guessed. A few bills floated on top.

The thought suddenly struck me that I didn't have a dime. I felt colder and hungrier. The impulse of grabbing a bill or two became aching. As if he had sensed my presence, he stared at me briskly, without stopping his maddening playing. And he winked, with a grin, not unsympathetic.

A warm breeze blew from the pine trees. It embraced me, a comfy, caressing tide. I would wait a while and then borrow. I hoped he wouldn't mind. If he did, well, I'd bargain. There might be something I could do for him, right? Why would he have taken me aboard otherwise?

As they left the tables, those red-cheeked, robust, jolly travelers came by, unfailingly dropping a bunch into the violin case. No coins. Only bills, piling up like autumn leaves. I couldn't believe it. A smile glued on his face, he kept playing, ending with a long, shrill vibrato after the place was cleared. Unfatigued, while I was tired and trembling.

Mute, he grasped a few notes between two fingers, as if holding a cigarette. He pointed them my way. I hesitated half a second. I felt as if I were pimping. Then I grabbed the cash. He was stuffing his wallet, looking satisfied. I walked toward the shop.

I came out biting into a hot dog, and bedecked with a whorish top of red plush. Whorish or Santa-ish… I had found nothing else in the crappy mall that would fit me. It was scarlet, over my lacy white gown. I had a glimpse of my ridiculous self in the car window. Something sharply familiar came to mind. The woods helped, perhaps.

But was he the wolf? Please. He looked innocuous. Resting against the Ferrari, he was smoking, staring at the languorous sunset. I could also appreciate it, now that my body temperature was restored to normal. Sunrise. Sunset. Had we been away for twelve hours? Apparently. It felt like a couple of minutes at most. Or eternity, of course.

Well. I needed to speak up, get things straightened out. Now. "Where are we going, dude?" Gingerly, he crushed the butt of his fag with his boot, then strolled around the car, caressing the hood with his knuckles, pleased, as if appraising its shine. Delighted. As he
opened the driver door (was it ever locked?) he said, "Thinland." My door was unlocked. I said, "Finland, you mean."

We zoomed out like a fuse from Canaveral, my hot dog tumbling up and down my esophagus, all tires squealing like mice. "Thinland," he repeated. Then he added the longest speech he had yet uttered. "No seals that I know of. They are just regular folks. Very thin,
correct. But no fins." How absolutely hilarious. Thinland… as you wish, dude, as you wish. Time for napping.

As I tried to wake up, a soft rocking motion pushed me back into sleep, lullabying me. In the end I came to my senses. We were cruising now, taking our time. He looked pensive and his eyes loomed larger. I hadn't noticed them yet. They were beautiful, with long dark lashes. Irises a color of mud. Striped and dotted. Green, gold, silver. A mushy kaleidoscope. Quite remarkable.

Christ! Were we riding on water? No wonder Jesus came to my lips. I had casually glanced through my window, and the ocean was there. I could not see the road on my side, only waves, thick and oily. Oh my, how was it possible? How deep…? Vertigo almost choked me.

I turned towards him. Cool, relaxed, he admired the waterfront on his side. Quite touristic indeed, a miniature Venice. Only, red. I mean, everything. Various shades. All possible tones. Red roof tiles, rosy walls enlivened by red shutters. Laced curtains festooned with red hearts, balconies filled with geraniums in bloom. Red awnings for stores, advertised by red lettering. Words I couldn't decipher. Tiny familiar pictures. Pigs and bottles. Dresses and pipes. Clogs, guitars, sausages, pitchers and pans. Dolls (were they girls?) and soldiers. Cigarettes and
syringes. Syringes? Bows and buttons.

He stopped dead. I instinctively ducked, waiting for the next car to rear end us. But no car was behind us, and anyway we were cruising. "Don't you need buttons?" he asked softly, as if whispering a romantic, perhaps an obscene proposal. What did he mean? Well, sure, I
could use a few. As a matter of fact, I loved buttons. I collected them, indeed. I couldn't resist them. How the hell did he know?

On my side there was water. Now that we were stopped, I thought I saw fish under the surface. Dark shadows. Maybe I just imagined them.

The impulse took me by surprise. The irresistible wish

to get out and swim. I should leave my plush jacket behind. I
almost took it off. All fear had deserted me. That's when he
grabbed my hand, gentle, but deadly firm. "This way," he said,
and he pulled me after himself through the driver's door.

We entered the button hole. I mean the button shop.
Truly, it was so small and so crowded it looked like a cave. The
walls were entirely packed with file cabinets, labeled with long
cardboard strips on which samples were sewn. A large table was
covered with crates, jars, and baskets filled up to the edge with
miscellanea of all sorts.

Behind an equally loaded counter, an old couple
took care of the customers. Mostly, though, they obsessed on
merchandise, shelving, storing away as if only that mattered. A
crowd bunched up at the center table where the bargains were,
greedy, intent, rapacious, enthralled.

I saw things pretty and precious. Pastel colors. Wood,
bone, ivory and horn. Patchwork. Lattice. Mosaic. Silk, satin
and velvet. Gold leaf. I saw coral, shell, mother-of-pearl. I saw
enamel, glass, fine embroidery and the tiniest of beads. Sailor
knots and forget-me-not, lucky
clovers of the most incredible green. My jaw dropped,
my hands itched with anticipation. Then, impromptu, that
multifarious grace gave me a heartache.

"I need air," I said to no one. I stepped onto the
sidewalk. The ocean lapped at my feet, and the impulse of
diving overwhelmed me again. He must have guessed. Known.
"You are not a seal yet," he said tonelessly. At my side, he was
lighting a cigarette. I pulled it off his mouth,
took a draft. It felt great, not sure why. I breathed deeply before
he took it back.

Then he took something out of his pocket (the
zippered one on his chest) and he put it into my palm. "What is
it?" "A walrus tooth. And a button as well, if you wish. I would
sew it to my favorite dress, if I were you." I mindlessly looked
for a pocket. My nightgown had none.
I just closed my fist. "I miss Mother," I exhaled.

What? My words startled me. Not sure what they
meant, why I had pronounced them, if they were even true.

"Was it because I watched myself in the mirror?" I
asked. We were back on the road. He said nothing.

I had lingered in front of the thing just the night
before, playing with my budding breasts. Noticing for the
thousandth time how the left one was larger and differently
shaped than the right, trying to decide which one I preferred.

"No, baby," he answered after a while. I had already
forgotten to what. "And you don't even know where to look. It's
more complex than that." He stared at my breast so frankly…
so briefly, I felt kind of slapped. I imagined his eyes dropping
between my tits like pickled onions, slimy and squishy, icy cold.

Well, his stare was unflattering, as if he had spotted a
scrawny steak on a market boot, a slightly battered apple, an old,
bad-smelling fish. He repeated, "You don't even know where to
look, do you?" and he laughed. I should hate him, perhaps.

I woke up freezing to my bones. It was pitch dark.
First, my fingertips felt the plush. I was wearing the thing, and
still freezing. I was lying on my side, curled up like a fetus. Did
he recline the seat?

Then a smell of dirt made me land, so to speak. I
was on damp grass. What on earth… Indeed. I sat up, spotted

a faint luminescence, a stripe, like a Milky Way. The road, doubtlessly, and passing cars. The road, so far away.

Had I fallen off? Please. I would have killed myself, while I was intact. Only dead cold. Perhaps a bit hungry? A hotdog was all I had eaten. Since when? Thinland… Was it what he meant? But I wasn't bruised at all. Did he carry me? Truly? I was clenching my fist, still
holding the walrus tooth. Damn it.

Suddenly, I remembered what I was at. When? That I didn't remember. I missed Mom in the most horrifying way. I recalled I was lost. Pardon, she was.

I recalled she had left, Stepdad said. To go where, with whom, he didn't say. "She is gone," he yelled, yanking at the kitchen table so hard, both his coffee cup and my bowl spilled all over. I sneaked out of my chair, went to grab a sponge at the sink. He didn't pay attention.
"Gone! Gone with the devil!" he screamed.

I had come all the way to Finland to find her. She must have gone back to where she came from. Maybe she was nostalgic. For sure. I should start walking, then, looking for Mother. Reach the road, then keep walking. I would find a village. A town. Maybe I would hitchhike. I had done it before.

Him? The hell with him! Forgotten, crossed out. Must be bound somewhere else, as I should have expected. It was certainly the fault of my breasts, irregular, meatless, too thin even for Thinland.

I started off at a steady pace, though I felt slightly nauseous. Courage, girl. Aim toward those asphalt lanes. You'll be there soon, then stick your thumb out.

Only, I got lost.

Hell

Deepening more and more into green. Endless meadows, edged by erratic patches of trees. The sun rose, then climbed higher. I sat once in a while. Must have been afternoon when (my head empty of thought, too tired even to feel it) I saw them in the distance.

They were quietly sitting on grass, as if for a picnic. In fact, Mother was fumbling inside a large basket, digging out a cluster of grapes she started plucking, tenderly feeding some to his mouth. I felt a pang of jealousy. Rather sadness. Also Mother's eyes (oh my, I had missed them so much!) had a tinge of melancholy. Not unlike her. More intense, though, than I recalled.

He was holding a huge sunflower. As I approached, he gave it to Mom with a theatrical motion, almost kneeling in front of her. Was he ridiculing her? She didn't exactly look pleased. But she put the bloom in her lap, lingering with her fingertip on its core, thick and grainy with seeds.

They both smiled at me. Still, I felt like an intruder. My sadness sunk deeper. Until suddenly a flash of genius lit my somnolent brain. How come I hadn't grasped it before? My eyes shifted between those two. My throat tightened. I hesitated, as usual, not sure whom I should ask, then I burst at him, "Are you my father?" He grinned. "Do I look that old?" Mother didn't laugh. She handed me a bunch of grapes from the basket. I devoured them.

At his side was the violin case, shut… well, locked, a key stuck in the keyhole. He reached behind his back, then presented me with a geranium flower, deep crimson. An unjustified happiness overwhelmed me. "From Thinland," he exclaimed as I grabbed it, and he openly smiled, for once. I noticed a bad tooth his lips tried to conceal. Might have been why he usually smirked.

I woke up with a whack on my face. My entire body tensed up in spasm. "What the…!"

"You can't fall asleep at the wheel!" he said. I was driving. Still wearing my nightgown and plush. At a glance, I spotted a branch of geranium lying on my lap, side to side with a walrus tooth. Clearly, none of it was a dream. It all had… was happening. Therefore, I should watch the road, should I?

The Ferrari ran as smooth as a spill on wax cloth. It glided. Soared. Right and left of us there was water, but it didn't scare me. Iridescent and muddy. By instinct, I sensed it was shallow. Maybe it was freshwater. Then a flock of flamingos took off, flew by, vanished towards the horizon.

I should ask where we were going, right? Before I opened my mouth I heard his breathing, rhythmic, soft. I had a quick sideways glance. His hands rested in his lap, fresh cig languidly hung between two of his fingers. Irresistibly, my gaze slipped toward his crotch, then abruptly stopped. "You don't even know where to look," he had said. I should watch the road, should I?

His head, without me noticing, had tilted. Now it slumped against my shoulder, limp, weirdly weightless. I couldn't help brushing his coiled hair for a moment. Nice. I took a deep breath. Go girl. Go with the devil.

part 3

Ulysses

Ulysses called on the phone, saying he was on his way but couldn't find my place. His accent (and a blur in the reception, perhaps) made it hard for me to decipher his words, as if he were calling indeed from an immense distance. I asked him to provide some landmarks, finally recognizing the name of a street. "But you are very close!" I shouted, probably with disproportionate enthusiasm, as I was simply speaking to a new repairman. "I know, I know," he said with the tone of one who really does.

When he passed the front door, I had a pang I can barely describe. Not because he was handsome. He wasn't. But his gaze carried that something that opens Pandora's vase, and then hell breaks loose. Or heaven, but you cannot predict which one. Something I knew well, but couldn't possibly define unless it smacked me in the face. From another face. There it was.

Indefinable age. Body worn by hard work. Bushy hair and fawn beard revealed in their midst eyes of depth unfathomable. Full of ocean, eyes that have seen it all but will forever guard their secret. Oh yes, I recognized them, though I didn't expect them…

I should have. Hadn't we exchanged a sort of informal warning? "You are close!" "Yes I know…" Come on! When we walked into the kitchen, I had shut the lid and secured it in place. I had donned my armor and sharpened my defenses.

His first gestures were almost shy. He smiled, thankfully, when I handed him a stepstool to spare him a trip to his van. Then he started to operate on my microwave, while I literally watched his back. Without turning around, he muttered, "How did you find me?" and I lost it for a second or two. I almost sighed, "Not sure… I waited, hoped, believed," but I caught myself and mentioned Internet.

I'm not sure he heard my answer. He had started mumbling a kind of litany… or a lullaby, a spell, both reassuring and strange, in a language I didn't know. Harsh, archaic and guttural. Ancient Greek, I thought, mesmerized. But it could have been Arab, Armenian, Hebrew or Turkish. Blond hair? Cobalt eyes? It had to be Greek. I drifted within its sounds, getting farther and farther from the place we were in.

He was fast. Quickly, he pinpointed the problem, tried several things in order to solve it, clarified all details I wished to understand, then did what I asked for. At one point he yelled, "You don't need me!" He referred to a task I could expedite without spending on him. Once again his words startled me, reaching me like a bullet. A small one, but still.

"You don't need me…" if he said so. Did he travel this far to bring me the news? That my ceaseless wait had been vain? That I could have managed without him? Was he right?

He started laughing. Not at me. He laughed at things and himself, at what was inside the wounded appliance, what he unsuccessfully tried, what he finally pulled out of his hat. He laughed throughout his muttering, singing, cursing in the mysterious language, and his laughter didn't bother me at all.

On the contrary, it confirmed what I already knew… that all
was a joke, unimportant and light.

When I asked if he did some other kind of repair, he
exclaimed: "You don't understand! I'm alone." "I am too," I
wanted to say, but my mouth knew better. Finally, he stuck a
business card on my fridge, and he went. I did not wish to keep
him. Didn't want to explore the hazards summoned by his sky-
looking irises.

Just for fun, I sought online critiques of his work. They
were dissonant, as it invariably occurs with customer comments.
Well… experience, even of a practical kind, is truly subjective.
Still, reports about him were stunningly opposite. Either he
was a saint, magician and savior, or a thief, robber, scoundrel,
in which case he was called "the guy with a thick accent."
Prejudice was at play. A tinge of racial profiling weighed on the
harsh judgments.

Overall, the picture drawn by those inconsistent notes
struck me as chameleonic… very appropriate for Ulysses, who
had said to the Cyclops he fought, "My name is No Man." His
poor victim kept shouting, "No man's hurting me! No man's
making me blind!"

His name is nobody.

I forgot… The positive critiques praised his being
"consistently on time." That is paradoxical for someone you
have been constantly waiting for. But it means what it means.
He arrives when he must, apparently. And he does what your
circumstances require… he informs you, for instance, that
you no longer need him. He suggests that you are sufficiently
strong, you can pull it off by yourself.

With a tiny, tiny bit of his help.

Afterimage

Of the man who couldn't see colors she recalls two things.

This is quite reductive, of course. More is worth recalling, for sure, but it remains vague. A shape, rather an area. A zone, rather an aura. A soft patch of vibrant, flickering something joining the two moments that so sharply reemerge, dwarfing the rest.

Perhaps they are right, after all, those two assertive, invasive memories. Perhaps they are all that counts, like two poles…

Little ones. Small sticks. Two short, robust stakes you'd plant in the ground, then connect with a tightly stretched rubber band. Should you take the stakes out, the band would collapse. Poof. Gone. Should you pull the stakes off the ground, nothing would remain.

There's a game of bocce on a summer afternoon, in the garden of someone she hasn't met before. She was brought along as a guest. She knows no one, but that doesn't bother her.

Perhaps there is a pool. Perhaps, when she first sees him he's wearing a pair of bathing trunks. Perhaps he's relaxing on a lawn chair. There is wine. Repeat. Wine. Yet another bottle, chilled, white, bubbling, as de rigueur in similar weather. All evaporates as soon as it happens, every sip, every drop of sweat, every word, until the game of bocce concentrates it all within the borders of its neat, rectangular court, filled with sand.

The owner of the house has produced the balls. A relic, an heirloom, wrapped in their original case. Large old wooden spheres, plus the jack. The paint scratched, peeling off but still bold enough.

Would you team up with me? Of course. Which color? Well, red… is it what she says? Correct. Is he wearing a red polo at this point? Yes. Red shirt, black hair and a nondescript mug, kind of oval. What her grandma would call "bovine" with a sort of fondness, because cows are good, gentle animals.

So they team up. To say magic immediately starts would be a shortcut. Couldn't happen like that. Well, it takes no more than a couple of throws for magic to start, then rapidly swell… Meaning that it's soon quite evident he plays bocce as no one else would. Meaning, as if he had no idea about the rules of the game or even that the game has rules. He throws casually, really casually and then he laughs. Then, on top of it, when the teams gather around the jack to measure which color is closest, arguing about hairbreadth distance, angle, radius and such, when discussions warm up and excitement…

That's the gist of the game, is it? In those moments he comes near the jack as expected, looms above the contentious balls but remains sort of vague, abstracted. Sort of absent, sporting a neutral smile, always, she can tell, on the verge of exploding with laughter. Yes, he laughs more and more as the game goes on, and his is a complex hilarity, both naïve and ironical, childish, and kind of sour.

  Mozart

When he's asked her to team up, he has told her that he plays poorly. That sounds weird, because he is quite fit. How hard can it be to play bocce? All the ninety-year-olds around the Mediterranean can do it. During lazy afternoons, while their ninety-year-old wives pour lace out of their crochets by the mile, old men's arthritic hands wrap themselves around wooden balls between swags of silver Pastis or golden Retsina. How hard…

He has said up front that he's bad. She is too, she has graciously replied, duly matching his obvious false modesty. He is bad for real, though, and that seems to make him laugh, perhaps of embarrassment. But his laughter is both infectious and charming.

They will lose, inevitably. He has known since the beginning. Truly, he should have asked, "would you like losing with me?" Had he been so blunt, so frank, what could she have replied? "Yes, of course, this and many other games, until the world ends."

Retrospectively.

So when his hilarity starts spreading, spilling over her (and she doesn't resist because it is fine, it's great, like a breeze lifting the inexorability of the afternoon sun), she starts laughing as well. Her good mood must reassure him, because the magic builds up. It becomes a fabulous sense of intimacy, as if they had known each other since birth. Maybe, in another dimension they have.

As if, bent as they are at ground level, eyes riveted on sand… or else meeting, suddenly, his diving into hers after a throw or at the very moment of counting score, a bit apprehensive, a tad questioning and then relaxed when she…

(Smile! She must. She has rapidly realized it and it isn't

difficult, as her mood gets better and better.)

As if crouching low, down to earth, had transmuted them into a sort of Hansel and Gretel, kids out of a fairy tale, brother and sister, little bro, little sis.

So how was it, girl, to play with a stranger in order to lose? Rather with no order at all, in the most disorderly fashion, happily unaware of the fact there could be winners and losers or even a goal to achieve, just floating.

Then the goal of that moment (how long did it last?) must have been another. Have fun? Lots and lots of it. Why? Because of the sudden lifting of rules, their unforeseen disappearing matched with the fact she couldn't care less. Or because the two of them, extraneous until a minute ago, were projected into a private sphere, a unique haven, unique heaven.

Were they drunk? Course not. Were they flirting and falling in love?

Perhaps they were flirting. Perhaps drunk. But not really.

The game shouldn't have ended.

The other team, the one with the green balls, played darn well. Perhaps they played normally. Still, she suspects they overdid it, just to counter the boredom of having hardly any opponent.

She had started playing in earnest, but she had rapidly, smoothly, imperceptibly aligned to his disorienting strategy, which of course wasn't one. Not-too-blatantly, and so the game lasted and the green side, irrepressibly winning, didn't comment about the absurdity of the red style.

The green, winning team included their host. He and her red teammate were best buddies. Then, the host must have known how things would turn out. This must have occurred before.

Did all of his previous partners have a blast? Did they feel the thrill? Did they drift as she did?

The game shouldn't have ended.

After that afternoon it was clear that they liked each other. They went out together a bit, she and the man who couldn't see colors. When he explained, she didn't ask for details.

She should have. These things are important. How we sense, meaning how our five senses work. It is different for each of us, and for some more different. The more different, the more important.

Very important. She should have asked, which colors exactly? How do you see them, or not? What do you see instead?

She did not ask, but he volunteered information when he said that genetic trait of his had radically changed his fate, x-ing him out of the family trade, which was tartan production. Very old, very famous industry, very flourishing, requiring precise expertise that was handed down generation after…

Not to him. He didn't have to choose if he'd produce tartan cloth or if he'd rather do something else. He did not have to choose, but he believed, indeed, that he'd like something else much better. Perhaps anything else.

So this confidence of his is also a distinct memory. She must have found it striking, defining… the only comment he made about his uncommon way of seeing. But was it uncommon? After meeting him, she realized she knew nothing about it.

We should better explore how we sense things. All of

us, each and every one. Understand how we use our five senses.
Each and every one.

At the other end of the elastic (giant rubber band,
perhaps scarlet like the bocce, the polo shirt, one of those
things movers utilize to bind, let's say, a mattress, a large
mattress, king-size…)

He was fairly tall, fairly robust. Average, nondescript
features but very sharp eyes. Very acute. Very smart, but he sort
of hid it. He downplayed it. And very black hair.

At the end of the rubber-band-kind-of-aura, kind
of blurred, undetermined time when they saw each other,
tentatively and still not sure if they should step forward
(although, clearly, they seemed to like each other, perhaps a
whole lot) there's this summer afternoon where they (not alone,
there's another couple with them, like another team, on the
backseat)…

There's this summer afternoon, less torrid than the
previous one because a month or two have passed, the season
has softened. Now it must be mild, meek, sweet September.

Not two months. Only one. Give it another month and
that would have happened.

Still, it must be September. The colors reveal it. She
(she, of course) recalls the colors unraveling by the side of the
road while they are bound to another villa, a cottage by the lake.
The lake's poignantly blue, dotted with white sails. In the fridge
a flask of Lambrusco is waiting, deep crimson. They haven't
arrived yet. She is driving.

At the last moment, though he was clearly elated by the
invitation, his thrill almost palpable, he has declined sitting in
the front. He has placed himself behind, on the opposite side

of her. Still close. She can distinctly hear him talk.

But she is cross because he has preferred the back seat, and as they go tension rises. A slight tension, nothing less than polite, wrapped within layers of irony and laughter. Giggles, humorous quips… She can tell, now that she has started acquainting him, that he's getting more and more nervous, uncomfortable. That is why he laughs, to shroud, veil, conceal the discomfort. Just like during the game, yet this time around no magic occurs.

It can't. He is not well because he is scared of her driving. She has perfectly understood. That's why he sits in the back. But she drives well, she knows it, she is proud of it. Why would anyone be afraid of her driving? This is nonsense.

At some point, as a joke, he equates her to a bunny, a young rabbit hopping around. Is he trying to say her driving style is too jumpy, too abrupt? He is the rabbit! He's the one with scorched nerves, chicken, wimpy. Coward.

Doesn't she realize he must be wary of all drivers, any driver? Doesn't she realize streetlights are a code he probably can't unscramble, so are stop lights in the back of cars, and the great majority of signals her brain processes without a blink? Doesn't she get it?

Not at the moment, or she does, but she's hurt and that overrides comprehension. At this end of the rubber band she feels stupidly yet atrociously offended. Perhaps she is too young. Retrospectively.

Too hurt. If he can't trust her… He can't. He has to! Like she trusted that losing a game wouldn't matter. She would lose any game of anything, till the end of the world, if they'd only team up for good. Lose forever, if he just could trust her to drive him to the lake, the chilled red wine.

Intact, perfectly safe on the passenger side. Relax. Take my hand.

But he has picked the backseat. Not trusting her yet… She should, she must give him time. A bit more, should she? That is when the elastic snaps. Little stakes, small pickets suddenly uprooted. Not sure how the evening ends… Oh well, it fishtails, insignificant. Not sure when and how they disconnect.

The Taste of Water

Please, can you describe it?
Not bubbly, not mineral.
Plain, flat water. Pure water.

Those square cartons… cubic I mean… I'll never forget them.

They were handed out after the show, backstage, in the rear of the truck whose front was the traveling theater that went town to town, suburb to suburb, favela to favela.

I sat there. I collapsed, exhausted like a beaten horse, not even removing my stilts, my complicated harness. Still on my wooden legs (those fabulous sticks I wore) I recovered my breath after the performance, having tramped gluey yellow sand for an hour, in full sun, in spite of the stifling weather.

When a member of the modest production graced me with a carton cube full of water, I ecstatically poured it into my throat, as if sipping the finest brand of champagne or else… What? Ambrosia? It was nectar to me. You see, I was thirsty.

What is special about it? As for many other issues it is degree that matters. I've been around a while, but I experienced the quintessential thirst in those Brazilian outskirts. Summer, midday, a soft muddy soil where we staggered on stilts, feeling,

I believe, the opposite of what astronauts felt on the moon. If
they floated, we sunk, sucked in towards the center of the earth,
lifting tons at the end of our fragile extremities.

Still, I looked like a butterfly in pink satin, sporting
feathers, pompons, bangles and spangles, tracing arabesques
with Chinese ribbons while galloping around, my gaze at roof
level, my accordion tickling the unforgiving blue sky. Miracles
of youth and adrenaline when they mix.

All that effort, that tremendous display of energy
and grace, wasn't worth a lot moneywise. But I felt perfectly
rewarded, believe me, when I was finally given that thing. I
mean water.

How could I love it so madly? There wasn't much
competition. I was lonely and sad, without even knowing it. See,
sadness was like sand grabbing at my stilts, hindering my step
as I danced, making it a tad harder, that's all. I didn't notice my
gloom more than I thought about sand while twirling.

But lonely I was. I knew I would be, from the start. He
had told me about an old flame, former lover living close by.
He had said she'd visit during our tour, and I shouldn't nag or
protest.

Did I ever protest? I took his philandering as a natural
flaw, like a storm or a drought you don't really wish for but, hey!
If they come, then what? I had been warned that I'd share my
guy with a twin, a double, a sub. I had seen pictures, and she
looked kind of like me. Dark and small, maybe a little plumper.
Oh, well.

Then he suddenly fell for a third gal, brand new, a local
actress. Local beauty? Not truly. I sincerely puzzled, night after
night, about what made that sweetie so much better than me.

But indeed, do our rivals have something that makes

them better? Do they ever?

Or is it another problem entirely? Is the question a totally different one?

As I said. Can you tell me what water tastes like? Can you, please, describe the taste of water?

You can't.

Water has none.

What you feel is the taste of your quenched thirst.

Sometimes it is all that matters.

Waste Not

When she wakes up, he's gone. He has taken his backpack. Not a doubt, he won't come back until night. Quickly, as if squeezing the hand of a naughty child, she puts her mind on hold and forbids herself questioning, brooding. Where. With whom. Why.

He's gone without a word, sneaked away without explanations. Now the day looks as empty as the bed, frightening in its useless, redundant integrity.

All colleagues have left or soon will (she can hear noise downstairs, in the hall). Excursions were planned. Today is the coveted break before the flight home, after a week spent between office walls. Restaurant in the evening, right… but dinners were tainted with work-related conversations, the team gathered around the same table, no intimacy, no true distraction.

After those lengthy meals they have returned to the room and collapsed in bed, falling instantaneously asleep. He hasn't even complained about the cheap lodging (she has enjoyed the thin mattress, reminding her of a boat, a train berth). Sunday would come at last and they'd go to the beach, stroll the local markets for trinkets. Get a tan in one day. Get drunk until the wee hours, uncaring of Monday's early start.

Taxi drivers know their way to the airport.

Saturday (was it yesterday night?) he has pushed her into a cab, mumbling something, tongue blurred by too much wine. Go ahead, I'll take the next one, he has said. After showering in the exiguous bathroom, she has dug out of her bags a silk baby-doll. One of those sexy wears, tons of lace and that's all. The trip had an exotic destination… which rhymes with, almost tastes of erotic. Truly, she has carried the thing in view of the weather, hot and stifling as hell. Now she lies in her diaphanous attire, sheets bunched and fan buzzing, while an emerald glare pours through wide-open windows.

Screams of tropical birds fill the night. Are these songs? Not those she's used to… these birds speak a different tongue. Their relentless chat has weird, haunting undertones. It inspires both longing and fear, makes her wish to do what the birds say, though sensing that it might be dangerous, bad. Go. Go with the birds.

She lies quiet, dead tired yet sleepless.

Lift the camera. Stop there, in midair. Now back up to get the best vantage point. She is stunningly beautiful. Darn desirable. You can't possibly miss it, no matter how inebriated you are, no matter how drowsy. It must be what the birds are yapping about.

When he comes back at dawn he fucks her, and how could he not? A light breeze brings an illusion of coolness. Three hours later, when she awakes from a brief but dense slumber, he isn't there.

*

He is gone for the day. Tonight he'll come back. Or else, since he took his luggage, tomorrow he will go straight to the airport. She has seen this before. Business travel means all sorts of business, local sex included. Like local cuisine, it boosts the experience. It makes it full flavored, complete.

She isn't that hurt by his defection. But, not having foreseen it, she's unprepared. Her colleagues' voices seep in through the open window. They are still lingering outside the hotel… but she can't run out and yell, "wait!" Too late for impromptu joining a party, for tagging along, let alone justifications. Then be it. She gets dressed, makes coffee on the kitchenette, throws a bag of nuts in her purse. She will spend the day on her own. It shouldn't be hard.

It is for some reason, in spite of her pretending the opposite. Abrupt anguish almost chokes her on a sunny plaza, among market booths filled with colorful, beautiful crafts. Such things usually catch her attention, distract her from trouble. Not today. On impulse, she digs for her phone, dials her folks at home. How's everyone? She is well, having fun. Yes! Back soon. She calls them so rarely… Surprise makes them giddy. Their pleasure, alas, doesn't bounce back.

In fact, the phone call breaks the dams, unlatching a valve in her throat, a hidden faucet now leaking a steady trickle of tears. She catches a random bus, needs to sit, to be rocked, be carried away.

Where? She didn't pay attention. A map is in her purse and the day seems infinite. She'll have ample time to retrace her steps. The bus goes wherever it goes, towards unfamiliar suburbs, leaving both downtown and the beaches behind. Buildings become smaller and paler, streets narrower, busier. People multiply like ants. So do houses. They come close, almost bite at the windowpane. But she doesn't feel crowded. On the contrary, she feels reassured. Cradled. Lullabied.

*

When did the guy sit? She has no clue. Someone else was there and then… Right, a brief commotion took place. Someone rushed towards the door, someone else pressed in. Not sure, though. She hasn't taken her eyes off the street since when she came in, enthralled, hypnotized. Now something has broken the spell, and she checks her purse, clutched under her arm.

The newcomer has caused her alertness, though he sits quiet and still. Small frame, not very tall, thin, breathes lightly, but she feels his presence as if an invisible hook had harpooned her innards, catching the soft corner of some main organ, lung, heart, liver, brain. A pinhole. A scratch. A thorn prick. But it stings.

She turns, has a look. He turns too. They exchange a stare of direct, calm appraisal. He wears blue, head to toe (not such a long way), pair of faded jeans and a cotton shirt. Same shade of his irises, light cobalt on bronze skin, under sable hair falling across his cheeks, shoulders, back, loose strands on his chest.

A wave of desire washes over her, of uncanny proportions. She recalls nothing of the kind, not recently at least. It catches her so quickly, she aches, as if someone had just slapped her. Rather hit her nape, the base of her skull, from behind. A shock, making her vacillate. She is drenched in sweat, little rivers soaking her breast and thighs.

She gives him a second look. So does he,

simultaneously. He must have perceived her intention, then promptly responded. They aren't smiling or exchanging any sort of acknowledgment. Nothing social. No need. He is sweating as well, his shirt patched, brow pearled and lips shiny. Her want has grown so intense, she feels like she is melting. Liquefying.

The bus empties as fast as it had filled up, convulsively squeezing people out. It must be close to the terminus. The guy shifts on the seat, prepares to stand up, hesitates. She senses it. Once more she turns to face him. His gaze is still firm, yet meek, the meekest she has ever seen in a man. Proud, and welcoming at the same time. Slowly, with a husky deep voice she didn't expect, he says one word only. Must be his name. On leaving, he is introducing himself.

On the doorsteps he's watching her still, his expression frank and yet not enticing. No nods, no invite to follow him somewhere, as she would have thought. From the sidewalk, he maintains eye contact as long as he can while the bus resumes its course, putting them face to face for a second, glass pane in between.

The impulse to rush at the door, alight, see what's next, has been hard to control. Like a mantra, she has kept repeating, "I can't." Can't risk missing tomorrow's flight home. Job? Colleagues? Her family? Her husband, whatever he's doing. Can't just leave, she has said as if she believed it. Was it duty burdening her, keeping her on track? Fear? Inertia? Did it all go too fast? She doesn't quite know. Sweat has glued her butt to the cheap vinyl of the bench until it was too late.

When the bus ends its course, she stays seated. She'll eventually get back to where she's started. The return route might vary, as sometimes they do. But she will find her way.

*

The bus stops near the beach, not far from the hotel. Excitement has deserted her body, leaving a dull exhaustion. Now she is craving the ocean, yet another thirst in her bones, a different urge. On the promenade, vendors show their multicolored fare. She remembers she wanted to purchase something, a few souvenirs, a few gifts.

The guy's name? She can't have forgotten already, yet she is blanking. Oh, that's one of those tricks that minds like to play... If you try to retrieve it, what you are looking for will further escape, hide more deeply. If you feign indifference, though, your brain will relax its spires. It will loosen its grip, let go of stolen goods washing them ashore, so to speak. Driftwood. Flotsam. Seaweed.

Sunset is approaching. Hurrying up, she'll be able to watch it from the beach. But a spread of flowers, lying in baskets of cane right in front of her, catches her attention. Not a thing to carry on a plane, but she never could resist sunflowers. She buys the tallest one.

She is holding it upright, like a candle. Such an eerie stance, loaded with memories... a procession, the smell of incense and wax, a monotone chant. Maybe a funeral? She walks towards the water, pale and foamy in the distance. A long way to go. Here beaches are huge, causing her to feel little and lost, but it doesn't matter.

Meanwhile, the sun sinks in an opalescent mousse. Disappointingly, it hasn't turned the bloody crimson she craved. It is tinged pink and gold, perhaps salmon and mauve, a shade of uncertainty and compromise suiting the sloppy consistency of the sea, today kind of ragged, stained, discolored. All of this, no doubt, has its melancholy charm… Staring at the horizon, she longs for the other side. Home.

But what is it? The place where she was last week? The land where she was born, where she usually lives? Her family? Her job, when this darn trip will end and routine resume? Her past? Remote? Recent? What is she missing?

She doesn't know, but she is restless, with a need to withdraw from people, though no one is disturbing her. Lots of folks are around but scattered, sparse, colored dots bunched up in irregular formations. It is late for bathing or swimming. Some have spread food on blankets, some play games, some are building fires. Music is everywhere. Bits of tunes mingle with adult conversations and children's screams. As she nears the shoreline, all gets dulled and muffled, a comforting background. The sound of the waves, overwhelming, swallows everything.

Here. Arrived. She kicks her sandals off, foam lapping her feet. As she walked, the flower has become a burden. She's tired of carrying it. She will not be able to bring it aboard… Might as well leave it now, yet the idea feels creepy. Quite cruel. Still. She kneels, digs a hole. Judging by the length and diameter of the stem, she needs to reach deeper. Sand is under her fingernails, hair over her face, her back to the sea from which a strong wind has risen. Deeper… till the tip of her fingers meets rock.

When she sticks in the flower, it stands. She is relieved. In spite of their looks, sunflowers are frail. They tend to collapse, fall apart, break their neck, their huge head a dead weight. But the hole she has excavated is good, profound, tight. The bloom stands like a flag. Tears have started to spill while

Mozart

she worked… mixed with sand and salt, they are caking her skin. Never mind. Just a residue from today's phone call, some got stuck in the pipe, now purging. Yet she can't get herself to stand up. On the contrary she'd like to keel over, let her brow impress itself into dampness.

Should she recite a prayer? To whom? Picture a sacred image of sorts? When she shuts her eyes, trying to summon a marble statue, perhaps, or a gilded icon, a hint of vertigo seizes her. Look up! Breathe! Again, she stares at the horizon, from which colors have faded.

She must pray, though, or the whole planting ritual won't be worth a dime. Possibly, the sunflower will die because… Yes, by her fault (she knows this is nonsense, yes, she knows). Still, is there an ocean-god she could appropriately address? Some old local deity. Ocean-goddess. One must surely exist.

"Our Lady of the Water." "Sweet Lady of the Sea, please accept this flower I'm offering." Is it true? Isn't she getting rid of the darn thing? Don't interrupt her. "I give you this flower, and…" As when she's called her parents, the dams briskly collapse. She irrepressibly cries for no reason. "And I give you myself. Flower, and myself."

"Our Lady, as I kneel on this sand, I promise. It's over. I am cutting and burying these chains. Here." Which chains? There are things you don't need to know, only pronounce out loud. Spit them. Vomit. You are done. She sits in the cooling dampness, facing out, seawards, her head cleared and clean.

*

She remembers the two of them sitting, watching the sunset like this. How come she didn't think of it earlier?

Well, enjoying sunsets on a beach is not quite exceptional. It happened dozens of times. But that one was memorable. That must be when she decided she'd marry him. A key moment, one of those when continuity is broken and you take a leap, no matter where to. A leap you can't possibly untake.

At some point of their clumsy courtship comes a ride to the seashore, dinner at a fisherman joint, further lingering on sand, unwilling to drive back. Then his long explanation, out of nowhere. She is in front. He's behind and has wrapped himself around her, the long-waited-for onset of intimacy…

Is it to ease probabilities of sex that he pours out his memories? No encouragement is needed, as he well knows. She is sure no scheme underlies his abrupt openness. And he isn't drunk when he starts telling things he could keep for himself. Slightly shameful, slightly painful, like the struggle to get rid of his baby fat in spite of an overfeeding mother, or the dreadful feeling when he lost the karate championship, disappointing his parents' expectations.

He has planned to kiss his first girl right after the match. That will be his secret reward, his real trophy. Somehow, he has attached his manhood, the christening of a new body, free of flabs and allowed sexuality, to his success. But he has lost. He goes home and shuts himself in his room with a batch of cookies Mom has baked for the occasion. One by one, he gulps them in rage, and he makes a pact with the devil. He will redeem his failure, or else…

Only, he forgets about it. But the devil does not. Did he hook sexual initiation to championship? How unfortunate. Both accomplishments slip further and further away, a package too elaborately wrapped. Soon he stops competitions and training, claiming they distract him from school. Mom, always afraid he'd get hurt, is pleased. So is Dad, looking forward to graduation and college. Truth is, after losing he doesn't feel comfortable around his coach and mates.

When approaching a girl, he is paralyzed by a shyness he didn't know about… like a tumor sprouted out of nowhere. He postpones with excuses. Postponing makes him feel late. Late makes him feel awful. Breaking the vicious circle gets increasingly hard. He believes he is stuck until, having finished college, found a brilliant job and left home, the spell simply subsides.

Yet the years of frustration, lasted into his twenties, took their toll. When he breaks free, he's eager to catch up on missed occasions. All of them. He piles up as many adventures as decency allows. Then he starts overlapping them, uncaring of decency. He has developed an addiction based on long deprivation, past angst.

That night, on the beach, he's honest about it. As if she didn't know. At work, everyone does. As soon as she started seeing him she was briefed, then constantly and lavishly updated. A new gossip blooms weekly, or more often. Is it why they haven't yet moved past the dating stage?

But she has never heard the whole story until when, before a sinking sun, he spontaneously, frankly, earnestly whispers it all. He is sitting behind her, face hidden. Doesn't have to look in her eyes. Easy-peasy, a confessional. On the spot, she decides she'll marry him nevertheless.

*

It comes back. The guy was called Claudius. That is what he said. How could she forget? So nice. And so obvious. God of clouds! "Dius" means "deus." Sure. Means god. Truly, clouds are called something else in the local tongue, and the Latin root "clau" doesn't hint at vapor formations. She should know from her school days, but so many years have passed… She can pick a new interpretation, all right. "God of clouds" justifies the blueness, the beauty. How he dissolved through the crowd.

He didn't. She did. He alighted where supposed, then waited for her. She could have gone with him instead of going on, going away. Well, he was an illusion. How could she have followed a stranger to a lost barrio? Into what would she have stepped because of a sudden fit of lust?

Longing. It wasn't lust, it was longing. Wait… she doesn't make sense. Anyway, her mind is out of control. She can't help wondering about what her husband's doing, which is perfectly insane. Where's the mystery? Didn't this systematically occur, travel after travel? He has followed someone to a lost barrio (rich hotel… it wouldn't make any difference). Someone he has cast his eyes on earlier in the week or met yesterday night at the restaurant, then rejoined this morning. An occasion he carefully looked for, yet he thought befell him by a chance he couldn't possibly miss. Isn't that the whole point? Never miss a chance… even the idea sounds blasphemous. Never pass on a possibility. It will not come back and you'll sorely regret it. Oh, you will.

Now, should she miss her flight, send her husband to hell, say fuck to her job… should she spend the next weeks, months, years, listlessly wandering the metropolis and searching for Claudius, would she find him? Probabilities are on the negative side. Statistics say she might never. She won't. Where is he? A few hours past, already, stuck still in the moment she omitted to live. On the bus, inches from her, the right place, right time, a combo never happening twice. See, that's something her husband wouldn't let occur, no matter the cost. That is what he's doing right now, live the moment, catch the occasion, reap another trophy, add a name and a date to the long list. Is she admiring him?

She never asked him to change. He never promised he would.

From her schooldays the notion emerges, tinged with the slightest discomfort, overlapping the features of a young boy, a classmate affected by polio. She knows what Claudius means in Latin, does she? It means crippled. The limping one. It means hurt. It means wounded. If he ever came out of the blue, he must have tumbled quite badly.

*

What do sunflowers do at night, when they are done craning their neck around the circumference, zealously worshiping their wandering star? Do they shut their petals, like eyelids closing, like joining hands? Do they lean on their neighbors? Stand alone? How will her flower cope tonight, on its own?

She only needs to look up. Dusk has filled the sky, the beach almost empty, all noise ceased. She only has to look up to know how her flower behaves. Besides, it's a cut one. Doesn't have roots, will die pretty soon. The whole planting is just a ritual, a fake.

Wouldn't it have withered one day, even if left on the plant? Flowers aren't permanent features. They carry seeds, become fruit, berries, pods. They dry up, metamorphose themselves. This particular bloom is no different, its destiny hardly modified. Please, stop worrying.

The sunflower has bent his proud rounded face, now reclined in modesty. As she walks away, yet keeps turning back, stalk and bent, drooping crown look like a single ink mark, elongated, angular, cast against thickening shadow. An initial? Rather an exclamation mark. Question mark. A note on a pentagram. A scratch in the middle of a page, meaning nothing. Something someone wanted to say, then they changed their mind.

The sunflower is a hieroglyph against the night sky, alone, darker than darkness.

Sergej

It was quick like a summer storm, and it came with scents.

The jasmine especially, growing up the wooden fence, drugged me with infectious sweetness, bringing up memories of my childhood and a treacherous sense of familiarity. Everything in his yard had a charming flair, sang a hushed siren call.

His brown chicken laid large, sumptuous eggs that he let me bring home. Quite a dangerous gift… Truly, only milk was missing from the nurturing dream I had stepped in. With a cup of fresh milk, just one, the spell would have been fatal. Thank god he didn't offer it. Still, escaping was hard.

In the house, soon enough, I met the flip side of his little Eden. In an old-style porcelain tube, perched on cinderblocks with its funky, ornate iron feet, lived a reptile. Extra large iguana? Not sure. A small alligator, he explained. He liked to take it for strolls, of course on a leash. Otherwise, he kept the door leading to the creature's den always closed.

It was the reptile that smartened me up, though not whispering into my ear, like Satan did into Eve's. That's a snake-kind-of trick and this was a crocodile. Alligator, I mean.

When Sergej left for the Cayman Islands, soon after our

fling had started, he asked me to feed the chicken and water the plants, could I? I had the keys to the house. Once, I walked in for a glass of water and saw…

I didn't, in fact. Almost stepped on it, because it was so silent, so still. Immobile like a sphinx, the beast sat on the living room carpet, blending with its muddy colors, camouflaged within its curly arabesques. Had his master omitted to secure the donjon? Good lord!

My heart started to beat a tad noisily, and I became uncomfortable. My legs softened, simultaneously urging me to run. Just a minute! Could the thing escape? Go outside, I meant… There was a cat door in the kitchen through which I deemed it could squeeze. Could it open the chicken coop and attack the fowl? I knew nothing about its habits or skills, but I felt imminent danger. Something seemed truly wrong, and I should do something.

Sergej had specified that he would be unreachable, as the heaven where he would reside provided no cell service. But the trip was paid for and couldn't be canceled, though it occurred, true, at a sort of unfortunate time and I couldn't join him. Oh, no. The folks with whom he'd go were peculiar, they would not, I would not… It would pass very fast, he swore. Alas, we wouldn't be in touch. Sorry. He wouldn't call and I shouldn't try.

Sergej had been crystal clear, but this seemed the kind of emergency asking for exceptional measures and I dialed his number, left a message. He called back in less than a minute, in panic, his voice near and distinct. Help me, he begged. Doodle (it was his pet's name) needs to be locked in at all costs. Wait, he begged.

Mozart

For what? I waited by the front door, phone in hand, dumbstruck by a sudden chill. Sergej said nothing more but I heard him breathe, and it sounded labored. I just kept my eyes riveted to the dark, scaly shape trying to morph within the furniture.

Maybe a couple of minutes went by that felt like eternity. Then, the animal slowly began to move. Like a snail, it inched off the rug and onto the wooden floor, crept across the room and leisurely crawled down the aisle leading to its cave. It kind of dragged its paws, with a touch of melancholy, I thought. Had it heard the voice of the master? Course not. In its den there was food. Maybe it wanted to munch on something… a snack. Prudently, I went along, following single file at a convenient distance. As the last of the tail was in, I slyly turned the doorknob behind it. "Done," I sighed. "Good," the cellphone exhaled.

So he had lied. Sergej could make and receive calls, no problem. Why had he claimed he could not? I suspected the lady he had met at the airport of being not a colleague's wife as he introduced her, but a lover or girlfriend he'd take on a previously planned vacation, zesty getaway he didn't wish to give up. Freedom was one of his absolutes. Sacrifice wasn't part of his toolset. He was a bird of prey and I knew it, because I was a prey.

A week prior to his departure, a stye had ripened under my eye. Something must have infected my skin, and I secretly blamed the poor hygiene of his bed, coated with dog and cat hair… or else our sleepless nights, perhaps causing my immune system to fail. Petty of me, but I hated that annoyance. It was painful. I felt ugly and depressed.

Sergej, in order to fix my mood, ran me a warm bath filled with balsamic salts. I should just relax, he insisted. He would wash me. Of course, we fucked in the bathtub, first tenderly and then with increasing passion.

He was wearing a quilt, that night. He looked handsome, like a kind of warrior. A pirate. As I said, he was a predator and that showed on his face. His body revealed other things. Childish plumpness, covert fragility. But he fucked me with fury, almost violently. That I liked, because I was a prey.

On the day of his return he urged me for sex, first thing, pronto. We made love, but I could tell he was absent, only anxious to reestablish his mark in case it had faded. Imperceptibly, sadness seeped in. Dumb, dull sadness.

He asked if I wanted him to come inside my cunt or my mouth. I hesitated for a second. He said, "I want you to get the taste of my cum," and I thought it fair, because I had just realized this was our last time. Then, it was fine for me to carry out something, like a goodbye note on my tongue. Deeper. Deeper. I remember driving downhill in a daze, leaving that intoxicating jasmine behind.

Then I mused about his chicken, sometimes, or his garden, or the frantic sex we had poured over our distinct solitudes since night one, when we almost made it outside, in a parking lot. Under flickering stars, his coat hastily thrown on the floor, the two of us on the coat. I mused about the first time and the last, and the island that came in between, and the poor reptile on the loose, unwillingly spilling the beans.

Four years later I met him by chance. He was exiting an Opera House, hand in hand with a stylish lady who resembled me a lot. He had aged, still keeping his ravenous airs, earrings, long beard, old-fashioned guru's poise.

As he animatedly talked to his partner, he looked charming, alluring. She looked fetched. She looked vulnerable, as she staggered on high heels… unlike me, because I wear flats. I adhere to the ground.

I walk fast, so I passed them rapidly.

ULTIMATELY

1.

Once, when I was in grad school, a guest speaker came in, a visiting professor of sorts. I don't truly recall details… but I'm sure he arrived on a Sunday, one day before the event, and that was unusual. I don't know why the administration agreed.

Nothing strange, no, with me being on campus on a weekend. I was a working student, and I had specific tasks to expedite previous to the conference. Here! The theme now comes back. "Art and Science" was the wide umbrella, with a few subtopics that will surface later, perhaps.

It was mid afternoon. I was in the first floor kitchenette. Otherwise, the building was empty. Most of the rooms were locked, and so were some of the double doors giving access to this or that wing. He still made his way to the kitchen, maybe randomly, maybe led by the light and noise amplified by the surrounding dimness and quiet. That small corner of life must have been a glowing lighthouse amidst the expanse of gray, mute architecture. I doubt the smell had traveled through the corridors, though I was cooking.

I was taking a break after fiddling with the electrical for long hours, substituting this or that piece of the obsolete system and crawling on all fours, tape in hand, fastening in place what felt like miles of wire. Well, at least no one would trip and end up headlong on the podium, especially none of the guests… That being finally over, I decided to have lunch. But I was simply boiling eggs. No smell. Maybe a clinking against the sides of the pot, maybe a gurgle of boiling water.

Suddenly, I remembered the confirmation calls. Oh my, I should have made them earlier, Friday the latest. Well, they were pure formalities, but I couldn't omit them. At some point, my negligence would be noticed. I should at least leave messages, right? On the answering machines of a few locked offices, far away, some already asleep, cocooned by darkness… I picked up the phone and I started, my cheerful, mellifluous voice floating like a ghost against my tired, washed-out, expressionless features.

That is when he came in, as softly as if treading on an invisible carpet. Slowly, quietly, he sat on the chair next to mine… necessarily, as the table was squeezed in a corner. Two chairs faced the free sides and I occupied one of them, phone in front of me. Gingerly, I played tricks with a pen rolling through my fingers as I crossed number after number down a typed list. Almost done.

I had pushed an oval placemat, crimson red, to the center of the table. Salt and pepper, two slices of bread, a teaspoon and an eggcup looked lonely. Aimless. Hopeful? Forsaken. As my pen cartwheeled on my knuckles, I leered at the eggcup. I had wanted my eggs à la coque. They were fresh. A rare opportunity, a reward for my drab day. Now they had obviously over-boiled. I must have looked pathetic.

If he startled me? Not in the least. I was rarely scared and he looked harmless, with the halo of respectability you'd expect from a member of the academy. No doubt he was

one such, and quite probably lost. Out of place. Out of time.
Obviously, he must be in need of directions I would gladly
provide. In a moment. I had to finish my call.

"be delighted… rest assured… extremely grateful…
our pleasure… warmest regards"

"…and go fuck yourself," he added, matching my tone
with a touch of mockery so thin I doubted I heard it. His voice
clear, distinct, loud but accurately timed, he spoke right after
I cut the line, as I lowered my eyes to cross the next item…
perfect chance to regain a composure I had momentarily lost
and decide if he had just insulted me.

He had not. I was sure, and yet not entirely. Slowly,
scrambling for some kind of reply, I lifted my gaze. His face
looked a tad hesitant, in-betweenish… like mine, I bet. Did he
regret his prank? Did he fear it might have been unsuitable? His
eyes were undecipherable. Well, no. They were serious and sad,
but so slightly I almost didn't catch it. Not quite.

Meanwhile I had gathered my wits. "Pardon me?" I
raised an eyebrow and smiled at the same time. He also smiled,
in a formal, almost histrionic way. "Isn't that what you meant?
I finished your sentence for you. Isn't it how it goes when we
need to pay those fake compliments—and dear this, and dear
that, yes sir, how do you do, have a wonderful day—but what
we really think is 'go fuck yourself?'"

He was good, I noticed, at faking the lackeyish tone of
my calls. But, "no," I answered, "really. I don't know those folks.
I don't care if I have to call them or not. I don't hate them that
much." He looked unconvinced.

Well, what kind of help did he… I should have asked
but, god, was I starving and I went to shut the gas under the
darn eggs. I could have gobbled them as they were, burning hot,

   Mozart

shell and all. As exhaustion kicked in I slowed down my pace, summoning an extra dose of calmness and patience.

I took ice from the freezer, filled a bowl, threw in the eggs for the thermic shock to ease the peeling. I put it on the table, then I went to the fridge for lettuce and pickles. As I turned around he was gently, meticulously peeling an egg. Would he like one, I asked while drawing a couple of dishes from a cabinet. Forks, a knife. Was there any butter? Napkins. Water. Two glasses. That should be fine. We started eating.

Then I noticed how wrinkled he was. Deep-set creases. His hair long, almost white like his beard and whiskers. Milky, gloomy blue eyes. Elusive. As I said, he looked, yes, respectable in spite of his opening line.

But, oh my, the kitchenette was so small, a bit like a train cabin… and the silence surrounding us, ominous. I wished I had turned on some kind of device. We must have been the only folks inside the entire building. The intimacy of our shared meal overwhelmed me, not sure why.

I watched him sprinkle a pinch of salt on the egg he had neatly sliced in quarters. He was careful, maybe too much, as if handling something extremely… precious? His attention was strange, peculiar. Eerie. Awesome… Again, I felt overwhelmed. I know it doesn't make sense. Then I fell in love.

2.

I had a podium to set up before I'd call it a day. Yes, it was a one-person job if you took it easy, and I had done it before. I had to drag a number of wooden platforms (alas, without any kind of rolling device) and then lower them side by side. I was relatively fit, my reserve of stamina fair, and lunch had energized me. Still, because I had time until the next morning I could linger a while.

After washing the dishes (he had offered to help, but I felt it was just good manners, and passed), I grabbed an orange and sneaked into a teachers' lounge, where I could peruse a laptop. I wished to refresh my notions about the event I was working, see who the guest speakers were. So I located his picture as it was my intention, learned his name and what his specialty was. Oh no, it didn't matter. Sheer curiosity, right.

The sound was faint as it reached me, a kind of broken murmur so subliminal it seemed to be… mine. Had I been humming to myself without noticing? It happened. But I had not, and as I neared the hall where the risers were, the tune became louder. Unmistakable. Beethoven's Moonlight Sonata.

Though… the pianist was making it less obvious, so to speak, by means of frequent, abrupt, random pauses. Not because of blatant mistakes. Maybe lapses of memory, maybe just passing thoughts. After a brief rest, the playing resumed with no sign of struggle or frustration, as if someone had opened a faucet and music, impassibly generous, had restarted to flow.

Right where it had stopped? Hard to say, since the thing kind of turns in circles. And most probably not. Each time, the mood had slightly shifted, as if a new source of light, a new shade had been added to the picture. Maybe the passing thought had changed the interpretation, steered it a tiny bit. And that, yes, made the piece more interesting, actually quite enchanting, as if it were hatched on the spot, composed from scratches.

The old black piano, pushed against a side wall… had I seen it open before? Certainly not in use, and I wouldn't have known if it was tuned. It was. From the back, he looked both straight and relaxed. From the back he looked somehow vulnerable. Maybe we all do.

I don't think he heard me come in. Or did he, because when I walked by, then started pushing and pulling platforms, he did not budge at all. Quickly, he glanced my way, yet his gaze passed through me, which was both unflattering and reassuring. Actually, reassuring.

As I focused on my breathing and motions, careful not to hurt myself, he kept pouring cascades of notes with perfect nonchalance. He sure wasn't flustered… Truly, what impressed me the most was the very opposite. Meaning I didn't hear him veer towards a more showy, more demonstrative attitude. Not the tiniest adjustment. No. His playing remained wholly natural, as if no one were there.

For some reason, his capacity of utterly ignoring the threat (or the lure) of a potential audience struck me as exceptional. I was awed. A little embarrassed (shouldn't he be? but wasn't)… once more overwhelmed by sudden intimacy. Then he stopped. Then he lowered the lid over the keys almost in slow motion, with a sigh that, I felt, had nothing to do with me.

A few minutes later, though, he asked if I could use a hand, his voice more convincing than when, a bit earlier, he had proposed to clean up the dishes. That must be why I agreed. Perhaps he was bored. Oh, he knew what to do, no need for instructions. He just mimicked my gestures (and my rhythm, my speed) matching them to a T. I loved working with him, I realized, the strangeness of it notwithstanding. After all he was a teacher, correct? Visiting professor so and so. Then he shouldn't… And still.

We each dragged risers by ourselves but lowered them as a pair, which lessened the effort and made it… pleasant. That way, it all went much faster. I was grateful for the impromptu gift, the blessing, the bonus. But at some point I saw him tense up, then slow down. "Enough done," he said matter-of-factly. "Sure." I couldn't suppress a pang of dismay (an unjustified sense of betrayal) as I carried on with my task.

Later, when I left the room, I almost tripped on him. He was lying on the floor just outside the door, as if he hadn't been able to go further. He was on his back, straight, still like a corpse, of course perfectly quiet. Yet alert. As I passed him, his eyes popped wide open and he grinned. While, again, I felt some embarrassment and a bit of guilt. Why had I let a guy of his age do physical labor? Clearly, he had worn himself out. Clearly, the effort required had been excessive and I had not understood it. Well, he had offered. Maybe he wanted to brag. He himself had misjudged his capacities, or the task, or both. Still, I should have known better. I felt uncomfortable and a little ashamed.

Later I was agitated and restless, not knowing what to do with my long lone evening. He must have gone somewhere, because I no longer bumped into him, or the other way around. But he was in my mind and he wouldn't leave it. The weird figure. Enigmatic, ambiguous. Both repulsive (because of his irony, his nonchalance that read as indifference, disregard) and attractive (because his lack of formality brought up a weird closeness, as if we had known each other for ages, as if…) I was young. I wouldn't have known how to spell such feelings. "Darn," I thought, "I must have fallen in love."

3.
That was it. I mean, that was it.
On Monday I was able to attend the conference and I

listened to his presentation. I don't truly recall the topic, maybe slightly exoteric. Vague, perhaps. I took notes, I know. Why? Whatever the subject was, it had nothing to do with my study plan. All the same, I took notes. Still have them. They don't make much sense anymore. I doubt they ever did. Here is one, "All illnesses ultimately heal." Meaning? I underlined it in red, did it strike a chord?

Afterwards I was on duty, once more, gathering badges as I sat at a small table outside and people filed out. I was bored. Surreptitiously, I doodled on a notebook I held upon my knee. He stopped by and he peeked, reaching across the table. "Nice," he said, looking at a complex hieroglyph I was tweaking with care. "I see…"

The inception of an indefinable thrill teased my spine while I waited for what he'd say next. As if what my drawing meant to him held precious insight, crucial clues to be treasured beside my freshly jotted notes. He paused, while he assumed the pensive expression I had noticed before, that sad undertone I sensed but couldn't quite name. His lips briskly twitched.

Instinctively, I knew he was about to leave and I felt… I felt panic. I blurted, "What?" and his face became elusive. A bit cruel, I thought, but was it? "Can't say," he almost inaudibly sighed. "I would if it weren't so personal." Bogus. Was he flirting? I was speechless, confused, and I closed my notebook. Hastily, as if remorseful, he gasped, "No! Please, I didn't… Keep drawing! It's gorgeous!"

There you go. I was paralyzed with embarrassment. "I… can't if someone is watching." He shrugged. I remembered his hands on the keyboard, then, steady, uncaring and free. Now he looked frankly annoyed. When he spoke, his tone was icy, a bit arrogant. "Do you have that much time to waste?" he said.

"Focus on your task, baby, for Christ's sake." Then he walked away. After all he was a professor, was he?

That night I looked him up again on the Internet. He wouldn't get out of my mind, or perhaps I wanted him to stay. I saw he was quite famous. I perused his whole teaching resume, publications, honors, awards and other achievements, then I backtracked to his biography. Early life. Wait. I must have gotten it wrong. Check again. Then check elsewhere. Oh, no. His date of birth made no sense.

I read everything I could scavenge about him, seeking whatever would mention his age at a given time. I found a few clues, graduation, hooding ceremonies and such. They all matched among them, none did with the reality I saw. Then I looked for pictures. None was there. Nothing, no, besides the headshot I had previously found, a pretty vague one. After all, he wasn't a movie star.

Based on the official data, he was in his forties. Based on what I had seen he was an old man, worn and weary, though still fit and certainly charming. With an aura of wisdom, due to age, I had believed. Perhaps not. Then he must have some illness. Some quite terrible thing. Would it heal? So he had said. I had documented it.

4.

I kept track of him now and then, through the scholarly press or online. I said he was kind of famous. I kept track after I fell out of love, which happened promptly, as he wasn't at hand or pursuable and I fell for someone else. Still, I couldn't take him entirely off my mind. He had a way of quietly, abruptly sneaking in, as he had when he popped up for lunch or woke up the piano. Ghostly. Out of the blue. On a Sunday afternoon, that gloomiest of times, and so magical.

So I learned that he died, two years later. He hadn't turned fifty yet. The last picture divulged seemed that of a centenarian. Did anyone notice? He must have been very infirm. In the last photo his hair was still longish, stark white. His eyes seemed of a sharper blue, but they might have been touched. And that halo of seriousness, of sadness, now was unmistakable.

Well, perhaps the fact that he had passed tinted my perception… Or else he had struck a pose for that particular shot, academic and orthodox, though in his heart he was going, "fuck yourself," and giggling. I am sure he was. And it must be what the phrase I dumbly wrote down (the sibylline quote) implied… that wink of awareness, both accepting and sour. "Every illness heals in the end." Yes, it does.

Mozart

    I began to go out with Mozart the year Mother came back.

    She reinstalled herself in the family home she used to rent out, her decision sudden, abrupt… Had she started to get weird? Hard to say. She had always been an oddball, never shedding the juvenile mindset (part rebel, I guess, part irresponsible) her coevals had dropped in due time. Not Mom. Some extravagance on her account was routine. And she was getting more private, more aloof as she…

    Of course, I rang her up, skipped by once in a while, checked on her in spite of her self-sufficiency. But we had never been intimate, and our visits didn't mean a lot. They weren't taxing either… she was so low maintenance. They just added a bit to my to-do-list, which was thick already. Fine, I'll take it. Mother. Around. Again.

    Did I tell him about her return? Not sure. When I got the call and rushed in, muttering a concise explanation, he was stunned. As I was when he stated, "I'm coming" with his usual meekness, yet not waiting for a reply or asking for permission.

Oh, not in the least.

When I started to go out with Mozart I was old. Not like Mother, though I'm sure she felt younger than she was, her small face bravely devoid of make-up, her long hair always sporting an incongruously flowered barrette. I had cut my hair short. I made up for decency sake, having no illusions about my looks, worn by age and by a variety of stressing agents.

Every day had a challenge in store, be it at work (I had a market booth of fruit and vegetables, my college degree notwithstanding), at home (which I tried to keep tidy in spite of my meager budget) or with my grown-up children (still needing more help than seemed reasonable). Challenges gave me purpose, though. I enjoyed fighting and winning, enough to keep me going.

I hadn't had a boyfriend for five years. After my divorce I had piled up one-night stands and casual encounters, seldom daring more consistent experiments, which were always short-lived. After all, affairs require as much energy as marriage does. Past the thrill of freedom regained, I got tired. My last fling was accurately chosen as a self-goodbye-present. I enjoyed the treat, then moved on without a regret.

In the night (the one preceding the call, yes) the wind had been horrible. Hot, because it was summer. It had calmed a bit in the morning, but now it resumed intensity. We had planned on our usual stroll. As we walked, though, the gusts got stronger and I felt uneasy, distracted. Wait, should we… The obvious option of entering a café didn't come to mind, or not soon enough, and I invited him to my place.

We had gone out for almost a year, always meeting

downtown, taking walks while chatting about a number of topics. So far, we hadn't had any attempt at intimacy. Honestly, the lack of it didn't bother me. I wasn't especially attracted. Was he? Could he have been just shy? Prudent, slow? To believe it would have been pretentious. I assumed he didn't feel desire either... quite a sobering thought, liberating as well.

Were we simply friends, then? We weren't. A strange aura, a bit of ceremony lent to our frequentation an undertone, as if it meant (or was meant to mean) something else. But, to tell the truth, who cared if it did or didn't? Our dates needed no effort. They implied no strain, no commotion. On the contrary, they supplied something I couldn't define but I kind of liked. I did.

As we arrived home I started a fire, in spite of the warm temperature. Outside, the wind hissed horrendously. It unnerved me. A fire would recenter me (us, because he was there, and such novelty added to my restlessness). It would give us something to do, lifting the slight embarrassment of impromptu closeness.

I let him set the kindling however he pleased, light it, then survey the first log as it burned. Oh well, he knew his way around it. Strange. I had figured him essentially unpractical. Now I spontaneously trusted his expertise. No need to double-check him.

I stepped into the kitchen, put the kettle on. I arranged cups, sugar, milk, lemon on a tray and was fumbling into my cupboard for tea, a nice, tasty brew, please, when the phone rang. As I turned to pick it up, I noticed the flashing. There were messages on my machine... when... They had tried to reach me for hours, they said.

  Mozart

I rushed back into the living room, purse in hand, to announce a brisk change of plans. He didn't seem troubled. Surprised, yes, a bit, when I sighed the word "Mother." Then he shocked me when, at the door, he said matter-of-factly, "Let us take one car," while directing himself towards his battered Volvo. I felt vaguely patronized and I didn't like it. I don't know what made me decide to surrender.

In the car I took charge again, giving him directions. Of course they were redundant. He knew where the County Hospital was.

I sat back and kept quiet. For some reason, his profile caught my attention… My mind craved a detail to bite on, as it happens when anxiety grabs you and you are trying to escape. I saw one, two, three coppery strands parsing his grayish ponytail. I had never imagined his hair other than the pale tint I knew. The idea he once was younger, different looking, flashed by like a shadow, an interference.

After talking with the personnel at the front desk we were ushered into a semi-deserted hall. A TV flickered in front of us, its volume turned down. The walls were a cold, frantic hue of lemon yellow.

When I sat, ready for a long wait, his presence felt wrong. Fraudulent, as if he had sneaked up a case on a table game, getting closer to the finish line thanks to my sudden weakness. I wished I could get rid of him, but I couldn't manage the nerve to let him know. On the positive side, this new familiarity allowed me to forgo conversation, I thought, and I closed my eyes.

As I opened them, minutes later, he had a book in his hands. He read quietly, almost religiously absorbed. I shut my eyes again.

His last name wasn't Mozart. Could have been. Someone must be called that way besides the composer. In his case I had picked the nickname, having met him during a performance of "Don Juan."

I don't attend Opera. Don't dislike the genre, but can live without it. I have mentioned challenges. They are not very conducive to theater going, a stretched, lengthy kind of pleasure, consonant with slow lifestyles, lots of free time and some affluence. Like cruises. I don't go on cruises either. I have mentioned early farmers' markets. They clash with late nights on hard seats, not quite softened by their crimson velvet.

But that was a matinee, and I had come to support a girlfriend whose date had bailed off. She was left with expensive tickets, no company, and a nasty mood. Normally, the incident wouldn't have sufficed to win my consensus… I had stuff to do, and didn't enjoy sitting still. Also, what to wear wasn't a question I wished to spend time pondering. "Don Juan, you said?" I don't know what made me decide to accept.

As we took off our jackets, slid our purses under our chairs, spread the programs over our knees and produced our glasses, she wanted us to exchange seats. Did the smell of her neighbor bother her? I complied on account of her probably vulnerable state of mind. I didn't even look at the person I landed by, just acknowledged his gender. And who cared.

There is a game I liked to play when I was a child, in the many occasions when Mom carried me along, parked me, then went on with her business-whatever-it-was (doctor appointment, hair dressing, endless try-on in department stores, looking for hard-to-find cheap-but-cute). She couldn't afford babysitters.

Bored out of my mind, I thought of a book I was reading, or a movie I had seen on TV during my homebound, only-daughterly weekends. I started looking around for the characters of the story. Embodied. I mean in flesh and blood. I accurately cast them, though I couldn't have named my activity. It took patience… I had to thoroughly scan my surroundings, sometimes wait a while for the appropriate looks to appear. I didn't mind double casting, adding up plenty of options for final selection. That kept me occupied.

Now the oddity of the situation, the initial wait, the long intervals, the sweet drowsiness assailing me during arias brought back such an obsolete pastime. I methodically started looking for Don Juans, the unrepentant seducers. I found many. Same for the scary ghosts of his victim (the outraged lady's father). Such conservative pricks are quite common. Leporellos, the cowardly yet critical followers, must exist but are trickier to spot. As for the female characters, bitter bitches and flirts were all over. I could throw my friend and myself onto the pile, ready for either part.

As I went on searching, bluntly ignoring the music, my next seat neighbor fell under my scrutiny. He sat straight and still, his face unmoving, intent. I discarded any Don Juanesque attitude. His gravity might have fit a revengeful dad, but something about him was delicate. Which would call for a gregarious role. The servant? Impossible. I was sure he lacked cunning.

All this musing occurred in less than a blink. I didn't openly study my subjects, especially when they were close. A look had been enough for concluding I had no use for the body at my left. I lost interest. Then an afterthought struck me. In the meanwhile, the light had gone down and the orchestra had resumed, introducing the following act with ominous sounds. I stole another glance, once more pondering the scant ponytail, gibbous nose, small chin, overall pointiness… not entirely unpleasant. Something clicked in place.

The man sitting on my left was Mozart. How come it took me so long to figure it out.

Now you wonder how Mozart's likeness could be so familiar it simply popped up, instantaneously finding its match. I had a college degree. I, believe it or not, was knowledgeable on a number of topics… in a strictly useless manner, as my notions were fairly remote from the stuff that made my daily life. They didn't help me with chores or with mothering, didn't attract customers to my fares. Also, my educated bits and scraps didn't form a whole like, let's say, a collection of neatly shelved, smoothly arranged, alphabetically labeled books, ready to be perused. No. My notions were a bunch of plastic bags abandoned in a closet, each holding unrelated miscellanea. I would chance upon one of them while seeking a screwdriver, perhaps, or a pair of pliers… something useful. Maybe inside here? I'd open a bag and find an old poem instead, a battle, a prayer. A saint, emperor, courtesan. A composer.

Let me fix this. What I just said doesn't apply to Mozart (Wolfgang Amadeus). I could picture the guy even if I had quit school in kindergarten, thanks to Dad and his gramophone (a miniature closet, pretentious all right, with small doors shielding the amplifiers). Dad liked listening to classical music on Sunday mornings. He had several records. He pensively shuffled the pile before choosing, but they all were by Mozart… a sheer monomania. All the sleeves displayed the same face, large or miniature, in full color, faded sepia, or a silvery silhouette engraved on a cameo. I must have seen it thousands of times.

Mozart's music had an effect of Dad nothing else achieved, not even red wine or a football match on TV. Both (wine and ball game) came close to the same result, yet with appreciable nuances. Something thicker, in the alcohol-induced joviality, made Dad's voice grow louder, easing out dubious jokes (I could sense Mother cringe at the other end of the table). Something angry tainted his yell each time that a goal went through. Based on which team marked the point, his scream had a different color, yet was equally explosive. I could feel Mother shake in the corridor.

Mozart's music put Dad in a lighter state of mind, clear of aggressiveness and coarseness. It made him look younger. With a stretch of my imagination I could see him dance, or more likely play a violin, perhaps on a roof. I could picture him gracious, un-embittered, unburdened.

Father left the record player behind, but took the records away. I don't think Mother cared.

I had no idea she had started sleeping outside. Yes, the season was hot and she must have grown unaccustomed to such temperatures. Let alone humidity. She had a big lawn chair of thick fabric, faded orange, a small table and a matching umbrella (superfluous, since I guess she came after sunset). The seat faced the back end of the yard, which once had been a wall.

Slowly, it had crumbled down while Mom was away. Renters never complained, not even informed her. The rent was pretty cheap and so were the renters, of the insouciant kind, only minding repair if strictly unavoidable… a main plumbing issue, a giant leak right onto the bed. Otherwise, they had no interest in maintenance. No, they didn't care. In particular, the backyard had caught nobody's attention. It had grown fairly wild, a sad jungle.

And the wall (a frail thing, not quite functional to start with) had fallen apart. Not a problem… Behind our yard was a vacant lot the city had seized years before, not sure for which purpose. One they never carried out. Behind our yard was a wide emptiness, more or less rectangular, bordered on the right and left with barbed wire and dead-ending into an impenetrable thicket, where the foothills began. Who knows why no lowlife ever bothered to cut the fence, claim the no-man's land for themselves. Truly, it offered no shade, no hiding place, not even a stone or a log for sitting and drinking, a rickety bench to nap on. At the far end, I said, the greenery was dense and it led nowhere. Our property (by the way, equally accessible from the front and sides) wasn't in the least appetizing. The local thugs knew, and the foreign ones intuited it at a glance.

What was worrisome, then, about Mom sleeping under the stars, empty glass hanging on the side table? Nothing. I don't know why the thought of it, afterwards, chilled me. Irritated me, perhaps. Did I envy her naïve, indestructible freedom? It felt irresponsible, careless. It felt as if she had stolen it, somehow. Oh, my… jealousy pure and simple.

Mozart happened to activate my forsaken cultural storage. As I said, we took walks, then we went for coffee and kept talking about this and that, a book, author, movie, songwriter. Something famous or something I never heard of. So what? I didn't care, because he didn't seem to care either.

I was smart enough to assess the extent of his

knowledge. He knew tons of stuff, and in depth, not like those folks who listen to the History Channel, see TV documentaries and peruse magazines. I had caught him sometimes, when he waited at one of our rendez-vous, book in hand. I suspected he always carried a paperback in his pocket. When I arrived he put it away, as if closing the door to an unmade bedroom when a guest comes in. Though, there wasn't anything messy with his reading. I'm sure. Yet I sensed the privacy. Its strictness. Its ferocity.

Oh, he must have known things, but his conversation was casual, only involving plain and understandable words (I was smart enough to realize it). I didn't feel diminished by his deliberate simplicity, tailored to my estimated level. I was glad when I could relate to a subject, fishing data out of my remote, jumbled storage. I could follow him on a number of paths, though as if leaping from stone to stone across water. My education was sparse, yes, small islands in a spread-out archipelago.

When we chanced upon something, alas, ringing no bell, he didn't change topic. Without showing a hint of surprise, dismay, condescension, he filled in a few clues allowing me to hop aboard. Then he kept going, nonchalantly. Thus, my notions expanded. They interlinked, forming more of a fabric, easier to unfold and display. Was he tutoring me? At my age…

The dangerous thing was neither sleeping outside, truly, nor the crumbled wall, but what Mom had done with it. Which, again, I only learned afterwards, as apparently during our visits I never… I don't know how she had summoned the strength. Maybe little by little, painstakingly, with the stubbornness of a troubled mind.

She had rebuilt the back wall, so to speak, piling up wooden crates as it was fashionable at the time of her youth. They made book racks that way... Where did she find the crates? God, they must have been mine. During my college years I had lived in the house. Dad was gone and Mom had moved out. I was trying to complete my studies while working at the farmers' market, full time. These must have been my crates, still stacked in the basement.

Hadn't they rotted yet? I'm sure. At least, partially. Mom had knocked off the bottoms. Not such a big effort... they must have been loose. Then she had built a tall shelf, one row above the other. She had connected the units with wire, neat loops, twisted ends. Well, not good enough... The wire barely kept the scaffold together. It ensured no stability, did she realize? Did she care? She had built a castle of cards.

What did she intend to make? Bay window? French door? Chinese screen? Did the thing have a practical scope? Was it meant for privacy? I doubt it. Anyway, we aren't finished. Mom had put inside each crate a clay pot. Those, she must have bought. They had bright colors, deep crimson, blue cobalt, malachite green. They were huge. I don't dare imagine how she hoisted them on the tallest row. She must have climbed on a ladder (there is one in the house, dating from back then) propped on gravel. She must have poured the soil and planted the succulents with the vase already in place. A balancing act.

Was it a kind of ritual? A challenge of sorts? I would be surprised. Challenges are my domain. Mom didn't traditionally excel at them, always choosing the easy way out. Yet, look at this. Did anyone help her? Of course not. Who would have shared in such senile idiocy without calling on a

Mozart

responsible relative? Look at this.

I didn't see it. My description is mere reconstruction. When we arrived at the house, later that afternoon, shards were what we found. Large ones… those pots were robust. They didn't explode, only split in large, sharp, irregular slivers. But there were many vases. Many slivers constellated the gravel, gaudy flowers of glazed stone. Of course, soil and bits of greenery were all over. The whole structure had miserably crushed, yet the wire still held wide chunks together, crooked, hard to pick up, maneuver, discard.

Judging by the ruins, the thing had fallen towards Mother. Was she asleep? She would have been hurt, maybe killed. Did she wake up and run? After further pondering, we guessed pots must have started to fall the other way… the wind blowing from the sea towards the mountains. When the scaffold lost some of its weight, though, it ruined face forwards, due to structural weakness or maybe a slight slope.

The first pots that broke must have woken Mother, giving her time to get away. Unless she had never slept. How could she have in such wind? True, the gushes had gotten gradually stronger. She might have enjoyed them initially. Might have found them refreshing. Nice and soothing, lullabying. Hypnotic, perhaps.

What had Mozart done (or was doing) for a living? He didn't say. I didn't ask. We met after hours, of course, or else during weekends. Technically, he could have worked nine to five. I knew he didn't. Not because of his age, which could have allowed retirement, or not. He just didn't exude that kind of pressure, kind of wear. Our evening strolls didn't seem a release

or a change of pace. They belonged to a seemingly unbroken
flow.

Not for me, but I managed a veneer of coolness.
And I cooled down, indeed, as the evening went. That might
have been another reason why I saw him… to let off steam
by shifting my focus. I mean, focusing on something else…
glimpses of a wider world he could access, and allowed me to
share.

Had he been a schoolteacher? I wasn't curious. Rather,
I didn't want to know, afraid that further info would subtract
from the ease, from the freedom. I mean, the less you know the
less you are responsible. Were I to learn something I didn't like,
something I should object to, I'd have to reconsider, maybe give
up on him. I would need to reflect, to make choices. Until now
I had spared myself the burden. After all there was plenty to
discuss, plenty to contemplate besides ourselves.

I hadn't asked for his last name. I preferred to keep
him remote, mythical, Austrian. As for me, he knew my name
and those of my children, what I did for a job, some practical
matters. No detail. Nothing personal. Didn't know I had a
mother in town, until the pots fell.

"She had wind chimes," he said softly, not looking at
me but at something he held on his palm. He was studying it
carefully, as for evidence found on a crime scene… a short,
frayed piece of string tied to a fragment of shell.

In a flashback I realized I had seen one or two, but
they hadn't impressed me. I mean I hadn't decoded them. Or
I had, the wrong way. Bits of string, some knotted… I must
have unconsciously assumed they had been used for assembling
purposes, in addition to the metal wire. Shells might have been

 Mozart

part of the planters, glued around the rims… quite a common feature… or Mom could have used them for decoration, spreading them here and there. She loved shells. She always brought back huge stacks from the beach, rinsed them and then stored them in jars. Did she finally want to display them?

"She made them," he said. How did he know? On my knees, I started rummaging for whatever would support his theory. Not to prove him right… I just looked for verification, which seemed suddenly crucial, though about an irrelevant matter. On the porch was a pair of gardening gloves. I looked for a bucket and found one. Back on all fours, I started a thorough collection… With hindsight, I reckon it was a quite insane effort, yet I couldn't possibly stop until I had picked it all. Tons of stuff, not just shells. Bits of dried branches I had wrongly attributed to the plants… they were driftwood, also gathered on sand, I'm sure. Beads and buttons, bolts, washers, curtain rings and beer caps.

Without saying a word, Mozart helped me. He did not crouch, just bent. Once in a while he carefully lifted his back, in slow motion. I saw his ups and downs from the corner of my eye, without paying close attention. But I took off one glove and handed it his way.

We must have looked like two nerdy kids working on a puzzle, on a rainy afternoon. The sun was gone when we stopped. I carried the bucket to the porch. It weighed like a corpse. I melted on the wicker hammock. Mozart joined me a bit later.

Mom had fallen on the sidewalk, a few blocks away. She had wandered out, walked or run before she collapsed. When? Not sure. Was it still dark? After dawn? It doesn't matter.

Someone saw her from inside a house, called an ambulance. She had taken her purse, that's how the police found my number.

A nurse mentioned some of the things she had been saying, incoherent, of course. The nurse didn't have to. She was extra kind, or just chatty. See, Mom had said "wind" about a zillion times. "Oh, the wind, the wind!" The nurse managed an ominous tone, full of terrified awe, without knowing it. No, she wasn't aware of imitating her patient… I'm sure.

Well, the wind was for real, as were other things Mom had uttered, "garden," "house," "flowers." Maybe "flower pots?" "It will carry us away." Did she say that? She must have been terrified when her mind snapped. Did it snap because of her fear? Did panic induce the crisis? Hadn't she already started to lose it? Otherwise, why would she have built the damn thing?

Suddenly, I had no doubt about the wall's nature. It was an art project. A giant painting, a sort of blown-up still life she had concocted and realized at great cost. I could feel it, and a kind of tenderness washed over me like a wave. Like a wave, it immediately broke into many fragments…

Many thoughts. Many moments. I pictured her going up and down the stairs to the cellar (tricky, slippery, with that misshapen step always catching you off guard). Eagerly appraising those crates, as excited as if she had found a truckload of the most precious wood, then impatiently dusting them off, getting a few splinters before even thinking of gloves. Had the crates first ignited her imagination? I felt sick, kind of nauseous.

I saw her sifting through catalogs for pots, hunting for the cheapest, but the cheapest that wouldn't look such. They had to be quite plain, and their frugal airs would pass for style…

          Mozart

a strategy she had refined for her entire life. The search must
have taken months, implied constant recalculation. A sentiment
I couldn't name squeezed my throat. It was neither compassion
nor sympathy. Just a kind of pressure, like a fingertip pushing
down.

She had chosen the colors, filled the order form.
How long did she possibly wait before... She had always been
thrifty, scared of spending, insecure and reluctant when it
came to money. For sound reasons, of course. I could sense
her dizziness when she dropped the envelope in the mail. Did
she phone instead? She would have grown antsy, confused. She
went to the post office.

Then the pots were delivered, and the succulents...
she wouldn't have bought them. Someone must have donated
them, tiny bits she only had to stick into dirt. Were they stolen?
I could figure her taking long walks, looking casually around,
quickly snipping a twig, hiding it in the tote bag she sported
across her shoulder. Short of breath, thrilled like a four-year-
old. No doubt, she had pilfered the succulents.

Rescued crates and pillaged plants made up for the
expensive vases. She thought managing everything else on her
own could justify the sum she had splurged on pottery. I could
feel her brain weighing things, fighting scruples and remorse,
incessantly negotiating, and it tired me. About the wind chimes?
Did she enjoy making them?

She did.
A trestle table was in the basement, with materials on
it, sorted in white enameled trays, hemmed blue, reminiscent
of medical equipment. Her tools (hand-drill, scissors, a large
needle still threaded with string, glue and a pair of thick glasses)

formed a weird starry shape in the middle. You could almost
see the pair of hands holding them. They looked as if they had
dropped from midair, the human body supporting them briskly
spirited away. Was she interrupted? Did she have to go pee?
Hear the phone ring?

Or was she one of those who leave the workshop
in chaos, don't plan on cleanup time, labor on their project
until they are entirely spent, and then walk away? I'd say
such a profile didn't fit the Mother I knew, eccentricity
notwithstanding. But then, this might be the Mother I didn't
know.

Something summoned me to go fetch the bucket I had
left on the porch, heavy as it was, carry it down the slippery
steps, lift it on the board, then (with an unconsidered gesture,
and much effort) turn it upside down. As it vomited its contents
on wood, I enjoyed the screechy sound, rattling, thunderous. A
sound of disaster, yet miniature. I clenched my teeth, squinted
my eyes, waved my hands to avoid breathing dust.

They would keep her for further exams. Her diagnosis
was of "acute psychosis." I could sleep on an armchair if
I wished to. It would be useless, they said. She was heavily
sedated, unlikely to wake up anytime soon. I could stay
nonetheless. Let me tell you, it is hard to make those decisions.
They are tightropes you walk on and you don't realize it. The
wire is wrapped in fog. Then the fog dissolves and you vacillate.
You know your next step is going to be crucial. You teeter, you
shake.

You end up making the wrong decision, maybe for
the right reasons. Anyway, reasons and instincts, motivations
and actions tend to contradict each other when routine has

　　　　　　　　Mozart

been kicked aside. When emergency calls. When someone
or something is hurt, knocked off, removed from its stable
location, compromising the overall balance, causing everything
to capsize.

I thought I should remain. Up to me, they said, I could
if so inclined. Of course, Mozart (he was waiting, perhaps
still reading) should go. I'd call a cab in the morning, as soon
as they'd release Mother. That, alas, wasn't granted, the nurse
said. That we wouldn't know until tomorrow. True, the hospital
is one of those places where things happen in circumscribed
fashion. You don't own more than the present minute, which is
crucial but also darn small, like the eye of the needle, the waist
of the hourglass. Actually, you don't even own that much.

I could not count on leaving tomorrow. Maybe I
should go home now, eat, get some sleep, change my clothes,
call my boss. Come back early in the morning, strong, ready for
combat.

In the car I felt a sudden weariness. When I spoke
there was a plaintive tone in my voice. I heard it and didn't like
it, yet couldn't control it. "Would you mind," I asked, "if we
skipped by her place for a second?" Oh, no. He shook his head.
I gave him the address. Then at least one hour went by, while
we picked up rubble. As if we both had fallen under a spell,
trapped by some incantation, sucked into a fold of time. Of no
time, I mean. One hour went by. Was it more?

When I emerged from the cellar, after dropping the
bucket's contents on Mother's workbench, Mozart wasn't
reading. I had a vision of him smoking a pipe… what a
banal thought. He was looking at the horizon. Bored? Tired?
Annoyed? I almost angrily shoved these worries away. I had

asked for nothing, and I had no room for concern, not now. But I didn't sit. I guessed we should get going.

How did we end up at his place?

That's actually an incorrect way to put it, since it seems to imply some meandering, some uncertainty. "We are going to my place," he said as he turned the engine on. The feeling came back of being pushed, somehow cheated on, of him moving forth in reason of my being kind of vulnerable. Why didn't I object?

I think I can answer. Nothing in his voice confirmed my suspicion. He was kind, gentle, meek as always. Just determined, maybe, to do the right thing. That's all… He was doing what seemed to be right under the circumstances, without asking too much for permission. Maybe assuming I'd stop him, should I disagree.

I did not.

His apartment was below the penthouse. No large windows, no view, but the height somehow brought in a sense of remoteness, isolation. I hadn't realized, hadn't known he lived in a building. It was slightly unusual, yet like him. The apartment was clean and barely furnished. It breathed out a sense of possibilities.

He went right to the refrigerator. As he pulled the door open, the light hurt me, too bright. Well, of course! The fridge was almost empty and its whiteness shone. He took out a half-bottle of champagne. Not the one you can find in a hotel room minibar. Not that little. Not a regular one either. A half-bottle. "They don't do many of these anymore," he commented with a sigh.

How much was in there? My mind ravenously bit at the

trivia… a raft in stormy waters. I delivered myself to the exact calculation of what such amount of alcohol would make. Two full servings. A good-sized aperitif. No refills. He had already two glasses in hand, stems squeezed between his fingers.

The bed was very large, with dark sheets. The room was lit only by a lamp perched on a nightstand, topping a tall pile of paperbacks, next to a tiny alarm clock.

He had removed his clothes in no time. I removed mine without thinking… didn't seem necessary. In the meanwhile he uncorked and poured. Had I been less tired, less confused, I would have recognized the expert ease he had displayed before, when he had started my fire. If I didn't properly acknowledge his nimbleness, I sensed it and it reassured me. I relaxed. He had handed me a glass then sat in lotus position, cross-legged in the middle of the oversized mattress. On taking my drink, I must have smiled.

His nakedness didn't strike me one way or another. It felt natural, or else everything was so unnatural, it blended in. He looked ageless to me. Kind of perennial. A fir tree. Yes, an evergreen.

Then I laughed, unexpected and startling. I was looking at him in the nude when I began laughing, heartily, incapable of stopping myself. He looked slightly surprised, on the positive side. He looked like he wanted to join, yet taking his time, making sure it was appropriate to share my hilarity, that I wasn't making fun of him. Not too cruelly. His face came alive, way more vibrant than I had ever seen it, especially the eyebrow he lifted in a puzzled, bemused manner, further fueling my glee.

With a franker smile he lifted his glass, briskly, lively, twice. I echoed. We silently toasted. The awareness that there would be no refill gave my drink an edge of delight, new, vertiginous, frightening. I tried brushing it off. I recalled Mother was in the hospital. What was I celebrating? He turned off the lamp.

To acquaint the obscurity took me a little while. It was compact. Velvety. Almost smothering. I held my breath. He must have noticed. We were lying down already, calmly, slowly starting to touch. "I like it this way," he murmured. He was talking about the darkness, I knew. I didn't answer. I couldn't make up a thing, not even a silhouette or a shadow. I felt claustrophobic. I felt trapped. Then it was as if someone had sliced a knot with a blade, a sudden delivery. Then I felt as if I could fly, a deep, weightless relief.

As we engaged in lovemaking he whispered once in a while, just a word, or maybe a short sentence I didn't try to decipher. Until I got curious, and paid closer attention. "I am scared," he murmured now and then. Sometimes twice in a row, "I'm scared, I'm scared." But there was pleasure in his tone, as if he wanted, welcomed, savored that fear.

Was I scared? Might have been, but would not have declared it.

Turning

1.

So the year when I sold the house, that year of peeling and re-painting, dismantling and rebuilding, searching and searching, and packing and then again searching…

Then not finding, and doubting, then fearing and then counting, all the counting never amounting to, never a-mounting, always kind of dismounting, teetering at the edge of something and always somehow falling below, always, a sixteenth of an inch, like a meringue never reaching the right consistency (when a fork tossed on top of the foam should remain afloat)…

A meringue constantly melting, and the muscles of your arm can't take it anymore, not anymore.

That year my arms hurt all the time, my elbows, my knees, but what most obsessed me wasn't fatigue or frustration. Wasn't fear, insecurity, impatience. What obsessed me the most was a kind of abstraction, rather a geometric pattern, perhaps a timeline. A time diagram, right, with added spatial elements.

What obsessed me was the triple motion of the couple (I'm calling it A) hastily leaving the place where they had lived a few quiet decades…

I pictured them quiet. A serene, modest, shielded,

perhaps monotone existence was what their house and garden
betrayed, quiet decades of a decent life for which I felt,
strangely, an intense sort of tenderness.

These folks of whom I knew nothing besides their
names, glimpsed at and promptly forgotten, were packing away,
pushed by an implacable deadline (my arrival), hurriedly clearing
the place of myriads of boxes that would be promptly replaced
by myriads of quasi-identical boxes.

Same cardboard. Same assortment of sizes. Same
labels, hand printed with a felt pen, bedroom, bathroom, pantry,
garage. Boxes of the same brown/beige color, the color of
travel, of transit. The color of train stations, gas stations, the
color of rain.

Then I thought of B. That was me and my son,
busy packing, our myriads of boxes about to be spat like an
avalanche, a cascade, like puke, like barely enrobed viscera on
the battlefield just freed of the previous lot, still punctuated by
war residuals and spoils, limbs lost from wounded bodies… an
old tricycle, a tire and a broken planter, an oil lantern, a broom,
a large spool of rope rotten by dampness. A birdhouse. They
had meant to take it with them. They had forgotten at the last
moment, our stuff a giant wave pushing their stuff ashore, their
stuff breathlessly running, running, then falling.

And I was obsessed of course by the immanence of
C at our door, Mom, Dad, teenage children ready with their
truckload of portable life all squared up, all tied up and like ours
beige, brown, the interstitial color.

How they threatened us, their mail filling our mailbox,
their contractor pacing our living room, tape measure in hand.
And I knew they were right. I knew that the pressure of their
dailiness (boiling water lifting the lid of the saucepan) was part

Mozart

of a complex osmotic movement.

Without knowing the next link of the chain, I could sense that something haunted C, rushing them towards the place that just yesterday, that today still was mine. They had to come and chase us away as we in turn were chasing A, the first couple. None of us could avoid this natural shift. On the contrary, we all feverishly allowed it. Though… were we a bit confused, a bit blurred?

Perhaps blinded. This I felt, sometimes… that we all, ABC, CBA, in fact groped a bit. My perspective, see, tended to rise up high, in order to encompass the three houses among which our disjointed team stirred itself.

As my point of view levitated to embrace the field of operations, people shrunk. We all became very small and so did our cars, vans, trucks, only made noticeable by their laborious transit, the back and forth shuttle, the turbulence.

Well, the metaphor is truly worn, but of course from a distance we looked like ants, carrying those things ants like to transport, a minute shred of paper, a fragment of straw.

Although, when my viewpoint lifted, simultaneously and strangely shifting in time, as if sucked into the future, I couldn't tell what A, B, C (these dark, creeping little formations, these m dashes, n dashes, ellipses) lugged away.

All the boxes, from up above, under tomorrow's gaze, disappeared.

So the awareness of our synchronous displacement, so momentous for each of the pawns switched around the checkerboard, yet irrelevant with regard to the large picture (seen that every square would be filled as it was before) didn't cease to occupy my mind.

The whole shuffling struck me as significant per se, something to be remembered not by the individuals concerned (who of course would never forget) but by a kind of external memory within which the new arrangement would be a sign, a marker, the head or tail of some micro-era, the beginning or closing of some historical chapter.

Do you recall the year when the As left their house on the hill and the Bs came in, rushing out of the cottage with the two maple trees and the Cs, after such a long time, sold the flat at the waterfront?

Yes, of course, of course. Meanwhile, someone would take the flat the Cs were about to clear. Someone I didn't know was already planning to occupy the Cs' flat at the waterfront, magnetized by its newly found emptiness, while I packed and packed and I was obsessed. Someone only scraping the edge of my consciousness, because thank god I couldn't see it all… the huge, constant sliding of particles. The small figure I had captured, a three-pointed star, modest comet dazzling through the night sky, was enough to make my head spin. I had to pretend that, while we were moving, something else (a big chunk of reality, I hoped) remained steadfastly in place. Then believe that somehow, somewhere, I would also find rest.

2.

Meanwhile, the woman walked.

I had noticed her when I first arrived in the neighborhood I was now about to leave. I had seen her walk, yes, countless times. Never still, sitting at a bus stop, for instance. Standing at a pedestrian crossing? Not once. Just didn't happen.

Right away, she had managed to capture my attention…

I had felt an immediate sympathy and an intense attraction, of the kind that you experience about perfect strangers you don't necessarily plan to befriend. You may envision having a casual interaction, a direct stare, nod, smile, maybe a verbal greeting. In times past, asking for a light…

Yet such contact might never occur and that would be fine. Even unacquainted, nice "regular" strangers have charm. They become part of the landscape and they enhance it, just as the tall pine tree, the hedge of jasmine, the curlicued mailbox do.

So the woman I frequently spotted (each time with a kind of spark, my attention aroused) had increased the attractiveness of the neighborhood since the start. Somehow, her presence had welcomed me in.

Well… she wasn't jovial, at all. I had never seen her, I said, other than in motion. Brisk progression. I should call it propulsion. She was bent at hip level, a very sharp angle. Her spine must have some kind of problem. Scoliosis. Arthritis. Severe. Due to age.

She was old, yes. How much, I couldn't tell. She dressed like a young person… nicely, I mean, variously and appropriately. She donned activewear, for instance, when she went for a run. She even sported a bandana, pulling back her scant hair, still quite long.

She must have run remarkable distances, judging by the large radius within which I randomly met her. Going that far, at that speed, must have cost her effort. I had seen sweat on her brow. I had noticed her paleness.

Each time I had seen her run, a slight feeling of incongruity had struck me. Sure, elders do exercise. Age wasn't the reason for my disconcertment. Something I couldn't quite name, though, made her activity look a bit odd, bit displaced.

What could have been less athletic than her frail, folded frame, those two segments so precariously joined, those thin, rigid limbs oscillating offbeat, the intent, pained gaze on the wrinkled face, the exiguous braid wavering in the wind?

I felt sympathy for her, as I said, and I greatly admired her stubborn training, though I couldn't suppress perplexity, as if something escaped me, as if I were missing a secret of sorts. As if she might have a special motive for working out so… so conscientiously, but I couldn't guess which.

What was she running for? I know it is obvious. Her health, her good shape. Oh please, that could not be the reason. What was she running for?

When she wasn't, her apparel showed her excellent taste. Her clothes were well assorted. Pieced together, I mean, but also assorted to the season, the weather, perhaps to her mood or the occasion. There must have been occasions. She must have gone somewhere. To the market, perhaps to church, perhaps to the movies.

Her gear was exquisitely complete. Nothing was amiss, yet nothing superfluous. She wasn't coquettish. She was thorough… the hat, the umbrella, the vest, the scarf. When she wasn't running, she clutched a purse (never large, always dark in color) close to the very point where her body hinged upon itself, the point of weakness, of fracture.

When she didn't run, she didn't stroll either. She walked very fast, her expression betraying exceptional focus tinged with strain. Tinged with a streak of despair, as if reaching her destination each time were a matter of utter importance. Extreme urgency.

Maybe it was. Although, paradoxically, I most

frequently saw her in cute verdant areas of our neighborhood (of which she roamed several square miles), treading tree-lined avenues bordered by quiet bourgeois mansions. Perfect itineraries for leisurely promenades. Yet she crossed such pleasant décor (in beribboned hat or in flannel coat, wearing laced boots or fringed moccasins) as if she were reaching the frontline with a life-or-death note in her bra, as if rushing to minister a last rite, deliver a firstborn.

Perhaps, once she had done such things. Her face had such fiery intensity. Meek ferocity emanated by her feminine attire mixed with her trooper stride. Yes, a ferocious meekness. And a complete abstraction, I felt, from her surroundings, notwithstanding the fact that she accorded her wardrobe to the weather, the season…

She displayed on her features (especially her gaze, pointed in front of her, never deviating) an impervious solitude. As if she were carrying along a separate universe, a mobile one that she deftly wove within plain reality, without puncturing the membranes dividing the two, without a single spill.

Sometimes I saw her among other people. I mean other than me. At a big intersection, by the gas pump or the carwash, next to the post office or near the mall. Even in those locations she never was still, never did something other than running or walking in haste. And I never saw her interact with anyone, anything except for her precious destination, to me of course obscure.

Her feet followed her head, due to the misalignment of her torso. That must have been tremendously hard.

So the year when I sold the house and then moved away I saw the woman walking, and the thought brushed the periphery of my brain, sweet and sour. The thought that I'd be missing her stark elusiveness, her arcane trajectories. Her moon-born evanescence, birdlike fugacity.

3.

That year I left the bad lover and found the good hairdresser. The two events aren't connected. Oh, no.

Shedding the lover was uneventful, one of those things sheer inertia performs. I, a person of strong will and conclusive action, that year was so drained by the meringue-making, egg white-beating act of losing and finding homes, that all other endeavors seemed impossible.

I, to save my life, couldn't face the responsibility of ending a relationship. Well, I didn't truly have one… just a worn, empty habit. Even that I couldn't unbutton, unzip, so to speak. Unless it would mercifully fall off, a dead skin, crumbling chrysalis.

Since the start, my lover had been spartan as it came to communication. He was fond of never calling, never connecting if not perfunctorily, right before the opportunity of an erotic session. Should his unpredictable schedule suddenly allow room for sex, he would let me know with the briefest of notes. I should reply with a yes or a no. Any flourish, such as offering a slight variation, a "shall we," would exceed his capacity and make him back off. Until the next opportunity, the next telegraphic note to which I should reply yes or no. I had soon learned my lesson.

Otherwise, my lover wasn't too bad. I mean, not a bad man, though so uncourteous that to call him unkind would be fine. Incapable of care or attention, he was mellow nevertheless. That, I believe, was the tricky part of it.

     Mozart

Because he wasn't mean (on the contrary, kind of armless) I was unavoidably tempted to nurture sweet feelings about him. Tender thoughts, emotions, even attachment…

I was prone to think of him when (almost all the time) he was absent, though I knew I shouldn't contact him unless a chance for sex was in view. An imminent one, within the next half hour. Then I should concisely ask, "are you free in thirty minutes?" Any addendum, I said, would throw that gentleman, gentle, man, into panic. So I preferred abstaining.

I remember acutely longing for him, yes, when butterflies went amok. It was mid-March and they were migrating. The butterflies. And I happened to be on their route, as I went South for a weekend job. That year I had rarely left town, being fully occupied by what I already described. So the brief trip felt exhilarating.

As I drove around for work-related reasons, swarms of butterflies materialized out of nowhere, like small clouds, sudden vortices, miniature maelstroms. Oh, the sound of their wings. Hush and murmur. Secrets whispered by many voices, screamed secrets, and yet undecipherable.

They appeared in groups of various sizes. Big crowds, sometimes, redolent of biblical invasions. Sometimes just a small bunch… four, five, twenty? Hard to say, as their presence was always so ephemeral and impalpable.

They had bright yellow wings with brown bottoms… this last a dull color, melting within the background. As they flapped around, for some reason the underwing tint was predominant. So the eye starved for golden flashes, craved the intermittent shine.

All that fluttering, I guess, pushed me out of balance. Sort of kicked, slightly dislodged my heart. I was stirred by

an acute nostalgia, a sharp longing. I called, left a sweet note.
Message in a bottle. If I knew he'd never reply why did I...
Then I knew I should let go.

Towards the end of the year, in the fall, I interviewed
for an interim job. I decided that prior to the meeting I should
have my roots touched, in order to be presentable. But I had
scrubbed and bleached the bathroom for my upcoming open
house, and I didn't want to stain the sink or the tube with hair
dye.

I hadn't visited a salon for more than twenty-five years,
my entire adult life. Such small luxury exceeded my budget,
and I could do my hair. Therefore, I didn't know where to go,
and I didn't want to devote much time to the search. I hoped
to chance upon a shop where I wouldn't be charged too much,
where the job would be decent and quick, and the lady in charge
of my head would be kind of quiet.

The guy, I mean. Yes. Cordero's shop opened on a wide
parking lot, empty, which was quite a bad sign. But the calmness
felt soothing to me, almost intimate, and it magnetized me
instead. When I stepped in, a girl was getting her color done.
Long, thin, straight hair rained down her tilted neck.

Cordero, all by himself, hovered upon his customer's
head. But he lifted his eyes, smiled and told me to take a seat.
He'd start working on my case pronto, no problem. For a while,
he alternated between the girl and me. Here a wash, and now let
it soak. Here a timer and I'll put you under the helmet, ok? He
attended to us as if managing a couple of simmering pots.

Soon the girl was all done, her mane shining gold. As
she stepped out, a client called to reschedule her session. And
so we were alone. The salon was darkish and deep, cozy and

crimson, a kind of Ali Baba's cavern. As I said, I hadn't entered one for a quarter of a century. Sitting there was as if having stepped in error into someone else's life.

Cordero had named his rate up front, a ridiculous sum compared to average. Because I used to do the job, quick and easy, by myself, I knew his price was actually honest. And he didn't try to sell me any extras. On the contrary, he immediately figured what I needed, touch of brown, good rinse and pat dry. Out! The sun would take care of the rest.

But he added proteins, conditioner and a scalp massage on the house. Perhaps he was trying to seduce a new customer. I doubted it. I believed he had well understood I was just an accident, and he didn't care. His next job had been canceled. He did not have a lot on his hands. Perhaps he was bored. He could waste some time and pennies on me.

Yet to me his extra care was manna from heaven. What a marvelous gift. My head and neck pampered? When had that occurred last? For sure, not in the company of the lover I had ceased seeing in late spring, when all those tiny butterflies had swarmed by. He would not have tickled my nape, dipped his fingers into my hair. Such erratic gestures would have been distracting, futile, superfluous and ludicrous.

"You have wonderful hair," said Cordero. Yes, sir. True. I had known it at some point.

I had hoped that while the dye soaked I'd be left in silence. But Cordero was a chatterbox and he talked. And no, listening wasn't bad. He was funny, smart and well traveled. He remembered faraway places he had visited in his past, places I happened to have seen as well, in my past. I enjoyed the idiosyncrasy of his impressions, how he had gathered unique details and how vividly he could recall them.

He was fond of international cuisine, which meant
he loved local recipes. He had tried all sorts of dishes over the
years. He remembered long gone tastes and textures. At one
point, as he expertly rubbed my neck, water flowing like tears
down my cheekbones, he described the best dessert he ever
ate. In a distant country where I had also traveled, in an ancient
town where perhaps I had sat at a bar.

Fascinated, I asked specific questions, but he needed
no prompt. He knew the exact words evoking the lightness of
the pastry topped by thin slices of orange and puffs of cream,
the exquisite contrast of crisp and dense, tangy and lacteus. The
dessert he recreated in words was a poem, a work of art. How
he had chosen it among all, how he had treasured the memory
of its tiny, incidental delight simply amazed me.

As we sat face to face, waiting for my roots to be fully
imbibed, he started singing a tune that sounded familiar, maybe
a theme from a symphony or such. That he would reproduce
a classical melody impressed me. I smiled, but he didn't notice.
Didn't react, at least. He was singing in front of me and in my
presence. He did not sing for me.

Soon I recognized the motif, the Moldau by Smetana.
It's a quite famous air inspired by a river. Oh my, I loved it
immensely. I got goosebumps whenever I heard it, the whole
thing I mean, as the composer scored it, not the bare motif
crooned by Cordero's morning voice.

And yet he sang well. Then we commented on the
music, which he loved, he said, exactly as I did. Well, of course,
if he could perform it impromptu… But why would I be
surprised? We discussed it, the flow, the liquidity, the polyphony
of myriads of lives, nature's cycles captured by… We were
almost talking philosophy while Cordero expertly toweled my

hair. I was ready. I reached for my purse, planning on a tip.

Then I briskly recalled that I had sent a record of the Moldau to my former lover, when we had freshly met and I still thought flourishes would be allowed, and of course he hadn't replied, not even acknowledged it. And I had forgotten, forgotten.

Now the stream had reemerged from some underground bed where it might have sunk. Yes, in Cordero's voice, the river, teeming with life.

part 4

IN COLOR

THE PIANIST

The sound. Fluid, and pixelated. The sound, sweated.
And magic. A suspension of breath, then the applause.

*

Fluid means attached, continuous, someone holding
your hand during a walk. Holding tight, never letting go. They
won't let you go… They have grabbed your hand while still in
the elevator, before reaching the portal leading outside.

It's a huge wooden door. You can't manage it by
yourself… it's too heavy. You have tried. Someone has laughed.
There are always witnesses to your poor performances, you
have noticed. It is tiresome. You see laughter about to burst on
their face and invariably you start clowning around, as if your
goofs were meant indeed for their amusement. They think all
you do is potentially hilarious, for some reason. Wrong. Most of
what you do is dead serious. You are learning how to live, what's
entertaining about it? You are trying to understand the ropes
of what seems an insecure trade. Don't they know? They are so
eager to have fun… and you oblige, play dumb and cut capers.

You have tried to push the darn door, thrusting your

entire body against it, palms spread against the wood. First, the thing didn't budge, then it crept an inch or two while you lost your balance. Someone laughed and then took your hand, slamming the door open with the other hand. Dang. When are you going to be strong enough?

Now, a walk is fluid because of the hand that never, never lets you go. Streets, you were instructed, are huge, nasty rivers you have to smartly and prudently cross or you'll drown. "Danger!" they have cried, "you could be run over by a car. Those machines don't see you. They are blind. You need watching!"

You can watch for cars. You aren't blind, you understand velocity, you can run. You think you are quite fast, but then, how can you know if they don't let you try?

There's a loophole in the system, you have noticed. You can't do stuff because you don't know how. But if you don't try, how can you figure it out? "Everything," they say, "will come in its own time." Well… What if some things are late? If they forget to come? Should you endlessly wait without taking action?

You take action. You repeatedly ask. You are denied.

It is one of the fundamental laws, so implied you don't bother formulating it. Things need to be asked for, then denied. It's a dance… You find it tiresome, but (who knows) maybe its lack would be boring. Anyway, they all seem adept at the game, seemingly unavoidable.

It's not that things are forbidden. At least you haven't thought that way. They only need to be pushed or pulled, like a toy your brother has grabbed at the other end. Things need to be dug out, as you do with sand at the beach. You are good at digging deep, narrow holes with your plastic shovel. What are you looking for? Nothing. Well, the middle of the earth, but of course you don't say it, to avoid someone's burst of hilarity. Truly, you are seeking the other side… it can't be too far. It's a matter of patience and determination. You haven't spelled it out, but you know. Things can be obtained with patience and determination, against resistance. Resistance is law number one. You push against the abominable front door separating the world of home from the slushy, river-like street. You pull on the hand keeping yours like a secret. You pull on your chain. It will end up breaking.

Still, you should thank the hand that ensures continuity to your crossing. You should, but you can't.

Your steps pixelate the crossing. Small, pointed, separated. Your steps are teeth, little dots, nails punched in by your legs. You hammer the nails on the street. Your steps are black marks on the page leaned against the piano music rack. You have asked what those words mean, as they don't look like those printed, for instance, on Dad's paper (that large screen he hides behind, to suddenly lower a corner and yell at you).

They are notes, Mom said with a smile. You have already seen notes, like the one she keeps in her hand when you go for errands (the other hand holds you). Not the same kind of notes. You like those on the piano better, their punctual, firm, percussive quality. You don't know yet they transform themselves into sound. They remind you of your black shoes drawing steps on the pavement. Your steps make sound.

*

 In Color

Now, the piano teacher is exceedingly tall. You
are cross. You don't want to be given lessons, sit on the
wooden stool, be quiet, listen to what he has to say. But you
weren't given a choice. Besides, you understand the thing has
implications. You mean it came attached, as some do. It came
wet and a little bleeding. Those things you can't just refuse…
you can, but not bluntly or blindly.

You need to apply some care, because they aren't
neutral. They are sticky, attached, you were saying. You have
understood that the piano thing is quite sensitive. You can't
frankly oppose it. Still, you don't want to sit with this huge,
unknown individual.

Not surprisingly, he is interested in your hands. He
claims them… how original. He starts by subdividing them,
parceling… Look! Now your fingers have numbers, and they
need to hammer keys for a counted amount of times. He's
concerned by your doing this daily, please, for twenty minutes at
least (how can you keep all those arithmetics going?)

Your hands, so free, so spontaneous, have been
regimented into a foreign army. They'll wear an extraneous
uniform, speak a language that sounds mechanical and of
little interest. Should you obey? Should you surrender to this
obnoxious routine?

As we said, the question is tacky. Mother is hooked on it…
this tall man as well. A promise of obedience escapes you.

You bitterly regret it.

*

Piano routine has grown to two daily hours. She is
gifted, the teacher has said after two lessons, while promoting

her to the written score, allowing her into the secret of those curly, ornate hieroglyphs. Is she grateful? Kind of. Scores have lost a bit of their magic. Now she has eyes for them.

She already had eyes. She doesn't want too many.

The point is, her talent (what is it, if not something someone says about someone else?) has gained her two hours of daily reclusion, cutting her out from toys, brothers, games, television. Two hours sat on a stool behind a closed door. A prize? Clearly, it isn't. Punishment? Well, what else, but the talent-thing fogs it, blurs the contours. Can you have talent and be consequently punished? Apparently.

Piano practice cannot be begged off by means of repeated asking. It doesn't respond to the rules of resistance. Something is unnatural about it. For instance, not all have to deal with it… it landed on her, alas, like an oversized hat, quite uncomfortable. It grows stickier and stickier. Mother clings to it like a jellyfish.

She has heard her play once. Mom knew how. Used to. Now she doesn't. Never will again. Why? This belongs to a set of no-answer questions, a wide coffer adults keep accurately locked. Mother no longer plays. Now she does, as if Mother's hands had replaced hers. By the way, isn't she Mother's possession? She is, though she's pulling out… patience, determination.

She can't beg her way out of her piano hours, though the weight of them swells as she grows older. She has more homework to do and the afternoon becomes shorter. Little time is left, and in such a tiny window there's more urgent, tastier, spicier stuff she wishes to do. Phone calls with her girlfriends. Movies on TV. Card games with her brothers. Or else draw,

 In Color

bake a pie…

She'd gladly give up school and play piano instead, the lesser between two quasi evils. She means bores. But that isn't thinkable.

She must deal with temptation, then. Skip practice? At least shorten it, biting off a tad at the end or at the beginning, maybe on both sides. Take breaks? Frequent ones. Lie about it? That's hard. Mother asks for daily reports and verifies her progress, of course, with the teacher. If she cheats, she will be discovered. If she doesn't score well, she'll be in trouble. How? Not sure. She's afraid she will become worthless.

While her hands (they have a life of their own) play the keys, her eyes wander over the wooden surface of the instrument, beyond the score. She could reproduce every stain, every dot by memory… She has watched the veined designs a zillion times.

She knows all the shapes that can be made out, clouds, trees, bridges, buildings. Most of all, faces. Many. Her gaze slips from the score to the shiny panels, where it lingers especially on this or that face. She engages in mute conversations. This naïve game entertains her. She starts nurturing a weird thought, perhaps to kill time, at least push it forwards. She asks herself if the figures are due to the wood's irregularities and strata, or if someone actually traced them.

Someone traced them. She knows it is a fancy (a lie, in other words) but she starts believing it. Then it isn't a lie anymore. It is the beginning of insanity. Overpracticing inevitably leads there.

She is insane. On the right side of the piano an

arch leads into a den, which in late afternoon (study time)
is vacant and dark. Daylight's gone at that hour, right, for
months in a row. A lamp draws the small loop of her supposed
concentration, beyond which obscurity reigns. This wouldn't
be a problem if the arch weren't there, leading to the creepy,
empty room she can't see and slowly starts to obsess her, to
haunt her. A cold breath is coming through, a threat of sorts.
Someone could hide there, jump out and surprise her, especially
if she gets too lost in the music, which meanwhile has grown
complex. (She is talented, her teacher keeps saying). She gets
lost anyway… the scores are more crowded, the arpeggios and
thrills faster and faster. Then she's suddenly startled. She stops
dead. She thinks she heard something. She shivers.

She has spotted a new design on the wood, squeezed
among the intricacies of auburn and brown. The score usually
blocks it, but one day she has found it. She hides it since, but
she knows it is there. A devil. A demon. Not only the face. The
full torso, a bit crooked. Not unpleasant. Enticing. Mischievous,
in a seductive way.

But a devil… right there, on the side, close to the
gaping mouth of obscurity. She's scared stiff. She no more dares
entertaining bad thoughts such as cheating on practice time,
skipping tedious drills and still checking them on her notebook.
Whenever temptation assails her, fear grabs her. Grabs her
hand, lifts it in midair and then solidly plugs it, you bet, into the
darn keys.

She is preparing for her first recital. She is ready, says
the teacher (who has become a friend, almost) and so is her
Beethoven. She will be a success and he's proud of her. Will
Mother? Perhaps.

                    In Color

He asks her to rehearse curtain bows. "Look at that arch!" he exclaims. "A perfect mock stage! Go back there, then come forwards, stop center, bow, count to three, lift up, smile!" But she is frozen. She needs to confess that she can't. While she thinks of lies, the truth just spills out of her lips. Her teacher laughs heartily. Sympathetically, "I'll cure you. Nothing is in the dark that wasn't…" All right. She has no choice but to leave the room, cross the TV lounge, enter the other end of the infamous office to finally emerge, as required, through the glorious arch. Like diving in cold water… same shiver, same thrill afterward. "Again," the teacher says. She repeats. Now she has done it ten times. She feels ten years older, a grown-up. "Bravo, little diva."

She knows she's learned something, at last.

Early on Easter morning she has cut her hand with a large, dented knife. She was tidying the kitchen first thing, to surprise her mother. Wraps and ribbons were all over the table. Chocolate eggs had been opened the night before, following tradition. Mother hadn't cleaned up because it was late.

She'd take care of it, then make breakfast. With the knife, she was cutting a golden cord whose knot couldn't be undone. She could have stored it knotted, of course. Hers was an excess of zeal. Plus, the knife wasn't the right tool. She needed a pair of scissors, didn't she?

The blade tore her palm, cutting all the way through, deep, zigzagging, a mess. Mother found her bent over the sink, unsuccessfully attempting to stop the bleeding. That asked for a trip to the hospital. Talk about a surprise.

She has cut her left hand. No more bass, no more accompaniment for the moment. They will take the opportunity

to strengthen her right hand, says the piano teacher, unscathed.
She still practices for hours.

When the wound scars, she sees how it interferes
with her destiny line. She keeps thinking about it. Wait. If the
crease has been modified (by her own hand… the other one)
will her fate consequently change? The scar overlaps the line
for a while… it makes it nonlinear, complicated, arabesque.
Then, towards the end, it sharply diverges. If the line were a
river (what else is it?) the scar would mark a crucial bifurcation.
Tributary… Emissary… A delta of possibilities.

Though it has perfectly scarred, the hand doesn't heal.
She can scarcely move it. It is knotted, a bit folded, as if holding
something it can't let go. Mother brings her back to the surgeon
who has sutured the wound. Maybe there was nerve damage, he
says. That, Mother replies, of course can't be. The girl plays the
piano. She can't stop.

She can't.

She suddenly realizes that the surgeon is exceedingly
tall. She had not paid attention, when her flesh was dangling
about and he was poking holes. He grabs her by the hand (the
right one) with a tone of authority. Not unsympathetic. "Come
on." He drags her to the sink he has filled with hot water. He
lets go of her right, gets hold of her left. Frightened, she tries
to withdraw it, but he firmly dips it into the water and starts to
articulate it. He pushes and pulls…

She starts screaming. This is hurting like hell. But
something loosens up. He laughs, lets her go. "Hopefully, it is
just muscles. Don't let them shrink. You need this routine, daily.
Hot water, then brace yourself. Move it! Move it!" Then he
turns towards Mother, "Don't worry, she'll play."

　　　　　In Color

*

After the concert's end (she went with friends of her age; the academy gives free tickets to gifted students, like her) she has climbed on stage, then respectfully waited on the side. She has begun to collect signed programs.

You see, she has embraced her musical destiny. She has made room for it. She simply kept practicing, progressing, and destiny made itself. Now she goes to concerts and collects autographs she then shows to her mother, quite proudly.

While she waited, she has noticed his scorched fingers. The flesh all around his nails is raw, profusely bleeding. Astonished, she has looked at the keys to see if they were stained. She has seen nothing. Perhaps she's too far away.

Now it's her turn. He smiles, automatically.She unfolds her program, smiling as well, and he signs with a flourish, quite an emphatic gesture. "I liked your performance," she says, meaning it. He keeps smiling. "I wonder," (this is inappropriate, please, stop), "how could you play so divinely with those wounded fingers?"

She regrets what she's said. This is embarrassing. She has brought up something… private, perhaps something… "Fingers?" He looks as if he were seeing them for the first time. Surprised, stunned. "My fingers?" Perhaps he's insane, she thinks. Overpracticing does it.

The proof, he starts laughing. What is such hilarity about? "But I don't play with these," he exclaims, giggling away.

Then what does he play with? Whose fingers, she means.

Loops

Kind of square, kind of squat. That's how she perceives herself. Compact, each part of her body a modest excrescence kept within a reasonable radius, magnetized by the center, enamored with gravity. All (her body, her mind) within reach… a small village where everything is nearby, cozy and snug like five fingers. Nondescript as well, like a ringless, slightly calloused hand.

When the visit of the older cousins is announced, she is thrilled. She reacts with the naïve enthusiasm due to all things new… a small village electrified by the arrival of a traveling circus. She has never met older cousins, neither these nor any. Of course, she understands they are relatives and what "relatives" means… essentially people, often smiling and greeting while expecting to be greeted in return. People who can be fully trusted even when (like today's announced cousins) they are perfectly unknown, and in spite of the fierce commandment "you shall never trust strangers."

But the strangeness of relatives, she has realized, is short-lived, like a candy wrapper of which you get rid at once. Their alterity expires as soon as they alight from the train at the station or emerge from the car and walk up the driveway (if she has been left home in trepidant wait). Their remoteness melts before you realize, liquefies between a big hug and a sweaty kiss.

So these cousins are relatives, and in a little while they'll bring exhilaration to her Sunday afternoon. She has been straightened up, her hair combed, her fingernails cleaned. Then she has been parked in her room and she has begun playing, oblivious. Lost in her occupation, the rumpus of arrivals has startled her. When she is briskly propelled into the living room, she is confused, as if waking up from deep slumber.

Nine, eleven, thirteen, the age of the cousins is spelled. She is taken by a sort of vertigo, humbled by the highness of these numbers. All odd (though she can't tell), sharp and slick (this she can perceive), climbing up and away as they leave her behind, a small, flat, helpless blob. These numbers, unreachable.
Does the age of adults impress her this way? Absolutely not. Adults are grown up, a different universe, of course out of her reach. But these cousins, like her, are still growing, yet they have gotten so far! She wonders how, when.
She stubbornly looks at their feet while the rest (gangly limbs, slim and elongated torsos) seem to escape and their heads sort of float, up above, bound to somewhere celestial, ethereal. Separated from their neck, superior, sublime.

They are polite. They all nicely greet her, but the nine-year-old boy is magnetized by a row of magazines piled on the coffee table, clearly intending to peruse them cover to cover. The eleven-year-old sticks to her mom's side, anxious to draw the line between girlhood and womanhood, eager to signify where she now belongs.

She understands she'll be ushered into her room, as it often occurs on these kinds of occasions, after the initial show.

To her greatest surprise, the thirteen-year-old pops in. She's embarrassed by his… stature, altitude? His boyish slimness seems to further accentuate verticality. His gaze hovers so high, it acquires a numinous quality and so does his smile. Actually, his smile could be rather defined as lofty and condescending, though in an innocent way. But she doesn't know, or perhaps that is what numinous means. To her, his expression as well as his looks are… princely, regal.

Indeed.

He has sat on a low stool, spread his infinite legs and bent forward, elbow leaning onto the miniature table where she likes to draw or play. He has come down to her level. She feels both blessed and humbled… the two states kind of melt, then blessing prevails.

Slowly, with a voice so breathy it sounds muffled (utterly fascinating her) he asks her to show him some of her toys. Suddenly, she feels shy. Also excited, and the two emotions mix up. Then exhilaration prevails. She rushes to her toy chest, eager to exhibit what she deems her most interesting possessions, two brand new sets of beads with which, she was told, jewelry could be actually assembled. How, she has no clue, but what counts is the possibility.

He will show her, he says. Will? He? She is wordless. Her eyes pop wide open. She holds her breath. Then she sighs.

Now, the boxes… one is already open, though she has done nothing so far besides watching its contents. The beads are fairly large, made of wood, painted in primary colors.

 In Color

Yellow, blue, orange, green. Mostly round, a few cubes, the right blend of diversity and plainness. They are pretty (the colors, so joyful!) and agreeable to the touch. They agree with her, yes! Good toys do. They match her own dimension, squarish, squat, contained and compact, small village.

The other box is still closed. It's "for later." Larger, or rather longer. Light, slim. Fragile, a dangerous trait. It's divided into small sections, all of different and unnamable shapes... in fact, a variety of rectangles, but she doesn't know and variety (when excessive, as in the present case) overwhelms her. These fancy rectangular cavities hold beads of all kinds and shades.

Shades are not truly colors. She can't exactly name them. Not with nouns. She must add adjectives such as "dark," "light," "pale" and so forth. Interesting pursuit, yet laborious. She confusedly feels such expansion of her vocabulary can wait. What all those shades (those beads) have in common is sheerness. They are transparent, which means... she cannot explain it, the idea is too scientific. Are they like glass, perhaps? Too hard a comparison.

They look precious. They look fairytalish. They are what a princess would wear. They cause her to hold her breath. Her chest hurts with unspeakable longing, a sort of reverse nostalgia. This is why they can wait. She can't handle such complexity yet. This is why the box is intact.

He has already torn the plastic film wrap. Of course, she hasn't protested. What she can't manage yet, he can do in a breeze. Right? He will guide her. That is what adults are for. Soon-to-be adults as well, here's the proof.

He has widened his eyes and gasped as he hastily indented the cellophane with his nail, moved by impromptu

greed. "These are marvelous," he has exclaimed, "these are
real gemstones!" His tone is a bit shrill, though his voice hasn't
lost the soft nasal quality (technically called "distinction") so
enthralling her. He is pretending excitement, sure, and she
knows but it doesn't bother her. Nothing is reprehensibly fake
about it. A convention, that is, by which adults abide when
dealing with children. Most adults, especially strangers, aka yet
unknown relatives paying short visits. Soon-to-be adults as well,
she sees.

"Your wrist! Let me measure it. I will make you a
bracelet." With a gasp of joy she straightens her arm, palm up,
in ecstatic surrender. He hooks his index and thumb around
her small bones with a frown, squeezes, then loosens his grip.
He repeats the operation once, twice, wrinkling his brow. He is
pretending, as if playing doctor. She laughs.

She has let herself slide on the floor right against
his legs, her gaze level with his knee, thus reestablishing the
immense distance between their faces, yet cocooning in his
physical proximity. She looks up.

He has cut a length of elastic cord with his teeth. His
hand fumbles into the box, wandering from a stack of beads
to another, fingertips diving here, there, appraising… Then a
sudden smile smooths his face. "Wait! Show me your favorite!
Which ones do you want?" Dreaded, difficult question. She is
mute, irritated by a knot in her throat, a tickle of sorts.

Then her gaze uncertainly shifts, pulled by a power
unknown towards a far corner, the one closest to him. She
points at a small lake of oblong, pale purple. "Hmmmm! You
have good taste! You picked the most valuable! These are
amethysts from Brazil!" She knows he's pretending.

     In Color

She knew a minute ago. Now she doesn't. These are amethysts from Brazil. The most precious.

How he has savored those words. How clearly and how lusciously he has spelled them, his voice high-pitched, clear of all breathiness, wanting to sound grand and yet, suddenly, a child…

He threads beads one by one, very slowly, with luxuriant precision and the solemn airs of a priest celebrating. His left thumb and forefinger hold the cord, the end of which he has duly knotted. His right hand lifts each bead in front of his eyes to verify authenticity, to enjoy its shine before deftly dropping it on top of its mates.

Her whole body has relaxed, heavy as if she were about to fall asleep, yet immensely alert. Her whole body sinks cozily into the rug while her head kind of levitates, mesmerized by the thread of purple hanging from his fingers, up there, a bait hooked to a fishing pole.

She drifts. Time is suspended. The confection of her jewel indefinitely protracts itself, seemingly occupying the entire afternoon.

"Done!" he finally exclaims. "Quick! Give me your hand!" Again, she extends her arm, this time less abruptly. Less innocently. Her wide-open eyes look straight into his, which imperceptibly squint. Then he lowers his gaze onto her tiny wrist, as he accurately ties the ends of the cord.

"Here you go! You are a queen!" A broad smile and he stretches his legs, yawns, stands up. One, two steps… he's out of the room. Noise is seeping in from the corridor. She understands what that means, but the languor that has filled her limbs is still lingering. In a trance, zombielike, she totters towards her mother who has appeared at the door, raises her bejeweled arm, "Look at what he made! These are amethysts from…" She doesn't remember.

In the hall, close to the coat rack, trapped within a tight bundle of loudly greeting, fairly rumorous relatives, he is whispering into his brother's ear. She does not…

Beads are cold, smooth, hard. A bit tight. They are poking rosy marks on her skin, tiny indents in her flesh, while the older cousins are leaving.

In Color

Her Wish

Red ballet shoes? No such thing existed. Ballerinas wore pink, black, or beige, and red was for whores. Well, maybe that was a bit hyperbolic. The wrong color, that's all, inappropriate, vulgar. There you go, vulgar. She liked the definition, she always found it conclusive. She was she, the mother.

And the one who wanted red shoes for Christmas, of course, was the daughter. Let us give them names, for practical purposes... Alma for Mom, because of Alma Mater. For the daughter, Borbora, with an accent on the second syllable. Because daughters can become annoying.

Where did Borbora's fancy come from, Alma wondered. She remembered, then. A story, a folk tale. Bor had mentioned it at the dinner table... red shoed girl who couldn't stop dancing. Something to do with hell, sin... she couldn't recall details at the moment, though her daughter might have provided them. But when Alma came home from the office, at night, she was tired, her mind full of more crucial matters.

Also, Bor expressed herself... childishly. Redundantly lingering, briskly stopping and needlessly repeating, a compendium of all possible rhetoric faults. Children are inefficient tellers, are they? Had she, Alma, ever been such? It would have been hard to believe.

Anyway, she couldn't recall details about the shoes story, if she had even listened in the first place. But the overall feeling was clear... a tale of compulsion.

Obsession. Alas, yet another flaw of young age... Why was Bor so insisting about something impossible to find? Unavailable, belonging to a realm of bookish imagination. Ballet shoes in child size were black, beige, or pink. Non-colors, neutral, discreet. Alma had visited a few stores on her way from work. Quite a time consuming detour, but she knew what her duty was. A package would be under the tree and the girl would be pleased. She would receive her gift.

Only, not red ballerina shoes.

Borbora had a thing with red, way before she met with the wicked tale, only fueling her passion. Not obsession... do you see the fine line? It is noticeable, but it takes attention.

What had fired the passion was a striking vision she had glimpsed once, when she was quite young. She was brought to a school play, during which an older cousin danced on stage. The girl wore a classical tutu, a large sphere of bright scarlet veils.

The intensity of the color was enhanced by the consistency (rather by the inconsistency) of the fabric, by its aerial quality, by the motion causing myriads of shifting reflections. Bor was mesmerized by the dance, the music, the applause... even more by the tutu. It was love at first sight, with its typical pang of longing, a blow right in the guts she couldn't yet name, but she could perfectly suffer.

Since then, the red tutu often came to mind. But the thought didn't imply things like wishes, wants, requests. Just

    In Color

a feeling, lifting Bor where… she couldn't tell… and then dropping her down, as if she had fallen from bed. And the fall was the longing, the indefinable pain.

When she first read the story, her emotion revived. Red shoes, though, seemed more concrete than a tutu, more accessible. They looked like a good start, a foundation. For what? Not sure yet.

If she could get the shoes, then tights, dress, necklace, even a tiara could follow (none of this was thoroughly planned… only a subconscious seed). She would ask for red shoes for Christmas.

Alma had sensed Borbora's bad taste on previous occasions. The girl being her first child, she wasn't totally sure. Was it just a phase all children went through? A fad, to be detected and pruned? She meant tutored, guided in the right direction, of course.

In Bor's case, an indicator was her greed for gaudy hair ribbons, barrettes, clips, you name it. Alma had painstakingly taught her how to match hair with accessories, for the sake of elegance. At least, decency. There were rules to go by, with a slight allowance. Dark or light brown, for instance. Why, good lord, wasn't it enough? Did all girls insist on over-decorating their ponytail? Alma couldn't tell if the annoying penchant was a passing trend or a stable, personal fail… (a lack, here we go).

As well as she didn't display natural stylishness, Bor wasn't graceful motion-wise, Alma had noticed when she picked her up after school. Rare occasions… Usually she had no time. See, she had to go directly from work, where it was fairly common for her to remain trapped. One call at the wrong moment et voilà, she was stuck. Sure, she had the presence of mind of ringing her secretary, who'd seek the delivery boy. Alma didn't need to explain. She just waved her left hand (the one not holding the receiver). Long and slender, emblazoned with a single pearl ring, her hand made cryptic gestures, but her faithful assistant knew… someone had to take care of Borbora. Alma couldn't.

The delivery boy was a grown-up. He had gotten old at the job, unfit for career advancement. Well, Bor's hand didn't approve of his… No, it wasn't distaste, nothing that visceral. The girl didn't dislike the man. She sensed his kindness. At her age such judgments are sound. Only, her hand disapproved of his grasp, pliers-like, as if the responsibility of his precious load overwhelmed him. As if he were afraid to lose the girl, even parts of her. His hand was damp with sweat. It felt slippery. They marched in perfect silence.

When, most rarely, Alma stopped by the school on her way home, she saw her daughter come down the stairs, each time, with a twitch of unease. Bor walked funny. She spread her feet like a duck. Her posture was misaligned. That gave out a sense of…

Vulgarity. It should be corrected if possible. Soon.

Alma thought dance lessons would fix the girl's gait. Ballet? Right. She should get that going. But the idea slipped out of her mind, coming back as an itch, then fading away. Definitely, she had a lot on her plate. Still, the issue kept surfacing. The girl should be straightened. She meant molded. Not corrected. Well, of course. Corrected in a good way. Tutored, here we are. Like a young plant that might grow all crooked if not helped. Redressed. Helped.

Now, things suddenly came together… The

subscription to a year of dance lessons would be the Christmas present. That would quench the weird red-shoes yearning, setting it in a more suitable format. The academy, an excellent one, was on the other side of the bridge. The hours were convenient. In the afternoon Nanny would bring Borbora to class, wait, then bring her back for her bath and dinner. Alma, of course, would be there for a goodnight kiss. A long kiss. The girl wouldn't sleep without it.

To the subscription card (a dry item, she reckoned, for a seven-year-old) she added a large, soft package. It contained a leotard, tights, slippers, plus a fancy headband (well, unnecessary, but still). She chose beige over pink, more sober and classy. Yet another lesson in taste. The girl would be thrilled.

Bor actually was. Scarlet longings simply melted at the sight (the touch) of those things, still scenting a whiff of brand new. She spread them on her bed, shaping a life-size doll. Leotard, tights, slippers as if tiptoeing, pointing down. Headband at the top… She tried curving it like a half-moon but it wouldn't stay, so she laid it flat, straight, in the proper place.

Dreamily, she contemplated her work, admiring the silhouette. Faceless, headless. Such lack made it lighter. Perhaps, it… perhaps she could fly. Borbora couldn't wait to wear the whole apparel and to begin her lessons.

Bor didn't like Nanny more than she did the delivery boy. Actually much less, though the feeling wasn't totally conscious. Nanny's hand, to start with, pinched her cruelly. It was dry, but that didn't improve things. Nana resented the afternoon walk, interfering with some private routine she would have entertained at home, nice and cozy, while Bor would conveniently keep to her room. She walked fast, dragging the girl who trotted beside her. She was quiet, but her disapproval was tangible.

Bor enjoyed her lessons, mostly spent at the barre, as appropriate for a beginning student. The barre was a safe, perfect place near the mirrors that lined the whole studio, wrapping it in a magic box, silver, shiny.

But Bor didn't see the mirror. Meaning what was inside it, herself. How come? Not sure. Suppose her eyes were still turned in, somehow… or else she was sheer, immaterial, her young body unable to refract the light waves. Children are that way, until someone's gaze strikes them at a particular angle. Then a switch goes on, at once and for good. Then the body becomes refractive, all right. Sometimes you wish it never happened. Only, it is irreversible.

Such gaze had hit Borbora, in fact, through her mother's eyes. But it had failed to work, perhaps because Alma was located too high. She loomed too spectacular in her daughter's perception. She was so very heavenly that her critical, slightly disparaging view flew above the girl, so to speak, leaving her intact.

But with Nanny Bor had worse luck. Nana was shorter than Mother, very short, or maybe age had compressed her. Borbora didn't know how old Nanny was (she had never considered the question), but her hair was pale grey, thin braids pinned around her skull. Her face was crumpled, corrugated, to the girl a mood indicator, a mark of authority more than a chronological clue. Stocky, bent, sadly wrapped in dull skirts and sweaters, Nanny was a concentrate of regretful discontent. Bor knew nothing about it.

She knew nothing of village gossips, broken engagements, smarter sisters, long years of domestic employment, envy, bitterness, tedium. She did not know what jealousy was and where it could find its outlets.

So when once, on the way home, Nanny spat her venom, the girl took it easy. As if she hadn't heard, truly. Nanny also took it kind of tangentially. She started off, "The girl behind you at the barre, the one with the ponytail, is a beauty as I was." She went on, "My hair was so long it reached behind my knees. It took Mom one hour to fix it. She had no time left for sister." Borbora pictured the scene. Nanny sitting on a small chair (dressed in grey like she presently was, only much younger), her hair spreading like a peacock tail.

She asked, "What color was it?" "My hair?" Nanny yelled. "Blond, of course! I had golden hair." Like Mother.

The next question trickled. Trickled up, if that makes sense. It dripped as if out of a faulty faucet, suddenly broken. But it dripped upwards, bubbling like lava, a thin flow, just a ribbon. A red thread, like lava, like blood. It dripped up from something that was down, stuck, heavy, guts, stomach, heart, liver… It started scratching her throat, then her tongue rolled the words out.

Like vomit. This is kind of vulgar, I know. "Am I pretty?" She asked. I wish she had put it another way. Nanny jumped in, "You aren't pretty!" she blurted. Then she specified, "You aren't blond. You are fat. You are clumsy. You look like a duck." No meanness was in her tone, only a statement of facts. Satisfied, she plunged into silence while Borbora pondered the verdict.

Just before the recital, Alma thought the dance

lessons should stop. There were at least two good reasons.
First of all, the subscription did not include costumes. Money
wasn't a problem, but things shouldn't pop out like rabbits.
Unprofessional attitudes irritated her. Then, the show would
imply rehearsals and the actual performance she, alas, was
expected to attend. Any addition to her schedule irked her in
advance.

Was the show really needed? On the contrary, it might
have unwanted effects. For example, luring the girl into weird
fashion whims… god knew what those costumes looked like.
Finally, lessons were meant to correct Borbora's deportment,
not to start a career. This consideration induced, of course,
an assessment that Alma, bless her heart, hadn't had time to
formulate for the past months. Had her daughter improved?
She focused. Not a bit.

Well, that got rid of uncertainties, especially since
Nanny had expressed discontent. Crossing the bridge back and
forth, especially in winter, was a bit too much. The wind was
truly nasty and she wasn't in her twenties, Ma'am. She would
catch a cold. Alma got the picture, all right. Then, Nana had the
nerve to add, the girl didn't do well in class. Dance didn't seem
to be her thing. Alma said nothing, as that statement was surely
beyond Nanny's competence. But she took her advice.

Bor's role for the show wasn't crucial. Yet it was,
in a way. The instructor had said that she would be a chick,
following mother hen with her sister birdies. That would be the
first set, featuring the youngest… an hors-d'oeuvre meant to
soften the audience, build a forgiving mood, to then welcome
the surprise of more skilled numbers. Such as an older girl,
maybe, a teen clad in crimson veils? Would there be such an act?

Borbora didn't know. She did not recall, didn't add two and two. She was dazzled, awed, lifted in heaven by the thought of her own passage on stage, lined up with a flock of small cackling things. Nicely tucked in the middle, no risk of being stranded. Shuffling with the tiniest steps in her slippers (sadly, they no longer smelled new, they had started to show the thread). Shuffling like a train and meandering as required, duly following the leader. Flapping her arms, elbows bent, which was slightly tiresome but well worth the effort. Fame, she understood, came at some cost, yet never too high.

How happy she was! Especially about the costume. Yellow, not her favorite color, but it quickly grew on her… Happiness requires adapting. Such wisdom (of course unformulated) was immediately acquired. Yellow, like the sun. Like the moon, sometimes. She started starving for yellow now, anything yellow. Would there be feathers? What would be over her hair? What did chicks wear on top of their little heads?

This time the girl was sad, and she tried to insist. Could she do the recital? The recital only, could she? After all, she had been assigned a role. As a chick, she was counted on. She tried making her point a rational one. She knew Alma would appreciate sound reasoning more than caprice or whining. But her mother didn't change her mind.

Then Borbora forgot. Novelty helped the transition… In the summer the house was sold and a new one purchased. She was transferred to a different school. Quite a revolution, the best remedy for any sort of regret.

Moving on. The new school was an all-female institute, while the previous was not. The fact didn't strike Borbora in a negative or positive way. She didn't give a great relevance yet to gender. Color, for instance, had such a stronger impact…

Speaking of which, this all-female school required a uniform, to Bor a new concept, sort of. The old school (where she had made such a poor impression, hadn't she, awkwardly strolling downstairs) was a public one. The new one was a private institute, fit to the better neighborhood where the family had moved.

Navy blue. Nothing like the sky or the sea, a dull tone, nearing black but without its sharpness and drama. Borbora wasn't crazy about it, but, hey!… The dress wasn't provided. Each family had to put it together, following rules with a tiny margin of freedom. Alma liked the concept… it echoed the light-brown/dark-brown formula she applied to hair ribbons.

The rules went like this. Skirt, pleated or not, one inch under the knee. Not too long (excess of all kinds was discouraged). White socks (not stockings, they are slightly indecent) one inch above the knee. They will keep slipping under… nothing is perfect. Blue shoes, strapped or laced. White shirt with no frills. Let us hammer the point, a man's shirt buttoned on the left side, lady's side. A man's shirt buttoned female wise. Clear enough? No necklaces, chains, brooches, nothing over the shirt except for a narrow tie. A blue headband. Wouldn't brown be fine? Wouldn't it be better? Alma thought she would discuss the point with the principal.

Bor, believe it or not, didn't have such garments. Alma hadn't had the time to… After all, the girl was still young. The new school was the occasion for tackling wardrobe issues. Things jell up on their own at the right moment, don't they?

Time for a thorough visit to the department store.

 In Color

Mom didn't mind a Saturday afternoon with her daughter. Hopefully, Bor wouldn't flash on something outlandish Alma, of course, should deny. She hated having to redirect her. Thank god, the child seemed to have outgrown that phase. Lately, for instance, she had lost interest in jazzy ribbons. Good sign.

All the items were found, three counts per category, to be free of worry for one year at least. Before checkout, though, the girl needed fitting.

White shirted, buttoned-up, bagged in a kind-of-straight-kind-of-bell-shaped skirt, fumbling with a blue tie, Borbora stepped in front of a full-size mirror that swung in its wooden frame, leisurely tilting back and forth. She was momentarily captured by that sweet, rocking mood. Alma straightened the thing and she steadied it, standing on the side like a post, her gaze lost in a vacuum, profile to the child.

What Bor saw surprised her. She had already been in front of a mirror, clad in beige dance attire. The memory, sunk for a while, popped up as memories do, uninvited. Brains love to be whimsical, mischievous, or devilish. Well, they can afford it… there's no way to stop them, correct?

The dance flashback dissolved as soon as it came. A pale girl in blue took its place. A strange one, cut in halves, white top and blue bottom. The white socks and blue tie (that she couldn't properly knot) didn't mend the fracture. A strange halved girl, un-blond and if not fat kind of large. Actually not even large, un-contoured, blurred around the edges, as if vanishing by rarefaction.

Obviously, she didn't put it that way. But the reflected image had an unsettling vagueness, and it didn't match the original. Meaning Borbora. This is what she realized, yet confusedly. And a thing filled her throat, kind of tickling. A question, again? On the very short side. It sounded like, "Me?" The word climbed, winked, looked around then it plunged back in. Silence came in its place.

Though a secular institution, the school was visited by nuns on occasion. Some of them taught classes. Religion, for instance, was part of the curriculum. The girl didn't make much of it, as she didn't of any subject (Alma had not yet detected this vacancy… she would get to it later, at the appropriate moment). Not that Bor disliked school. She adored, indeed, a small parcel of it, and she waited for its intermittent delivery. All the rest was, let's say, a container, a bowl. In the bowl, a few tasty morsels came afloat now and then. She patiently waited, then she savored them with delight.

Such as the music hour, when they all single filed to the chapel, sat in the wooden pews (nicely squeaking and cracking), chanted a number of songs (easy melodies hammered over and over, seasoned with slightly different words). Bor really enjoyed singing. Weird, as soon as it left her mouth, her voice no longer sounded… Once exhaled, it belonged, sure as rock, to a different person. Stronger, bigger. Belonged…

Bor liked it so much, she sang a tad louder. Then she reveled in the gap, slim like a knife cut, between her volume and that of her closest neighbors. A thin halo seemed to surround her notes, wide enough to single them out. What a thrill… Awed by the phenomenon, Bor assumed others would notice as well. She unconsciously expected the teacher to lift her eyes from the keyboard, trying to localize that… what was it… that pure, shiny silver bell. Bor unconsciously expected to be asked in the first row, perhaps be given a solo as some other girl was.

But she wasn't.

We suspect that, carried away by her enthusiasm, she sang a tad brashly. Maybe not exactly in tune. It is an assumption. Finally, she didn't mind.

A nun directed the choir, also playing the piano with long, nervous fingers spreading over the keys like thin spider legs. Nuns were good with their hands, the girl had remarked. See, another nun taught domestic economy. That was also a class that Bor truly enjoyed.

But the name of it remained quite a mystery. Kind of dry, reminiscent of dusty accounting books, columns, rulers, plus and minus signs. Or else real estate, the selling and buying of property, the girl thought, in the wake of her recent relocation. Salaries given to nannies and cooks, proper management of tabs at the grocery store, possible allowance to children.

The name of the class was displaced, like the label of a jar that has been promoted, let's say, from containing rice to holding abalone buttons, pearly and precious. But it still says "rice" in Grandma's faded handwriting, almost disappeared…

During domestic economy class (taught by a nun, we said, of all people) girls made crafts, toys, and various gadgets. As soon as the materials (always a surprise) were delivered, Bor started breathing deeper. Her lungs sort of expanded, her chest opened.

Recently, the project had been a black ballerina. Black meaning from Africa. In her past school, where genders were casually combined, an African boy was in her class. From Somalia, he was extremely handsome, his skin a dark cappuccino shade. His name, hard to pronounce, was mysterious. All the girls…

But the felt for those dancers' bodies was black. Didn't have that warm, chestnut lusciousness. Pitch black. Raffia was distributed (Bor had never seen it) and then metal wire coated in different colors. Some embroidering thread, glue, needles and scissors.

The nun who ran the project had just returned from Africa. Missionaries frequently came to teach, maybe while in transit. As they waited to be reassigned, their order dispatched them through local institutions to serve interim jobs.

Missionary nuns (most rarely a priest) were quite special, Bor had noticed. Their peculiar qualities were hard to pinpoint, or else she lacked adequate words. They were tanned, sure. Sunburned, and that made the white of their eyes intriguingly shine. Yes, there was that glare, indefinable, and then something else in the motion, the way they crossed the courtyards together, as a flock (she saw them during recess, lifting her gaze from a half-nibbled croissant) aiming toward the street. Yes, they moved like birds… not exactly flying… maybe gliding. Ducks? No. Chicks? Not at all. Again, a fleeting, disturbing memory.

Nuns coming from the missions (exceptionally a priest or a monk, their male version) were joyful. The birdlike quality the girl saw but couldn't properly name was lightness. It was ease. It was happiness, though this concept still escaped Borbora's capacity, or the classroom walls. Like a cloud, it frayed at the edges, slipped away, evaporated.

The African dancer had a twisted-wire body (its pose standardized, but with flexibility) topped by a round head embroidered with perky features. Over the head, black hair was propped in pineapple fashion. A string of flowers (they had been fun to cut), incongruously Polynesian, was around her neck. A full raffia skirt constituted her garment, matched by a feathery puff on her bun. Skirt and headgear were the bulk of the project. Strings of raffia of different lengths, in large quantities, had to be threaded then ruffled with great patience… clearly, a quality in constant need of encouragement, as most girls were soon frustrated and lost.

Not Borbora. Well, she was frustrated at first. Raffia came in green, yellow and red. She had a thing for red, still, you know… The nun delivered the packets, starting with the front row and alternating colors. Bor sat in the back. Her eyes bouncing from the nun's hand to the bag containing the booty, she held her breath.

But red didn't land on her desk. Yellow did. The nun stopped for a moment. She smiled, "You are lucky. Yellow and black make a nice contrast. They are dance itself." Quite a statement. How did she know? Borbora felt better.

She sewed her doll's skirt in a blink, her hand fancying the right-to-left motion. She looked up. The nun nodded from her desk, "Bring it here. Wow, this is well done! You are good. You are going to help your companions." Bor kept gathering skirts for an hour, all colors, and a bunch of red ones. Which skirt was her doll's didn't matter. Which doll she'd bring home was irrelevant. Her lungs worked at full steam.

The doll's feet were a loop of wire. That simple, but it worked. A turn and a bend, the flat surface then fastened to the base of thin cardboard. Good. The figure would stand, no problem. While carrying it home, Bor realized the nuns had a feature in common with the dolls. Missionaries were shoeless. They wore sandals, of course, made of leather, squared and stocky, in all seasons. No socks.

Nuns, and the occasional priest, also sported a white rope surrounding their waist, with three knots, large, evenly spaced. The knots were elaborate and beautiful. Did they make them every morning, anew?

Borbora was curious. She could ask the nun who had her sew the skirts, if she came back to teach. Their assignments were usually brief, and she didn't. But Bor saw her the following week during recess, in the courtyard. The girl almost choked on her snack, her croissant ruining down her blue outfit in a cascade of buttery crumbs. She started running… the nun was going out to the street where the girl, of course, wasn't allowed.

Out of breath, Bor caught her right at the door, pinched the back of her robe, almost slipped, and then grabbed her hand. The nun stopped. She turned towards the girl, her smile sudden and wide. "Yes?" she said, looking at Bor. In fact, through and beyond her. But the indefinite quality of her gaze (that frightening openness, overwhelming) didn't bother Borbora. She was preoccupied with her question.

It trickled up, scorching her throat, like a frog gasping for its dose of oxygen. A frog, slimy. Uncombed. Pajamaed, perhaps. A totally unpresentable frog. "What are those for?" she said, grabbing the knots, hiding them in her palm. "Those," the nun said, taking her time… "Those," she paused again while Borbora recovered her breath.

Her throat eased. She straightened up and she waited.

"Those," said the nun, "are my wishes."

 In Color

THE MOTH

I couldn't believe it let me come close, trap its wing between the wall and my finger… What, now? Catching it under my cupped hand wasn't possible. It was huge. I had never seen one that size. But I was afraid of scraping its pigment, as it happens with butterflies, if I kept applying pressure. Slowly, I switched from index finger to thumb in order to verify. Nothing was on my skin, or else the light gray, evanescent, was too pale to be seen. Maybe it scattered in the air as soon as it was lifted, just disintegrating itself.

Pale gray? Well, the insect's beauty didn't need color. On the contrary, its monochrome garb highlighted the fine textures of body and wings, carved with different patterns, webs of delicate hieroglyphs, here spirals, there figure eights, here a beehive… Most amazing of all were two circular reliefs, like huge buttons hand-sewn by a fancy seamstress. They looked like giant eyes, which of course they weren't, being placed on the lower wings. Were they mere decoration? A mimetic device? Perhaps.

My thumb frozen in place, my gaze stuck upon the creature, I reached over to the bed stand with my left hand. I wanted to grab something, not sure what. My glass for the night was too small in diameter, and so was anything in reach. Wait.

Without loosening my grip I managed to crouch down, stretch out, get hold of a shoe. Hurray! I applied it against the wall like a sucker. And I heard the slightest of noises, a leaf falling, a page furtively turned.

I sighed. I had been holding my breath for the last few minutes. Because of a moth? An exceptional one. A rarity, I thought. Well, Grandfather would know. Later, Grandpa would tell. What I needed, now, was something I could cautiously slide between the shoe and the wall. Maybe a piece of cardboard… (That was easy to find. Books were everywhere. Blindly, I took one of them from my bed stand, utilizing of course its hard cover while the rest hung limply on the side. It was an old edition of Andersen's fairy tales Mom had given to me. She had owned it as a child, long before).

The operation succeeded. With Hans Christian lidding my shoe I could finally move, and I carried my snare into the kitchen, leaving it on the table as I searched the cupboard. Substituting a salad bowl for my shoe was quick… Satisfied, I contemplated my prey, slightly enlarged under the transparent dome. Then I thought of Grandpa's magnifying glass. I could borrow it from his desk. No one was home at the moment. I was all by myself, the house dim and quiet.

Playing around with the magnifier, I focused on one of the buttons. It was furry, made of minuscule stems packed against each other, like velvet. As I moved the glass to the other side, an eye came into sight. I was stunned. I remembered I could turn the lens, get a larger close up.

Round, a miniature globe, pea green… was it emerald? A dark dot in the center, the moth's eye looked human, though its sphericalness also made it mechanical. I kept staring, until I felt… Was it staring back? I felt watched, uneasy. I forgot I was

 In Color

the one holding the lens, looming over the captured insect. I
was the one in charge, yet the eye iced me in place, as if it had
caught me at fault, witnessing some embarrassing truth.

Yes! Its sheerness suggested perfect awareness, and no
mercy. "I have seen you," it said, posing as god the omniscient.
Truly, the moth's eye resembled Mom's eyes, also green and
uncannily beautiful. But Mom's weren't that pure. Hers were
mossy, opalescent, with a slight hint of earthiness, while the
moth's green eye looked celestial, if it makes sense.

Not sure leaving the upturned bowl on the table, with
my humongous find underneath, was the best idea. But I left
it, feeling suddenly exhausted as if… Had I been hypnotized?
The thought briefly brushed my mind. Oh, no… I was tired
beforehand. I was heading to bed when I spotted my visitor
and went hunting instead. It was time to resume my trajectory. I
picked up my lone Mary Jane and rescued my book, realizing I
had lost my page mark. No big deal.

The glass salad bowl had smooth, even edges. The rim
had neatly adhered to the table, said Grandpa when he found
my trophy in the morning, sealing the moth into a tiny death
chamber. Unconvinced, I checked (though I never doubted
Grandpa's words), but there isn't a striking difference, truly,
between dead and live moths. All I had gotten from mine while
it still breathed was a faint rustling sound (as it gently fell into
my shoe) and a femme fatale kind of gaze.

Grandpa lifted the bowl without hesitation. "A
magnificent sample," he said. "It would be worth keeping."
Then I'd put it inside a box, in my drawer, I said with
excitement, and I'd show it to Mom whenever I'd see her. I
would show her the amazing eye, yes, through the magnifying

glass… unless the dead moth had closed it. I preferred not to verify.

"Ultimately, it will disintegrate," Grandpa glossed. He had turned around. He was at the door, headed to the television room. He had mumbled to himself and I didn't immediately register his words, preoccupied with finding a cute container. Then the sentence came through. "What will disintegrate?" "The moth. You will find little pieces, then a fine dust. You should put it in formaldehyde to preserve it. It is fairly complex. Perhaps, one day you'll be an entomologist…"

A slight twinge squeezed my throat (it happened, sometimes). I hadn't fully understood Grandpa's statement. It contained too much unknown data, such as entomologist, formaldehyde, ultimately. This last sounded interesting in its vagueness. It sounded wide, open-ended… shifting, cloudlike, nicely remote… Mom would certainly come before "ultimately" occurred. "Ultimately" everything would disintegrate, but that didn't concern my present or a future I could reasonably conceive. I put the jewel box I had found (it had formerly hosted a chain and a cross, gifts for my first communion) in my bed stand drawer.

Mom and Dad had solemnly presented me with the thing, minutes before we left. It was winter and a drizzle came down. I was hurriedly pushed on the back seat of the car, out of caution for my immaculate dress.

Not that I cared for it. Momma did. It was her idea I should wear it. It had been hers, but she had received first communion in wartime… the austerity of her attire had made perfect sense. Grandma had had it cut out of a bed sheet, a good piece from her trousseau she willingly sacrificed. Mom

 ⟶———————— In Color

kept praising the excellence of the fabric, that to me felt just like a kitchen towel, thick, dull, quintessentially opaque.

The style was disappointingly simple, monastic (only garb, an embroidered tassel, white on white, on the chest, minute and geometric). Classic, as if for a Greek amphora, Mother kept repeating with pride. A Greek vase? That wasn't how I had wished to look on communion day.

I had wished… I had waited for the occasion since kindergarten, year by year, anticipating the fourth Sunday of May. When the roses exploded with color in the yard of the nunnery (where I attended elementary school), the annual ritual was celebrated. After weeks of frantic excitement, second grade girls and boys single filed from the classrooms to the chapel, shining in their stunning outfits. Boys wore mini tuxes, with candid bowties. Girls wore satin gowns loaded with lace, ribbons, tulle by the mile. Year by year I had spied the procession, my gaze riveted to the long trains of the girls' dresses, most of all to the veils pouring out of neat flower garlands, pinned on top of their nicely combed little heads.

My sharp longing was dulled by the certainty (was it faith?) also my turn would come. But it didn't. In the spring of my second grade the teacher called me aside, carefully breaking the news. I would skip communion. Mom later explained she and Dad had different plans than to have me mixed up with a bunch of schoolmates. Why, I didn't inquire.

I received the Holy Wafer in winter, on a Sunday, in the company of Mom, Dad, my brothers and sisters, Grandmother. Grandpa didn't attend. Mass was celebrated for us only, in a private chapel. While I was getting dressed I managed to feel happy, as elated as Mom expected me to be. I was thrilled by a small purse she put in my gloved hands, filled with a silver rosary, a kerchief and a missal bound in white leather, filigreed with gold thread. Those three items were given like talismans, or I took them that way. I was also presented with the chain and cross in their box, but I shouldn't wear them. Mom would keep them for later. Sheer simplicity was required at the moment.

I avoided glancing in the mirror when my hair was pulled back, then hidden under a bonnet. That medieval contraption, edged with a modest zigzag, was my headgear. No veil and no garlands.

I was kneeling in the front row of the chapel (dimly lit, snug and tight like a boat, with dark walls and ceiling) when someone from behind pushed a small bouquet into my hand. I had never seen those flowers before. They looked like little stars, their smell so penetrating I felt dizzy. But I loved it. I inhaled, as I squeezed the stems into my fist. I inhaled over and over while, slowly, the ceremony unspooled.

For the entire day I didn't let go of the flowers. Breathing them down and deep.

I have another treasure in store in my bed stand drawer. I am thinking of it while rearranging my stuff to allow the moth in. I have a number of things, but the one of which I'm talking is precious, relatively new, kept for a special purpose. I will give it to Dad as a present.

I have found it while wandering alone in the forest (Grandpa and Grandma believe I'll never get lost, always showing up for dinner on time, my hands thoroughly washed. They are right. I'll never get lost. I have a compass with me and I take note of landmarks. I have learned at an early age. Please, don't worry on my account.)

I have found this thing in the forest, sticking out of the

trunk of a tall pine. I couldn't believe its proportions, so big I decided to take it and save it. For Dad. He'll be amazed.

Dad adores antique and bizarre. He is a total fan of estate sales. He comes home with furniture, frames, various oddities Mom does not approve of, you can tell. But Dad doesn't care for approval. I have noticed over the years that he's fond of bulgy, curled, curved, and gold. Baroque, Mother says. It's her usual remark, whenever he lands his load on the dining room carpet. She exhales the word with a sigh, each time… I don't think he hears it, lost in contemplation of whatever treasure he found.

Well, this thing I have discovered is curved, curled, swell and golden. It is sap, Grandpa said, somehow fossilized, petrified. It looks like a humongous drop of honey. It is also translucent, like stained glass, and you can see inside it, little veins, dots, cracks, a sort of geography.

Grandpa said it will disintegrate. He means crumble. I can't truly believe it. It looks healthy at the moment. I still check it now and then, just in case. Ultimately, I know, everything falls apart, but I'm sure Dad will visit earlier than that. Well, of course.

Staying here for so long (what an unexpected vacation!) has advantages. One of them is the liberty I enjoy after dinner. I am allowed to stay up until late, in the TV room. At home, that would be unthinkable. I bet Mom and Dad aren't informed, or they wouldn't approve.

I'm doing nothing wrong, though, only following the rules of the house. It's known that grandparents relax when left in charge of grandchildren. They know better than…

I remember the moth's eye. That color. Do dead

insects close their eyes? Do they have eyelids? I should take the magnifying glass, and I'd know for sure. Later. Now the movie has started.

I sit on the rattan couch, Grandpa and Grandma on the sides, on separate rattan armchairs. Furniture is fragile and small in the TV room, which looks fake, like a dollhouse. Tiny and snug like a boat. But both Grandma and Grandpa have shrunken, I guess, and I don't take much place. All is dark, so we can see the screen. It is magical.

I have arrived a bit late. Fumbling with my belongings sidetracked me… well, it happens. I don't really care. If I've missed something important, Grandpa or Grandma will let me know. There is a gorgeous lady, dark haired, in the middle of a busy street. She looks lost, surprised… Then there is a shrieking of brakes, and white flashes repeatedly crossing the screen. This occurs at various moments as the movie goes on.

A bit patchy, a bit enigmatic. I like it. The doll (woman I mean, but she looks like a robot) tries to reconstruct something from her past, but her memory seems to be interrupted, each time, by the flashes, the shrieking sounds. I got that. I've understood… a lot, I believe. But I have missed the title.

"Amnesia," Grandpa yawns. He's already at the door, and heading to bed. I have to ask Grandmother what the word means. Hopefully, she will know. A condition wiping your memory away, she says. You forget very important things, such as your name or where you were born, because of a trauma. In the movie, that blast on the screen, a car accident. I put two and two together. The dark lady had forgotten some because of an accident. She remembered thanks to another car crash… correct?

Grandma confirms. She is extremely good with movies,

novels, stories in general. She remembers details. I am sure she
never got amnesia, not once. Does it often occur? Grandma is
vague about it. Now a line in the film comes to mind, ripened
to its full meaning. When I entered the room the lady on the
screen looked stunned, her gaze glassy, and a passerby (neatly
attired, double breasted, fedora on his head) asked, "have you
lost something?" "Yes," she said, "ten years of my life."

This all vaguely scares me. I hope nothing like this
ever… But, tell you the truth, I am enthralled by the name.
Amnesia… I wish the protagonist were called that way. I keep
murmuring it in bed, in the dark. Amnesia. I could give it to my
daughter, as soon as I have one. I wish *I* were called Amnesia. I
would love it.

Most movies we have watched, this summer, kind of
looked alike. Do they all? Women are always brown haired, kind
of… statuesque. Intense, and unhappy.

In tonight's script she waits for her husband, who
has gone to war. When he comes back he is hurt, a bit crazy,
forgetful. I mean almost amnesiac, like in yesterday's movie.
He can't quite glue before and after together. Then and now.
So he wakes up during the night and runs to the forest. Not
sure he will return. That is hard for the lady, who in this case
remembers it all, crystal clear. I like her. She is patient and
strong.

Her very last line sticks to my mind. "Winter," she says,
then she stops. "Winter, winter will bring him back." I guess she
is still hopeful, but again there's a glassy look on her face. Now
"Gone With the Wind" comes to mind. They have broadcasted
it last week. This is how it ended, "Tara! I'll go home and think
of some way to get him back. After all…"

All the movies we are watching, this summer, are one and the same.

I have noticed Grandma's taking a hankie out of her pocket. Sliding it under her glasses, she blots a few tears. She's so easily moved. She cries over nothing, these days.

Cʜɪɴᴀ

"For Talia. Do Not Break," says the note. The box… Wait. She sees that her younger siblings don't have one such. Ah! Then it is a mark of age, a privilege of seniority. Those laurels always come with a challenge. But it doesn't matter. They are worth it.

Under the Christmas tree (huge, good smelling and glorious, just a bit incongruous perhaps, in daytime, with its lights turned off) there are few other gifts. Yes, there's little cash in the household, seldom a superfluity. That is why everything… thing new, thing packaged, beribboned…

The box is well wrapped, but kind of severely. A piece of plain paper, no frills. What singles it out as exceptional is the handwritten note. The handwriting is Mother's, she knows, though a part of her brain lends it an impersonal voice, wide, diffuse, remote, thunderous.

She opens it at last, with some trepidation, and she registers en passant that container and contents don't match. The box isn't… Oh, it's beautiful! Thick cardboard, lid held by golden hinges, but isn't… It must have contained fine cigars, fine chocolates. There's a brand on the side and tiny, hard to decipher print.

Doesn't matter. So much straw, so much tissue paper. First her fingers are shy, then they become nervous. A small butterfly tickles her throat. All this stuffing might hint at one of those grown-up jokes, when they trick you with a sparkling lure just for fun. Meaning, for the sake of seeing your chin quiver, your eyes veil with dismay as you realize…

She has no time for worrying. Doubt keeps silent and coy under her solar plexus as she feverishly undoes the shrouds of white tissue, burying a treasure smaller and smaller.

Two minuscule cups with their matching saucers. Cute and snug, the size of a thimble. She could wear them on the tip of her fingers, and they wouldn't fall. They are the pawns of the set, though, the infantry, common soldiers. There is more and better. Go on.

Here's a pitcher for milk. Here's a sugar bowl with symmetrical handles, its lid carefully taped on. With those, slightly bigger, she almost falls in love. But wait for the teapot! A large version of the sugar bowl, same enchanting roundness, yet the serpentine of the spout, the small hooks accommodating the handle (an arch of woven reed) make it so…

The teapot is the masterpiece. She admires it in awe, transfixed by a stupor clear of ownership pride. She doesn't appropriate it. She is won.

She hasn't seen a teapot before. Meaning, full-size. Teatime rites do not belong to the local culture. They all drink tea, of course, cold, during summer. It is brewed once a week, loaded with sugar and lemon, bottled and stuck into the fridge. Hot tea, truly, is meant for the sick. If they run a fever, let's say, or have stomach trouble, water's boiled then poured into a cup where a small bag hangs. Looks and feels like medicine. She knows nothing of five o'clock ceremonies.

Here, look. A printed label is tucked under the goodies, slightly crumpled. It says, "Toy Tea Set." It sounds like an incantation. A spell.

"Do you like them?" says Mother. "Be careful! It's porcelain! Treat it well. We thought we could trust you." She'll turn five in two months and she already knows how to read, a sure sign of precocity.

She can't take her eyes off the miniature china. She has never seen ware of such finery, such color, not even full-size, as we said. Blue on white, and the blue draws intricate arabesques, eerie, enchanting, lacey and soothing like a Sunday dress.

Back in the kids' quarters, she displays everything on the plastic table she shares with her bros. Then she brings pitcher and teapot to the bathroom, intending to fill them with water (pretend-milk, pretend-tea) while pondering, still, what might do for sugar. On her tiptoes, she opens the tap. First, milk. Careful! The pitcher's so tiny, it keeps overflowing. Slowly, slowly… She needs just a trickle. Now the teapot. Pay attention! Full! Stop!

Butterflies have abandoned her guts. Her chest widens to allow a wave of happiness as she firmly, solidly grasps the arch of woven cane and then lifts her arm.

The crash makes her knees buckle. Here she is, petrified

between the sink and the door, elbow still up in triumph, fingers wrapped around the treacherous twigs. The handle and her palm have remained one, inseparable. The teapot has slipped underneath them, taking on a trajectory of its own. Now it lies on the floor in pieces, while a puddle of water spreads out like blood on a battlefield.

Broken. Spilled. Quick! Before Mom arrives. Pick up shards! Mop away!

But she can't. Can't let go of the reed, which adheres to her right hand by magic. She needs to understand what just happened. Look how these things are made! The handle threads into the loops of the pot then curves back, its ends slipping into small rings of rattan… kind of loose, as when you tie your shoelaces without double knotting, when a button is a bit too small for a buttonhole.

When she carried it a minute ago, the pot was light enough for the handle to remain in place. But as soon as she filled it, its weight caused the ends to slip out. Treason!

She feels cheated, not sure if by the reed or by water. Water, likely, as by nature it is accident-prone. Surely not by the teapot that, alas, gapes on the tiled floor, forlorn, wounded and mute. Vaguely menacing.

Dead? It can't be.

Again, for a split second, she feels she was betrayed. By whom? Cheap manufacturers? She doesn't know toys are made. By the adults who didn't tell, didn't explain… They don't have the time.

Then she simply feels bad. Ashamed. "Do Not…" Her mind balks like a frightened horse before the last word of the

In Color

fated note.

She eventually glues the toy back. A grown-up must
have understood her pain, if not fully, enough to provide glue
as a form of consolation, plus some summary instructions.
With adult assistance, all right, she has done a good job.

The handle ends are locked in, sewn in permanent
fashion. The teapot is all patched, but bears a triangular hole…
a piece couldn't be found or else had shattered too much. No
big deal (someone's patting on her shoulder). She can turn it
around and the hole won't show. No one will suspect there is
one. Except… And the scars! Those glued cracks are visible,
interrupting the pretty arabesque. Because of the hole, she
cannot fill the pot with tea, meaning water. It has become a
fake. A pretend-pot.

Mother hasn't been extremely upset by the accident.
Talia expected worse. Either she looked too contrite, too
humiliated or (the thought only brushes her mind) the tea set
wasn't terribly precious, or…

Maybe Mother was busy, and she let it go. She moved
on to some other problem, right?

Talia can't. She keeps her toy-tea-set in the box.
Sometimes, all by herself, she airs it briefly, turning the teapot at
a convenient angle, hole in the back. Also managing to conceal as
much as she can a ragged, huge, diagonal scar. She pours nothing
into miniature cups. She has long given up on pretend-sugar (a
clear sign of emotional disengagement). The milk pitcher is still
smart and cute, a joy to behold. But it looks kind of lost.

In Color

She doesn't remember. If not for that shade of brown, warm and pleasant.

It's called home. It comes with a smile. Brown, warm and pleasant. It is also called light. Brown vibrates. Light vibrates. Light and brown are warm. Warm is home. Warm is pleasant.

Brown distends itself on the sides of her, horizontally. Perhaps rises a bit… anyway, has a tendency not to stop. A tendency to stretch, yes, which is promising, exciting, pleasant. But it doesn't stretch down. It can't…

Down is where she is. At the bottom. And she can't stretch. She is stationary, a dot, a period in the center of that dynamic expanse. Brown. Promising. Luminous, full of particles. Vibrating. She can see the particles. She can see.

She can see self. Can she? Probably. Parts of self, not brown, somehow more discolored. Let us call it white. A dress. Fabric. This is a dress. It comes with her, always, for what she can track. When she is, properly speaking, when she can situate herself as a dot, a period mark, in the center of the fugue of brown (and she smiles, she can't help smiling, the thought is so pleasant, so homey)…

When she can define self, an anchor in the middle of
brown, she has a dress. Fabric. White. She is mostly white fabric.
Soft. Fresh. Very fresh, about to seep into brown. She can't yet
explore brown, welcome its invitation to stretch, to expand,
to explore. Not yet but very soon, of course. All is soon. Very
soon, she, the brown… all is happiness.

She is not in the very middle of brown, and it doesn't
matter. She is in the middle of nothing, she has noticed.
Everything has the tendency to be offset. That means falling,
somehow. Everything tends to stretch further on a side,
resulting in more pleasantness. A dynamic effect, meaning
an urge to go, to peer over the protruding side, or indeed the
opposite one. To experience the unbalance. All is like that,
unbalanced. All is very wide… Unfortunately, the sole part of
all she can securely manage—recall—define—witness (for now)
is the brown light of home that makes her smile.
At least she thinks so. Does she think? Of course.
What else is there to do? This is what she does all the time.
Think. Simple enough.

Outside, they say. She is carried. She's not sure about
that. She doesn't remember.
She lies in her stroller and can only look up. Up is
made of oranges, pierced in a roof of leaves, many. Many
is important. It is exhilarating. In the garden, they say, she
keeps smiling. She smiles out loud, and makes little cries. Of
joy, they say. It is possible. It depends on the multitude and
the oscillation. Multitude is exploding. A call for possibilities,
an eccentric force. Multitude is like fingers… something
so extreme she can't reach it. Still, at the sight of oranges,

her consciousness inches in the right direction. She has not
arrived yet. Not her. Fingers are not her, nor are oranges or
consciousness. Does she think? Yes. Isn't she conscious? Not of
fingers or fruit. They are too many, too multifold. She's alone,
after all. Alone after this all.

Mother. Is not there. She is passing by, quickly. At least
so they say. She could confirm, probably, but with some reserve.
To be honest. She doesn't remember. Almost. Maybe she should
confirm. Mother passing by, quickly.

Doors. Tall openings. Very complex. Ambiguous.
Vertical, like cuts. Vertical implies some danger, some
unpleasantness. It has the tendency of imposing, looming over.
She is always down, always at the bottom. She can move…
she can, but quite horizontally. Nothing should stretch vertical
without some horizontal attempt, horizontal allowance. Doors
don't oblige that way. They stay upright and do their funny
business.

Mother is connected with doors. She does things with
doors, appear, disappear. Mother is mostly unstable, and that
makes her more precious. She means longing. Mother is longing.
Longing is like stretching, only you stretch nowhere. A tiresome
stretching. Without end. Stretching without end. Cold. It doesn't
make you smile. Actually, it tugs you sideways, briskly, then pulls
you down. I mean your mouth, down. Your tongue, down.

This is too extreme, of course. No mouth, no
tongue… she hasn't gotten that far. But she's heading in the
right direction. Longing makes her. Mouth, tongue. No words
yet. Does she think? Of course. Not in words? No.

Longing is not like brown. There's no warmth in its

                    In Color

light. It is cold and silver. Not less beautiful. What is beautiful? Mother. Silvery. Moon. What is moon? Mother. Has she seen moon? No. What is Mother? Moon.

Mother is feeding her moon. So they say. She doesn't remember. Mother is feeding her moon, but there's no milk in moon. She can't recall, can't confirm, cannot testify. Mouth, tongue. No teeth. Throat. Mother is gone, the taxi waiting for her in the street. So they say. Mother will return to work, where she's waited for. A matter of doors, again. Baby didn't eat. She did not suck. Baby is tiresome. Mother is tired. Baby is tired.

Mother fell out of brown as you'd fall out of grace. As you will.

She has fallen out of grace. Grace is brown.

The maid is feeding her a bottle. Later, the maid's feeding her food. She doesn't recall bottle. She recalls food… it is brown, but another kind of it, entirely lacking vibration. Cold. Food is cold because she doesn't eat it, or slowly. Maybe food hasn't been warmed up. Mother/moon is not here. Maid is Mother yet isn't. Mother, maid and moon are all conducive to mouth. She will reach mouth soon. It has a bad taste. Mouth is mean.

Baby spits. She vomits. So they say. The activity is not clear. She does it without cries, or smiles. She is impassible. She keeps food in her mouth for hours, the maid says. Maybe minutes. She doesn't swallow. She spits. Very far. Food lands on the opposite wall, the maid says. It is hard to believe but the maid is mad.

She doesn't recall.

Maid is the one putting her in the carriage, bringing her outside where gold is. It took time to reach gold, to understand gold. It's another version of brown, yet more dynamic, further expanded. The unruly version of brown, which makes her laugh and make sounds, they say. She doesn't know what sound is. She knows oranges… they are a version of gold, dancing into gold. She knows dancing. The roof of gold dances. Gold rotates. It is the air, outside, after doors. Doors are dangerous, and they lead into gold. Gold is dangerous. You can only approach gold from a carriage, where you are safely caged, lying on your back. You don't crawl into gold. Especially not.

Besides, some things do. Crawl in gold. Things. That is a mistake… she doesn't know things. Things would be like fingers, and she didn't reach fingers yet. Aren't oranges like fingers? Almost, but not quite. Oranges are dots, concentrations, knots of gold. Not really separated.

Those crawling are black. Black moves and cuts gold. Black has nothing to do with brown, but she loves it as well. Love, what is it? It is black, in motion, and noisy. Love makes music. They say she can look at birds for hours, from her crib or her pram. They don't need to further entertain her. They can take a break from trying to feed her. Eyes wide open, she stares at birds, smiles and vocalizes. As she does when she sees oranges on trees, but for birds she vocalizes more.

Well, she has also grown. Maybe she has discovered mouth. Yes, she has, but for taste and spit. Not for sound. Sound is not in mouth or tongue. Ears? She doesn't have ears. Where are ears? What? Sound is falling in eyes from above. She has eyes. It is where the black sound falls. She drinks black, she drinks sound. It is better than food. She doesn't spit sound. She swallows it. Swallows.

Baby likes swallows. She's in awe. Just put baby where she can see birds. She seems to understand. What? What the birds are saying. We should try feeding her while she looks at birds (listens to them?) She will get distracted. Maybe she'll swallow.

Father is a green distance. The side of the road. Father drives. She is carried in the moving, the motion. She is sick. Mouth again. Throat. She doesn't spit. Spit is her, spit becomes her. She doesn't know. She is mouth. Where is Mother? Mother is mouth. Father makes motion. Father is an engine of green. Green constantly moves sideways. Green is dangerous. More dangerous than gold, and totally different. Quite different. Green snakes, it is sinuousness. Sinuousness is unpredictable. Instable. She doesn't know unstable. She doesn't trust green.

Father comes with green, and the balcony. Someone holds her in his/her arms. She doesn't know someone. He/ she is behind her. She can't worry about behind her, truly. That is asking for too much. She knows arms… they come in front and around, like a carriage. A cage. Arms hold her up. Here's the balcony. It isn't like door. In a way, more direct, simpler. Doesn't play tricks. She's on the balcony, warm brown in her back (that is home, now we've nailed it), kind of silvery gold in front. Sun/moon/out, a pixelated surface. Out is getting more defined, more complex. Also streaked with green… that they call road.

Road is Father. Road contains Father. Sometimes

it spits Father. Father has the tendency to become road.
Sometimes road holds Father. Father should return. Father
doesn't return. It will return later. Later doesn't exist, or indeed
all is later. Later is now. They say she reaches to the balcony on
all fours, always, at teatime. How does she know? They say she
takes speed, rushes towards the balcony, tries to sneak away. She
doesn't.

She is only looking for later. Someone grabs her and
holds her high. She looks out, she pulls later out of the golden
maze. She pulls later. Not with her fingers, though she is now
sprouting some. At least thumbs… they are enough. But she
doesn't summon later with thumbs, she does it with eyes. Eyes
call later, then the sound of it falls into them. They say she
vocalizes when the car climbs the hills, peers out of the last
turn.

Father scares eyes. Father comes too close and he is
unpleasant. Horribly unpleasant. More than door, more than
Mother, longing, danger, later. Horribly is a concentrate of
danger. Father has become a concentrate of horrible danger,
coming too close to eyes. Also doing something else, she is
not sure what. Something shrieky that makes eyes and mouth
suddenly come together. An explosion. She is crying, that's
slimy and confusing. Crying is red, and it chases Father. She has
never seen red before. She dislikes it. Father has turned away,
meaning he has disappeared.

Darkness. Red crying has caused darkness. It is not
black, not brown. Darkness is something else… the absence of
color. What is color? All. What is darkness? Nothing. Falling,
she means. Nothing, falling. Father fell.

He fell from the grace of god. She also will. We all fall

     In Color

from the grace of god. Father has. Each time she sees Father, she cries. Father becomes darker and darker. He keeps falling. She keeps falling. She couldn't fall any lower.

part 5

Alter Alter

The orphanage is perched on a hill made of lava rocks.
No trees, besides risible puffs of conifers, dusty and bent by the
wind (around here it is horrible, screaming as it rushes down the
canyons, towards the beach).

The orphanage overlooks a desert strip of shoreline,
jutting out in a sort of peninsula. Why so far from the closest
village, not to speak of a town? Why so lonely, so remote?

I don't know if there's a reason. Maybe a combination.
The nuns who own the place didn't really choose it… it was
bequeathed to them, and they didn't say no. The rich family
who built the estate, long ago, carefully picked the location. Like
a sentinel, the mansion surveys land and water, always aware of
newcomers.

The gratuity of the mansion, though, isn't all. I'm sure
forlornness befits the orphanage in the common mentality.
So preserved (like exquisite marmalade) the girls are spared
temptation, that most abhorred evil, worse than melancholia,
depression, even madness.

Three sides of a large courtyard are screened by the
building's walls. The fourth one looks toward the mountains,
tapering into a slope, a ravine where goats graze, scrawny and

bent like the conifers, their perfect companions.

We are going up the winding road on a Sunday morning. It's a sunny day (they all are, year round) and a windy one, obviously. Dust is raised by our newly waxed four-wheel drive, shiny black. Afterward, it will be waxed again. But the driver has all the time in the world, as we drive only on special occasions. This is one such.

Daddy likes to ride with the windows open. He has a high body temperature and he sweats, especially when in formal clothes, waistcoat and jacket. Even more when flustered by an important matter. This is one, though he's trying to downplay it, I think.

Dust generously pours in, getting into my eyes. I'm alone in the back, my suitcase for company. Two large trunks are tied on top of the car, which is panting uphill… we proceed at the leisurely pace of a mule. Not a problem, only a matter of bearing the dust.

My straw hat, quite large, shields my face (the brim hangs like a veil if I tilt it forwards). Still, I had to remove my glasses and clean them, meticulously, more than once, with the kerchief I keep rolled in my sleeve.

When I did it for the fourth time I noticed the initials, white on white. Kind of subtle, hard to see… at least for me. I realized I had taken Mother's kerchief, by mistake. The maid must have put it in my drawer. My stepmother had a moment of distraction, apparently. She stacked it in the wrong pile. (The maid cannot read).

*

The operation has been extremely costly, but Father is rich. That is why we have the four-wheel drive that gets waxed before and after each outing, always shining like a pair of dancing shoes. Dad is rich and my appearance counts, for the uglier I look, the harder it will be for me to get wed, despite all the money. Still, money will prevail. It always does. I am young, younger than I feel, but I know this.

The operation was performed on the mainland. First we took the ferry, then the train. Our cabins looked the same in both transportations, padded, leathered, curtained and fringed. You had to pull the curtain to see a flash of landscape, discreetly, possibly when Father was hiding behind his paper, Aunt behind her fan. Too much sunlight disturbed both. Father started to puff and sweat, Aunt to cough (I wonder why). They preferred the curtain closed.

Aunt and Dad accompanied me. Aunt for comfort, I guess, Dad for talking to doctors and paying the bills. I only spent a day at the clinic. I was way too scared to notice my surroundings, though I recall a park with tall pines. Very different from these scrambling bunches… Those were bright green, their canopies shaped like perfect spheres. I remember the color through my one open eye. I remember the smell, embalming.

Father didn't want to stay longer than was needed. All went perfectly well, the surgeon declared (I was healthy, and so young). It was safe to travel, he said. Our family doctor would take care of the rest. Sure, he'd know what to do, no worries.

We left on the same night, half of my face wrapped in bandages, stark white, scenting of disinfectant. We had couchettes and I slept in the lowest one. It was screened by curtains, like a kind of cocoon. Aunt slept right above me, Dad

in the next compartment. We would reunite at the station. All
was under control.

Mother didn't travel with us because she was ill. Now
I wonder why she wasn't brought onto the mainland instead of
me. Why a cure wasn't sought for her from those continental
doctors, so bright. I don't have the answer… I can only assume
she was more expendable than I was. She had already produced
me. I hadn't yet done my part.

Anyway, those doctors weren't that smart, as I'm about
to prove. My bandages were to come off one week later. I could
not wait… our weather, I said, is hot and windy all year round,
with little variation. I started itching. I wanted to get rid of that
mummification, wash my face.

On the eighth day our doctor cut the gauze with a pair
of small scissors… a barber trimming a beard. I would give I
don't know what for the look on his face, which I missed, for
I shyly stared down with my unencumbered eye, breathing as
quietly as I could. Well, Doc must have looked mischievously
satisfied. He said nothing.

No one said a thing while I stood up and went to the
threefold mirror, vainly gilded and as shiny as Dad's car. My
usual face met me… My eyes, same as before, out of sync,
diverging, the left one kind of stuck at an uncanny angle.

It was still stuck. The surgery had not changed a thing.
But we never went back.

I will find a husband no matter how, because of Dad's
riches, properties, factory and all. I am not worried, besides
the fact I'm still eight. This should give me another ten years,
hopefully, and yet not certainly… Mom eloped at thirteen.

But Mother was beautiful. I am not. I can notice it even
with my defective eyesight. Anyway, I won't have to look for a

husband. He will find me, or Dad's bank account. Perhaps he
has already.

*

The orphanage… I should not call it so. I should stop,
right now. It isn't an orphanage, though the girls who live there
are orphans, Stepmother said. I heard her mention it to her
daughter (from a former marriage, Stepmom is a widow). Still,
the place isn't an orphanage. It's a boarding house, as Dad said
to Auntie last week. A strange word… it evokes upholstered
cabins and some moving devices. In fact here I am, all packed
up and in my traveling suit. I look so much older than I am.

*

Mother died a month ago, giving birth, they said. The
weird thing is I hadn't noticed she was expecting. For the last
year, I saw little of her, briefly visiting morning and night.
When I entered her room (that she never left), she sat by the
window. She had her fluffy robe on, pale gray with blue flowers,
enhanced with small golden beads. Quite enchanting. I so
wanted to grow up and wear it. I knew she would give it to me,
although I never asked. But I knew, and I couldn't wait.
Mother's hair wasn't done in the morning, or at night.
I'm not sure it was during the day, when I couldn't see her. It
must have, but when I came it was down. I kept staring at it. My
eyes switched from the brocade of the robe (those little blue
flowers) to the long hair I assessed with a kind of greed, proud
as if it were my own. As she sat, her hair brushed the floor. It

looked tired like she did. She had her sewing basket close by, but she never sewed. Her arms hung on her sides. She wore no rings.

She smiled while I gave her a long, good hug. No sitting in her lap... that was no more of my age. But since she never joined us in the dining room or the kitchen, since we didn't walk in the gardens, since she didn't come to Mass or in town, I longed for her lap again. I knew I shouldn't... so I hugged her as much as I could. I would have hugged her all day, all night long. I hung in there until Aunt coughed, and that meant we should go.

I don't know if Mom was informed of my surgery. When my face was dressed I wasn't allowed to see her, not sure why. I was glad when the bandage went and I could resume my visits.

But they didn't last long. She died very soon. Father married in less than a month. Summer, still... Leaves were on the trees. They fell afterwards. Suddenly, all became a slippery carpet of rust. When the leaves fell, all had already occurred.

It is fall now, though you can't really tell. On the hill there are only these scrawny conifers, and they look the same in all seasons.

*

I remember the night when Mom died. It was horribly hot. Aunt had been complaining all day, putting her mending down to wipe her brow, shake her fan. After dinner she read a story to me, one I already knew. I said nothing. I could hear it again. Then she sent me to wash up and change. No visit with

Mother.

In my room the window was open and the shutters pulled, but not tightly. Still, no air circulated. I lay on top of the sheet, incessantly turning my pillow, holding my rag doll at arm's length. I must have eventually fallen asleep… I always did.

At four, I was awake (there is a clock in the room, a tall, dark kind of tower. I have learned how to read its hands long ago). I heard screams and I knew it was Mother. I heard steps and other noises, but I didn't move. I sneaked under the sheets. The room was much cooler now.

I had already been up at four, twice, because of earthquakes. You know, don't you, they come at four in the morning? I have asked why, but I haven't got an answer. Not one I have understood. It is the quietest hour. Everything is at rest.

I'm a light sleeper, Auntie said. I hear noises and can tell where they come from. Growing up, I have also learned what makes them or who. Until three (the clock's hands tell me… I like things big and far, they are the ones I see)… Until three there is sound from the dining room right below me. I know it's Dad, at the table. He does things with papers. He counts up. He also drinks from those crystal bottles with a million facets, like rubies.

Until three, sound comes from Aunt's room, next to mine. Especially in summer, it is very distinct. I hear the scratching of her pen on paper. She writes. Not numbers, like Dad, I don't think. She must write to someone and she sighs a lot. There are other noises, of course. I'm not listing them all.

Then a thick silence comes. The rooster breaks it as soon as four-thirty. It is not that precise… it can also croak at five, six, six-thirty, or never. Roosters can't be used for telling time, they are approximate. But the maid isn't, or the driver who opens the garage door, or the gardener headed to the tool shed. They are up at five. I hear the maid all year round. I hear the others quite often. I know what happens and when.

So if earthquakes are meant, as they are, to take us by surprise, there's no better time than four, the still hour… though the animals seem to know in advance. They fret from the previous afternoon, and the gardener says, "Earthquake's coming." Then he looks at the sky and says, "Earthquake sky." I look at the sky and it's empty. There's no comet, I mean, like for baby Jesus. No signs. What does he possibly see?

He (the gardener) often says these things and then nothing happens, so he is like the rooster, approximate. But sometimes the earth shakes and that puts a smile on his face, and he brags, "I told you." I still think it is guesswork. If earthquakes are supposed to sneak on us, I'm sure they don't advertise. Still, the chicken, the cows, they…

Earthquakes happen a lot here. Not on the mainland. They are our special thing, in a way. They are usually small, though the second one I recall smashed all of our porcelains. And the cow mooed more loudly than I had ever heard. The toolshed was hit… it remained crooked and stuck, a bit like my left eye.

The first one shook the light fixture, that's all. Right above me, it started swinging to and fro, as if an altar boy were going nuts with incense. Did I say how large are those chandeliers? But I wasn't scared. I enjoyed watching it.

*

Around four I was awakened by Mother's screams. They were sparse but scary. Long wailings, not like her, but I recognized her voice. I slipped under the sheets and tried to fall asleep. I think I succeeded.

She died giving birth, they said, but I never saw the baby. All was very chaotic. Aunt cried. The maid cried as well and everyone was red-faced, gardener and driver included. Our doctor came, then a priest, then more people until I lost count. I sat in the kitchen with a cup of milk for what seemed like hours. Aunt, then, sat me in the drawing room, on an armchair with a tall back, turned toward the window. I stayed still. I doubt anyone could see me. I preferred they didn't, because I was scared. I'm not sure of what, but I was, more than when I had surgery in the middle of those scenting pines.

Strange smells, by the way, came and went. Strong drafts, pungent, like perfumes but also medication, then something else. All was upside down as if we were going to travel, as if a much bigger earthquake had occurred.

At some point the maid redirected me to the kitchen, pushing a bowl of soup under my nose. But I never ate in the kitchen… She turned towards the stove, busy with pots and pans. Food smelled good, covering the extraneous scents. I always liked watching the maid cook, but not then. I did not touch the soup.

I heard people upstairs, noises, voices. Doors were opened and then slammed shut, opened, slammed again.

Evening came at last. Aunt took me by the hand. I'd stay with her sister, she said, yet another aunt who lived in town. I didn't know her well. I did not want to go but said nothing. Auntie pushed me onto the back seat of the car that was ready in the alley, facing the gate. Just the driver and me… that had never happened. I closed my eyes.

*

My other aunt told me Mother had died. Again, soup was in front of me, but we weren't in a kitchen. We sat at a long mahogany table in a dark mournful dining room. The two of us (Aunt didn't have a husband) plus the maid, who went back and forth with our dishes. We hadn't started eating yet. Aunt said Mother died, all in one breath. My reply was shorter: "Why?" "She died while delivering." That didn't answer my question, but I kept quiet.

At the funeral (after another day, then another night of quiet boredom) I looked for the baby. I expected to see it, all white with his little cap, in the arms of Auntie, perhaps? There was none. I knew I shouldn't inquire, but I wanted to.

Mommy's casket was closed and covered with flowers. Bows of large ribbon, trimmed silver and gold, had things written on I could read. Also my name was there.

Now, you want to know if I was desperate because Mother died. I wasn't. Not then. I have been very sad later, when the leaves started falling and Dad married again. I have wept every night in my bed, also during the day, but not at the funeral, when I was looking for the baby who was nowhere.

I asked Auntie as soon as I dared. Maybe I shouldn't have, but I couldn't resist. We were coming home from the graveyard, the two of us sitting in the back of the car. I whispered, "Where's the baby?" She didn't answer, and did not look at me. I was wondering if I should repeat, when she said,

"The baby is dead." I said nothing.

Then I said, "But I didn't see the white box." I knew how babies were buried… lots of them passed. They got those cute little white caskets. She said nothing. I wondered if I should repeat. I repeated. She sighed, then she said, "The baby was buried with Mother." That made sense. I figured it in Mom's arms, a Jesus with Mary like those I saw in paintings, on the small gilded images I was given as bookmarks.

Still, I wasn't sad. I asked, "Was it a boy or a girl?" She sighed. Then, "A girl." Then she burst into tears and murmured something that I couldn't grasp until later. But later I did. She had said, "Victorina."

That was a brash lie, as I knew as soon as I was brought to the graveyard by Aunt herself, by the maid… not by Father. We went every day, for a month. Aunt had lied, because only Mother's name was on the grave, and an angel of stone. Tall, impressive, but one… no small angel, as it should have occurred if also a baby was buried. Only Mom's name was carved on, with the dates of her birth and death. I could make sense of those, no problem. Mother died at twenty-one.

*

Victorina (I will call her Vicky) is not dead. Why didn't I guess it before? The thought strikes me as we have almost arrived. Yes, the boarding house is in sight. A few more hairpin turns (sickening me with vertigo) and we'll see the main gate, the nuns, maybe.

She is alive. Why didn't I figure it out? I must have been distracted, confused… First, the marriage, my dress to be sewn

in a week, fittings every day. Lots of things to be done and no
one in charge, the house a wild rumpus. Mother's clothes were
taken out of her room, put in trunks and carried away. Where,
I do not know. And I don't know why. Shouldn't they be mine?
Well, of course.

I thought of the robe with blue flowers only when it
was in a trunk, god-knows-where. (I shouldn't say "god" in
vain, but it's fine. I don't truly believe, since Mom died. I only
pray to the Virgin and Baby, before he grows up. Alas, the robe
is gone.)

For a couple of days, I feared Aunt would leave us
as well… everything, as I said, was upside down. Walls were
painted over, curtains pulled down, furniture shifted around.
Aunt remained, and quite busy. She stuck flowers in each vase
the earthquake had spared. Hundreds, thousands of blooms…
When the newly married came in, the house looked like a
jungle. I came back from church early, in order to help her.
Guests started arriving. There were hired maids.

I'm not sure why Aunt didn't come, today… just for
company, to say goodbye. I am alone in the back with my
suitcase. I keep cleaning my glasses, but the dust is blinding me.
It is making me cry… my kerchief is soaked. I wonder who will
do the washing. Who will do the ironing.

I haven't seen baby things when Mom's clothes were
packed. There should have been a trunkful, at least. Mother
must have necessarily made them, in those months when she
never came out and never was combed. Truly, I didn't see her
sew… hands limp in her lap, two dead birds… but I wasn't
there all the time.

I haven't seen baby things, but of course they are gone

with Mom's stuff. Why weren't they given to me? I'll also have babies. I should have those, together with Mother's dresses, jewelry, and all. Where did baby clothes go? They must have been green, yellow, white, for boy or girl, never know. I regret not having seen them, I terribly do.

I haven't seen the crib either. I have asked Aunt about it… At first she said nothing, then, "The baby was premature." Early, I guess? It sneaked in like an earthquake at four in the morning. This is not what she meant, I know. They hadn't bought yet a cradle. It wasn't time yet.

Still, I think Victorina isn't dead. They have sent her somewhere as they're sending me. Did they send clothes and crib along? Possibly. Only, I have to find where.

*

The orphanage is a boarding house… Pardon me if I keep changing on you. In fact, it is a convent. There are too many nuns to call this place otherwise.

I have spent ten years in this convent, in the company of the waves splashing against the rock we are perched over. As you know I hear night noises, I always did. How could I have missed this one? But it didn't bother me. It helped me to sleep, kind of a shush, shush, baby.

I have been home for visits, though never for long… I mean there was no such thing as summer vacations. But we went home sometimes, those who had one to go to. Those who weren't totally orphans, only partly, like me. Our driver came up on Saturday morning (once per season?) He brought me back on Sunday after lunch.

At home, I did not sleep in my previous room. I had a

new one, small, neat, next to the kitchen. An immaculate bed, a table, a chair, plus a closet where I hung my coat, put my hat on the top shelf, my bag on the bottom one. Nothing else was needed. I came properly attired for Mass. I left as I came.

In the closet I kept an apron, mouse gray with a trim. I had sewn it. I have sewn all of my clothes in the convent. Dad sent expensive fabrics in huge packages, wrapped in paper and tied with a rope. Aunt must have purchased them in town. I never asked.

I liked visiting home because I liked the room. It was close to the kitchen, I said. The maid slept on the other side of the corridor. Her place was even smaller and certainly not as clean. My new room reminded me of a couchette, on a train or a boat. It was like being always in transit, always traveling, and I liked the feeling.

Aunt didn't live with us any more. She stayed with her sister, the one I was sent to when Mom died. It made sense for them to be together. In the house there were Father, Stepmother, and her daughter from a previous marriage. With me, that made four around the dinner table, one per side. I liked the geometry. I liked having lots of elbowroom, a nice change from the crowded refectory where I usually ate. But I enjoyed the refectory as well.

Nothing happened when I visited home, nothing bad, nothing good but the pleasure of the little room, the wide table. The maid was getting older. Same was true for the gardener and the driver. Not for Dad, Stepmom, and Stepsister… through the years they looked as if they were frozen. I suspect it's because they were kept in shape, combed, powdered, nicely dressed. Dad, impeccable with his rimmed glasses, shiny mustache, black hat and so on. Those things make you perennial.

How did I look to them? I wonder. No mirror was in
my room, but I glanced at the large one in the hallway, though it
was screened by too many flowers. I checked if I was in order. I
always was. Like Dad, I wore glasses. I always will. My eyes only
get worse. They tire easily.

*

I was not sent away for educational purposes. Stepma didn't
want me, that's all. I was never told such a thing, but I knew
it on the wedding day. That's why I came home early, under
pretext of helping Aunt with the flowers. No one gave me
permission, but no one cared. No one even noticed, I'm sure.

I sneaked into the car with Aunt out of panic. That's a
big word. Confusion perhaps, and a sense of distress? When the
newly married arrived (in a hired carriage, snow white, leaving
them at the gate), Stepma bent down to pick up her train, while
Dad held her by the forearm. I noticed her very long gloves.

She laboriously gathered her veil, then she stood for a
while, straight and tall, before marching towards the house at
Dad's side. First her eyes had a quick, anxious spasm, as if she
had spied something invisible. Then she smiled, a sharp, toothy
smirk that made me feel queasy. I was by the main entrance.
Her eyes met mine rapidly. Her face remained still.

On the day of the wedding I knew Stepma didn't want
me, but she wasn't unkind. She said nothing. I was packed
on the following Saturday. Sunday morning we drove to the
convent. Very soon, Aunt went to live with her sister. It was
as if a rock had fallen into the water. A few ripples and then
the surface is sealed. The stone lies at the bottom. It was as if

a rock had crushed something, very small and no one would know, nobody would find it. I don't know what it was.

I've remained at the boarding house for ten years, with all of those visits, identical. I don't know where these years have gone. I'm not leaving because I have finished school. Just as there aren't vacations, there aren't diplomas. I am engaged and I will marry soon.

It's not really a surprise. This is how things go. What else could I wish? I'll be happy to be married, I guess, though I never doubted I would. I've known since I was eight, and before.

Suddenly, while we drive downhill (same car, same trunks tied on top, full of different dresses, all sewn by these hands of mine), I think of old baby clothes. The ones Mom must have embroidered and knitted. The ones I never saw.

I feel nauseous. It's the turns, of course, the speed, the sun dazzling over a sea that gets closer and closer, almost frightening me. I think of those clothes because I should have them… I will have babies too. And I think of Vicky… I have not, for ten years. I haven't wondered anymore about her being alive, dead… it all disappeared, sunk, swallowed away.

In the convent the days were so full, they slipped by like beads on a rosary (well, that's what comes to mind, force of habit, I guess). That is how ten years went down the drain. It's not casual… it is how an orphanage works. You do stuff all the time, so you don't think too much. Only moderately.

You are not tempted… You aren't sick with nostalgia. You don't want to get out. You have no longing. You do things so you'll be ready to marry, with some luck (for sure, in my case). Day by day, you get prepared. Just follow instructions…

it's a deal. You comply and you feel comfy. A lulling sensation, repetitive, like the waves when they do not crash.

Like a tunnel, you know? Like a train. I mean a train in a tunnel. You only need to lie quietly on your cot. Ease up. Close your eyes. The train will bring you there.

For ten years I never went to see Mother's grave. Why? I have described my visits home, the rituals, immutable. Saturday we had lunch and a quiet afternoon. Read a book, mend your stockings, take a walk in the gardens, always within the gates. Dinner, then. Sunday Mass in our best clothes.

In church I saw people, people saw me. That is how I met my to-be-husband, though I suspect he had already found me. Sunday, at lunch, my betrothed was unfailingly invited for the last year or two. He never missed. Then I was driven back. Too short to be boring.

Yes, I've thought of the graveyard many times, at night, in the room that looked like a train. But I haven't asked to go, I don't know why. If I think deep and strong… I guess I didn't want to please Mother. Sure, I knew she was dead. Still, I didn't want to please her. I did not want to visit her grave, though I knew it was there (the grave) and probably waiting. But the stone couldn't call, the angel couldn't. Mother couldn't. I am sure I didn't want to please Mother, but I wasn't aware of it. I was aware of nothing.

Now my throat knots itself. Luckily we have arrived in the flats.

*

Unlike Father, Stepmother, and Sis, Aunt looks older.

There's this thing about lies. They split. That is why vipers, with their bifurcate tongues, are not to be trusted. That is why you say of a gossiper he or she is a viper. I've learned it from the nuns… they gave me an education, though I wasn't there for such purpose. It is weird how things work out.

Now let's analyze this. Aunt said Baby was buried in Mom's arms, but there's no trace of it (her, a girl, Victoria) on the epitaph. So the baby isn't dead. Where is she? She would be ten by now. I could take care of her, like the elder took care of the younger in the convent. Boarding house. Orphanage. After all Vicky is an orphan, is she? Even more than I am, since she has no Dad either. I mean, does she know Father is Father? Was she ever told? I believe not.

Where is Vicky anyway? How can I find her? Who would talk, assuming I'd dare inquiring? Or that they'd tell the truth. Father? Please… I don't think I ever asked him a question (I'd be terrified). I only answer to Dad, when he bothers to interrogate me.

There is Aunt. Aunts. Since they live together, I could ask both at the same time. Would they dare lying in concert? Maybe they'll contradict one another. I think I should try. They look so much older.

*

I have asked. I was invited for dinner, the three of us around the mahogany table, in the dark room that didn't get any jollier. I was blunt, I guess, but didn't know better. After dessert, I simply put down my fork. I did not think of gingerly

lifting my wine glass, to look casual. I haven't learned that kind
of finesse in the convent. Stiffly, I proffered, "Is Vicky alive?"
There was silence (as expected).

Aunt (the eldest) was eating. She kept her eyes down,
but after a forkful she said: "Who?" Auntie (my dearest)
coughed (that was a good sign) then puffed under her breath,
"Of course, not." She at least knew what we were discussing.

I guessed it was a now-or-never occasion, so I
summoned up my courage. "Why isn't her name on the grave?"
Auntie left the table. Aunt said nothing. I didn't repeat. There
was no point.

Lies have been told, to me at least. And they keep
bifurcating… I mean there's a possibility I haven't considered.
Maybe Vicky is dead, and she is in the grave. Only, it shouldn't
be known. They (Father? Aunts? Doctor?) didn't tell anyone
besides me that Mom died of childbirth. But why would they
conceal it? Wasn't the girl registered? Should I verify… I'm not
sure I'd know where to start.

Or, the baby could have been earlier than I thought.
Auntie said she was premature. Maybe she wasn't a child
to speak of, not quite. If so, why was she named? Was she
christened? A priest was around when Mom died… that I recall.
He was there for Mother, but he could have baptized Victoria.

I could check the books at the City Hall. I know Dad
wouldn't like it, and he would find out. I'm not sure the clerk
would let me anyway, or if I'd dare going. Not all by myself, I'm
afraid.

Or, the grave could be opened. Well, one day. When
they all will be dead and I will be old. Then, I'll have the
grave opened. Then I'll dare. Only, if in the meantime Vicky's

somewhere, alive, I am missing my chance. See how things become twisted.

See how the lie keeps splitting, like a river into more and more rivulets… Let's say Mother didn't expect at all and there was no baby, just as there weren't baby clothes. Mother never sewed a single one. She couldn't, more than all she had no reason. Then what did she die of?

That isn't the point. Maybe they didn't know. Sometimes doctors don't. They are approximate, like roosters when they tell dawn, gardeners when they predict earthquakes. They have no clue about why Mother was ill, why she died. But why did Aunt make up a baby, and she named her? Who's Victoria?

*

The earthquake. That would clarify it, of course. Earthquakes can uncover graves, it is known. Not frequent, but heard of. I've been catching myself praying for an earthquake.

I said I don't believe in god. The nuns didn't change my mind… they never suspected they had to. I'm not asking god for this simple calamity to happen. I'm not sure yet who I'm calling on this. Maybe I'm only wishing, but I'm wishing hard.

Nothing tragic, but a very strong one. Epicenter right on, in the graveyard. Four a.m., all asleep, no one yet outside. Cattle in the barns, chicken in the coops. I don't wish for casualties. A good shake, one. Then the aftershocks, tiny. But the tombs upside down, the dead scrambling out, bones all over.

Not too messy! They can't be too scattered. I've to see that cute, dainty skeleton (Mom's), with a bundle niched against her ulna and radius. Vicky in Mother's arm, pearly white.

Unless she was so small, early, premature, her bones have already crumbled like talcum.

Let's hope not, or I'll never know the truth.

BABEL

The balcony.

How could I have considered it a safe place? Don't believe I haven't pondered the question. I have since I was a child. See… my compulsion of hiding on balconies, wherever I might be, began early, then never truly subsided.

It's a more common feature than you would imagine. Modest flats have at least one annexed to the kitchen, the storage, the laundry room. A small ledge of concrete surrounded by bars, an output for nasty smells, a place for hanging a rag or hiding a bucket. Well, I systematically find it and it becomes my corner, my abode, my sanctum.

I squat laterally, my back pushed against the bars. I like the sensation. The bars make me feel safe. They are stronger than me. They contain me. Still, I've wondered about what would happen if a piece of this cage suddenly gave up. Why not? After all, men put the contraption together. And men are imperfect, are they?

Men make balconies. My own grandpa forged many of those I have explored, here in town, in the countryside, at the beach. His wouldn't be those in the back, opening to the courtyard or the alley. No. They would be living room balconies, curved and curled. Grandpa was a skilled ironsmith. Well, a kind of magician. Truth is, I'm in awe of all smiths, having seen one at work. I have seen the forge... Let me tell you, it takes strength to do that kind of job. Metal is a huge beast, a wild creature. You have to tame it. It takes brains, muscles, a fearless soul.

But (that's where awe comes in) the things that you build then look pretty. When we go somewhere (all packed in the car, Father at the wheel), my eyes hunt for garden gates, fences, lampposts. They exult at the sight of balconies enlivening façades, otherwise mere displays of dullness. Balconies are the garb of buildings, the flourish, the lace, at least in the colonial South where we live.

They look like needlework, braided ribbons enhancing the chalky walls. Still, I know how sturdy they are. It is not the bars, really, worrying me. It's the pavement, this strip sticking out of the architectural body like the tip of a tongue. How do you trust the connection? It feels quite improbable, if you think about it... that I do, sometimes, and it gives me a thrill. Of the pleasant kind, I don't know why.

I enjoy my balcony stations at sunset, a time I find oppressive indoors. There's a brisk change of pace. However the day went, we start wrapping it up. Someone heads toward the kitchen, someone lights up the living room, turns on the TV. Dinner lurks on the horizon. Family gels around evening rituals. That is when invariably, unreflectively, a magnetic pull draws me out.

When my back pushes against the bars, in that small womb embracing me, I look at the sky changing colors. I immensely like it. I get lost in the permutation. I forget everything else. I just float.

*

The last thing in my eyes are squares. Not many. Three rows? Rather two. I can't tell. Why? I sure had the time to figure it out… But I didn't.

Two or three rows? Two, I believe. The space is exiguous, a cradle. Old tiles, forming a checkered pattern, white and blue. They are called azules. On the blue squares is the worn trace of painted lilies. French lilies. Why those? I have no clue, but I have often run my finger on them. Their petals are cute, tender, frail.

I have chosen this balcony because it's the highest. It belongs to the tower. That is an overstatement… I should call it turret. Quite a modest cylinder, but it dominates the rest of the building, sticking above the roofline. Like the ornate ironwork and the painted tiles, it is a Moresque reminiscence. Not uncommon around here.

The turret is a tube, occupied by a staircase leading to the room at the top, Father's library. No, there isn't a telescope. Only a desk, books entirely lining the walls, and a miniature sofa where two people could squeeze. Here and there the shelves allow closeted areas. One of them keeps a collection of liquors. A small fireplace faces a narrow balcony, on the left. Obviously, the glass doors open inwards. Thick drapes screen them. They need to be pulled or the doors won't open. They are dusty rose, a color of flesh, like the sofa. Old flesh… this room doesn't get lots of cleaning.

I steal on Dad's balcony whenever I can. I sit there at twilight, waiting for a spell to get hold of me. Nothing magic…

no talking birds, angels, fairies, all the peterpanish nonsense
you're fed as a child. The spell seizes my limbs, telling them not
to budge an inch, please. Then it reaches my tongue, and I savor
silence.

If I look down (that I avoid not because the view scares
me, but because I prefer the levitation, the groundlessness)...
If I look down, now and then, I can check the kitchen window,
a few stories below. When it lights up, too brightly, I tense in
a gradual manner, sending energy in rivulets to my extremities,
filling up my torso, arms and legs with a flow of pulsing blood.
I regain awareness of my muscles and bones, but I stay still until
my head placidly returns from its wandering. Nothing magic,
I said. My head says goodbye to the open, to the enchanting
expanse where it fluttered for a while, like a feather. I stand up
and get in, without looking back.

What gives me the signal is not just the kitchen light,
but the shadows I glimpse through the window, brisk and
snappy like puppets. One more poised, my mother. One, a sort
of twirling jack-in-the-box, Isidora.

*

I am Xenia. As you know, it means the stranger. I
am not one. I was born and raised here. The exotic name was
selected by Grandpa... Not the balcony maker. The other one,
Mother's father.

He had a huge collection of stamps, his favorite hobby.
Well, his devouring passion... he spent every scrap of free time
at it. Heavy volumes, bound in different colors, were devoted
each to a continent split in myriads of nations, some of them
occupying many pages, some a couple of rows. None was

missing.

Grandpa brought me along when (after pondering over cryptic catalogs) he went shopping. He also allowed me to soak envelopes in water, wait for stamps to come loose, lift them carefully, and then lay them face down on a blotter until perfectly dry. The same caution was needed while moving them through the page with a pair of long-handled tweezers, closing ranks, so to speak, to invite and welcome newcomers.

They looked just like the books on Father's library shelves, but I liked Grandpa's microcosm more. Everything was enthralling... the paraphernalia (china bowls, blotting paper, long tweezers), the preciousness (with its undertones of mystery), the erudition (a thick tapestry of interlocking geography and history). Most of all, the beauty.

How I loved those cameos of a thousand colors and styles! How I enjoyed picking and switching favorites, following variations in mood and the gradual shift of my taste (which, of course, with age grew more precise and more personal)... When I was permitted to browse, albums spread on my knees, I progressed, let's say, from periphery to center, leaving what I most liked for the end. I savored it all, lingering on each page. But I drooled for dulcis-in-fundo Magyar, Indonesia, Arab Emirates or Central African states. They amazed me with their parades of butterflies, strange masks, fabulous animals.

Grandpa had traveled locally, both for work and for war. He had not been abroad and he didn't care. His collection fulfilled a mathematical mind, quenched an obsessive bent... perhaps was a financial investment. It still meant the whole world to him. The entire planet, yes, in his hands. And he wanted his first grandchild to be Xenia. Mother didn't have an opinion. Father agreed.

I'm Xenia and I am not. Deep in my heart, I'm aware my name is a fancy, a caprice. I was meant to get Grandma's name, Titia. Not a lot better, way more common, but it sort of lurks in the background. See, I'm attracted to the letter t, for instance. It sticks to me like a shadow. I often feel like a t. I relate to t-shaped things, like this tower… turret. Or to stilts, those long sticks with short crossing platforms actors wear during pageants, or when circuses are in town. Crosses, obviously, where Christ and martyrs are nailed, open arms, head reclined. Crutches for the crippled, old-style, made of wood, as you see them in paintings. All those things feel familiar… See, I have always been skin and bones, and so angular. Maybe that is why.

*

Isidora was born when I was six. Mom and Dad chose her name. At first, it sounded pretty. In the long run, I liked it less. It is made of two parts, and that seems excessive… I only figured it out when I saw the Egyptian Pavilion.

The entire school went. Kids love mummies, evil eyes, hawk-heads, all of the creepiness. But I was already a teenager, not so easily impressed. Still, I found the display quite dazzling, a bit like Grandpa's stamps. All those figures and stories, traced, carved, sculpted with such elegance, shining turquoise and gold, filled my eyes.

And I thought I resembled those folks. We had something in common. Wasn't I cut like them? My body, a bunch of sharp lines. My jutting profile… My hair matched theirs, long, watery, indocile and raven. Also the letter t, with which I identified, came up often as I browsed names of gods, pharaohs, pyramids. My Egyptian phase lasted a while, so I discovered that Isis was the moon. I got envious of Sister… Of her name, I mean.

See, I felt kin to the moon. I do, that's why I worship the time when the sun obliges, giving its nocturnal partner a chance. At birth, Sis was emblazoned with both stars, because of the "dora" suffix, the gold. She's the sun and moon for my parents, no doubt. Shouldn't we have split? I wouldn't have minded the dimmer luminaria. Having none seems unbalanced. That's how I started to resent Isidora. Her name.

As a child, I fainted twice. The first spell happened when I was six. Isi was just born and I was about to go to the hospital, to finally see Mom and the baby girl. Nanny parted my long hair. As I said, black, curled, rebellious and nappy. It required tight braiding, and depending on who performed the task (grandmas, aunts, nannies, but never Mother), tight could veer from efficient to cruel. With each crossing strand, my whole mane was pulled from the roots so sharply that my neck tilted backward. I endured. I had to be groomed.

But that morning, excited or rushed, Nanny truly overdid it. I lost consciousness. She got scared and left, perhaps to seek help. When I awoke, my cheek soothed by the cool caress of the bathtub, no one was there.

I always loved tiles. The bathtub was trimmed with a bas-relief, white on white, nothing fancy, but every square sported a bee… When I came to, my eyes spotted one of the insects, very, very close. I heard a buzz, which of course didn't emanate from the tile. I was still confused. But the buzz matched the bee, and I liked it, and it all made some kind of sense.

I fainted for the second time at my sister's christening, on the wooden bench where I stiffly sat, clad in velvet (white collar, white cuffs), my feet aching inside my black varnished Mary Janes. I'm sure the incense did it. The altar boy swung his nasty thurible in my face. I can't think of another cause.

*

Grandpa (the one of the stamps) died a couple of years ago. He was old. Still, I miss him plenty. He has left me one of his albums, a country, and not quite my favorite. Rows and rows of popes, saints, madonnas, a few buildings and churches, then flags, the most boring. But it doesn't matter. It is worth some money, and I'm glad. I'll know what to do at the right moment. Isidora has received an album as well. I haven't asked which.

I had borrowed something from Grandpa shortly before he died. I have kept it. No one's claiming it back. It's a green pair of tweezers, long-handled. He had lent them for me to fix one of my earrings. They worked very well.

At the funeral, a cousin showed up whom we didn't know existed. I say we, because Isi was surprised as well. She couldn't stop watching him. Neither could I. Red-haired and red-bearded, he has just returned from Chile, where he has spent about two decades. I don't know the details. Mom and Dad have often talked about him, but in that pinched manner of theirs. He popped out kind of awkwardly… He's the one who should bear my name, though I never heard a male version.

My room is in the basement. It wasn't always the case. Things have shifted four years ago, when I finished high school. Grandpa was still alive. That is unrelated, I know. Until then, Isi and I shared a bedroom, large and looking toward the back. Behind our block, the town ends and the beach begins. The room had no balconies, only windows screened by puffy curtains.

The view wasn't too bad. The beach, there, is closed to the public. It's a muddy strip of black sand filled with I don't know which worthy mineral. Once it was a quarry, now abandoned. Something's gloomy and forlorn about it. Kind of charming, as well.

The room never felt like mine, though I did my homework in there, and of course I slept. But you know where I spent my sweet time.

When my folks fixed the basement (in order to give me some privacy) I was glad, but the library became kind of remote. Well, I don't mind climbing stairs. There's no window in the basement.

I sit at my desk, a long table where I do my crafts. I have good lights, sharp and focused. I have learned how to make jewelry. Metalwork. With the tweezers Grandpa lent me (the green-handled ones) I can ply the thinnest of wire. Copper, which is most tender.

Father doesn't approve of my crafts. He's afraid they'll distract me from college. They won't. I'll graduate and then take off. I will travel. Sell my album of stamps (just one country, but pages and pages) to buy my first fare. Let my name mean something at last. Of course, I haven't told Father.

He is worried about me. He thinks I didn't notice. I did, and I know the cause of concern.

*

I am falling. I mean I'm fainting again.

I don't like the sensation. It's ugly. Luckily, it doesn't last. It's precipitous, like they say of my delivery (Mom doesn't talk about it. I don't think she liked it. I was fast. I engaged in the channel when she wasn't fully dilated. It must have been truly painful, that is why… I have lost the train of my thoughts).

The feeling, I said, is precipitous, which is probably better. Then, don't think I stop feeling. Don't think I am nowhere until I come to. I am some "where," of course, just hard to describe. Always thinking of stamps, I'd say it fits on one page but it's colorful. I have mapped it… there are recurring items… wild horses, probably white. Dirty white, a bit gray, bit silvery. They run over me. I hear them coming from far, then the noise gets closer. They gallop over me. Hundreds. It's thunderous but doesn't hurt. Heavy, but it doesn't smother me. And the herd never ends, somehow it rarefies. Then I come around.

I have seen a neurologist, yes, who asked several questions. He asked things I couldn't answer, if I froth, if I bite my tongue. There's no mark on my tongue that I can notice. But I'm usually alone when I fall, so I don't know about frothing and my recollection proves nothing. The EEG came out clean.

I have passed out more than once after Grandpa died. That is why Dad is worried. He doesn't like trouble. He does not like anomalies, not in the family, especially not in the head.

I have also resumed my balcony habit, which I had almost lost when I moved downstairs, to the basement. Not entirely… I said I don't mind climbing. But my trick seemed suddenly childish, immature, so I kind of let it go. Until,

recently, a lack of air grabs me at twilight worse than it did
before. I sneak out, sit on checkered tiles, lean against the
bars with my eyes shut, or else staring at the sky (that's equally
restful). Call it meditation. Whatever.

I still fit. I'm still skin and bones. I fit laterally, of
course. If someone saw me from outside (they can't, there's
no vis-à-vis, the turret sticks out in the heights) I'd read like a
hieroglyph inked against the wall, interlaced with thick iron bars.

*

Something strange occurred a few weeks ago, while
I was there, that I haven't yet figured out. It has troubled me,
though I'm not easily scared. I have no idea how that happened,
but I was trapped, locked out. When I saw light through the
kitchen window, I began my ritual of slowly gathering up,
coming back to reality. When I turned towards the door, I
smacked my face against it.

It was shut, obviously from the inside. No other way.
And the curtain was pulled. I saw a compact wall of darkness.
How come I hadn't heard a thing? Well, I was… I had let
myself glide. It could have occurred in a time of complete
absorption. I mean absence. But it must have been done in the
quietest, slowest fashion… A millimeter at a time, as a thief
would.

I panicked. I turned out, my back pressing against
the glass panes as if they could absorb me, as if I could melt
into the building, engrave myself. I tried keeping the landscape
under control… now it threatened me. I took long and deep
breaths, then I turned again, banged and called to no avail.
Then I shouted at Mother, whom luckily I could spy, down into

the kitchen. It was summer, the window was open, my voice
carried. Mom didn't come up, Sister did.

I was pale when she let me in. She was flushed. She
must have run up the stairs. "What happened?" I paused, not
too sure about what I wanted to say. "I don't know. I was locked
out without noticing. Please say nothing. Say I fell asleep in the
library, and I had a bad dream." So we said.

And another time, sitting there, I heard laughing. I
think so. Smothered giggles, they startled me. I was deeply
relaxed, kind of hypnotized. I did not budge and the noises
barely registered… just an oddity I'd think of later. Noises?
Yes, there were more than laughs. Something else, nondescript,
thumps, like furniture pushed around. Lightly. Murmurs,
perhaps. A voice I didn't recognize, not Father's, for sure.
Maybe the cleaning lady. In the late afternoon? What an oddity.

As I went by, I noticed the sofa was caved in, as if
someone had sat there. Someone heavy.

*

Recently, Isi and I had a row. It never happened before,
and hopefully never again. We were eating lunch when she left
the table. She must have gone to the toilets… We have no other
excuse for leaving the room. When she returned, she was livid.
She grabbed me by the arm, dragged me into the corridor.

She said I had messed with her make-up. No idea what
she meant. She insisted about a tube of lipstick I had stolen.
I was shocked, and couldn't make head or tail of her words.
She had grasped my neck, fingers digging like prongs. When I
clawed at her face, she reciprocated. Then I grabbed her neck.

We both screamed. Mother appeared at the door, stupefied, but she didn't have time to speak. We had already let go. I have left a round bruise above her collarbone. A scratch runs down my cheek, like a tear.

I have found the lipstick. I'm quite sure it's the one she meant when she got cross. I had not taken it, of course. On me, it would look awful. I can only wear dark and matte (it goes with my olive complexion, my black hair). She likes shiny and light. That fits her skin tone and her age. The gold tube (not cheap, I can see why she lost her temper) was on the library sofa. Rather, in it. Yesterday I realized someone sat there, once more, without bothering to straighten things as they left. Or else badly, in a rush. Mother wouldn't be pleased by such negligence. Mother never comes to this room… Still, I couldn't help fixing the couch, pressing down the bumps to smooth up the creases. And I met the cold metal tube, in the fold between seat and armrest. There it was… I unscrewed the lid and enjoyed the apricot smell. I put it into my pocket. I've no use for it, as I said. But I'll keep it, for now.

*

I haven't told you this yet. It's coming to mind because of the lipstick color. Salmon, lobster, peach, coral, what should I call it? It's orange.

I have been making love to my cousin for the last two years, since the funeral. Not exactly. We started about a month later. In the meantime, he was invited for dinner twice a week. Not too weird. Guests are frequent. Still, it was quite clear Mom and Dad had a thing for him, not sure what. More than sympathy, something tied to family history, something I can't unscramble. I haven't tried, for I got to know Cousin on my own terms.

The first time surprised me. After lunch, on a Sunday, he asked me to go for a walk. That was not unusual, and fun… he had such charming stories to tell. He had traveled all over South America and I loved to hear about it. Kind of casually, we headed towards the beach, the black muddy sand in the back, the abandoned quarry. There are nooks and crannies, of course, and that forlornness I described. We began as soon as we got out of view. I say we, for I didn't oppose.

That was quick. I can't say if good or bad. I'm not sure I have the competence. It was dull. But then I had made it once, with my high school boyfriend, and it seemed just as dull. This was a bit different. I might tell you how, sometime.

I liked it enough to repeat it, always there and always on Sunday. We still go to morning mass, the whole family but not Cousin, who joins us for lunch. After lunch, Isidora has a swimming lesson. Mom and Pop nap. The two of us head out for a breather. Everything falls in place, does it? That hour (between one and two, no matter the season) fits our intercourse like the balcony fits my body at twilight.

Not that the two moments compare. No. The sex thing is something I want. It provides the right mix of adrenaline and release. It makes me feel different, more Xenia than Titia, somehow more than a hieroglyph, fuller. But it doesn't bring ecstasy (should it?) The balcony does.

*

I made love for the first time at our vacation house, a

small villa surrounded by orchards. That is where we routinely celebrate my birthday, which occurs in midsummer. Quite a short ride from town. No one minds. For my quinceanera we frolicked until dark, dancing, obviously, and we were allowed beer… Isidora was nine. She was put to bed with much fuss. Mother had to employ some persuasion and that kept her busy, long enough for me to disappear in the orchards with my boyfriend.

We lay in one of those squares dug under the trees… Maybe it was round, a circle, wide enough for two bodies. A small lake, usually water-filled. Not then… it was dry, the soil crumbly, but we saw grass and thought that it would be soft. While he scrambled on top, I felt stinging under my butt and thighs. Our mattress was a spread of nettles. I started giggling. I don't think he noticed. We never switched places, therefore he felt nothing. I mean he wasn't stung. But I was.

I have better understood Father's worries. There's some background I didn't know about.

A grandaunt, on Mom's side, had seizures. Long ago. She was quite messed up but they kept her home, in the country house, yes, the same one. She liked to sneak out, wander among trees. She did nothing bad, nothing dangerous, but to let her loose wasn't safe, because little by little she had gone insane. Namely, seizure by seizure, or so they believed. So the doctors said.

The more she lost her mind, the more she liked escaping. It was as if a mischievous spirit, a small devil had gotten hold of her. She ran, trying to reach the end of the property, where she stopped dead at the barbed fence. And she lifted her fists, a kid ready for a tantrum. She did not scream, though. She sang bits and snips of opera songs (that is what the radio played at the time). She smiled at the barbed wire as if it were a full house. She bowed at distant ovations, among chuckles of crickets and frogs.

Once, Dad reminisced about it over dinner. Cousin was invited. He sat on the other side of the table. The other side of me, I mean, next to Sister. Dad went on to deliver the tasty morsel… he described the time when Grandaunt left during the night, in her bedgown. I can picture those yards of lace glittering in the dark, bathed in moonshine.

She met someone with whom she had intercourse, as they learned when they finally rescued her. Not because she said it. They weren't so sure she understood, Father commented. He does not think the guy was identified. They must have opted for discretion. They found her outside, half asleep, with an angelical smile. Then she sang all day. Father was embellishing, I guess.

Anyway, she had passed through the window, as the door of her bedroom, the one leading to the corridor, had been carefully locked. The other one opened into her parents' room and she didn't go by, they swore, while the door to the balcony was wide open. And her knees, both of them, were scraped, swollen, bruised. But she sang all day.

I had never known Aunt had seizures. I had never known of this aunt. Grandpa's elder sister, she had died before I was born. So I couldn't remember her, but I did recall something else.

*

I remembered (just a fragment, but it blew my mind because of its sharpness, and how fast it disappeared. I tried to fish it back, but in vain. I had to make do with the brief, instant flash that struck me—try to fill it up, repeating its content as you list bits and pieces of dreams before they dissolve).

I remembered being small, in the country house, and being picked up by a tall person who wasn't Grandpa, though Grandpa was there. Someone lifted me, who looked infinite to me, head as high as the leaves topping the veranda (a green roof, as remote as paradise).

The tall person was laughing. I recall being excited by that laugh, loud, explosive, a cascade of shattered glass. I remember that laugh like a sunbeam, and myself (when I went up in those arms) as if being swallowed by the sun, sent out into space.

Now the exhilaration came back… I could sense it… And I pictured the dress I had on, dotted yellow and brown. I recalled how I loved it, how I wanted to wear it, and how I felt when I did… a flower, a bloom. I remembered, but later, Grandpa saying, "Yellow becomes brunettes." He was smiling.

About the person's face… teeth are flashing while words are pronounced that I have forgotten. An idea of purple lips, almost violet. Blue eyes, vaguely scary. And the bright orange fire of the hair.

I know it was Cousin. Sure as rock, it must have occurred just before he left. He had to be in his twenties, or younger. And I must have been two. I think I remember an odor, sharp and musky. Maybe he had been smoking cigars with Grandfather, who always did.

I am sitting on the library sofa when this comes to mind. Why now, here? And why did I stop? This is not a comfortable place, and in fact a smell lingers that is slightly bothering me. But this one I can tell. It is brandy. Thus, the liquor reserve has been recently tapped. None of my business.

I go back to my just found memory. Does he also remember? That moment? The polka dots? Me?

It is Sunday. He will come to lunch. He will sit in front of me, next to Sister. We are perfectly neutral in public, I mean around the table. No one knows, and by the way what is there to know? Nothing, no romance, no plans for the future.

I will travel to South America as soon as I'll finish college. I'm sure I will love it… architectures and landscapes resemble those we have here, but they are bigger. I have been listening to what Cousin said, but I already knew. There's no country in the world that feels truly extraneous, thanks to the stamp collection.

We have sex most Sunday afternoons. A… routine of sorts. I suppose it could be defined as… crude? Unadorned, for sure. Perfunctory, and on the rushed side. But week after week, month after month, it has become less dull. I have taken the due precautions, of course, and he knows. No worries. Soon I'll graduate, I will leave and this will come to an end. He knows. I guess he doesn't mind.

*

The last thing in my eyes are tiles. Blue. And white, a checkered pattern. Azules. I was lingering on their color and shape before getting ready for downstairs, for the family and dinner.

I'm not sure, now, if my eyes are open or closed. Darkness is really thick and my sensations are blurred. But I have come around, I know where I am, no more horses are tramping me. And I'm really, really cold. I don't know for how long I have been unconscious.

It has happened again, and this time I've panicked more. I remember, but I'm still confused. Most of all, I am weak. I hope I'll fall asleep.

When I tried to get in, the glass door was closed. I think (not sure… it feels as if centuries have passed)… I think I heard rushed steps. Someone running away, and that made me furious.

I banged with both palms against the glass panes. I yelled, "Open, open!" Then I turned around. Lights were on in the kitchen, but the window was closed. I could scream my lungs out. Nobody would hear.

They would know where I was, I thought. If not right away, quite soon. When I'd fail to appear for dinner they'd know. Obvious, wasn't it? I had no reason to worry, but rage made me whimper and fret. I felt trapped. The balcony suddenly scared me. Could I trust such a cage? So frail, stuck in midair? The locked door had severed it, cutting the circulation. No more blood came from the building, to feed…

No blood got to my extremities, to my head. I felt dizzy. I knew I should calm down, summon patience, but I couldn't. I banged against the door, I started yelling.

I don't know when I fainted. Maybe then, because that's where memory stops. Which way did I fall? Maybe towards the door… there's shattered glass. I don't feel pain, but itching all over, like nettles. I don't feel like moving at all.

If I've broken the glass, I could stick my hand in, turn the knob. Only, I don't feel like moving. I need to stay put. They will come.

My head… I must have banged it. Getting my arm to move (not sure which, body parts remain vague) takes forever, I swear. An eternity later, my fingertips have reached my skull.

My skull? There's a wound running down the back of my head, like a tear (this cannot be true). There's a cut, very deep, very large. I brush my fingers against it. They get sticky. I can feel the lips of the cut… lifted, thick, swollen. They remind me of something else but I can't say what. And between those pulsing hems, at the bottom, something hard, something bone.

I remove my fingers. My hand, slower than a slug, slides cautiously back, mapping out a geography of broken crystals. Was the moon up tonight? Was it full? Did I see the moon before falling? I saw French lilies, on tiles… Does the moon make the broken glass shine? I see darkness.

My hand also feels dampness. Lots of blood around me. I must have banged my head pretty badly. How long have I been out? I'm colder and colder. I know Father, Mom, maybe Cousin and Sister will come. Will they? Cousin.

So the balcony is holding all right, this small ledge, sticking out like the bar of a letter t…

I am enmeshed with the rail, like a hieroglyph.

So the balcony is holding, and I am the one who fell. But things happen.

Girl With The Purple Hair

I only saw her once.

She was rushing into a car stopped at a red light, entering from the passenger side. I recall her brisk motions, and still flexuous… her wild, fluttering mane, those long auburn… Well, kind of. Her hair color had some puzzling nuances. Notably, a streak of purple. I mean lilac. Periwinkle on rust, the weirdest match I ever saw. Unforgettable.

I saw her once, and it was almost too much. Almost troubled the quasi-perfect knowledge of her I thought I already had. The aural one, from the other side of the wall.

Day by day I had built an intimate portrait… Well, no intimacy and no portrait. I had built a coherent map of her gestures, rhythms, habits. Sort of an abstract pattern, outlining a credible personality. For example, I expected the abruptness she displayed while she jammed herself in the vehicle, clumping in such exiguous space a whole arsenal of bags of all sizes.

I knew her impetus from the thump of her purse landing on her desk, every morning, as if parachuted from an airplane. From the slam of a drawer (top left) where her

certainly long-nailed fingers dug (blindly, I'm sure) some
urgently needed possession (mints? gum? cigarettes? lighter?)
Something that apparently didn't travel with her, but was
unfailingly sought as soon as she plopped, with another familiar
thump, on her chair.

At the same time (she did many things simultaneously)
she kicked off her shoes. Hurriedly, her toe fumbled with an
ankle strap while something toppled away, stopping dead against
a solid barrier (the desk's leg?) An equivalent noise promptly
followed, overlapping, asynchronous, syncopated, sibling but
not twin, bent (as sound can be) in a divergent direction.

I imagined sandals even in winter, wooden high
heels (the heavy noise), intricate strings, metal hooks, sinuous
braiding. Just my fantasy and yet, based on such in-depth
acoustic experience, it chanced to be true or to come close.

She was in nine to five, often spending her lunch break
on the phone, though I could distinctly detect eating routines.
Clinging of silverware (real one, not plastic). Peeling of lids
(perhaps yogurt). Tossing of squishy wrappings into a trash can
next to the wall… Yes, whatever came into the disposing device
(I figured a basket painted white, thin and tall) had an intrusive
quality, as if it were thrown at me. Unavoidably, it made me
jump on my chair as if someone had entered the room.

That never happened, indeed. I was alone all day and
bored out of my mind. It must be why I feverishly recorded
every trace of life from the adjacent quarters. If it weren't for
such entertainment, I would have gone insane. I almost did
anyway. Luckily, I didn't last at the job… I was not made for
clerical tasks, those involving a forced seated position and long
hours of nothing.

I was not made for such a life. Danielle wasn't
either. The girl... I had named her, of course, long before
our fulminous encounter. It is hard to be so acquainted with
someone and leave the presence anonymous. You end up
qualifying it one way or another. So I had christened her
Danielle, for no particular reason.

Well, Danielle was irked by her nine-to-five chore as
much as I was. See, the very script of her motions revealed it.
Nervous. Frequent. Impatient, as for a caged lion.

The auburn mane! Right! There was something leonine
about her. Something fauve, though when I heard her pace
beyond bars, so to speak, I had not seen it yet.

Danielle scribbled a lot. Not on notebooks. On pads,
top bound... I could hear the distinctive lift of the paper, then
rolled back, slipped behind, pressed down. Very different from
a simple page turning. She wrote lots, and yet discontinuously.
She wasn't the focused, disciplined type. Volatile, abrupt, she
allowed frequent interruptions, passing to something else as if
her train of thoughts liked sharp angles. As if her mind enjoyed
zigzagging... a nice mending stitch.

Drawers were often opened, fumbled in and then shut.
Especially the top left where, no doubt, some essential feature
resided, needed frequently, like a vital supply... I went nuts
trying to decode its nature.

Is curiosity bad? Mortal boredom might be a valid
excuse. Anyway, the detail increasingly puzzled me, by contrast,
as the picture of the world-beyond-the-wall assumed greater
vividness. Yes, such clarity... I could call it splendor. It sure
brightened the dullness of my routine. Each noise, little by little,
acquired roundness and exact meaning. Still, I couldn't figure

out the thing she kept in the drawer, the object of her quick, nervous rummaging.

Back to the notepad where she wrote. Oh my, she was fast! I could tell by the way her hand brushed the paper. The rasp moved away from my ear, then jumped closer, then again moved away, as lines certainly filled the page in rapid succession. Well, if it was poetry (I didn't think so) it must have been visceral. Urgent. But her inspiration was… frail, short-lived?

Trust me, I'm pretty sure Danielle was no poet. She drew, though, quite often. No more left-to-right strokes… her hand stayed in place and I heard circular rubbing, insisting, minute. Cartoons? Perhaps fashion, possibly both. Was she simply doodling? By mere exasperation? I doubt it.

She had many markers or pens. The on-and-off of their caps was cheerful. They popped like miniature fireworks, then rolled in all directions… her desk must have been a scatter of tools. I was envious, I admit. Intermittently, she drew all day long. She must have carried home a whole bunch of sketches, a collection, an entire portfolio.

Could I have done the same? My employers seldom peeked in, though they unpredictably did, and wouldn't have liked to find me distracted by personal stuff. Still, they checked on me rarely. Someone else would have taken the risk. I did not.

What about Danielle? She risked nothing. I sensed she could do whatever she wanted. She, no matter who employed her, was her own master. Technically she was bound, like me, but just temporarily. She was waiting for something else that she knew would come. Soon. I could tell with absolute certainty, see… I also was in transition. I could relate to the disquiet, the impatience I perceived in her gestures. Only, there was something affirmative in her restlessness that I entirely lacked.

That's the point. Though, like me, she was trapped in a nonsense clerical job, the purple-haired girl had a future. Clear as day, it shaped her every breath, made her dance on her chair. Future, so to speak, drooled into her present, pulling forwards the hands of the clock I heard tick, slightly syncopating the one lurking above me (a sad oval of pale against the dark wallpaper). Mine dragged behind, a bit. It was slower. It wasn't even mine, after all.

Danielle had a future and I envied her for that, just as I envied her spread of multicolored markers, her supposedly impressive portfolio. What an artist she was! Her behavior (impulsive, spontaneous and passionate) undeniably betrayed it. I also wanted to be one, but I didn't dare. And I didn't think I had a future. It was what I most missed. I hoped someone would hand it to me… a future, a scrap of it, large enough to pull me out of the goddam job.

The art gallery where I worked was in a cul-de-sac squeezed among tall buildings. Luscious mansions, old downtown, built a long time ago, inhabited by fading aristocracy and nouveau riche. Light was scant among ivy-covered walls, ornate balconies, and somber façades. Little entered our front rooms, where art was exhibited and sold. At the end of an L-shaped corridor, my office was entirely windowless. Lamps were on all day.

I had guessed that Danielle's shop must have a similar floor plan, just reversed, her room being the most internal, like mine, the rest specularly spreading towards the other side of the block… a wide, crowded boulevard, sunny and bright.

Obviously, I could have verified, walked around the

block and looked for the corresponding entrance. But I would
have found the store closed. Our working hours matched.
She actually arrived after me (and I waited for the reassuring
thump of her purse, as I waited for her to leave before I'd start
packing, at night).

Still, I could have checked in what kind of business
she worked, and that might have shed further light on the sonic
landscape I was finely charting. I am not sure I wanted to. My
fantasy of her being employed by art dealers, just as I was,
suited me well. After all, the area pullulated with galleries. Hers
was quite successful, I mused, though apparently she was bored
just the same. She might have wanted her own gallery, or none.
She might have wished to fully devote herself to her creative
work. Objection… She wasn't the devoted type. That I knew.

I was sure the gallery she worked for, opening on the
bustling boulevard, not on the back alley, was thriving. Mine,
instead, was so derelict I had started to suspect it might be a
cover. For what, I didn't know. But I wondered about it just as
I did about the mysterious contents of the top drawer, on the
other side of the wall.

My employers were a strange pair. Him, a maker of
black-and-white movies, old and shabby-looking, though often
harboring a kind of sly smile, as for one who knows more than
you can imagine. Her, much younger or so she wanted to look.
Her hair, a pinkish copper, so unreal to be pathetic. Pinkish, not
purple. I mean not the heavenly periwinkle I mentioned. Oh no,
not even close. This (my lady owner's hair) was a tomato-stained
straw, meant to enhance by contrast her once pretty and still
huge green eyes. Ex belle of the ball, she worked the occasional
client with the remnants of her killer charms.

I didn't truly like them. They paid my meager salary.
They quite rarely entered the room where I did what they asked
me to, dust a couple of frames, copy a letter or two, organize
a very thin bunch of files. I was done in half hour even in the
most studied slow motion. Then I was supposed to answer a
phone that never rang. Or to open the door when Madame
went to have her nails done, Monsieur to the barber, when she
left for an errand and he took an afternoon nap.

Sometimes, she got friendly. It rarely occurred and it
was so unlike her, I invariably assumed she must have had a
Martini with lunch. In those cases, she expounded on a specific
group of local artists, once hot-selling and fashionable, now on
the wane. She had known them quite well. She still represented
a few. Sadly, they all were involved in hard drug consumption,
dying one after another, quite fast. They produced art to pay for
their addiction, often in direct form, a sculpture, a painting for a
fix.

Of course, she wasn't part of the sordid bargain. Of
course, she didn't pay them that way. But she was well informed.
Why she shared her knowledge with me, I have no idea. Excess
inebriation, I'm sure. Her stories troubled and affected me.
Artistry as a career became more precarious to my eyes. More
attractive as well, endowed with a romantic, suicidal halo.

I was sure the gallery-in-the-front didn't represent
such burned generation of losers. The owners must sell glossy
abstract or colorful naïve. Hyper-realistic still life or gentle
erotica. Hard to tell, since I wouldn't go check.

During lunch break (while Mr. and Mrs. Boss met
friends, colleagues or family at a nearby restaurant, lingering
around coffee until mid afternoon) I bit into my dull but

coveted sandwich and listened.

Danielle was on the phone. I couldn't decipher her words, not a single one. Not that I wanted to. I found pitches, rhythm, intonation sufficiently enjoyable. It was like a concert, and it often lasted accordingly. She was tireless in her zest for conversation. Animated. Vivacious and teasing. Prone to laughter. Never cross, never irritated.

I had no idea whom she talked to, but I knew it wasn't always the same person… There are variations of tone when we change interlocutors. I agree, the nuance can be infinitesimal. Still, if you pay attention (and god knows I did, having nothing else on my plate) you can't miss it. A small change, and yet critical, like the code for a safe, a key matching a keyhole.

Whom did she talk to? Lover? Sure. Mom? I suppose. Friends, how many? A ton. I said she never was angry, whiny, or preoccupied. That I constantly was, back then, though I don't recall what about. It must be why her peculiar lack of anxiety struck my ear… I envied that as well.

Now I'm sure you know what envy becomes when it builds up, do you? Mine began to get thicker, a long mental list, plenty of bullets. Drawings, pens, a future, a carelessly brave state of mind… Envies, when stacked in a pile, become hatred. Well, I swear this wasn't the case. In my case (or Danielle's) those amassing jealousies were hazardously morphing into something else, mostly resembling love. But I didn't know that was happening. Or what love was.

Once, during one of those tedious lunch breaks (breaks from what, I wonder), I heard a word. Don't ask me how the prodigy occurred. It's a mystery of physics I haven't yet put my finger on. There is no logical explanation. Why one word, in nine months of constant exposure? How could that meager cluster of sound travel a path of its own? Borrowing an invisible crack, a fissured pipeline? Let's not try to rationalize the impossible.

The word wasn't shouted more loudly than the rest… I don't think so. It came after a burst of laughter. That I know. A long, hearty, contagious giggle. Then the voice, in fact, tapered down. But I distinctly heard the word "hoods." Right.

It isn't the entire truth. I heard other words. Two more, to be exact. I have omitted them in the above confession because they emerged later. I mean that I recalled them with considerable delay, as when you reconstruct a dream and the more you think of it, the more fragments pop out, lining up in full daylight. The same happened with the two additional terms, which indeed came earlier, but promptly faded, blown away by the impact of a single monosyllable. Hoods.

With no further ado, the side words were "small" and "four." Pardon, in reverse order. All in all, four small hoods. That's what I deciphered in nine months… I guess it was enough.

Four small hoods made my envy escalate at an impressive rate. Tiny things have such power… Think about diamonds, for instance, or rubies and such. I immediately pictured them in red velvet. Thus, Danielle was a costumer in her more-than-real life. I mean, outside the gallery.

All made sense now, the pads where she first scribbled notes (lists of characters, materials and prices, store addresses) and then poured sketch after sketch in a creative frenzy, her abundant phone calls, meant to keep her business going while she was trapped in the office. And her own taste in fashion,

the super high heels that I had guessed about, metal dangles,
baroque strapping and all. Plus, the hair I discovered later,
way later… the auburn mane with the purple streak, clearly,
a theatrical thing. She must have been an actress as well. Her
tuneful voice betrayed it. See how everything falls in place when
you finally get a clue, irrelevant as it might sound? Four. Small.
Hoods.

Knowing Danielle was involved in the theater (maybe
the movie industry… our town swarmed with studios) added
to my feelings a pang of sharp longing. See, the artistic dream
I timidly nurtured was indeed bent towards the performing
domain, a universe about which I had long fantasized. Also, a
universe from which I felt locked out for various reasons. I saw
it like an island in the sky, floating over whipped cream-looking
clouds. A magnificent island, but all ladders had been pulled up
and I couldn't fly, of course. I just ambled under the thing, so
to speak, staring up through the clear bottom, meant to entice a
desire as keen as it was desperate.

But Danielle belonged to the island. She had access.
She could go in and out. She had found the invisible elevator,
or maybe she had wings. The passcode to the gate was right in
her pocket. And how could I doubt it? She seemed to possess
whatever I wanted, but I couldn't possibly get.

Next to our gallery-in-the-back lived a famous movie
director. I knew about it before I accepted the job. Not that I
could have refused it… Let's say the information sweetened
the pill. The guy in question had nothing to do with the
gloomy shine (if that makes sense) of my own black-and-white
filmmaker. Mine (the gallery owner) was virtually unknown,

having won a prize and then just rested on his laurels. The other
was a myth, a national glory. Also, he was a master of color.
His movies were like paintings… like harmonious rainbows, in
fact. You came out of the theater, each time, with eyes full of
wonder.

Several books were written about him since he had won
his seventh Oscar… I had borrowed one of them at the library
and I carried it at work, tucked in my lofty bag. I browsed this
or that page, the tome lying on my knees, hidden under the
desk. As I said, I wasn't daring. But it was way easier to shut a
book (and then dump it into the bag I kept on the floor) than to
make a bunch of colored pens disappear.

I skipped critical texts and eagerly sucked biographic
details. Of course, the star was married. Who cared? He and
his wife lived… No, not that near. They lived in the penthouse
of one of those castle-sized buildings of which our cul-de-
sac brushed the rear side. Certainly not the façade, which of
course graced a wide, tree-lined square. Even if my room had
had windows, a peephole, a vent of sorts, I still couldn't have
glimpsed at their precious quarters. Shielded from my curiosity,
the penthouse hovered in the heights, enjoying a limitless view
of our town and beyond. I imagined spacious corridors and
exquisitely furnished rooms, filled with artwork as colorful and
bright as the star's own creations. I imagined entertainment and
music. More than all, I figured light, pouring in cascades. Rivers,
torrents of light.

In the book, the photographs especially caught
my attention. Freeze frames from movies I had watched
several times. I was pleased to recognize scenes I recalled. I
observed details. I hungrily scrutinized actors, even lingered
over hundreds of extras (the maestro was very fond of

picturesque crowds). Slowly, I started absorbing his taste. To me it was medicine. Or drug. The colors he liked, faithfully reproduced, enthralled me. Gradually, I identified a recurring combination, making his palette unique and exceptional. A weird juxtaposition, concealed within a variety of other tones, a distinctive chromatic signature. I'm talking about rotten orange (was it rust?) matched with a kind of tender wisteria, between purple and cyclamen… Periwinkle, that is.

I had no way to see the penthouse, despite its enticing proximity, let alone the master himself. Just a peek at his wife would have thrilled me… His butler or his maid would have satisfied me. I had no chance, still I dressed for him every morning, nurturing the insane hope he would meet me. Not the other way around, for some reason.

I knew it was more impossible than improbable. True, they all (he, his wife, the maid and the butler) surely went outside, then returned. Not by the back alley, alas, where they likely never set foot. Still, tremendously aware of threading his close surroundings, daily, I dressed for him.

The rite didn't involve much complexity… I didn't have much of a choice. I wore the prettiest outfit I owned, a Chinese jacket embroidered with flowers. That's what I recall but, because a long time has passed, I will take the liberty of adding sequins, gold thread, a tad of extra spark, meant as an apology for my young, pathetic naivety. The jacket was red. Not his favorite color. Still, I thought it attractive on me. My black hair in a single braid, my bangs straightly cut fitted the jacket. I knew I wasn't beautiful. I also knew I was exotic, striking in a way.

Once he had seen me, I was sure, he would pick me as an extra for his next film. Don't assume I was totally delusional.

There was more than a grain of salt in my hypothesis. I had studied the pics. I knew he liked my type. If he only could meet me. If he could fancy something in our dim little shop, a painting by one of those addict bohemian dudes, then everything would just fall in place, like Danielle's multifarious soundtrack.

See? The star-in-the-penthouse apparently could distract me from the girl-beyond-the-wall. I believed he could be the one meant to hand me the future, the small scrap I needed. I expected it from him, clad in my Chinese jacket, my hair neatly coiled, trusting the unusual slant of my almond eyes.

The idea that Danielle might know him surged at last. It came with a delay, as if I had pushed it at the very bottom of a drawer, while it should have been in plain sight. Those markers… that furious scribbling… Way before the fatidic words (four small hoods, remember?) I should have figured out she designed for him. He must have employed herds of assistants, costumers, stage and prop designers. They had to be energetic, creative and confident… Danielle A to Z.

I was sure that every day, after hours, she brought him the notepad. Once or twice, he kept her for dinner—candlelit, on one of those pergola-covered balconies, jasmine stubbornly imbuing the air, the wife smiling as she did in the magazines.

Maybe Danielle went in the morning, before work, to gather instructions. That is why she was always late, in a rush, parachuting herself and her purse as if landing from high. In the purse was the pad where she had noted the assignments for the day. He exacted those visits, or rather pilgrimages. Stars need you to be generous in time and availability, in exchange for a tiny share of their radiance. They ask for infinite patience.

That must be why I detected the opposite when my friend stepped into the office. She had given her dose of meekness away.

But I didn't doubt my capacity of being patient as wished, when I would be cast as an extra for his next film. Imminent and already in the news although, as always, production would take a long time. Complex settings, humongous crowd scenes, expensive decors… Famous actors on the ballot for the main roles. Gossip and curiosity. His upcoming creation, I had heard, would combine a medieval tale with a futuristic dystopia. Middle age was one of my favorite periods.

Then it clicked in. Small hoods… for the falcons! I had got it entirely wrong. No red velvet. She had been trusted to create hoods for the falcons. Black, minute… the word small now acquired its proper meaning. Not a big task, all right, but quite delicate. Would she slip the hoods over the falcons' heads or just pass them to the manager of animals? Maybe she was the manager… A tamer… she had it in her. Would I dare such a task? I didn't think so. All I wanted to be was an extra, a nonspeaking walk-on. Asian looking, that's all. Tartar. Turkish. Mongolian. A slave. Yes, that would satisfy me.

Suddenly, one late afternoon, dead and stale in spite of the rather interesting turn of my deductions, a new idea sneaked into my mind, quite incongruous… Those hoods! They were for the canaries. See, the word "small" kept bothering me. Without being a detective I could sense that, stuck in the middle, it played a key role. Those hoods had to be incredibly small to have slipped through the sound barrier and alone reached my consciousness. Suddenly, I was sure the new masterwork would be shot in the Canary Islands and involve an exceeding number of canaries. True, the press didn't tell. The press doesn't know it all. By the way, he notoriously kept aces up his sleeve. He adored delivering mesmerizing in-progress surprises. Genius does.

Canaries have nothing to do with the Canary Islands. Well, it mattered little. Poetry has its own rules, and my guy was a poet. Danielle wasn't… again, it mattered little… this was his creation, not hers. She was asked to provide hoods for the canaries, period, though the species didn't truly belong. She would do her very best.

See, my mind had gone overboard… it was the tail end of an endless day. I had started to think in zigzags, like my invisible neighbor. I had begun to dangerously morph into her. Or the other way around, which is the same thing. We were merging.

And (that should have warned me) I envied her no more. Bizarre. Now that there would be reasons for unleashed jealousy, I felt none. How did it happen? See the previous paragraph… the wall was crumbling down, at least on my side. We were merging. At least on my side.

Now back to the canaries. A few things need clarification. First of all, I must have missed a word… well, among the vertiginous quantities I never heard. I must have missed one in the fatal sequence, which for sure must have been "four hundred small hoods…" Right? What would he do with four canaries? Such a skimpy quartet would only befit a new-wave-conceptual-minimalistic project of sorts. While, in line with his spectacular vision, you'd expect a flight of four hundred… four thousand canaries. So, that is what I had missed. The word "thousand."

Yellow multitude. Numinous, bright like the sunshine that I missed as well. Oh so miserably. Eight months. How much longer would I resist? They would be capped with thimble-sized hoods. The canaries. A surreal painting... how like him! Black hoods? Striking, but obvious. Red, the shade of my jacket? Perhaps blue, yellow's complement on the spectrum.

Any color he'd choose. Why would canaries be hooded? Wait. The idea struck me for a reason... I must have recalled something. Was it for them to sing louder? More melodiously? To such scope they used to be blinded. No hoods were employed... that would have been excess courtesy, and a kind of nonsense. But we are talking movies. Poetry, to be exact.

How would Danielle find the patience for sewing thousands of hoods, each with two pinhead holes to match canaries' little eyes? Especially since she left her limited dose at the star's place, every morning and night. Well, she didn't have to sew them, I betted. That would have been menial work, out of character. She had to design the model (such a perfect miniature), order fabric and thread, find a bunch of seamstresses.

That... I could do. It didn't take daring, didn't imply risk. I had patience in overwhelming supply. In fact, I would be honored to sew some of those costumes. Those hoods, even four thousands, why not? Not under the desk, ready to drop them inside my bag... which would have been feasible, seeing the weeny dimensions. But I'd swear the thing required focus, precision. I, at least, wanted to provide such qualities. I didn't want to handle it carelessly. On the contrary, I wanted to excel at my task because, you have guessed it, that could be, that would be my ticket, my way into the island. Not the Canaries.

The one I have described, the inaccessible universe I longed for, where Danielle belonged.

If I obtained the four thousand hoods job I would leave the gallery. All that sewing would pay. Even if each hood were a trifle, quantity would compensate. The job would take time, be repetitive… I could use it like meditation, while I planned on a future… In fact, no. The job would be the future, the loose end of it I had been waiting for. I should go ask Danielle, as simple as that.

Does it sound absurdly farfetched? Only from the present perspective. Or from any perspective other than mine, past or present. I had come to my conclusion, deduction after deduction, or invention by invention (is there any relevant difference?) No room was left for doubt. I just needed to walk around the block, find the nerve… Move it, girl! I also needed to concoct a lie for arriving late, or else leaving early. It took me another month.

Meanwhile, on a weekend, I was swept by an impromptu wave of creativity. I made a pair of dolls, wooden balls for heads, scraps of silk for clothes. They were puppets, complete with strings, crossbar, and a large hook for hanging them when at rest. Modestly, very well executed. Spurs of action so rarely occurred to me, this one left me in a state of exhilaration. I wrapped my offspring in tissue paper and I proudly, carefully stored them inside a shoebox.

Monday morning, I couldn't resist bringing them to work. My babies! I showed them to my boss, who was in one of her chatty moods. She took them in her hands to my trepidation. She spent half a minute in awe. Maybe that's not the right word… Then she scornfully dropped them into the box (luckily, the tissues softened the shock) saying, "cute, my dear, but this is not art. You have a long way to go." As if I didn't know.

The day after I left work ten minutes to five. I do not recall what I said. No one cared, I realized. I believe I had the guts to transgress because, down and deep, I was bruised by the cold shoulder my boss had given to my toys, never mind her unflattering comment. The spell tying me to my desk had finally loosened up.

I turned right at the corner, then right at the next. I had counted the doors I passed on the alley before reaching the corner. Nine. My eyes rushed to anticipate the tenth door opening to the main boulevard where I advanced, dazzled by the very start of a sumptuous October sunset.

That is when I saw the car stopped at the light, the girl dashing in. A split second, a flash… My brain had to gear up in order to process it. But I already knew. From my toenails to the tip of my pitch-black braid, I knew it was Danielle.

I was mesmerized on the spot. The tall figure. Slim, I guess, but no doubt large-breasted. The auburn cascade of hair. Wide sunglasses, uncannily dark. High-heeled shoes just as I had pictured them (secret smile, secret smile). Rainbow-varnished nails. Cream colored miniskirt and long calves, bottle shaped, very powerful.

Those calves stabbed me, somehow. My eyes lingered over them, while… Wait! The light turned green. Now she was in the car, door half-open, pulling in the last of her paraphernalia as if vanishing inside Ali Baba's cave. What she carried confirmed my lineup… pencils, pads, thick samplers of fabric, patterns and magazines for sure filled those totes. When she slammed the door I feared her hair wouldn't fit, so imposing was the feathery mass. Then I saw the streak. Periwinkle.

I had fallen in love, and I couldn't stand it.

I didn't ask about the four-thousand-canaries' hoods, and I never saw her again. She kept her job for as long as I was able to hear. I did not keep mine. Not because I ever dared to say, "goodbye, I'm going to get a life." Oh no, I didn't have it in me. I wasn't a tamer of destinies, not even my own.

Our gallery shut its doors, not sure why. My boss' health was the official reason. He looked old. He probably was. His long afternoon naps might have had other causes than boredom. His omniscient look, so out of context, might have betrayed something getting loose in his brain. That could have been why he didn't shoot a thing anymore.

The official reason for closure was the owner's wish to rejoin his small province, weary as he was of the stressful capital town. Stressful? So the wife said, and though she was a socialite she would go, for love's sake. About love I knew nothing except for a cinematic delusion, an aural infatuation and an indigo vision, none of which I could even honestly categorize. About love I knew little and so I believed her.

In the meanwhile, the group of formerly hip artists that we still represented had finished dying. Invariably overdosing, as if following the same cheap scenario. They all died in straight poverty, having used every penny they had made. Often paid in advance, and alas in kind. Plowing through the piece to get it done and then ask for another advance. Working slave-like in increasingly dark, cold, uncomfortable premises they still called atelier. That was horribly sad and might have had consequences on the fragile economy of our small, claustrophobic salon.

Anyway, the gallery unexpectedly closed and I lost my job. Nothing then (until I'd find the next hide into which I'd wait for the future) prevented me from walking the boulevard up to the famous gallery-in-the-front that, not selling the doomed generation of freshly deceased painters, had to be still unaffected and thriving.

Danielle wouldn't be in the showroom. I knew where she spent her day. In the very back, just a membrane of bricks away from my ex prison cell. I could ask for her, say I was a friend, though I wasn't. I did not even know her name. And she had no idea of who I was in case someone would announce me. The girl with the Chinese jacket? The girl with the braid?

Then why would I want to see her? At this point, the job of four thousand hoods was certainly taken. If something doesn't wait, that's show business. Should I just tell her I could sew and, in case, was free? Since she worked for him… though I wasn't so sure she did.

There was no point in going to see Danielle unless I were chasing ridicule, some kind of mortifying humiliation. I had sense enough to understand it. No point, besides the fact I was sickly in love, but I didn't know and so it didn't count.

Then he died as well. The famous director. Without notice… another ace up his sleeve. Quite a tragic loss. He did not finish his last movie, which had nothing to do with the Canaries or with any island at all, need I say. It had medieval sections, though. Falcons, I guess. Hooded, probably, as they usually are for hunting purposes. No smaller birds.

I ended up working as an extra in the industry, highly enjoying it. It thrilled me to be part of the picture, to appear within the tableau. Darn, it made me feel… I don't know. In the moment, as they say. It made me feel present. Alive.

Girl By The River

I started off towards Miraya's house in my nightgown, quickly throwing on top of it a kimono I found by my front door. Not its place, not sure how it landed there, but thank heavens it did... The nightie is old, sheer, torn, and the wrap I had the good sense to grab at least ensured decency.

This usually occurs in dreams, does it? Being inappropriately clothed in a public place. Pointedly, in the street. A classic. Recently, alas, it has happened for good, in the occasion of an emergency or two. Was today one such?

It wasn't. But when I stepped out to the backyard, half-asleep, coffee in hand, the birds were too loud, too restless. They must have unnerved me. They were doing a hell of a rumpus, drawing frantic figure eights around the bare branches of my two maple trees. I can usually find the cause of a bird commotion. A predator invading territory, a disturbed nest. Today neither seemed to apply.

The airborne excitement must have fueled my previous anxiety about the maples. Were the birds... Was there anything else I could do? I should seek Miraya's advice, I thought. Oh, not on the phone... In person. It is a short walk.

See, a couple of weeks ago the trees were attacked by a plague. I called the forestry agency, which was well informed, as the bug had already spread over a considerable area. Many specimens have been treated at this point, and mine were as well, but hopes of survival are slim. They'll die sooner than later.

So will I, unless a miracle (let's say unforeseen development) takes place. But I have reached the stage where I am not perpetually scared. A sense of detachment, a dumb disbelief coexists with painful awareness, sadness and despair. I am thin, my body inconsistent. Putting clothes on myself isn't yet unpleasant, but less satisfying than before. That is why I can be found in my nightie at all hours…

Let me reword this. I cannot be found, as no one ever shows up. Well, I could be if… Hypothesis nil. My isolation is chosen. This is a time of life (rather, an ante-chamber of non-life) I don't wish to share. The only company I seek is nature, you have guessed it. That is why I have returned to the cottage, in the blessed middle of nowhere.

A few houses are scattered around mine, not too close. Mainly secondary residences of town dwellers, they are empty. Is such scarcity of neighbors a risk in my present state? No. I can communicate with the world via phone and via internet. I can drive to the village in about half hour, to the hospital (thrice a week) in an hour or so.

And there is Miraya. Her proximity makes all the difference. A fifteen-minute walk and I am at her gate. A five-minute climb up a graveled alley and I have reached the mansion. The slope, I must admit, has become demanding. I run out of breath, my heart pounds in my chest. I slow down. I take short breaks as if fascinated by a wild flower, a butterfly, a ladybug, you name it. But I'm sure that my act doesn't fool

Miraya. She has begun to meet me at midway, where a bench is conveniently placed.

Today I made it all the way to the house, then we walked together to the back, where the orchards occupy a concavity… Rather, a miniature valley enclosed by smooth, rounded hills. Oh my, Miraya's backyard! I have loved it since my teens. It always sent chills through my spine, of the pleasant kind.

Once I stepped in, everything else disappeared. The place was its own universe… island… secret garden. Don't all kids like these natural havens? Why, though? What do we wish to escape? Isn't the outside world desirable, rich, full of promises? To me it was, and yet I found the orchards adorable. They made me ache with something I'd call nostalgia for lack of a better word. The unnamable longing.

As you pass the mansion, you'll see a spread of green velvet (or a sea of white and pink, following seasons). Such lush, vibrant carpet ends against a background of rocks, brown and mauve. The hills are also part of the property, which they enclose within a sort of conch shell, coffer, treasure box… Not too small. Not alarmingly wide.

If you turn around, you'll get the same illusion, as the hill on which the mansion is perched blocks most of the vista. The house sticks out like a nipple atop the curvy mound of a huge, lonely breast. From the back you'll notice how large is the building, though it manages to look almost… light?

Time ago, its irregular silhouette (a mixture of pointed roofs, turrets, terraces) was the only manmade presence against the sky. Now other constructions lurk in the distance… the profile of recently sprouted condos (they are summer houses, just cheaper)... squarish, drab, bunker like, the hospital (kind of pale, yet detectable because of its size).

But it isn't hard to cut out those fringes, to isolate the villa as a single hieroglyph tattooed into the blue. At night, especially in moonlight, it must be even easier. In the foreground, the house must loom as an opaque, somber shape, while darkness obliterates the beyond. One could assume, why not, that years didn't go by, that things didn't change... At night, though, I'm not around.

True, days are getting shorter, but my visits never go after teatime. Actually, never intrude on it. They, Miraya and Carlos, are as private as I am. They also don't need company. I breeze by. They like it this way.

When I arrived, she was fully dressed. Well, it wasn't that early, but did the hour matter? Is she ever less than impeccable? She was wearing a tunic of linen, thick and pale, a tint of discolored rope. Although, sparse threads caught the light in a striking fashion, sparkling like metal wire... perhaps, mother of pearl. My gaze was magnetized by those filaments, further glowing as she gestured towards a pair of trees, on the side, I hadn't noticed before. Like mine, they were suffering.

"These aren't fruit trees." Of course. They were maples, like those in my backyard, though the fact wasn't immediately evident, because they had lost their leaves. Way too early, in regard to the season. Upon closer examination, something else appeared wrong... branches were also scarce, their design less intricate than expected. "They have started falling," said Miraya. She didn't refer to the foliage, and I noticed the crack in her voice.

Was she about to cry (or to fight tears) because of

dead flora? I didn't think so. But there was a strain in her throat, perhaps due to age, I hadn't heard yet. "A lot came down already," she went on, pushing twigs with her toe. Just a few small sticks… She and Carlos must have removed larger debris. They employ seasonal help around harvest time. Otherwise, they proudly take care of all maintenance. Oh, they keep the place as clean as a jewel box! Well, they have no other burden… the land is their offspring, their child.

She bent down to gather the fragments she had bunched up with her foot. A bin, crate, an orderly pile or heap ought to be somewhere. As I watched, the color of the wood struck me, shiny and light, not so unlike the threads parsing Miraya's dress. But the twigs didn't remind me of metal. Rather, polished bone.

"Careful!" She almost screamed. A branch hung above us, severed from the trunk, still held by ramifications entangling it. Stuck, trapped as if within a cobweb, it looked haunting, unreal. I could clearly see the cut section, and I noticed a core as bleached as the splinters I had under my feet. Like a tendon, a string of neural substance, a marrow, gleaming with that same insane candor. "Is that color normal?" I asked, knowing it wasn't. But Miraya is such a good source for natural matters… She would clarify. "It's the sickness." She was grabbing my arm. "Move, quickly! It might fall."

We walked towards the house. Should I ask if the plague threatened the orchards? I knew it didn't. Plant bugs are selective, and they choose their victims with care. Their targets, I mean. Those neat, orderly rows, quite packed yet duly organized, surely weren't at risk. They would happily thrive, unaware of the maples' misfortune. They'd survive Miraya and

Carlos. Of course, they'd survive me.

Not sure if the fleeting thought of their longevity compared to my precariousness pleased me. Very probably not. But I didn't linger on such melancholy note. As I said, I have trespassed into a phase of intermittent denial. Rather, denial pure and simple, ruptured by sporadic spells of angst and revolt, coated by a thin layer of blurred, irrational hope.

I didn't linger, I said, on the orchards-in-the-valley's rosy future compared to my quite grayish one. Truly, I was busy planning my route, thinking I would walk home by the riverbed, still dry after the summer. It runs parallel to the road, out of sight because of the bramble bushes separating the two. Also, because it is a ravine, carved below street level.

But I know where the slope is smoother, where the hedge has gaps, allowing access… In my teens I have perused that back alley, so to speak, many times. Not only am I familiar with its mood, eerie, lunar, a tad desolate and yet pleasantly wild… frankly, today I was nostalgic. I felt I hadn't teetered on that patchwork of rocks, gravel, mud and sticking out roots for too long.

Yet my present (and pressing) reason for choosing the riverbed was, you bet, my stupid nightgown. Right, if I kept my kimono tied at waist level (with the string concealed under the satin lapel) nothing would be wrong with my appearance. Miraya had said nothing. Though… had she ever seen the kimono? I don't think so. It was Mother's. I have recently dug it out of a closet. For no reason at all, just a fancy… I have started following them with little restraint. You do that, as soon as you're weaned off immortality.

No, Miraya had never seen the kimono. A bit worn,

rusty color, striped peach and pink... I guess it looked decent.
Only I knew about the yellowing gown it concealed, sheer, and
no underwear. Still, that bothered me now that the sun was up,
now that I was lucid, present, awake.

What runs through the ravine during the appropriate
seasons, never deeper than a couple of feet, is a modest creek.
Still quite beautiful, when at its fullest. The peak of the flow
coincides with the awakening of vegetation in spring... buds
and buttons, then small, tender leaves. In my green years, I
liked to go there at such times, follow the water's edge, wade
on rocks. I fell more than once, to no harm. Just mud-soiled
clothes, a few scratches.

Did I love the creek as much as I loved the orchards,
clasped in their mystery canyon? It was a different feeling. True,
both places had a quality of seclusion. They were sanctuaries
of sorts, but not in the same way. The orchards had a peculiar
stillness, as if under a charm. If you'd linger in them for too
long you'd be trapped, like Ulysses at Circe's. You would never
find your way home unless, obviously, you didn't need to. Unless
the orchards were it, I mean... a totally different story.

While the small stream was free. A way to freedom,
I mean. As you neared it, you sensed it... in the wind playing
among the greenery, in the water sliding along, slow but foxy,
full of stubborn resolve. Yes, the river was a way out, at least a
possibility.

That is where I met Carlos for the first time. By pure
chance, and then we did it on purpose. Meaning we knew we
would, at least I did, though we never openly planned it, never
specified when. For a while, we met almost daily.

When I saw him, he was turned the other way. His head was bent forward, still, intent. His hair, already graying, was tied in a dangling ponytail. I think the ponytail caught my attention. It was fashionable in those years, but I hadn't seen lots of them. Not around here. Not in the village. Then I saw the cane.

He heard me approach, but he didn't budge. I knew he was aware of my presence. His large, frozen back… his very stillness betrayed him and yet he took his time, as if stating his lack of concern, before deliberately looking over his shoulder. He gave me a long, blank stare, then he resumed looking down, the tip of his cane digging cautiously among the tall grasses.

"What are you looking for?" I blurted out without introductions. "Eggs," he said. Formalities could be postponed. "Not here," he muttered, his eyes scanning around with a piercing gaze, to me slightly ferocious.

He started walking upstream, pretty slowly, because there was no trail. And he constantly stopped, digging, hunting. I noticed the funny leg. Kind of floppy, it trickled away when its turn came, after the good one had advanced and anchored itself. It unfolded from the hip, dripping askew, until finally the shoe met the ground.

I don't know why I followed him… It seemed the best thing to do, sort of unavoidable. "Eggs of what?" I said after a while. He answered without turning, slightly annoyed. Herons. Egrets. Cormorants (two of them, huge and black, flew by). These birds nest at ground level, sometimes. Eggs for what, I thought, but I didn't ask.

In the following weeks, he taught me everything about the winged creatures thriving by the water, or just visiting as seasonal guests. I was still at the age when such topics could mesmerize me. I'm not sure I ever surpassed that phase. As I said, we met daily. Spring was ripe. Our thing lasted until summer.

When he had come back from war and looked for a job, he was hired as a gardener at Miraya's. He didn't belong here, didn't have a place or a family, therefore he was lodged. Not inside the mansion, of course. He was assigned his own quarters, little more than a toolshed with an outhouse. Fine. He was the kind of man who could have lived in a cabin. Maybe he had. And he had just been at war. Finding his current job had been lucky. I'm sure Miraya's folks didn't regret having him, though. He was knowledgeable, reliable, good.

Carlos was good to me, no matter what anyone might have thought or said. In fact, he was the best, which I'll never tell him. There's no risk for such conversation to occur.

Nothing would have happened, I think, if I hadn't come into the workshop. Had we kept to our strolls, solitary as they were... Nature was so enthralling to him, he wouldn't have paid attention to me, not in the same way. The season would have ended. I would have resumed school.

Maybe I'm wrong. Maybe something was already on his mind when we sat on rocks, waiting for a flapping by silhouette, his cane briskly pointed at the sky. Hiding behind a bush, breath suspended, spying an egret perched on its nest. Maybe I'm fooling myself.

I had noticed that yearning of his, even when we walked in nature, that intensity in wanting whatever he wanted a bit too much. Still, his want wasn't greed, and that set him apart from anyone else I've met. By then, I didn't know.

I didn't know he was different. He had a hunger for beauty but he wouldn't eat, only contemplate. Not religiously. Ecstatically. Esthetically? Ecstatically. The eggs, for instance...

he only wanted to look at them. Not exactly. He wanted to find them. Because it was hard? Perhaps. Because they were hiding, and he relished spying on them incognito, without causing harm, without…

I have been sidetracked. The workshop was in the mansion. He had the keys. Besides his botanical duties he took on whatever his patrons requested, following the genteel notion that all hands should always, obviously multitask. Truly, he could fix about anything. He had keys and was allowed in, though certainly not in Miraya's workshop (more precisely her studio). But not only had he trespassed… he had dared to use the easel, perching upon a stool that enabled him to quasi-stand without cane. He was very skilled at steadying his body, freeing both hands in order to do whatever he wished.

I don't know if the small canvases and the oil tubes were his. Where could he have bought them? No store sold that kind of supplies in the village. Had he carried them in his army backpack? Had he had the nerve of stealing Miraya's?

I hadn't met her. She had left two years before my birth. I had heard about her, of course. My parents had known her. But she had married and gone to live abroad with her spouse, a baron of something. I hadn't seen pictures either, until when I entered the mansion with Carlos for the first time. As I crossed the dim hallway, as I tiptoed through somber, thick carpeted dining rooms, my eyes fell on a few silver frames. No doubt, they contained the girl-of-the-house.

I didn't pay close attention. Was she pretty? Why should I care, since she wasn't around? I don't know if Carlos had noticed the pictures. Must have.

I remember the scar on his pubis bone, huge, shaped like a cross, ropey and bulging. My fingers ran over it many times. Not sure if that pleased him or not, but he never stopped me.

He said he was ten per cent of a man. I was old enough for understanding. Once I asked him which percent I was. I didn't specify of what. He took his time as usual, and then said (I can still hear it), "A hundred. No," he added, "hundred and ten per cent of a girl." He didn't say woman, and I didn't catch the nuance.

The cook found us, on a Sunday when she was officially on leave… But she had overslept in her quarters, which alas belonged to the mansion. She had a tiny cell on the floor where the bedrooms were, and Miraya's suite, huge, stretching in length, its separate chambers (one of them was the painting studio) nested within each other like Russian dolls. A large parlor led to a library, which led to the atelier, which led to the bedroom… the most internal room except for the adjacent bathroom. Well, her bedroom (where nobody had slept during fifteen years) was really kind of remote… Like the orchards, like the riverbed, a separate planet, quiet, cocooned and soft. Sweet dreams, darling.

I am sure the cook is the one who saw us, though we haven't seen her. But we heard a noise behind the door, and then hurried steps. We got up in a rush, unsure of what would follow, and it was too late anyway.

Nothing happened on the spot. I had time to fix the bed as usual. We had barely indented it… we were always so quiet, so prudent, so careful. We got dressed, I went home. Obviously, the cook reported us. I can't imagine why Carlos wasn't fired. I got the thrashing of my life.

Afterwards, I used to pat the pillows, pull the coverlet tight, smooth it down to the tiniest wrinkle. Was I sure no one would check under the bedspread? Or did I believe sweat and spills didn't leave marks on the sheets? Did I minimize such marks by wishful thinking, making them so pale they would not… I was fooled—reassured—blurred—comforted—confused—by the fact nothing major ever took place. It couldn't.

Bland erections, as if his penis remembered something that should happen, but what? Still enough for my entertainment and instruction. After all, I was at the discovery stage. No ejaculation. Never more, he said. Kaput. No orgasm as far as he was concerned. I got bits and pieces, small tokens. Not too bad, for an absolute beginner. Yet, believe it or not, I lost my virginity to his little finger, a millimeter at a time, with just a tinge of pain, and no blood.

From the orchards, if I look at the house stubbornly clamped on the hilltop, so distractedly huge, I can easily identify Miraya's suite. Oh no, she no more inhabits it. I can point at the bedroom's balcony we never opened, at the uncurtained window of the studio, with the naked glass pane I used to look through during poses. I only saw the sky, sometimes clouds. Posing wasn't hard. Anyway, that all lasted so briefly.

I got the thrashing of my life after my escapade (rather my trespassing, my intrusion) was reported to my parents. Why didn't they pursue Carlos? Those were still times when, in such instances, fault was asymmetrically assigned. I had done all that I shouldn't have, since I first talked to a stranger instead of running away. Of course, my folks knew nothing of our strolls, never learned about them. They only were informed of the latest episode, devoid of details. They must have thought refraining from further digging was best.

Luckily, on the evening of revelation my period came in flood fashion. I was bent over with cramps and yet jubilating, as my parents' most horrific concern was dismissed. My ears rang after four of five blows to my temples, duly delivered by Father, nearly unscrewed my head from my neck. I lay in bed, pain sieging me from above and below.

I said I felt relieved, because my not being pregnant was proved. I could hope I wouldn't be killed or maimed, perhaps not hit again. But I was sure I wouldn't be spared severe punishment, interdictions and all sorts of disastrous sequels.

Besides such apprehension and physical pain, I had no feelings. Just a cool, impassive awareness of irrevocability. As if (forgive my banality) I were a small boat at the creek (yes, that's where I wished I'd be) and the ropes tying me to the shore had been briskly cut. No one was aboard, and I wasn't a good boat either. Maybe I leaked (I bloody did at the moment). I had no sense of directions. Boats don't.

I lay still, listening to the drone in my ears (a chorus of crickets, almost a lullaby) when Dad entered the room. I didn't expect him, didn't dare meeting his eyes. I could sense his embarrassment. Mine was worse. Later I thought he might have felt guilty, maybe scared. He might have feared he had hit me too hard, although righteously. Without saying a thing, he left a blank envelope on my bed stand, and went. Afterwards, I looked in. It contained a few bills. I did not understand, just wanted to sleep.

I woke up now and then because of my profuse

bleeding. I was sore all over the place, and numb at the same time, if that makes sense. Strange thoughts crossed my mind, kind of lazily. I couldn't formulate thorough plans. Dad had given me money. A gift? Was it possible? Was it a kind of pardon? Could it…

I thought I'd go to the village in the morning, first thing. I'd buy myself… something. Crazy of me! Still, I was up early. Paradoxically, exhaustion made me restless and edgy. I just pocketed the bills, then rode my bike into town. The air was crisp. I wandered on the main street like a zombie, my mind an empty shell. I didn't even look at the windows. The rail station was a few lights away. I took a train.

I didn't miss Carlos. Didn't think of him much. I had not been in love. Romance had never happened. Nothing tender or passionate was said that could have sparkled ambiguity. Little was said in general, tell the truth. Of course, he had given me an avian education, and in bed he had taught me things… perhaps more than I needed for a start, and less, certainly less. Let's say he had taught me "other" things. Our affair was at least eccentric.

He was good to me in many ways, yet I wasn't grateful. I forgot him with determination and care. When I am around him now, so much later, in such different fashion, I am forgetting him still.

Shortly after I left on a northbound train, Miraya returned. She and her baron-husband had split. Not divorced… They had got a papal something, one of those tricks allowing wealthy Catholics to get rid of unwanted mates and remain immaculate. She came home to her parents. Did she resume her quarters? I don't know. I was away.

Yes, I kept in touch with my family. My folks sent the money I needed for as long as I needed it. They supported me through boarding school and through college. Oh-so-slowly, I understood Dad's envelope was meant for the very purpose it served. My folks wanted me out of the way… understandably so. Still, in summer I came for an annual visit, and so I met Miraya. Well, I saw her. I liked her in person more than in photographs.

She started living with him after her folks died. He moved into the house, but they didn't marry and villagers gossiped. I heard a tale Miraya must have fed to the priest, who zealously fed it to the community. The buzz went, because they weren't married (maybe Carlos already was and couldn't get a divorce) they did not sleep together. Who would care if they did? A whole bunch of people. She must have felt the need of releasing a formal statement to keep reputation intact. Then truth, like lies, has many facets. She had mixed fragments of truth in her lie, I could tell. Only scraps, though, Miraya.

And why should I care? Wasn't the way things had shifted bizarre? How we had exchanged roles. How I had been the girl in her bed, somehow stealing her place and then, when I had vanished, she had… kind of stolen mine? I never told her. I am sure Carlos didn't. Did she hear rumors? My removal was meant to minimize them. I think it succeeded.

We have become acquainted, then friends, after my folks moved out. Now the cottage is mine, and I have come for long periods of time. Ever longer… I enjoy peacefulness, quiet. Always did, even before I fell ill.

I have befriended her first because of the weaving, which is what keeps her busy, besides the cares of the property.

I heard about the large looms that were shipped, in pieces, from wherever she had lived. Carlos must have put them together. Here, they couldn't be found. They are rarities and I was curious, I guess. I showed up at the mansion without previous notice. The ice was easily broken.

Three giant things, wide like king-size beds. Something was already stretched across one of them, a blanket, a towel, a shawl… Without need for me to ask, Miraya sat before it and started picking up threads, as she nimbly guided the shuttle to and fro. I was mesmerized by the complex pattern she formed as the piece imperceptibly grew. I'm easily enthralled, but her weavings, truly, were marvelous. They still are. Now that I think about it, she must have made the dress she wore in the morning. The pale tunic with a shiny glare. Must have woven the cloth, and then sewn the pattern.

She has given up painting. She likes the loom better. Carlos paints in her studio… It all has worked out. He portrays her, as I can see by the canvases hanging around the house. He paints her fully dressed.

I admire her being… perfect? A joy to behold. So refined, and simultaneously grounded. It's a rare combo, and you cannot fake it. It needs generation to ripe. Is it what long-lived privilege does? Education, good manners, good habits pile up so neat and tight, they become a kind of second skin. They fit, effortless, smooth, unobtrusive. The luxury of simplicity ensues.

Unless I'm wrong, and the grounding comes from the ground itself. From the land her family has owned for so long, the paradise-orchard that has cradled her in its womb. Still, I admire her self-control, poise and calmness, wisdom, grace, though I'm not sure her qualities motivate my fondness of her.

The fact is, being her friend I also belong. To the property, the orchards, the mansion. In a way, since the two of us are close, I…

The riverbed wasn't the smartest of choices. Had I told her, Miraya would have discouraged me, and she would have been right. No, the roughness of the terrain didn't matter. Climbing down the slope was a joke and so was climbing up. But there was no shade, and I got short of breath. Perhaps dehydrated. I arrived home in a sweat.

The scar on my head is also cross-shaped. Ropey and bulging but, the doctor said, as long as I have hair nobody can see it. I have hair. It has thinned, not too much. Oh my, the maple trees in my backyard… the sight of those naked branches, the falling… Should I have them cut down to the stump? The removal of spoils… I am not looking forward to it. All this saddens me beyond measure.

There is no final prognosis. Not yet. A number of (a few) things might still happen. I have passed the stage of perpetual anguish about myself. But I'd like the trees to be spared. I know it is irrational.

The birds yapping and fluttering put me in a state, this morning. Like an omen. Not necessarily bad. Undecipherable. Undecipherable for some reason was bad. I meant to ask Miraya about the birds' panic, then I forgot. (It is happening. I tend to forget. Not the past. Current trivia. Details. It is the medication).

And how lurid was the whiteness of the sick wood. How repulsive. It made me forget the birds… I recalled as soon as I got home, and still wondered about the commotion, what might have possibly stirred it. Fallen nest? I would have seen it, for sure.

In late afternoon, when I dragged myself to the back (around sunset I like sitting there with my laptop, a book, a forbidden drink) birds were around, of course, but calm. I mean, normal. My eye was attracted once more by a soft sparkle. Intermittent, minute luminescence.

I'm annoyed to confess I was smashed with tiredness from my morning walk. The way back, especially, had squeezed out my residual juices. Damn it. I had collapsed into the lawn chair, espousing its shape, cozily cradling in. My hands were occupied by my glass and a paperback. Why should I move? Should I? Well, I couldn't resist. I had to extricate myself and go check.

A few fragments of shell were in the grass, indeed. Crumbled, yet unmistakable. Eggs had fallen, were broken. Maybe they had precipitated together with branches. Oh, no! What did the birds think of this odd catastrophe? Had they noticed the spraying of chemicals, just a few weeks before? The obnoxious smell? Then the abrupt loss of foliage, the pathetic stripping, the sad, unseasonable nudity.

Birds are far from stupid. I'm sure they fled when the trees were treated. Must have. But then they returned. And now, again! In spite of the fallen nest, of the smashed eggs, look… I suspect they'll stay until the end. They will stick around, yes.

Around the maples, I mean.

My Beautiful Slum

The minivan drops me at the curb. That's when I realize I have seen nothing. Right, I have totally missed it... the vista, the townscape and all that it does, how it fixes me, how it takes away my thoughts and feelings and returns them clean, pressed, an orderly pile.

I guess it is the motion. The beauty? Oh yes, the town's beauty, so spread, so abundant, so free (well, normally I'd need a bus ticket, today was a bonus). You should try, my dear. Watch the buildings (doors, windows, roofs, chimneys), the cars, tramways, lampposts, the fountains and bridges, the squares with their gardens, the bars with their tables outside. Watch every corner. There is so much to see while you're wheeled around. Just sit back, they say.

Still, beauty isn't all. What makes me breathe better, feel better, think better, it's order. Perhaps, orderly beauty. I'll tell you. Trees, river, boats, seagulls... and people as well, they link in. They are connected, they belong, though they seem randomly bunched, like the toys (do you recall?) we threw into the basket when Mom begged us to please tidy our room.

The tall, huge wicker monster... We liked to overturn it and hide underneath it. It became our cabin, our hut. Mother didn't know. At night, when she arrived, our toys were all over

the floor and we trampled them, sure, as we fought (pretending
or not), ran after each other, leaped, tumbled or otherwise
expressed both our zest and tedium. Poor Mom showed at
the door and she lifted her hands to her hair, short and neatly
bobbed. I held my breath, afraid her bangs would be messed up.
Kids! Kids! Put those toys away! We complied, still screeching,
still sweaty from our wild exertions. Without loosing energy or
speed, as loudly as usual, we grabbed and tossed, grabbed and
tossed. It was kind of fun, quickly done, the room clear and the
basket bursting, lid tipped on the side. It couldn't close properly,
of course.

We ran towards her, then. Someone grasped her legs
in a desperate hug. Not me, who being taller could aim a tad
higher. And I arrived late.

Not truly a fast runner.

Why am I… This city, I was saying, looks like a bunch
of toys tossed inside a trunk with no ratio, uncaring of what is
near what. But then, strangely, each thing finds a place. It gets
organized. It makes sense. The town makes such wonderful
sense to me, when I am in motion. It is like a prayer, you know?
You sit in church for an hour, all is said out loud that should be,
then amen. No need to understand. Or else like a rosary, though
I have never said one. I have one, made of corals. I used to.

Today I have kept my eyes closed until they shouted
my name. Then I've grabbed my suitcase (my old brown leather
bag, yes, still holds) and I have alighted.

Not sure where this area is located. I have never seen
it, but this town is huge. There are tons of outskirts I haven't
set foot in. They look alike, kind of, and I find them just as neat

as downtown. The point is the same. They are a mixture, things collapsed together, loosely arranged, but a magic touch gives them meaning, makes them come alive. This street, for example, this row of little houses…

Quite small. Do I care? A house, any, is more than I've had for a while. It's more than I need. I don't know the effect it might have on me. I anticipate it, not truly with pleasure. With fear? I'm afraid. Does such sentence work? Can you say, "I'm afraid I'm afraid?" I'm digressing… fear makes you do that.

Mine is the second house from the corner, larger than the others. More dilapidated as well. The paint's peeling off. Two boards run across the façade, giving it a patched feel. Don't know what they are meant for… they do not look great. And yet, I will know right away which one is my place, should I get here late, drunk or such. My house is the patched one, bandaged with boards. The one hurt by something, then kind of sewn up.

The house next to mine, on the right side, is empty. How can I… Come on. It took me two seconds, a side-glance. I'm good at this. I wouldn't have sur… All the other huts are inhabited. Did I say huts? Kidding. They are houses.

Only, very tiny. How wider are they than the front door? One more foot per side? No worries. They are little but cute. Now what did you expect? To the left of mine, they are all equal. Same width, and originally—I am sure—same design, same paint on the façade (is façade a face? We're talking of noses here, snouts…) The snouts, I was saying, initially sported the same shade, the entire row, but not anymore. They have been painted over, each one in its fashion, if the word applies. The outcome is a feast of mismatched beiges and grays enlivened by a random splash of pea green. A touch of sour

  Alter Alter

pink. And not a good job at that, nowhere. You'd think a three-year old had colored them in, a large crayon squeezed between chubby fingers.

Each house was its own microcosm through the painting fever (whenever it happened, perhaps not at once). You are shocked I used that word? Yes, microcosm. Wait, you'll be shocked again. I'll give it away… Be stunned for good, darling. I have read tons of books. Hold on! They allowed us one hour per day in the library, all week besides Sundays, and I never missed. Do the math. I didn't quite finish the library. A lifetime wouldn't have sufficed. So much was crammed over those shelves, and not very orderly at that… Yes, sure, there were labels. They named areas, regions, I guess. A map, was it? But I couldn't figure it out. So I went kind of randomly. I jumped around often. I grabbed stuff I was mainly attracted to, I admit, because of the cover.

But doesn't it count? Like a dress! You would care about it, would you? I used to. Now look at this bag! The damn case weighs more than its contents, and that says it all. The old, thick-skinned thing, made to outlive you. But still, it weighs more…

Oh well, no one was in the library. No instructor, assistant, however you call it. Him. Her. It should be librarian, I know. There was no librarian. We were left by ourselves… Steal books? No way. We were frisked afterwards. They let us free and loose in the library. Let me, because I was always alone. See, books weren't popular. Not there.

The above is called flashback, though it doesn't imply darkness, caves, a hunt, someone tailing you or such. The word means that kind of regressing in time… Being sucked in, a vertigo blurring you, slowing you down. The proof, I haven't finished explaining how each house self-painted, almost, uncaring of what you could see, let's say, from above, from a helicopter… of all things. Just walking around, just seeking a bit of perspective. The street in its whole looks a mess. Frankly. Uncannily assembled, but that trick I pointed at saves it… that skill towns possess of self-ordering no matter what. Dear heart, those ill-tinted façades look pretty together if you take a step back, or else wait a moment. They do.

You ask me how people can fit in such boxes, as narrow as caskets. Forgive the comparison. Ah! The things expand lengthwise. Like for Russian dolls, each chamber leads to the next one (without hallways, which would eat up space). Two, three rooms, perhaps? It's more than enough.

Then notice how people are small, here. Proportions work perfectly. It looks as if things have been planned, does it? Here people, as I've learned at a glance, are tiny. Of course, dark. Smooth hair, pitch black, oily. The size includes me, not the hair. Mine is grayish and faded. Now I'm worried this house might be large for me. Too much. Let's wait until I get inside.

Not yet. I stand by the door, at an angle. I seem to be watching the door. I barely see it. I'm watching around, comrade. I'm checking what I need to check, before I get in and lose touch, at least visually, with my new surroundings. Well, you… I… never lose touch, not quite. Can't. You'd be dead. You could… it depends… Why am I telling you?

You know life rules, do you? The basics. Self-explanatory. Life is like a highway, and you watch the road, yes? You scan every lane simultaneously, behind, ahead, right, left. You have the whole picture in mind even in those instants when your thoughts drift away, or you mumble a song, or you aren't thinking at all.

You have a snapshot of everything that goes on, but in motion, because it is always changing. Not just on a highway… that technically was called a metaphor. When you take a stroll, it's the same. When you sit at your kitchen table, eat breakfast. At night, when you slip into bed. When you brush your teeth, you open the door to grab the daily papers, when you walk the dog. Always keep that camera on. Why? Please.

Before I step in and obscurity… I guess power wasn't turned on for my arrival. Of course. Who would have done it? That is where a flashback… a flashlight, I mean, would… There is daylight, still. It will last a good forty minutes. I shouldn't waste time.

I am wasting time. Taking time. I've lowered myself on the steps, slowly, slowly. Stairs lead to the front door. They are in surprising good shape. I've counted the steps, nine even. I mean, odd, but evenly shared. All stairs are identical. I've spotted it. No one painted them over… some might have cracked, crumbled… most haven't. They are solid granite. I ask myself why nothing cheaper was used. Here? Granite?

I sit on the ninth step. My bag (it looks like a doctor's case, but I swear no scalpel is in it, not even a syringe…) My bag sits beside me. My arms, see, cross over my chest, relaxed and tight at the same time. I've a fair sense of how I look… Like someone who'll not get much talked to. That's fine. Don't want conversation. I am listening to something else.

You would be surprised how this works. I've done it, you know, many times. Sit on a front porch, not yours necessarily. Anywhere you can sit without being disturbed.

Sunset's best, then wait as long as you feel like, until dark, if you can. Until silence. The point, truly, is getting the shift from daytime to night. Listen to the sounds, catch the motions, the patterns, the things said, the looks, the whole landscape. It's all organized… It has meaning. You'll learn all that you need to learn.

That won't keep you safe, out of trouble. In fact it could help you into trouble, if that's what you want. Which is the whole point, you agree? What is it that you want.

Right now I'm insecure, and I shouldn't be. It must be avoided. Be uncertain just once, and ill luck will spot you from hell. It will come and catch you. Perhaps it will take time, but you won't escape. You cannot be uncertain. Don't ever doubt. Being wrong is ok, unavoidable. We are all wrong at times, perhaps all the time, and it doesn't matter. We are wrong now and again, but we manage as I have been describing, repeating… all jells, all colludes, finds a place, bunched up in a basket of sorts. If you're wrong, you are average, human. Keep going, do not hesitate.

Right. I am in doubt about when and if I should enter. Oh, I will. There's no alternative. Why am I stalling? Could the place I came from be better… Such thoughts are pure blasphemy. Nowhere could be worse than the place I was in, in spite of the library. No, not even death, although I didn't choose it, not sure why. You see, I'm even iffy as I flash-back. Let's sit on these steps, until I clear up. Pull myself together. I will.

Sunset is very close. My eyes fill with beauty. It's my weakness, I know. It has been my pitfall, my Achilles' tendon…

See? Here's another erudite tidbit. What for?

Beauty, what for? The lawns shine at sunset, like emeralds. Should I look at myself from… Yes, dear, the lawns shine. These houses have lawns, one each. Little patches, identical, verdant… so bright and so luscious, my eyes hurt. Of course, they are miniature. They run parallel to the stairs, on both sides. Thin strip on the right (the façades are slightly asymmetrical), room for a flowerbed. No flowers, grass only. Same thing on the left, a tad wider, kind of an oblique square, askew. The lawns, I said, frame the stairs. They are inclined, smooth, velvety slopes.

How could people who so awkwardly painted their façades tend these pristine yards? They don't. No one cares. No one knows what those slopes are for, how they are meant to look, in whose fantasy. The rain season is barely over. This grass is a free gift of nature, exuberant, juicy and rich.

But how could it stay the right size, how didn't it spill, overgrow? Not yet. The rain season just ended and this is its still perfect product. Don't worry, grass won't overgrow. It will wither and die. The season of draught has begun. It will happen fast. Soon, these patches will be as sloppy as the rest… But we've come at the perfect moment. We are looking at the perfect sunset. All shines, green like emerald, and the street looks beautiful.

How I wish you were sitting here. These stairs are too narrow, of course. No man is at home anyway, not a single one. How do I know? Swear to god, no male is around except for the babies, and an elder invalid or two.

Men will arrive later. That is why I sit on stairs, watching, waiting. When men will return things will change, the patterns I mean, and I'd like to know exactly. Have to. Could this wait a day, maybe? Not sure.

No men. Doors are open and the grass is punctuated with babies. Small women (black hair cut at various lengths, oily and slick) appear at the doors, sit on stairs, squat, stand, go in and out, chat across the lane. Many live in a same house, as tiny as it looks. You see the slope, do you? Those nine steps, the angled lawns. The front door is higher than street level, but we aren't on a hillside. We are in the flats, dude, you couldn't do flatter… it is flat until the horizon, immensely plain. That means there's additional space under the ground floor.

A garage? Course not. There's no access. In the back? Not an alley to speak of… the next row of houses is practically pushing against us. Side entrance? No room. You could not fit a trashcan, not even a child by profile. All side windows kiss other side windows, no shutters, no allowance, no need. Dirty glass panes, old curtains. There is no garage. There are basements, where more people dwell. An old man might be napping downstairs. Tomorrow I'll know.

Women are at ease at this hour. I'm sure dinner is ready, though I do not smell much. It is me. Smell is one of those things I have lost. They say it happens. I have read it on a magazine, in the library. Goes away, the fifth sense, but it could come back. I'm not sure… again, doubting… Well, patience. I won't miss the scent of cut lawns (I loved it, did I?) because grass won't be cut. It will wither.

Women look relaxed. They walk in and out of the houses. They leisurely check on the babies, without fretting. You could say without care. False. They care. They have no reason for fretting.

The babies are resting outside. They are plenty. On the

grass, no cribs and no hammocks, not even a basket like Moses'.
Wrapped in bunchy clothes, serene, they rest and do not slide
down. How come? The slope isn't steep. The grass keeps them.
They are light, very light, don't you...

Oh gosh, I can't look at those kids without feeling
soft. I wish I were like them, which is frankly nuts. But that
peacefulness on their faces, when they sleep... or when their li'l
eyes are open, and look up. The sky doesn't hurt them. Sunset
doesn't hurt them. Perhaps they can't see yet. I don't recall. How
old are those babies? Can't tell. Of course, none of them walks.
They are freshly made. You wouldn't believe how many... That
tells you about how many folks live inside these dens, what
they do all night long, what happens when the men come back.
These babies... dot the lawns like those ceramic dwarves I've
seen elsewhere. Other suburbs I've visited.

But those dwarves are quite ugly. Angels, then? I look
at the baby on my left, in the neighboring yard that, I said, is
practically attached to... Mothers don't mind (I can't tell who
Mom is, they all are). They don't care, and I'm discreet anyway. I
know how to steal a glance.

Peace is what I feel. Please, believe it. I had almost
forgotten, but then did I know the first thing about it? Maybe,
when I was a kid. This is ridiculous. Unexpected, peace lowers
on me. Because I've arrived? Right here? Like a parcel, I have
been delivered. Because it's the end of the line? Yes. What could
be best?

My patched, bandaged house is almost the last one. Or
first. First, last, same thing. Remember? Turn it upside down,
whatever it is. It works, always. Peace, whatever it is, lands on
me a bit too heavily. Crushes me down on these steps. Yes, it

melts me. My limbs and muscles don't respond as fast as they should, as I have taught them to do. Oh, I was no longer slow when I grew up… no more late arrivals. I learned how to hug what I wished, to reach what I wanted.

I don't like this weight in my limbs. I should stop my drooling at newborns. And I don't care for sitting. I've learned all I need for now. Stand up, get in, see what's inside. Check out if the power is on. (It isn't. I'll deal with it, and the phone, and the gas, tomorrow. Tonight I'll sleep in the dark. It will be just restful. I need rest. I need to go through my suitcase…)

In the bag, besides toothbrush, comb, and my papers, there's a snapshot I had forgotten about. I will turn it face down. When you enter, first thing is a kitchen. Here's a kitchen table. I am turning this picture face down. I'll deal with this later. Now, I want to get changed. Let's see. A skirt and a blouse, neatly folded. Damn, I haven't worn a skirt… for how long? Did I have this on?

Matter of fact, I did. The skirt is sky blue, bell shaped… There's a lot of it, more than needed. But I pull it up and it stays. I'm wearing it, pal, because I have no choice. I need changing. I am starving for another skin… if it's old, re-used or recycled, fine. The blouse has small flowers. Good god, did I have this on? Matter of fact, yes. I am wearing it. It fits. Bit more than it should… I mean there's too much of it, too.

Too much of the house. I know already, though I haven't set foot beyond the kitchen. Bedroom, is there one? There must be a bed, a mattress at least. Maybe some bed stuff, maybe not. I don't have pajamas, and who cares, and I'm very tired. I haven't stepped out of the kitchen. This house is too large for me.

I am getting cold. Slightly. I won't be… I know the
draught season has started. It will be as hot as hell, a question
of hours. But the rainy season has washed through the house. It
has soaked roof, walls and foundations. Chill has bitten down to
the core, the core of my house. Only time will get the chill out.

Tonight I am cold.

Outside it feels nice. Without thinking, I have stepped
outside. I have stretched myself on the lawn, exposed,
unprotected. I shouldn't, I know. Left of me, the baby I have
watched earlier (still there) is a patch of fabric, light, dotting
the green. On my right is the currently abandoned house. Yes,
empty. A vacuum, I should call it.

This slight bent I'm on doesn't bother me. I like it, in
fact. The soil is damp, wet, but the grass is warm. I look at the
darkening sky, with scratches of purple, dissolving. They'll be
gone in minutes. If someone looked down, now, she'd see a
kind of pattern. A blue skirt, all spread like a bell, parachute,
swimming pool, maybe? A flowery blouse, arms wide open, like
a cross.

That's me. Looking beautiful.

Tanked

Daniel was on top when I heard rasping at the door. Knocking… lightly, that must have been what she meant, but didn't quite dare. The closed door intimidated her. She wasn't accustomed to barriers, especially not between us. I was still flesh of her flesh, was I?

She might have thought a doctor was in. That would have commanded her respect, her obsequiousness (all things uniformed did). Maybe more than one doc, a few, and nurses as well, performing a procedure of sorts. Such a doubt would have stopped her in spite of curiosity, eventually sent her back to the hall. She would have sat on the sofa, waited like a good girl.

Was she listening, then, for a scrap of conversation? Whispered orders, to confirm her guess? A sound? Surprise! We didn't make any. I was so weak I could barely breathe, certainly couldn't exert my muscles and simultaneously vocalize. For the time being I had given priority to motion. Tension, to be exact. My entire energy concentrated in my open arms, fully extended, wrists locked, fingers clamped around Daniel's fingers.

Hands had to be out of the way. Lips, tongue, genitalia… No hands, no. Maybe later. Now I wanted him crucified on the cross of me, and the other way around. We both arched like a double bow, rose and fell, every inch of our skin making contact. Besides hands.

Mute… We hadn't exchanged a word since we'd met, meaning three fucks ago. No way to tell time otherwise. Curtains were always drawn, lights always turned on, only lowered by a dimmer a nurse shifted on occasion, not sure why. I assumed Daniel had always arrived during nighttime. I couldn't be sure.

He was clean, his skin smooth and dry, rubberlike. The air conditioning prevented us from sweating. Its low, constant buzz isolated us in a kind of capsule… the room was that tiny. Yes, we could have been in space. Anywhere.

D had no body odor, not a distinctive one. He had a hospital smell, bland and faintly sweet, sanitized yet vaguely rotten. The same smell I exuded, I guess. We could have been two Barbie dolls out of the same box. His head was fully shaved, a hint of regrowth pleasantly brushing my palms. Not now. Hands weren't allowed…

I sighed noiselessly. Her presence outside had returned me to earth, interrupting my flight. I was cooling fast. Alas, Daniel caught my fading vibe. He slowed down, then he lay beside me on his stomach, his face niched between my shoulder and ear. I felt the whole of him, not only his penis, deflate. I hated those aborted rushes, miscarried ecstasies. Yet our present posture was the closest to tenderness we had ever shared, our fingers relaxed, still entangled, unwilling to let go. We said nothing. I waited for my mother to leave.

She should have gone for good, not just to the adjacent waiting room, to allow for Daniel's exit. Would she? Were we stuck? Would we be discovered? Not that such eventuality troubled me. What could happen that hadn't already? Could I be punished? More? About him… if he took the risk of ignoring regulations to come frolic with a female patient, he mustn't have much to lose. I shouldn't overworry for Daniel.

How did I know his name? He hadn't spoken a word since fuck one. You assume it was penned on his gown, do you? I never checked. He dropped the thing on a chair, by the door, as soon as he came in. And I couldn't have possibly… Had I wished to get up, I couldn't have. Not walked, not…

Daniel yawned and I lost the train of my thoughts. My eyes wandered around, then fell onto the crowded surface of a minuscule bed stand. The glare of my amber ring (such a cute perfect egg) caught my gaze, as if concentrating all brightness the dull, somber room contained.

And I suddenly knew what Mother came for. The amber. She wanted it back. She must have looked for it without finding it. Suspected, then realized I had stolen it. Borrowed? Giving back the ring was the way to get rid of her. Could D slip into the bathroom, hide awhile? I'd let Mother in. I would give her the ring with due apologies, then I'd ask her to go. Should I tell Daniel…

How did I learn his name? I didn't. I don't know how he calls himself.

I know I have fallen on a plane.

Not "from" a plane, dummy. On it, more specifically into my seat, seatbelt duly buckled. I remember being sick, a part of me desperately wishing for help. A doctor! Isn't there always one on board? This sure was no exception. By the way, even a nurse would do. Someone help me! I was sick like a dog. I remember, though I can't feel it right now. Those states evaporate. The picture fades out and only the caption remains.

Your brain stores a few stickers, brief descriptions, adjectives such as "awful," "unbearable." A simile, "like a dog."

I remember I was vanishing, liquefying yet strenuously trying to stay seated, hoping no one would notice my (temporary, I hoped) defection. I had decided, after all, I shouldn't get aid. The sicker I was, the more paranoid I became, for some reason. Terrifying scenarios accompanied my vertigo, my nausea, my cold sweat, my tremor. I shouldn't attract attention. Shouldn't let them know, or I'd get in trouble. They'd send me… Would lose my carry on. Should I… At that point, the subject of this frantic monologue left the stage.

When I reemerged I didn't recall who I was. Not my name, though it mattered little… I could have dispensed with it, but I missed some general information, any kind, for operative purposes. Knowing nothing about myself made it hard to imagine a possible course of action, decide what I'd do next. I didn't dare moving. Luckily, I was still sat and buckled.

I knew I was in transit. Sort of in between, which implied as well after and before. Yes, that much was clear. Slowly, the idea of a vehicle came forth. Getting that part right reassured me. Grounded me, so to speak. Only later I puzzled out that I was in flight. An airplane! Now I had a where. Not a when.

"I" was coming back, though. "I" (yet unnamed but present, comrades, present!) was on a plane, transiting from an origin to a destination. When? Oh god. My vertigo promptly resumed. Many references fluttered through my brain (which felt as mushy as a pudding someone forgot to refrigerate). I mean, I saw bits and pieces of facts, but I couldn't tell which belonged to the present. Didn't know which ones I should grasp, hold on to…

When was I? The search was exhausting. I gave up. Meanwhile, words were on the tip of my tongue, struggling to come out… in different languages. Yes, I apparently could speak more than one, and such skill seemed redundant, embarrassing. I was frightened of expressing myself in the wrong idiom, irrationally convinced my mistake would have had nasty consequences.

I tried to pay attention, listen to the words others spoke. Why hadn't I yet? I saw people talking. Uniformed ladies and guys stood by a metal door, busy in conversation. Hostesses and stewards? Was it a door? It looked like a gate. My sight must be still blurred… As hard as I tried, I could not properly read those folks' lips. Wait… Then I realized they didn't make sounds. No one, nothing did. All was perfectly mute. We were fish, sealed inside an aquarium, underwater.

I gasped for air. Then I screamed.

I must have dozed off. I thought I was recollecting the events that led me to this place, putting them in a row for your perusal. But I have fallen asleep. For how long?

Daniel is gone. No surprise. It has happened before. We have napped after sex, like two cherubs. I have heard him snore… gently, like a cat, each time… then I have snoozed away. When I later awoke, he had left. Then he came back. I can't measure time in between. He is my watch.

Now I'm all alone. I feel like a half moon. A sick sickle. I shall sleep again.

Then I see her. She is sitting on a metal chair, in a corner, close to the curtained window, far from the bed. Far from me, yet staring at me like a bird of sorrow. Could you stop, Mom? Cease being yourself, could you? Of course I don't ask her.

She still has her coat on, neat and tight, wide lapel emblazoned with a cameo. Winter coat, color of petroleum. Her hands clasp her purse. How like her. Her hands… I glance at the bed stand, a chaos of bottles, sparse tablets, empty boxes, tissues, powder and spills, even a tube of lipstick… What a mess, and yet I can tell the amber is gone. Mom! The scream scorches my throat. It hurts like spitting blood. Did she hear me? I'd like to sit, prop myself upright, but I can't. I am furious.

She stands. She looks uncertain. Her features betray anxiety, then panic. Should I pity her? She is coming towards the bed with such tiny steps! Unbelievable. Why does she walk that way? She'll never make it on time.

I am dizzy. Come here, for Christ's sake! Where did you put the ring? Why did you… I know it's hers. I know how much she cares. But she could have asked.

Where do you go when you lose consciousness? When we sleep, we dream. We go into dream world, kind of a separate realm, yet not indecipherable. When we faint, have a seizure, fall into a coma, where do we… What's there when awareness fails us? I wish I could tell.

When you fall unconscious you don't die, don't vanish… Well, the "you" does. The "I"… I told you how long it took to come back, on the plane. So the subject of the conversation (of the monologue) is cleared out, but something remains. Quite dense. Struggling. Aching. Laboring. Sweating. Trying to make it back to the surface from the very bottom where it seemingly crashed. From the gluey, muddy hole.

Something, not "a" thing. The article is missing. Multitude. Legion… don't they call the devil that way? From hell, multitude tries to climb, crawl, creep up the abyss walls. Legion is determined, strong, frantic to become one again.

I remember such effort, such desperate tenacity. Such absurd optimism, until all that pixilation reached my upper edge, made it to my skin pores, and I opened my eyes. Tell you the truth, I like those crumbles of being, all scattered, all nameless, more than I like myself. They are so innocuous. So pure.

When he first showed up, I had just returned from one such. I mean seizure, fainting spell, whatever they are. Still trembling. Still marveling, contemplating the sight of those little spots swimming towards reality. Starlets, fireflies of mine.

Quietly, he pushed the door open. When he dropped his hospital gown, he was in the raw. When he lowered himself upon me, I felt refreshed. Happy, about that? Of course, I kept it shut. In my mind, I knew who he was. I had already named him.

Daniel was a prophet. He climbed out of the pit where they had tossed him. Food for lions. A penance of sorts. Who decided it, and why? Those questions never get answers. Climbing out is what fucking with Daniel feels like. Here, now. Only, I'm not sure I want to.

I have stolen a bunch of her jewelry, piece by piece. I have sold it within the hour, you bet. Had to. Atrociously unfair. I know how much she cared. I know I'm unforgivable. I deserve what I got. No excuse. On the contrary, Mom, please accept my apologies.

Still, do you remember Cornelia? Don't look at me that way. Those tears in your eyes, always on the verge of spilling, yet stuck. How I wish you would cry, period, instead of giving me the lightning and thundering.

Cornelia, I was saying. I don't recall details. Don't recall much, I'm not even sure I liked the gal, truly. But she went out to some balcony, her kids in her arms, right and left. She said, "These are my jewels." A proud thing, maybe a rebel thing, a great sort of thing to do. Mom, you could have said nothing of the kind. Did you ever hug me? If you did, you sure weren't proud.

I stole the amber last. Didn't have time to sell it. Damn! You got it back. So be it. Would you let me sleep? I can't, unless you leave this room. Come back tomorrow, maman.

The last time I saw my girl, she looked fine, well groomed and dressed up. We played all afternoon, drawing on huge, multicolored sheets of construction paper. I had bought the largest pad at the dollar store. And markers, and scissors with rounded tips.

I had stuffed a whole bag of mess inside my carry on. Mess is ribbons, barrettes, candy, safety pins, stickers, make-up, you name it. I pulled out a golden braid, slipped it through the loop of one of the scissors, knotted it, then hang it around her neck like for a professional seamstress. Same for myself. I had found scissors with plastic handles, mine red, hers pale pink.

First we drew trees, flowers, boats, houses, people and every beast we could think about. "We say a thing, we draw a thing," I had told her. She loved it. She kept singing with her little bell of a voice, the prettiest of sounds, "Now we make… a birdy!" "Now we make… a lelephant!" "Now we make… a duck!" First her pitch went up (now we make), then it remained suspended, like a kite, then came down like gentle rain. Time flew.

I was about to leave, and we hadn't started cutting yet.
Can she sense how long are my visits? All the same, between
two shuttles. She said, "Mom, what's the most important?" I
chocked. "Uh…" My brain raced and felt mushy at the same
time.

Is it love? No. Believe? Believe… Faith? Come on,
she isn't yet four. Loyalty? Is it me coming no matter what, no
matter where from, going to the dollar store, bringing this bag
along? Isn't this the most important? Must be. Yet, shouldn't
this change at some point? Could it?

Hope? Is it? Why are you asking, doll? Because you
already know? Are you testing me? Haven't I failed yet? Then
something lit up. "You mean, what's the most important among
these, like… houses…" "Houses!" she said. She was smiling,
her fingers smeared black, tenderly caressing the contour of her
drawing. "Houses, flowers, eyes, faces. Birds and trees," I said,
still uncertain. Maybe we should just enumerate. Maybe she
didn't care about a first prize.

Now I did. "Baby," I asked in turn, "what's the most
important?" She pensively scratched the top of her head.
"Fish," she said. I sucked my cheeks, puckered my lips, making
tiny invisible bubbles, sending mute kisses her way. She laughed.
So did I.

Bird Of Joy

I'll never forget the joy when the sledge took up speed, and we realized we had made it. Yes, we were together and safe, headed no-matter-where as long as it was away. The animals were draped on our laps, braided in a harmonious wreath. All looked good at the moment.

I had only provided the rodent (what was it, small sable, rare weasel?) and the bird, which I stubbornly called "dove" but didn't look like one. Maybe a hybrid of sorts? Slender, curvy, its plumage strangely mottled. I was fond of it. Carefully, I brushed its wing with my fingertip, afraid it might fly. But it seemed at rest, wrapped around the rodent, this last wrapped around the flamingo. The flamingo necked with the piglet, which cuddled with the pelican. A medium-sized turtle and a fawn completed the set.

Thus, the Queen had procured five pieces… No wonder. She was older, stronger, smarter than me. But she loved me, and it was all that counted. I reciprocated her feeling.

Pure joy. Exuberant, bubbling, it was piercing my skin like a bunch of arrows… what a pleasant itch. The world around us looked pristine, sparkling with contrast. The Queen's raven hair, with her white streak (a tattoo making her unique, unmistakable) almost glittered. My hair, less dramatic, was sufficiently in tune. Plain white… I'm the albino gal with faded lashes, invisible brow, freckled skin, eyes the color of chowder. Way less striking, I admit, than my partner. But this morning I matched her, like a minor chord, allowing the main theme to unfold and resolve.

The glory of our success wasn't mine. I had only followed orders. Waited for nighttime. Ignored the rain. Picked a lock. Unplugged the alarm. Stolen the bike with the large front basket. And in the meanwhile didn't think, didn't flinch, forgot about fear.

Wasn't it easier than I thought? Not sure, but the animals gave me courage. I wrapped them in a towel Mom had given to me. Rough cloth, a bit prickly. So thick, it would feel like a nest, I figured, and keep them cozy. Also, dull the sound if they'd make any.

And I liked the towel. I carried it with me like a talisman. Printed in gaudy colors, it portrayed the province Mom came from (as I did). The island that doesn't exist anymore, one of the first regions to sink. When general evacuation was ordered, Mom, among a few others… Mom refused to leave, yes.

As I said, the Queen's older than me. More experienced. She could be my mother, or else a big sister.

All the doors were marked. As I rode, I kept my head down, trying to focus on the pavement in hopes of keeping my balance, pedaling as fast as I could. But I saw red patterns with my peripheral vision.

Blood? Bullshit. They wanted us to believe it. Just

pretense, intended to scare us. So much like them, such trickery
of dubious taste. Who knows what they used in order to obtain
the dark crimson, the irregular texture… Didn't look like
spray paint. The effect—creepy—because of the quantity—
massive—the mere repetition—imagining—as if—a legion of
demons

> Legion
> Legion
> The ominous word
> Lambs

A lamb would have been nice. None was around, I'm
sure, or the Queen… She collected a fawn (still a ruminant), a
flamingo and a turtle, a pig and a pelican. While I contributed
a rodent (small mammals are covered, then) plus a nondescript
bird. Enough for a start. I mean a segue.

Nothing pulls the sledge. Animals, as I said, are safely
inside. We are rescuing them. No engine, either… I doubt fuel
could be found anywhere. Sails are up. The wind nicely blew
when we started. It still does and (the Queen says) won't cease
anytime soon, while the rain subsided at sunrise in favor of this
icy sparkle.

Will the joy resist a downpour? Be there after darkness?
Why worry? I am getting the most of the present moment.
Who cares about later, as long as the creatures are fine? Warm
and breathing. Alive.

Past the south gate, straight on. I see where we might
be directed, though the land-shift is happening so fast that
geography's a guessing game, unreliable. The isthmus might
have already split… we are fighting with time.

Destination is hypothetical, yes… News have been
polluted, and then frankly withheld when those in power
no more needed compromise. We are not sure about what
happened south of the isthmus. We know about the shifts, the
huge slide of tectonic plates, faster, faster. And the sudden
collapses, sunken islands and coasts.

This is history already. As both transport and media
started failing, people busy with evacuation and losses…
Why am I saying… Doesn't anyone know? Just as all know
who made profit from tragedy, those who do not care for
tomorrows, who—I must have heard it somewhere—"sing and
dance at the edge of the chasm."

How appropriate a metaphor… if you think of
the isthmus, cracked open. Only, they (our local looters and
buzzers) don't sing or dance. They stay inside, snug and comfy
as (surprisingly, after such massive melting) this terrible winter
has come. It is killing many.

Not them. They have sieged themselves into mansions
the telluric rumpus has spared. Double walled, armed sentries
polka-dotting the stuccoed façades. What do they do inside?
They consume whatever resource they have sacked from
terrified us, as they promptly realized we'd soon lack it all. They
are hastening the end. Isn't it a classic scenario?

Indeed. Just like war. But no war is needed. They have
kept us at stake with a hastily declared Martial law. They have
weapons. We, the common people, were taken off guard, busy
escaping, relocating, grieving. Adapting. Now I guess we have
adapted to them.

Not quite. Some of us still believe this might not
be global, as rumors (what is left of news) pervasively
imply… Some suggest this state of things might be somehow

circumscribed. Could there be a haven somewhere? An area, a region, a town where a different story took place? Where perhaps people shared? Helped their neighbor.

To be honest, what we care about are the animals. They (they) are eating whatever still moves. They are killing what cold hasn't yet. They have weapons. They shoot and devour. They'll end up feeding on their kin, I'm afraid, but I'm not contemplating it yet. Does the Queen? No. Slaughtering animals is as bad as it gets… You can wait for the end, or else you can trace the finish line.

Sanctuary. One must exist. We will make one, as soon as we get out of reach. Maybe we won't be pursued. Maybe (this is why the exhilaration) we are free. If only these pets could survive.

Sanctuary.

Colors aren't absent, just pale. The change has been gradual and still, within due proportion, quite fast. Those sparse fir trees aren't black. Look again. They are barely soaked in sepia, enough to remind you of green. You hold on to this chromatic suggestion as for someone losing her sight, glad for whatever hint…

We are losing our sight. Collectively. Slowly. These poor conifers are mnemonics of green, like a picture book damped in water, ink melting away. We have got months of downpour, I said, yet the fading colors (this change in refraction, this shift in the air carrying light waves, in light waves themselves, molecules falling off sync, fragile mechanics destroyed) isn't due to the rain. But rain and the fading are symptoms of a same dysfunction.

That's why pig and flamingo aren't pink, though

I picture them so… I imagine them shiny and throbbing, psychedelic, cartoonish. They are a slushy caramel, naked and vaguely indecent. It isn't their fault.

*

The above (some of it) is a lie. Well, almost. I was trying a larger scenario, something less domestic, less trivial, I could frame our breakout within. I was making it up while joy filled my lungs, fueled my imagination. You heard me think, that's all.

Let me put it straight. Then, of course, believing me or not is your choice. I know, once you lose credibility… Listen. Some of the above is pure fantasy, and some is the truth.

We have run away, sure. And we are running still. There's no "they," or there is but only consists of the Institute administrators, directors and staff… aka nurses, instructors, counselors, evaluators and guards. Yes, it is a correctional facility. Also, a kind of rehab. It is private, which allows for blurred contours. You are right, we were basically inmates and we have evaded. Which means we'd better get going, try to pass the border in haste.

True, we have been out of touch with the news. No internet, no television, no phones. Sounds like extreme measures, but I have told you where we belonged and those were the rules. We got filtered information… which is a contradiction in terms. What is filtered doesn't inform. It's pre-formed. It's a fairytale, like the one I freshly concocted. Only, way more boring. We stopped paying attention quite soon.

The island sank and Mother did stay. Kataria and I had left already, ferried to the mainland, come to the capital, started fooling around. Mother had given up on us years earlier. I suspect she was relieved when we went… we were quite untenable.

We weren't relieved about Mother's. It was very sad, and I rarely think of it. The submergence occurred a week before we were caught. Maybe… It's the last piece of news I recall in full Technicolor, so to speak. The last I remember, perhaps not the last I heard. Our arrest wasn't immediate, but after the sinkage things seem to collapse in my memory. They also dull away, as if a giant eraser were blotting them, making a whole mess of the page.

This rag, yes, belonged to Mom, and the map on it pictures the island. I have always liked it. I snapped it from where it was hanging, damp and soiled, when Kataria and I left. And I grabbed a pig… the bank Mother kept on a kitchen shelf, piggy shaped. How naïve she was, how predictable. I snatched it on impulse, wrapped it into the towel. We crushed it as soon as we passed the corner, filled our pockets with heavy and unpractical coins. Just enough for the boat. Then I crumpled the towel, shoved it into my pack. I have it still. Some things stick.

Truth can overdose you. Let me take a breather. The air is so crystalline it fosters contrast, I said. You know how, do you? Light draws a thin halo around things, and makes edges shine. It's all about contour, like meticulously cutting figurines with sharp scissors. Cutting them one by one, and all becomes clear. I am thirsty for neatness. It rests my brain.

Kataria, the Queen, is my sister. She isn't older. I am. We have always been close. She loves me and that makes me happy. I reciprocate her feelings. Is she smarter? Hard to say.

I'm supposed to be the smart one. Yes, she's taller and prettier, which takes little effort. She has the raven hair with the white streak, since birth.

My diminutive size comes with my albino looks, two facets of the same malfunction (should I call it so?) Mom and unknown Dad have passed down. That ticktack bomb apparently chose to explode just for me, hardly brushing Kataria on the side. Her discoloration (a star on a racehorse's brow) is all she got. No symptoms so far.

Looks didn't truly matter in the life we led. Not back in the island, where we grew up unleashed, single Mom unable to rein us. Even less, since we came north and urbanized ourselves, so to speak. Or maybe looks counted… they came in handy. All considered, I think my freakish allure made me fit for the role I played. Without need for tattoos or piercing, I was naturally outlandish and so was Kataria, in a different way. We kind of completed each other, the sisters.

Yes, the weather has changed. Don't know about shifting land or continents cracking… Such things could have occurred after the island sank. Explanations were contradictory and vague in the immediate aftermath. I heard theories I didn't quite ponder. Facts were shocking enough.

Then again, we were caught, and news was withheld since. It was sparsely injected, so futile and fake, any average brain would just block it. Queen and I lost track of the world. We stuck with inside trivia. But, no doubt, the weather has changed. It has rained for three hundred and sixty-five days. I don't know what's up with the oceans, out there. We will find out.

I have picked a lock, stolen a bike. The plan wasn't

Kataria's. I instructed Kataria, and as usual we acted in sync. Which is what makes us unbeatable… see, this concerted soul we possess, how well we harmonize. Not a glitch. Few people can function this way. They all diverge at some point and that is when the mess occurs. While… we are unison.

How come we were ever caught? Think about it, please. The island was gone. That must have upset us, rattled us quite a bit. Oh, it must. But today! All went slickly like butter on toast. Where's the towel? I'm burying my face in it, breathing… Not a scent, not even an animal one. Are we losing olfaction as well?

Nothing was painted on doors. At dawn, while I rode… The rain had miraculously stopped, as if this all were planned, not just by the two of us. As if our story belonged to a larger frame, I was saying.

Wait. While I rode, I looked down, slaloming among pond-sized puddles, wary of muddy spots. Aiming at the driest segments of pavement, as if wading on rocks. I barely noticed the town. It slid by, a vague, slightly frightening movie. I had missed it for a while… seen it only in pictures or within narrow window frames, at a distance.

I had not been *in* it, submerged by its vastness. Now I felt like a goldfish tossed out of its bowl and into the sea, scared, agoraphobic, at loss. I purposely didn't pay heed to the landscape, if not to make sure I'd get where I should. I had foreseen disorientation. I had figured out every turn I'd take, over and over and over. Believe me, I had rehearsed. I had had all the time in the world.

Nothing was painted on doors that I know. Why would it? It's a piece of fantasy I gathered from Bible studies (the most boring of our forced routines). No crimson, especially. Not that

I could tell.

Oh, the petting zoo. It saved the day and got you going.
We had grown up with animals. Mom didn't possess
a farm, but we were surrounded by them, and of course
by wilderness. Then, I'm the perfect size for horse riding,
which I have done for cash since I was twelve. Going to the
hippodrome at the break of dawn, providing the animals with
the first bout of exercise, substituting for busier and better-paid
jokers.

Of course, we had cats and dogs. Mom was permissive
with pets, though she didn't raise a finger to help. Poor thing.
The two of us were a handful. And we didn't need her. Our pets
were our babies. We had canaries and parakeets. Goldfish and
turtles. Baby goats, ducks, and rabbits until they came of age. The
entire array of rodents… guinea pigs, hamsters, mice, and even a
squirrel. We stopped short of monkeys and snakes. Such exotic
stuff costs a fortune, and Mom would have lost it for good.

Oh, the petting zoo, pathetic and dear. It was in a shed,
the shed in one of the courtyards. It stank. I wished they had
assigned some of us to the cleaning. We would have done a
better job. Barely supervised (one guard for the whole place,
which had various sections, not all cages and playgrounds
simultaneously in sight) we had an hour to sit and play, cajole
and caress, feed a leaf of lettuce or a bunch of seeds, stay put,
contemplate.

The visits were optional. You'd sign up on a list affixed
in the cafeteria. You could sign for every day of the week,
if open spots were available. Someone would pick you up at
the appointed time. You'd be escorted to the place, then left
on your own. A guard would be at the door, dead bored. Or

daydreaming, perhaps.

Weren't they afraid we might damage pets? Hurt them? You are kidding, pal. None of us would have. I mean none of the inmates. They (the instructors and such) knew it perfectly well.

As time went, the animals got scarcer and scarcer. A sign, but of what? Budget cuts? A slack in therapeutic impetus and educational zeal? Or was something occurring outside, in the larger frame I was mentioning? Extinction. So fast? That would sound farfetched. But animals wound down to nothing. We have salvaged whatever was left.

Sleds with sails that wind can propel on land (even on muddy, slimy, swampy country roads) don't exist. The car was in the shed where we had left it on the fated morning. A miracle. A can of gas was nearby. The car's body was rustier, the sunroof wide open and stuck. No big deal, as long as it wasn't raining. It would not for a while, said Kataria, licking the tip of her finger and then feeling the air as fishermen did, back home. Wishful thinking, but she's a glass-half-full gal.

We will get as far as the gas does, unless this trap dies for a different reason. It slept in the shed for more than two years (thank god it was spared the rain). But it started off the bat. Boom. A prodigy. I heard you. As if this were planned, as if it all belonged into a larger frame.

My lies… To put them all straight (I might forget some, it's a work-in-progress), I am the one who can't see colors. I used to. I still grasp a little. It's a work-in-progress.

*

Why is the gas never-ending? Because we drove smoothly, always in the fourth gear. By the sun, it's late afternoon. We still have a quarter.

The air is cooling. We are wearing all clothes we possess. We have blankets, one each. We are heading south, right? Strange. Slight traces of snow mark the roadside... as if maybe, over here, rain had not been so constant or had ceased earlier, time for the barometer to drop a few grades. We aren't ready for driving on snow. We are ready for nothing, in fact.

Food. Oh my. I have left room for improvisation, have I? I did not... What about money? Overall, I didn't think further than to where gas would lead us.

At the wheel, Kat is whistling a song I recall. The title escapes me, which of course drives me nuts, but keeps me awake.

The animals, I said, are wrapped around, across and within each other. We have shifted them from our laps to the dashboard, where they squeeze against the windshield. The glass pane is chilly, but I guess adhering to its surface makes them feel safe. Otherwise, the wind blasting through the sunroof might blow them away. Oh, no, they aren't tempted to escape. Not even the avians? Well, I'm not surprised about pelican and flamingo (they are lazy, having been captive for ages). I avow that I'm stunned my bird didn't attempt a move. But I'm glad.

While Kat salvaged the petting zoo, I got my samples in nature, in the flower patch beside the building. I hurried there as soon as I passed the door, before heading towards the street, and I spotted them in minutes. I suspect the bird might be wounded, though no injury is visible. Both of them must have been paralyzed by dampness, freezing, hibernating almost. That is why they've allowed me to catch them, easy, as if they were stuffed toys.

We'll take care of them, promise.

I've been watching the needle. I have nothing to do besides glancing at things, the landscape, the road, Kat's profile, our seven puppies in turns. And the dashboard lights, obviously. All this staring takes incredible effort, and it keeps me alert.

I have been watching the needle, my heart steady and strong… I know how to keep it that way. I have worked on it, yes. Got an early start, maybe when I decided to ride horses without much of a training, also knowing how frail are my bones.

I was sure they would hire me, because of my size. Subs for jokers are often teen and female. There isn't a bunch of competition. Still, my looks don't exactly open doors. Didn't, in the island at least.

My looks helped, indeed, the heart-fastening techniques that I learned so well. I know how to make myself unattainable. Deaf to comments and mindless of stares, impervious to those feelings (judgmental, demeaning, hostile) people don't express, yet are just as lethal as poisoned arrows or stones.

Well, the steadying of innards (heart… guts, stomach, liver, you name it) turned useful when we arrived in town and started fending for ourselves. I had developed a pretty cold blood, without knowing it.

Picture this. Before starting my day (sometimes before getting up) I hang my heart (the muscle) with safety pins. Here is one. Visualize it. Watch metal pierce flesh, come across, hook a rib (they are tiny, like fingers). I repeat it all three more times… yes, the thing looks pointy but has four chambers, correct? You need to secure them all. I proceed with millimetric precision. It is painless and foolproof. Before heading outside, I clip my heart in place, metaphorically. Then I am invincible.

Was I saying? I have been watching the needle with my usual poise, and yet with great focus. I don't want the engine to sputter, spatter, exhale. Not of its own will and not in the middle of nowhere. I want to find a place, get there with the last drop of gasoline, park.

Here we go. A small lateral path leads into the forest. Here is a picnic area of sorts. We avoid benches and tables, spread a blanket out on the ground, save the other for cover. It must shield nine of us... but these puppies are small and so am I.

The silence is thick, and quite beautiful. Kataria has stopped singing. She hasn't said a word for the last several hours, which is usual and not at all worrisome. Her face is as calm as the moon. Is there one, by the way? The thinnest of slices, a beginning.

Suddenly, the joy has resumed. Paradoxically, my weariness has summoned it back. What am I tired of? I did not drive a yard. Well, I've done things... biking in the morning, then looking, which is really tiresome, alas. Still, the joy has resumed. For no reason.

But the lack of food slaps me in the face, a well-deserved blow. Idiot. Why didn't I?

A cramp stops my brooding. Yes, my period is coming. No, I couldn't predict it. It isn't periodic. Goes away for a while, then catches up on me, like a private Niagara Falls, when it so decides. Tonight, why not? I look at the moon's nonchalant, subtle wink. Can't believe it might be responsible for the flood about to be expressed by my uterus. I haven't thought of pads either. All of this seemed collateral.

I am sure the Queen and I could stand a day or two. Fasting, I intend. We have, more than once, though not quite intentionally. But the animals! How could I have been so negligent?

The Queen's whistling. She's soft. Still, she startles me. She holds the pig in her lap. I am sure she trusts I… Does she expect me to make a basket of goodies materialize? I burn with humiliation. Chill out. I will explain. She will understand. We will think of something. She will.

She has pulled the box out of her pack without me realizing. Looking forward to a little fun, then. I feel dampness between my thighs. Though I am sitting, the pain in my pelvis pulls me down. I am tired again.

*

Celia has asked me to bring the make-up kit. It is small, a diminutive box I mindlessly lifted (an eye-sees-hand-catches reflex, spinal level) at a dollar store, shortly before the arrest. Didn't get a chance to try it out for the last couple of years, but they let me keep it. Doesn't come with a brush. Nothing pointy I could stick in somebody's eye. It comes with a miniature pad of foam. Why did I feel an urge to snatch it?

Well, the spread of colors, of course. Rainbows are irresistible. I don't think Celia could tell the shades apart, even then. They must have already looked quite mushy. For sure, she can't tell them now. But, when she gave me instructions, she insisted for me to get this item so much, I understood she had a thing in mind. Today, while I drove, she specified what.

Here we go. I think it is time, before daylight entirely

fades out. I know it doesn't matter, but I want to see what I'm doing. I will start with a sedate, natural layer, complementing the buff of her freckles. Olive green on her eyelids. Periwinkle and gray close to the temples. A charcoal line under her non-existent brow. Hazelnut above it. She is pointing to another and yet another tab, like a four-year-old. I think she wants them all.

Then, I'm not going to stop. Her skin has grown smoother. I hadn't noticed yet. It is silky, slippery and cold. She is relaxed. I guess the small circles I draw with the tip of my fingers soothe her. As she asks for more, I'm going baroque, painting her like if she were a goddess. Or an Egyptian queen. Wait, that isn't possible. I am the Queen. She wouldn't want this to change.

I am painting as if the halves of her face were butterfly wings. That she would like. Of course, she has kept her eyes closed and we haven't talked. We don't have to.

What Celia has been telling you isn't the truth. Well, it partially is and I don't wish to contradict her. Let me fix a detail or two. I'm younger only in the sense I came out first. She was conceived earlier, therefore she sat on top, so to speak. I was closer to the exit. With twins, things get confused. First born, first conceived… strange primacies.

Celia often discussed the point. She might need some kind of logic to explain the gap between us, so wide. Dizygotic twins aren't identical, but our case is extreme due to her illness, which doesn't depend on delivery, or on any suffering she might have endured while lagging behind, in the second row.

The thing is inherited, and because we didn't belong in the same egg, we got distinct sets of chromosomes, genes, alleles, whatever. Perhaps. The malady isn't well researched yet.

It has quite a peculiar name.

I'll let Celia tell you.

*

The name of my syndrome is unspeakable. It belongs to the (German? Dutch? Scandinavian?) fellow who figured it out. It sounds like the intermingling of two animals that don't quite go together. I don't ever speak it out loud.

Rare, uncharted maladies (when they become popular, they usually get a mouthable moniker) are named by the scholar who found them. Which is kind of unfair, because what do discoverers do? They detect some cells under a microscope, weirdly acting or looking. They observe a few patients, collect data and symptoms. It's not as if they climbed a mountain, stuck a flag on its top.

Diseases should be named by those suffering them. Those living with them, dying or not. There's a bunch of sufferers, kid. How should we choose one? Whoever first tells the story. The first one who speaks. Then it is his sickness. Her story.

*

You've digressed, Celia. And I know you don't care about the illness' name. Or about the illness, in fact. It was barely a deal until colors faded. Your small size and white hair were cool, or so you let us believe.

But the loss of sight poked a hole. I'd say "I know," but I can't imagine. Loss of tone, loss of contour. The fuzziness drove you crazy. For a while you didn't tell me. I had noticed you spent lots of time touching pets.

But what is a petting zoo for? Sitting there, smoothing the back of delighted suckers, trying to surprise the reluctant ones before they'd run away. Still, what caught my attention was how long you tormented the turtle. The poor thing must have hated it. You always cornered it against the retaining fence, held it captive and lingered on its scales, tracing them as if trying to memorize a code of vital importance. Your doing didn't look affectionate, not even pleasurable. I started wondering.

*

I was losing my sense of depth, Kataria. It is scarier than you would imagine. It makes moving around hard and frightening. That is why I was terrified biking, this morning. The ride took the breath out of me. When we met at the shed, I thought I would faint. The animals kept me going and, of course, knowing I'll rejoin you.

That is why you did all the driving.

Sorting among my lies… Stop using that word, Your Majesty. It's the truth we are delivering, all the way through. We are unwrapping it, taking our time, a lingering kind of pleasure. We are peeling it like an onion, one transparent sleeve at a time.

*

Still, I was about to point out the animals were—are—stuffed. Who'd believe birds would stay put on the dashboard of a convertible, sunroof wide open? Not even lazy ones, flamingos or pelicans. Were they flesh and blood, I swear they would fly. And Celia's simil-dove would surely lift its quite skinny self, even drugged by hunger and cold.

The animals are all-too-real, draped around each other in a harmonious skein, arching like a bridge, part on Celia's lap, part on the dusty soil against which their colors (even dulled and worn) luridly stand out.

But their hues are well the only thing that stands. These are stuffed toys, I said. Double-stuffed. Mother made them, filling them with scraps of old stockings (way to go, Mom). Then she stuffed as many as she could in our backpacks when we took the road. Not that she would miss us, as Celia pointed out. But I guess a mix of blurred sentiments flooded her. A gluey, sticky compound of regret, remorse, guilt, nostalgia, sprinkled with a tad of self-commiseration, made her eyes swell. No, she didn't cry. She'd have had little chance of getting our attention. But she frantically pushed these creatures she had made inside our luggage. We didn't protest. Didn't care.

We did later, at the facility (should I call it so? I guess there's some kind of ease in that peculiar lifestyle). Celia brought them to the facility, and she was allowed to keep them (not much harm can be done with plushies of that size). The five Mother gave us, plus two Sis had already packed. Correct, they belong to different lineages. Celia has made the rodent herself, and the nondescript bird of which she is so proud.

Lastly… but this is my theory, still to be verified. I don't think Celia (as she might have confessed already or will soon enough) has poorly planned our evasion, leaving a number of crucial factors to chance because of distraction. Whatever she did was… on purpose. I might not be the smartest, but I have always been able to read her mind.

*

I have dipped my finger into the avalanche, the thick, lively stream poured out of my womb. I have done it quite often. Blood is one of the most beautiful things… This looks very dark. It is stringy, dense, full of clots, as it happens when it breaks the dam after a long hiatus. It is old. It has been withheld. The young, scarlet supply will follow in a matter of hours. This is my dark blood, packed with nutrients.

I have smeared it over the tips of my fingers, both hands. I am tempted to lick it off. Wait. Here is a better thought. I will start with the bird. Sip it from my pinkie, love. Gently. I'm sure this babe's no predator, doesn't feed on flesh except for some mushy worm. Blood is different, though. Please…

I'll try to feed them all, one by one. They look drowsy, kind of inert. I wonder why none has reacted to the smell. Rodent, piglet? Are they losing their sense of olfaction? I am not sending this bounty to waste.

Do you recall Grandma and the bear? I am asking Kataria. It's a story we used to know. Nothing to do with us or the present situation, but it still comes to mind.

*

Nothing to do with the present situation, but I do remember. You are the one who loved this tale when we were much younger.

Grandma knows her time has arrived. She leaves home on a crisp morning, all clean and dressed up. She goes out to the wilderness, to the place where she knows the bear will soon come. She also knows her first son, the great hunter, will follow the bear. He will shoot the bear, bring the spoil home, roast the meat, share it with the entire family. But the bear in the meantime will have gulped… This is what Grandma wants, to be eaten by the beast her offspring will feed on. You loved that story, Celia. But you don't have kids. Never will. So this doesn't apply.

She has long overshot her average lifespan. There is average only, no exception. She has long overshot the longest verified lifespan. She doesn't believe in miracles. Everything had plateaued until her sight started deteriorating. Then, all went pretty fast.

She has to take her pills every twelve hours. At the Institute, they dispatch two doses each morning, that's all.

*

I remember the porcupine, all of a sudden. How did Mom get the brushy part? Wait. The memory is vague. We must have been really young. But it comes to me, I mean to my palm. I can feel it against my skin. I am not inventing it… I can see the color, dark underneath, light on top.

Mamma had gotten it wrong. Porcupines are the other way around. But she did it that way, I'm sure, because she used an old broom for the prickly part. Then she made the body maroon (was it felt?) for contrast. It looked like the negative of a photo, correct? We were too young to tell.

The porcupine was my favorite. I recall sleeping with it for a while. Recognizing it in the dark was a joke, was it? Too bad I have no idea of where it went. I believe I remember it losing stuff… the inside, I mean, whatever Mom used. Stuffed animals tend to fall apart at some point, an inherent weakness. Although, these are holding up pretty well. But then we aren't children anymore. We have developed a different kind of relationship… more contemplative.

I keep my eyes closed, focusing on that tiny, far, sunken porcupine. It went down with the island, of course, wherever it was, bottom of a closet or else the municipal discharge. I can visualize it quite well, but here's what happens. How strange! It goes double. I see a mirror image as well, light beige with dark prickles, as it ought to be. Two small porcupines, facing. This is what I see.

*

Not sure of what Celia has in mind. She has placed the toys in a circle. Rather, a rough oval. Seven puppies isn't much. I wish we had more. She had to distance them quite a bit, in order to close the loop, although she's pretty small. Yes, I wish we had more.

Previously she has pampered them at leisure, in turns, smearing her menstrual blood all over the place. Now they are nastily marked crimson, rust, brown rapidly veering toward black, though those changes are lost to her (and they don't matter, of course).

She has wiped her hands with the towel she always carries along, then she has pulled it over her face, where she has kept it a minute or two as if inhaling fiber by fiber, thread by thread. Now, remember the outrageous spread of eye shadow I have plastered on her skin. Add blood. The result is an indescribable mess.

And quite festive. There's no mirror around. None in our backpacks… by the way, no hand mirror's allowed in a place like ours. The car has none either (worry not, you can drive without them, I swear). But she hasn't asked for mirrors, and she won't.

She lies on her back with the ease of one who's getting a suntan, letting herself bake without a care in the world, lulled to sleep by a gentle murmur of waves. Look at her, and you'll get the picture of a lazy, blessed summer noontime at the beach.

Besides, it's getting colder and colder. I don't know how her body can master that kind of calmness. Yes, she has always been in command. She has a will of steel. But curling up, shaking, quivering should be reflexes, right? How can she control them? Unless she already…
Seen from above, she must look like the Virgin of Guadalupe cast in her rounded thing… A halo? Looks like a shell, for what I recall. Or a vulva, perhaps. Doesn't the Lady stand on a slice of moon? There you go. We got one in tonight's sky, quite charming but insufficient, a bit stingy, somehow. Are there angels around the Virgin? They must. Celia has several winged creatures with her. Her bird, in particular. Elongated, she says. Skinny and frail, just like her.

The bird that she calls a dove is a crow. Honestly, that's what it looks like. She has taken enormous care making it (oh, so many years ago). Wings and legs are mobile and fastened to the body with buttons, which make the thing look fancier but less birdy, alas. More equine. More human. She has painted white zigzag stripes over the black fabric, like flashes. I suppose they are for decoration. Perhaps, also a tribute. To me, I mean to my mottled mane.

Anyway, the bird is a crow. If it could croak its little

song, you'd recognize it, no doubt. Someone should break this silence. I can't.

Let me step away. Close by, to the parking lot. Is this one? Scrawny grass has invaded it. The concrete is either submerged or crumbling away. Is this due to the rain? Looks like, though it must have stopped a bit earlier, here, than it did in town. The air is dry and very, very crisp.

Yes, the petting zoo exists. What was I saying? I have stepped away, I mean to the car, and I am fumbling with the damn sunroof to see if I can possibly unstick it. I am freezing. I'd like to get in, push the seat back and rest. Sure, the petting zoo is real. Only, we haven't stolen a thing from it and it doesn't host fawns, flamingos or pelicans. There's a pig, and a turtle to which, right now, I'd wish to come back. Sit down where Celia used to, run my fingers through the creases and spikes of her rocky carapace.

Shut my eyes, imagine those are mountains and valleys, a landscape. The earth seen from above. As if I were on an airplane and could—with my hand—from the inside—ideally—brushing—the closed window—giant—below.

I have never been on a plane. But the ferry, when it is far out and the island recedes while the mainland, the other side, closes in.

The ferry, in between

part 6

LONG DISTANCE

THE CROSSING

They call me Nina.

Not Niña… that would be Spanish, and the name of
a boat. Geez! I don't care for boats, ships, whatever travels
on water. Not a bit. Hopefully, your story is on dry land. No
seafaring…

Just kidding. You know you can say whatever you want,
do you? Sit down while I make you a cup of coffee. Then you'll
tell me everything. Yes, whatever you want.

Spain is spread all over the place, but invisible. A bit
like Africa.

Africa is a purple shadow on the horizon some folks
say they see, and you screw your eyes and see nothing, then you
feel bad, but still you see nothing. It is strange voices they catch
on the radio, strange songs they don't understand but, they say,
make them cry. Only, they are heard offshore, during nighttime,
when the fishing crew goes far out… and I'm not around. In
the middle of night I'm not on a boat, for Christ's sake. I am in
bed.

Relax. Why do I put the crystal ball on the table? No,
do not look inside. Leave it covered, please. Relax. What's the
matter? Hear this? Coffee's coming up! I'll be back.

I said Africa. Invisible. Smell of jasmine brought all the way from Tunisia, impregnating the air like a cascade of sperm… Forgive me. I speak plain. You also should. Coffee's ready. I said Africa. I said smell, radio waves with lost songs (songs that make you cry or else scream with longing). I said purple shadows and wind. Wind, of course, covering it all with a yellow patina of sand, straight from Egypt, straight from the Sahara. Were we not on guard, the sand would just bury us, like Pompeii's sleepers after the naughty blast. It would bury us alive.

Now, what's the problem, my son? Either you tell me or I'll tell you. Do you want me to tell you? Let me get the cards. Here's the sugar. Help yourself. What did you bring me? Let's see.

After the word "see," she has closed her eyes. Look at her face, rough and stony. Large features. Coiled hair, heavier than a crown. Her hair, patched white, snowed upon the raven as if out of spite. The white, white. And the raven, raven. No middle ground. Her hair, mottled like night and day, evil and good, luck and misfortune. Small golden rings at her ears, punched in at birth, long ago.

She was saying Spain. Spain is all around, but invisible. There's no Spanish here that we know of. We do not speak Spanish. But the names pursue us. Sanchez, Rodriguez, Torrez, Lopez, Martinez. Those, of course, are the rich. Names of places, La Mesa, La Costa. Villages, rivers, wells, castles.
Her nickname is not Nina, as she claims, but Niña… at least was in the beginning. La Niña, the girl.

Where does this kid come from? How did he land
here? They must have sent him from the pension where he's
certainly lodged.

And how much should I charge him? These are not
the ones I take from. I only charge those with bulging purses. I
can see the cash even when they don't carry it (and they usually
don't). I can see the wallets even if they come straight from
work, rolled up sleeves and soiled fingernails. They cannot hide
money from me. No one can.

Those come in to know where the water is (without
paying for the rhabdomancer, who costs more than I do and
is often wrong. I know where the water is). They come by to
know if Esquire such and such they're about to call is angel
or devil. What about the judge? They wonder if they can trust
the veterinary. If the tumor spreading in their groin must be
cut out. If the railroad will pass through their property. If they
should sell the land, or buy more.

Boys like this one, here, always want to know the
same thing. If she's cheated on him, if the baby she expects
is another's. That I probably know, as I know the rest. How?

That's easy. I'm the only one in the island. I know because they tell me. When you've heard everyone's secret, there's no secret left. I only need to add two and two, search my database. I file the information in the correct folder and the folders are here, in my head. Nothing goes lost, believe me… They tell me what they don't tell the priest.

Why? I give absolution but don't ask for repentance, that's why. And I'm no informant. I don't give out their secrets. I shift them around and pull out a snippet, now and then. Nibbles, crumbs. Hints and innuendos. Nothing bad ever happens because of what I said. Because (you got it, right?) I say nothing.

Grandpa has given her the nickname. She hasn't known her mother, who's died while delivering her. She is number ten, after nine brothers. Of course, she's come at the wrong moment, wrong place… there's been a shipping error. Who's made the mistake? Who's to be held responsible? No one. Still, her poor mother died because no girl was timely sent to help her raise nine boys, who, as soon as they walked, were out of the door. On the fishing boats, working the land, to the market fair selling fish, eggs, milk, produce. On the motorcar, when Father bought one.

But then they were back and they needed feeding. And she fed and clothed them all, and in the meantime she was pregnant. She has been pregnant until she was dead. Nina came too late. She might have remained where she was.

Nina knows it.

Grandpa calls her "the girl," in Spanish, because he has been in Spain. Indeed. He went to fight a war, then came back to fight another one. The girl grew up in wartime. She was very young when it started. Grandpa was old, too old… after less than a year, they sent him home. Dad and all nine brothers were called, even the kiddos. None of them returned. Not all were declared dead. Some were lost, but no one returned.

Now, this is the point. She knows where water is, but she hasn't a clue about her lost brothers. Did anyone add two and two, anyone figure out she's an impostor? No. But she knows she's one.

Brothers went to fight on the northern front, on the continent. Not on the island, that no war ever reached. You could argue her powers can't go as far as the continent. It is foreign land, in a way. There are limits even to the irrational, the paranormal. You cannot expect her sixth sense bridging over the strait, can you? Tides and wind would sweep it. Brothers vanished in foreign territory when she was young. She has forgotten them. She never had any.

That is why she's not La Niña any more. Please, oblige, call her Nina.

He has blond hair, that makes him foreign, I mean from the continent. Northern. I will know more by his accent, when he'll manage the guts to start talking. What he has to say really bothers him, really burns him and makes him feel ashamed. What the heck. But I shouldn't be worried. It can be one thing only… is the baby another's? Very probably, or he wouldn't doubt it. If he doubts, he has a reason for it. Unless jealousy eats him for fun, unless he's jealous of shadows, sick at heart. But he's not. That kind has a damp madness in the eye this one hasn't. His eyes are dry, shifting, vague. He doesn't know where to start. Coffee, hopefully, will do him good.

If he keeps mute like a fish, I'll know what I'll do. I'll reach over, put my hand over his. My right over his left (I need my left for the cards). I will keep my hand over his (mine is so much larger), steady and firm, heat seeping down from my palm slowly, slowly. Until his tongue will melt…

In the meanwhile, if we don't want to grow old at this table, I shall shuffle the cards and pull something, just for a start. Here we go, Wheel of Fortune.

The war lasted forever. She lived with her grandparents. Grandma took care of her, but she preferred Grandpa. Not sure why. Twice a week, he went to the continent (the main harbor in front of the island, and few neighboring villages) to sell fish and produce. He had a small motor van, a covered motorcycle, handy for carrying stuff. It was fun going with him in the motor van. She always wanted to, and they let her. Grandma never said no. Grandpa never said no. She always went.

Until when they got stuck. On the continent. The news was that the front was lowering, coming down, creeping south bit by bit. The radio had chanted it for days, weeks, months, but the girl didn't really know what that meant. Grandma did, and sighed. Grandpa did, shrugged… The news said the front was receding. As the war was about to end, it sank at a precipitous rate. It fell, closer and closer.

Without warning, the ferry service was cut. When they arrived at the dock with the motor van, they found uniformed people and a sign the girl couldn't read. Grandpa couldn't either, but the soldiers explained. She wondered where they had hidden the ferryboats. They must be all docked somewhere, but she couldn't see them, and the sea looked empty. It looked suddenly terrifying. She stared at the sea, wiped clean like a desert, the island all alone on the other side. Lost. Unreachable.

Grandpa grabbed her by the hand and climbed into the motor van, clattering with boxes and barrels. He rode along the coast to the next village, spying the beach while he drove. They went village to village like a Joseph-and-Mary. Nina didn't know why. It was late, after sunset, when Grandpa stopped. He had found what he wanted. He grabbed her by the wrist, crunching it, pulling hard. She ran as fast as she could. Grandpa had spotted a rowboat on the beach. The oars were inside. Before she could think, she also was.

Grandpa stole the boat. They left the motorcycle behind. Grandpa rowed all the way to the other side while she sat behind him, always watching his nape, always, always. She kept watching Grandfather's neck, the back of his head, because she couldn't watch the sea. She was scared out of her mind, also colder and colder. But she didn't move once. Grandpa rowed for three hours, never turned, never said a word. They arrived in the middle of night.

I am wrong on this one. There's no girlfriend involved. No fiancée and no baby. This boy… I'm not sure about what he wants. Maybe he doesn't know either. Maybe he's just killing time. Maybe he wants me. Let me think about it.

Meanwhile, I have pulled an entire set. Seven cards. Here we are. The Star (it means solitude). The Priest (well, of course, he's always nosing around). The Empress (it is me). The Fool (it's the client). The Tower (it's the problem, the thing that's befallen him, the thing he can't shake off his shoulders). The Wheel of Fortune (the first one I pulled, it means change is occurring. Or it must occur). Lastly, the Chariot. Indecision? Whose?

What does this babe want? Whatever he wants, today I'll give it to him. Today he'll find it.

News of the missing brothers arrived, one by one, inside yellow letters. Their house is a bit off the road. There's a gate (sort of… it doesn't close), then an unpaved alley, dusty, leading to a ramp of stairs. Their place is on the hill, with a little patch of terraced vine and a few olive trees.

The postman hates it. He always puffs when he arrives at the door. In fact, he starts shouting as he passes the gate. He singsongs

Grandpa's or Grandma's name, kind of casually… truly, out of despair. He's not going to climb all the way, please.

Nina knows. She has gotten into the habit of running down when she spots him, then she grabs the mail from his hands. She has sprouted in this last couple of years. She has become very tall. Boney, of course. They all are. Food is scarce. She's down there in no time, back up just as fast. The postman is grateful.

Normally, there's not much to deliver. Since the war, a bit more.

They have received ten yellow slips in three years. Father won't come back. No brother will either. But the thing has occurred at once, with the very last note she carried upstairs… Grandpa waited on the front porch (Grandma never came out). She gave him the envelope, closed. He didn't look at it.

He stared at her face. Her forehead. He stared and said nothing. Then he tore the paper, and she read. She already knew, of course. Little brother. Then they got inside and had dinner. Nothing should be done. Nothing urged.

The next morning she saw what had caught Grandpa's attention. What he had seen, the night before. In the mirror, after she washed up, those streaks of white on the raven, those patches of discolored hair.

And so this is the problem. He doesn't like… Right. That happens. At least one per village that we know, and a few more we don't. There are ways, as long as… This kid is uncomfortable, very worried. What does he want to know? If it is a disease and will pass? If he should lie? You bet. If he should still marry? Well, he is asking me… imagine…

Please, Nina! Say something.

Sure. Travel, son, travel. Let me throw a voyage in. See? The World… Foreign lands. Go, son, where nobody has a freaking clue. Leave your folks behind. Avoid the church and the army. Stay away from doctors and priests… Board a train, a plane, even a boat. Move! Only, you came in the wrong direction. Don't come here, it won't work. Get back to the continent. Head north.

I will charge you nothing at all.

Don't feel like it. I… need more coffee. Nice kid.

Grandpa died as soon as the war ended. He passed quietly, in his bed. Afterwards, Nina and Grandma went to the sanctuary in the mountains, on a cliff overlooking the strait. They had to climb on foot, slowly, slowly, Grandma shuffling her feet and leaning on Nina's arm (she was so tall, so strong). It was a sunny day, also windy, as they all were. The wind carried sand, and some reached into their eyes that got teary, but it didn't matter. They were going to light candles for Grandpa's soul. Grandpa deserved candles. They lit ten of them, then they stopped in front of the Virgin.

How gorgeous did she look… Pitch black, her skin a piece of coal, shiny. Her features, so fine. Baby as black as she. Their mantle was gold, silver, studded with myriads of jewels, like stars. They couldn't stop looking. Nina wished she could be that beautiful. But then, you'd need to be a goddess or a baby god.

The statue had landed on the beach, right under the cliff, probably after a wreck. The ship lost god-knows-where, only the wooden doll had floated ashore, quietly swimming, mom with her kid in arms. Relentless, unstoppable, like Grandpa on their stolen boat.

Our lady with her enigmatic smile, lips sealed over some untold secret.

That is something else I don't know. Where the Black Madonna came from, how she floated ashore. Who she really was, because she must have been… someone. I mean, someone else. But I have no clue. I am an impostor, all right.

        I said Africa. This small town we live in was founded by the Egyptians. I have not made it up… the whole thing is etched on a bronze plaque outside the City Hall. Not that many have read it. Those who have don't recall. The story doesn't stick, doesn't mean much.

        To me it does. This once was an Egyptian colony… Very long ago, the plaque says, they came all the way from Africa in a frail, tiny boat. Who was in it? Men? How many? Did women come along? One, at least. Sure. Must have.

        As soon as they arrived, they built a village and thrived. They did. They became us. Sure thing, a woman at least came along. In the boat, right? Young girl. Sometimes I think I have known her.

Postcard

I have lingered on the dock until I started shivering
with cold. First, it was kind of pleasant. I had no wish to come
back, especially not for dinner… but I needed to, or else they
wouldn't start.

They'd sit, rigid, trying to keep nervousness under
control, the impulse of doing something tensing their muscles
while the soup would cool down, jell up and get slimier. Then
Father would explode, crying something like, "Where the hell is
he? I'll kill him as soon as I see him." The idea makes me laugh.
I mean smile. Am I cruel? I don't think so.

See? I'm already gathering my backpack. I'll be just a
bit late. I will probably make it before Father screams. I will just
have caused an ache, a few stomach spasms. Nothing serious…
the soup will be gulped more rapidly, to appease the cramps.
Then we'll leave the table and vanish, some outside, Mom at the
sink, moaning. Dad, of course, at the bar. And I might return to
the docks, though the dampness at night is on the thick side.

My bones tend to stick out. I am too thin. I don't like it.
I don't want to look frail, that is why I wear long pants and long
sleeves. Also to stop the cold, true, from reaching deep down
into my chest… The wind blows all the time here, sometimes

from the sea, sometimes from the mountains. All the time, but I like the wind.

Grandpa has left for the island on the ferryboat. He will not come back till next winter, if he does. Although he's strong like an oak tree, he is old. I've watched the boat sliding away, getting smaller. Truly, I wanted to see it disappear, but I'd be late for dinner. As I said, I don't care. Still, watching the boat wasn't vital. In fact, it irritated me. Sentimental, was it? That I am not and don't wish to be. It would be as inconvenient as being thin. I'm not looking forward to thin, frail and sentimental. Well, the opposite.

I am looking forward to embark with Grandfather and the fishing crew. Make money. Even better, join the Navy as he did when he was young. Possibly, don't come back.

The sea has the dense thickness of petroleum and its color, a greenish black, almost vicious. Water in the harbor is scary. It's a glue that gets hold of you, gulps you down, makes you vanish. Stinky and soiled, but still kind of pure, if that makes sense… Whatever you toss inside, even all the trash of the world, water eats it, devours it and remains pure. How? Well… The ocean is like god, see what I'm saying? I mean, like a confessional. You throw evil in it and it swallows it, and it returns it clean.

Where the boat cuts them, the waves change their color. In the ship's wake there's a turquoise wound, bleeding blue instead of red, a whole scatter of gems with frayed, foamy edges. Seagulls peck as if it were whipped cream. Where does the turquoise come from? Where did it hide? How does it squirt out of the petroleum mass? It's a mystery, of course. The sea has many.

I stare at the cut as it stretches, far, far, towards the horizon. As it lengthens, its closer end heals. Yes, the surface quickly seals up… water sews itself back in haste, then it feigns indifference. Loss of memory, oblivion. It is magic, again, how it all gets smoothed as if nothing happened.

There is much to learn here, though I couldn't say what. I watch the wound open, stretch forwards, then patch itself. Seagulls (crazed and drunk) peck at the pluming edges, paparazzi running after a royalty. They are nobody, those birds, just crowd. In a bit, the dolphins will join them. I like them better, though they fit into the same category, loud, inanely jocular. Dolphins are good for nothing but to tear nets apart, ruin the fishing.

*

I remember the fan falling on the floor. I heard the sound. It was embarrassing. How it resonated, how it echoed, probably because the silence was thick. Gluey, tight, compressed, because of the incense. Incense squeezes your throat, fogs the air, makes the silence so dense it breaks, then, like an explosion.

The fan fell during a moment of stillness, the priest quasi-transfixed in one of those crucial poses, hands up, chalice held high, host above it, crushed between his thumb and forefinger. You see? The priest looked at the chalice in awe, as if it were the face, the head of someone and the host were a crown, a halo, a top hat…

That could be distracting, I know. It isn't. Thanks to the priest's stillness, to the silence, the scene is almost frightening,

I swear. In that fragile expectancy, in that tremor, I heard the noise. A gunshot… it could have come out of one of those tiny pistols ladies keep in their purse. Those abalone toys, carved with cute little flowers as if they were hand mirrors, or combs. As if they didn't carry bullets, small as you wish.

The fan fell from a purse, indeed, and the noise echoed through the nave. The girl stood (we all did, it was consecration time) in the last pew of the genteel enclave. I stood in the first row of the non-genteel zone. Too close. The fan slid right under the pew, towards me. Not far. Those things do not roll. They don't have much of a life.

The fan, so to speak, tried to escape but had nowhere to go. It lay, half hidden. I bent without thinking, picked it up, gave it back to the owner. While I lifted my head, my eyes met with the brocade of the gown she wore… or was it silk? It was turquoise, shiny, and it almost blinded me.

I haven't been in church since I turned twelve. Only women and children go, plus the rich men. Lower-class males with common sense grow out of that stuff. I did. The above is just an old memory. I don't know why it came back.

Let me tell you, instead, about Grandfather's birds. He has three of them on the island. I haven't seen them in a while, but they have been around for ages. I guess they live old, like people. They looked wrinkled and scrawny from the start… at least, since I can recall. Still, they haven't died.

Two parrots, quite large, one more than the other, and louder. Well, they are both loud. They scream intermittently. Unpredictably, you never know when. They scream when the whim takes them, not for food, not for any reason. Inspiration comes suddenly, and they yell at the wall, the ceiling, nobody.

They yell quite convincingly, the same things they've learned I'm not sure how. Did Grandfather teach them? The same stupid things, "You rascal," "You old drunk," and "The hell with you!"

The huge one, larger and redder, has a thing with hell. Sometimes it goes on forever, as if reciting a rosary bead by bead, "hell, hell, hell, hell, hell, hell…" with a singing cadence, as if lulling itself to sleep. When it goes on and on, the smaller and greener intervenes, as if it couldn't help commenting on such amazing news. It does sharp coughing sounds, sort of, "yes, yes." Then it reiterates, "yes, yes, yes," from the very back of the kitchen, where it usually hides, shier than his companion. More modest.

Grandpa lets them loose in the house all day long, but at night locks them to their perches, tying a chain to one of each bird's feet. They consent to be caught and shackled with a little ruffling of wings, only formal. They endure being cuffed as if they were putting on jammies… Don't know why Grandpa does it. Maybe it is just a ritual, reassuring.

He has a raven as well, younger and more recently acquired. Huge. It doesn't talk. It barks like a dog. In fact, it lives in a kennel Grandpa built in the backyard. Alone, like a Montecristo, a rebel of sorts. Grandpa feeds it generous chunks of raw beef. That crow eats more meat a day than we do in a week, minced and soaked into Mom's ineffable soup.

Grandma died long ago. Grandpa lives alone. I mean with the birds.

Let me tell you about Venice. It is far. I don't know if I'll ever be able to see it. You have to get on a train. Maybe several trains, I am not sure. Anyway, it is a town by the sea, like this one, with docks and a harbor. Truly, I have no clue.

All I saw is a framed postcard Mother keeps in her bedroom, face down over the closet. Black and white, yet you see stones shining. Buildings pierced like lace, sparkling, foaming.

There's a square. The buildings, I mean, make a square, full of pigeons. Wouldn't you expect seagulls? They are pigeons, same kind of guys, followers. A sea of pigeons fills the square, punctuating those sheer, lacey palaces. If I close my eyes, I see color… silver, gold and green. Perhaps pink. I don't know why Mother keeps the card in a frame, why she has it turned down.

Grandpa has gone to Venice, he says. He was everywhere with the Navy, so it is probably true. The ships went throughout the Mediterranean, past Gibraltar, around the tip of Africa. Dock after dock, Marseilles, Barcelona, then Tunisia, then Greece. Grandpa's memories are vague. He's fond of details, but they kind of hang in the air…

He insists he has visited Venice more than once. I have asked if it was beautiful. He was hazy. He mentioned islands, a lagoon. Each time I bring up the subject, he tunes into the same song… the lagoon, he says, was eerie, wild, magical. It was dawn and the island came out of nowhere. The fog was very dangerous. Aren't those islands creepy? They are. I've asked about the square, other things I heard mentioned, bridges, gondolas, carnivals. He repeated his nonsense about dawn, fog, the lagoon, the island.

*

The deck's pavement is slimy. Dirty. Foamy. I have cleaned it over and over. I hate this rag and this bucket. I'm on all fours, and I don't like this position. True, there's some kind of comfort in looking down, eyes fixed on this little portion of landscape, those boards that, close up, become almost beautiful. Not irrelevant, as they look from high up. I mean, the most you look at something, anything, the most…

I hate this posture. I hate losing control of who might hang over me, impending like a bird of prey. On the side, or behind me… I'm aware of the presence, but I'm not allowed to stop and look up. Well, the fellow is checking on me, of course. On my job, that is cleaning. I don't like my job.

Mother had that beaten dog look at the sink, after we finished eating. She might have had the same at the stove, before eating, when she warmed up the soup, and those morsels she tossed in at the last moment. Only, before eating I didn't notice. Hunger might have distracted me, or maybe I was late. Afterwards, when she washed the bowls and the spoons, I could see the glare of her sadness, like sweat. How can you guess people's feelings, when they turn the other way? You just can. Course, you can tell things from behind. I wonder what my back says when I'm folded over, rag in hands, rasping off this filth. Nothing, I hope. I hope my back stays sealed.

You should keep at the job, Grandpa said, and I will, at least for a season. Though, I already feel it has been forever. This posture kind of wipes time away. Kneel down, bury your face and you'll figure… as soon as you start, it becomes forever. I swear.

*

He was right. Grandfather, I mean.
The island loomed out of nowhere. My heart jumped

in my chest. We had not seen it… I hadn't, though I was leaning against the rail, getting washed by the prickly night air. I had lost track of time. Dawn was close, but fog blurs you. It makes you lose touch with reality, a bit.

There's a lot of fog here. You need expertise to dare venturing among these waters. Our captain, obviously, is a pro. So is the crew. I'm the newbie, and I don't count anyway. I am just cleaning deck, cabins and stove. Home, I never cleaned a thing. Mother did. Now I feel I'm becoming her, and I don't like the feeling. But it's needed, I think. I'll keep the job for the moment.

After I cleaned the kitchen, last thing, I didn't go to my cabin. I came here for a smoke. Nothing, nothing was visible. How can they keep the route in this fog? But the air was cool, rich, invigorating. I let it wash over me. Clean me, for a change. Then tiredness won me. I was so tired, I couldn't get to my cot. So swamped, I couldn't move.

Now the fog shreds away and the island appears… so flat, it seems fake, a cloth laid on top of the waters. A few houses, a church in the middle, a steeple so high it doesn't make sense, piercing through the sky like a needle. The bells ring with unbearable fracas. We have docked in what must be the harbor, I guess.

We will stay a few hours, what for I don't know, but we are allowed on land. There's a bar where most head for beer. Someone has already come out. No beer and no wine, they say. Only a clear alcohol brewed here, on a neighbor island. Strong as mighty hell.

I'll pass, thank you. I haven't slept and I'm already light-headed. I need to take a walk.

My feet bring me to the only target in view. There are

steps to the church entrance, and the door is open. The bells
called for an early mass. I get in. It is cool and dark.

A small person in black, a woman, lights candles. I like
watching the flames. A rosary will be said before mass… it's the
usual routine. Only, who will attend? How many souls are there,
besides us, the bartender, this old gal, the priest?

I was fooled. A hamlet hides behind the church. The
island might be larger than it seemed on arrival. What do they
live off? Fishing, probably. We are delivering stuff to these
folks… that's why we have stopped.

A few women file in, clad in black, nondescript like
the candle lighter. Then, two taller figures, erect, richly dressed.
They wear boots and are veiled (they all are, but these have their
face screened as well, by a dark net, sheer enough for a stolen
glance. I see eyes, shiny and furtive).

Some rich people live on the island, all right… and
need praying. Something might have occurred. An illness?
Rosaries are often said for the dead. Did someone die? When?

Go away. Get out of this church. It's the wrong place. I
will head to the bar and taste their aquavit. It will do me good.

They are saying we won't stop in Venice. We will not
have the time. Know what? I will fake it. When I will return
home, I'll say that we did.

*

Grandpa has passed away. Father told me as soon as I
landed my bags on the kitchen table, empty and relatively clean.
It was mid-afternoon. We had arrived in the morning, but I had
loafed for a bit. Not eager to make it home, not for lunch. I

have money enough to buy food and drink at a bar.

Father said Grandpa passed while I was away. Fuck, then. I don't feel sadness right now, but a burning disappointment. I've been out at sea, doing the freaking job, because he told me so. I came back, I feel, to report about it... About Venice, though I haven't seen it. The lagoon, how weird it was, and that creepy island with the church.

Of course, it doesn't matter. It isn't the point. Grandpa's passed, Father said, and as soon as he did he looked older, wasting under my eyes. "And the birds?" I almost yelled. He didn't know and didn't care. I will go to the island. I'll look for those birds. "What about Grandpa's house?" Father didn't know, didn't care. He is just a drunk. I don't know how Mother bore with it.

On the ferry, I was on deck all the time, pressed against the rail, distracted by the silly rumpus of seagulls. A whole squad of dolphins is after me, bouncing fins and bodies submerged, nosy and coy like a bunch of widows.

Grandpa's door is unlocked. The house is next to the beach where his boat should be, but I see none. Maybe he has sold it before he fell sick. The house consists of a kitchen, a bedroom, an outhouse, and the kennel Grandpa built for the raven. All is empty and smells old, funny, slimy.

There's no bird, but two perches are crammed against the wall, and I'm tramping a crumbly mess. Mostly, sunflower seeds, nibbled, broken, sad, dusty. I am tempted to grab a broom, but I don't. From the perches, two long chains are dangling.

I get into the minuscule bedroom that Grandpa, of

course, shared with Grandma when she was alive. I have known her, but my memory is blurred… Just another bag of dark clothes, turned towards the sink.

Here's the bed, surprisingly in order. Where did Grandpa die? On the bed stand is an empty glass. A bulb hangs from the ceiling. Here's the narrow closet. In a weird burst of rage (what am I mad at?) I slam its doors open. Inside, a single jacket, dark gray, kind of disintegrating. I frantically search the pockets. What for? There's a rosary, black, and a piece of paper with unreadable traces of ink. For no reason, I reach over the closet, and my hand meets a frame. Overturned. That makes me laugh, I mean smile. It's a postcard of Venice, quite similar to the one Mother has. The same one? It isn't. But there's a lacey palace, and pigeons. An obsession.

*

Last night I have dreamed.

I am back home, though not for long. Back in my small bed, pushed against a wall where pious images are pinned for decoration. My bed is even smaller, I notice, than the cabin's cot on the ship. I can't wait to board again, do the cleaning, little as I like it, get paid. The point is, I've grown muscles. I'm not that thin any more, and my bed feels tinier.

Anyway, I've dreamed in color. Gold, silver, pink, orange, turquoise. Very glamorous, but I can't pinpoint what… feathers, probably. A huge flight of feathers. Were they clouds, instead? Something light, immaterial. Bells were ringing, brash, clattering, and they woke me up.

On my way out, I saw Mother at the stove. I almost

startled her, kissing her close to her neck, from the back. I don't
recall ever doing it. I don't know why, today… She dropped
the wooden spoon and rubbed her palms on her apron, as if
she were about to… What? Hug me? Hold my head, my face?
Caress me?

I looked at her hands. At her apron, stained, soiled. She
hesitated, doing nothing, saying nothing. I kissed her again, on
her forehead, where her hair begins, showing for an inch or so
under the kerchief. She kept her gaze down. I heard her breathe.
Her breath was like a wave, dense and oily.

How small did she look. Did she become so?

I have grown so much taller.

Narcissus

And of course the thing about vanity was an artifact.
Just a lame excuse, a cheap gossip they rolled over their tongue,
like candy, trying to soothe the dull ache lingering below,
between their chests and guts.

They said that he was vain and death had been his
punishment. "Vanity doesn't become boys," they kept whispering,
for the legend to take a life of its own, for the myth to enthrone
itself and bear responsibility, shaking fear off their shoulders.

Truth is, they had been unkind to him and they knew,
but they had been unable to help it. Maybe, if chance had
allowed tête-à-têtes… They only met him en masse, at the
pond, where they arrived with their loads of laundry and their
garrulous mood.

Well, their chirpiness wasn't properly happiness.
Contrary to common belief, youth is rarely glad. It is busy with
ripening, and all those stretching cells itch when they don't
hurt. They itched, all of them, with a vague wish to claw at
something other than their own skin.

So they scratched him, not badly, on the surface. I'm
not sure he realized.

When they arrived, he was there. He must have come

early in the morning. He stood planted on a rock, line cast,
fingers loosely wrapped around the fishing pole he held lightly,
with ease… using balance, a quality that he had in great store
and irked them big time. Especially since their own had grown
flaky, bodies sprouting in unexpected directions at once,
without previous notice.

He stood tall like the oak tree that spread its roots near
the water… knotted tangles, like arthritic fingers stubbornly
grabbing dirt, crumbling it as they relentlessly advanced. The
roots brushed the rock, wood and stone melting in mossy
alliance just like muscle and bone.

The tree wrapped him in shade, further accentuating
his darkness. Was it truly required? Didn't his olive skin and
black hair obscure him enough? To the girls' eyes, yes, they
obfuscated him, as well as they singled him out.

He was not called Narcissus. Please. Boys don't get
named after flowers, the most female of symbols. So that's
where malignity started… with the nickname they picked
instead of a word they couldn't pronounce.

Strangers get annoying, don't they, from the start. You
are neutral, perhaps well intentioned. Then you shake hands and
trouble begins. They casually introduce themselves with some
gibberish you try to reproduce out of courtesy, and your tongue
stammers, your brain cannot piece together that weird sounding
nonsense.

Who said Narcissus first? Not sure. They muttered
flower names and they laughed. They laughed more than they
muttered, bashfully covering their mouth with their hands.
Daisy, Pansy, Lily, Chrysanthemum. Amaranthus, Narcissus. The
last one stuck, because they were giggling so much they could

no more talk.

Of course, they were embarrassed. No other boy would come to the water and stay, at least not in sight. That was where gals should be among themselves. They believed he purposely tagged along. But he arrived before them, correct? Well, that didn't count. He still managed to be in the wrong place at the wrong time.

They named him when, once, he passed them on his way back, basket full of fish and pole on his shoulder. Long cadenced strides and not even a nod, a smile. Was he too shy? Too proud? They were struck by the waft of scent that he left behind, the intense flowery smell. Did he perfume himself? That fired the irresistible giggling. Whispers rustled about, hands squeezed hands, elbows punched hips, waists, ribcages.

Did he perfume himself? He oiled his hair, that dark nappy jungle, each morning, from the jar Mother left on her bed stand with other belongings. With a mirror, a triangular shard. Such a useless thing… it reflected no more than a fragment, a slice. An eye maybe, or half of his mouth. Upper lip. Lower lip. Stupid shard of glass, only good for cutting your wrists. Was it why Mother kept it?

Three gold ringlets in a coral colored shell. A chain, long and thick, and a folded napkin embroidered with letter L. A long-toothed comb he used as well, dipping it into the jar. The everlasting oil had slightly thickened, turned a caramel hue, honey-like.

Quickly, he plunged the comb into the jar, which was wide and tall. The stuff spread like a magic potion and loosened his knots. He took care of tightly closing the lid, then he passed his fingers through hair slick as ribbons. Now he could weave it in one long braid as he had seen Mother do. He tied it with a piece of rope.

What did Mother add to the oil? Myrtle, rosemary, clover and sage. No narcissus, of course. Narcissus, come on.

Mother died three years before Father, who survived a while. He only went at the end of last winter, when the snow started melting. He did not see the spring.

Fine. If there is a good time for dying, that's not spring, though Dad probably didn't care. Not about seasons, the weather. Not about a thing, truly. He had been sick for too long.

He was sick before Mother was. Illness got him as soon as they arrived. A slow poisoning of the blood, his skin yellowing like parchment, his strength sucked away. Mother took care of him and she did the washing for people. At the pond, but she didn't go with the girls. She went at the crack of dawn, on her own.

She always brought him along, as far as he recalled. Since he was a small child, she brought him along. She helped him on the rock, where he stood until she was done. He liked fishing. They didn't talk. He heard her sing now and then, bits of tunes interrupted with no reason. Never mind. He loved those songs, even…

Mother didn't teach him to fish. Someone else must have. Dad, before he got sick? He didn't remember. He knew how to fish with a pole since they had arrived. Before? Didn't remember.

After Mother passed, he kept coming. He always caught some… that is what they ate, lunch and dinner. Father only wanted soup. He sipped a tiny bit, then turned towards the wall, leaving a half-full bowl on the bed stand. When his breathing grew steady, the boy took the bowl and eagerly drank what was left.

He was thin, but muscular. As for balance, if you'd pierce a bullet hole at the very top of his head and drop something (coin? marble? tear?), it would hit the ground right between his feet. Now… why would you want to pierce a hole? You could sense, almost see, the line traversing his body, straight but flexible like his fishing rod.

Who gave him the rod? He didn't remember. It must have been with their stuff when they came. Father neither gave it to him nor demonstrated how to use it. He fell ill as soon as they arrived, as if he had preferred not to. As if he would have liked it more to perish at sea. Or else earlier, over there, before they escaped.

Daddy's soul didn't make it through. Clearly, it got stuck somewhere, but it took them time to understand. Understanding wouldn't have helped anyway.

He wrapped Mother inside the striped rug that came with the fishing pole, in the bundle Daddy had carried on his back, all the way, until they reached their landing. Because Dad used to be quite strong, he suddenly recalled.

He rolled her into the striped, thick, prickly, colorful rug. He knew she would have liked it. Every night she kneeled upon it for prayer. Well, he couldn't really tell. She squatted on the rug, her face tensely facing the door where she had spotted a crack, long and thin. That is where she looked, mesmerized. Moonlight seeped in, a blade, sometimes dim, sometimes almost blinding.

Just a shard, like the piece of mirror she kept at hand.

By her bed, on a crate she had managed to barter or buy, from whom she didn't tell. She brought home three of those, over time, one for each of the mattresses. She and Father didn't sleep together. Never had since they arrived.

Every night she looked at the luminous crack, that scar breaking the darkness, fissuring its compact embrace, and she muttered prayers or something else. He stared from his bed, eyes wide open. Didn't sleep, just rested, relaxed and quiet. Sick Dad made the air stuffy… That dampness was familiar, securing. Its sour odor meant home.

Mother rose before dawn. Without making a single noise, she sat up in bed and opened the jar, combed and braided her long hair. He woke up at the scent embalming the air, briefly, a draft of prairies in bloom. They stole out in minutes. Laundry was already stacked by the door. While he grabbed it, she carried board, soap, and bread. They ate on their way, two large slices. Fresh, she had wrapped them the night before within the embroidered cloth. She had kept them on her bed stand, like a sacred something. They bit hungrily. They slowly chewed.

He wrapped Mother into the rug and then dug deep under a pine tree, on a naked hilltop surrounded by the widest of views, kind of infinite. Swept by wind… he knew she would have liked it. He could tell by the way she looked at the crack, at that secret window. He could tell by the way her nostrils flared when they walked to the pond, each morning, as if sucking in the crispness, the chill.

He didn't ask permission for digging. No one saw him. Someone might ask later, or not.

She died after three days of cough and great weakness

that she spent in bed, profusely sweating. He cooked food
that was already in the house. He didn't go fishing, didn't leave
the two of them for a single moment, feeding both, but they
needed little. Mom turned on a side, quiet as always. Breathing
became hard but never got labored. She passed fast, with no
agony he could detect. She slipped between his fingers.

When he knew she was gone, it was almost night. He
did nothing. He lay in bed until dawn cleared the sky, time to
wake up, their time. He rolled her into the carpet.

Then three years went by. Father withered slowly, at his
pace, while the boy kept the same routine. What he caught at
the pond was about all the food they needed. In the afternoon,
though, he worked mending nets in the village. That came easily,
a breeze… someone must have taught him, but he didn't recall.

He was good with needle and thread, and that made the
girls giggle. Sewing was women's work. But he was better than
them all. He worked fast, in order to get done before sunset.
Leaning against whitewashed walls, sitting on a bench or a
barrel… they would never call him inside, where they got ready
for dinner. Mending was an outside job.

The girls peeked at him from the windows. They
whispered half words. But he focused, head down, and he didn't
notice.

He had never been out on a boat. No one had invited
him. He had no friends, though of course he could speak the
language. So did Mother. She had to, because of the washing.
Mother could understand, but only talked in case of necessity.
Otherwise, she sang in the old language and she murmured
things inaudible, looking at a single string of moonlight. Now
she was under the pine, which smelled almost like the oil she

left in the jar.

Besides, sure, the one that brought him there, he had never set foot on a boat. Meaning, for high-sea fishing. He just cast his line at the pond for freshwater fish, good enough, and he always got some. The pond froze in winter. During wintertime, all nets were thoroughly mended.

He had grown very tall, straight, perfectly aligned, like an arrow. Not a man yet. Will he ever be one? Lingering, as he did, where the women-in-bud came to wash their laundry… And he didn't see, didn't mind them. As if they meant nothing to him. He did not tease, did not engage in conversation, sulking out of pride or timidity, they thought.

Not a man, uncaring of other boys' company, quietly sewing his nets or staring hypnotically at the water… Waiting for the subtlest whirl, ready to yank the line with a tinge of ferocity no one saw.

His long braid, his exotic perfume made his maleness doubtful. Scent was the culprit. It was what earned him the fame of being frivolous, which of course he was not.

Someone said, when they came back to tell he had vanished from the rock…

He was there, they could swear, and a minute later he wasn't. Jesus, nowhere in sight. A splash? How could they tell? They were washing laundry. They were splashing their heart out, also chatting, yelling and laughing. No splash that they heard and no motion over the greenish surface, not that they saw but, hey, did they watch? Pole and line were left askew on the large stone where he had perched all morning, basket leaned on its side and no fish.

He was there, his skin beaming its tawny, warm halo, sharply singling him out. Still and mute, a statue, a tree. Then, a moment later, he wasn't. One of them said he looked down to fix his hair, leaned too far, lost his balance and fell. But we know he was balance itself.

The pond was said to be bottomless. They believed it communicated with the ocean through an invisible channel. The old folks said it. They must have some kind of proof. Something was lost there (a sandal? a tunic? a bird cage or a wedding ring?) then was found stuck inside a net. The pond flushed its secrets into the sea.

He had looked at his handsome face and had fallen for himself, see, as he didn't care for lassies. So they gossiped, to release the fear grabbing at their guts because of that mystery. In fact, he might have levitated. Disappeared into thin air. Disembodied.

They had never learned his real name. They couldn't recall it.

Later, when spring truly marched on, narcissi were all over the hill with the lone pine. Where he had buried Father as well, wrapped in nothing. There was only one rug. Sheets and blankets were worn, soaked in dried sweat. After Mom went, not much laundry was done. He had buried Dad in his clothes, and it didn't matter.

Wild narcissus is white as china and nicely shaped. Its perfume is acute and pierces you like a bullet. It spreads your nostrils open, shoots straight into your brain, bursts like a single, sharp stab of longing. As for what, you have the choice. Or you don't.

Wild narcissus' scent is strong, but it doesn't travel. It

stays put. You have to come close. You have to crouch on dirt. On this naked hill, it might be unpleasant. You have to kneel and lean forward, face down.

Higher up, the pine scratches the air with a pungency that spreads far and wide, like a wish, an invocation, a song or a lament. It comes in fits, in gushes, then is gone. All of this is immaterial. Intangible. None of this lasts.

Landing

She needs not to hear the name, the mother whose child has died on the ferryboat.

She isn't looking at the sea when the officers step on the pier and come forth, two small, forlorn figurines. No one else has disembarked still.

She has her back towards the sea, because she and her husband are hurrying towards the promenade, intending to get something to eat. Most unusually, the ferry hasn't arrived on time. It has lingered in sight of the harbor for a while. No idea what the matter was… certainly a technical issue. In such cases shouldn't a repair craft be sent? A scooter has gone out at some point. Someone must have been hoisted aboard, some exchange must have happened… from shore, they couldn't tell. Finally, the boat has moved. It is nearing the docks when they suddenly decide to go grab a bite.

They have already rented a car, bought what groceries could harmlessly sit in the trunk, parked the vehicle in a convenient place. When the rest of the party will land, they'll drive to their destination together. Time has flown so far but now, briskly, in spite of their joyful mood, exhaustion has kicked in. They haven't eaten since morning. Hunger is making him irritable, she can tell. She feels weak, almost faint. Quickly, they head on foot towards the nearest bar. A question of minutes.

She hasn't seen the men walking, but something makes her turn at once. As she notices them, her knees buckle and bend. She staggers, she stops.

Though he asked to remain with his aunt and cousins, though he was excited to stay and wait for the next ferry, she shouldn't have let him. Now she is stabbed by the memory of when she climbed aboard, leaving both her children with her sister's family. She waved. From the dock, they waved back. Then she watched them trotting away, adults chaperoning them. Where to? Trust. She wasn't in charge anymore.

She recalls the instant lightness, a sense of unburdening. Sweet relief, perversely savored. Now the feeling comes back and chokes her. Burning fingers squeeze her neck in a deadly vise.

Earlier, while they were driving to the seaport, he complained he didn't feel well. As she asked for details, he said his head ached. Then his throat did. Knowing that he still wasn't able to pinpoint the source of disconfort, she always paid attention to his words, even when inconsistent or vague. Children easily forget about pain, hence she never omitted to inquire in the aftermath of a claim, meanwhile looking for clues (blush or pallor, a fever, a sweat, lack of appetite). Did she, this afternoon? Of course, not. They were separated. But they shouldn't have been.

Earlier, in the car, he whined, "Mommy!" She turned toward the backseat. "I feel…" "How?" "I don't feel…" His voice tapered down. "What, love?" A cousin was poking his waist with her elbow. He started laughing. She had lost him. She hastily assumed he was fine, maybe a little nauseous, a combined effect of excitement and fatigue.

Now a spasm squeezes her throat, as she reckons those were early pokes from whatever monster was haunting him. He sensed it and duly informed her, asking for help from the one supposed to provide it. She shouldn't have left him.

He was wearing a checkered shirt, green, his favorite color. She imagines him on the boat… Later, they will say he first fell in the dining room, close to the pool table, where he waited for his uncle to play. He was eager to watch Uncle play, and proud, perched on a tall stool, then dizziness must have tumbled on him like a fog, sucked him in like a maelstrom, vertiginous. God. Oh god. She shouldn't have left him.

Before melting down with a twirling motion, as if wishing to screw herself into the wooden boards, unremovable, nailed to a square foot of dampness, a puddle, a patch of moss… Before being overwhelmed on her turn by darkness, she has time to visualize a strange object shining in the sunset. The sight bursts out of nowhere, while her mind and her eyesight fade. A vision, a visitation, a ghost.

She immediately recognizes the spiral binding of her son's first-grade notebook, the one where she daily checks his homework. She has, for the past year. Now they are going on vacation. Here! The spiral flies closer. Her son likes to play with it, sticking his index finger between the curved metal and the side of the pad.

Just before she passes out, she feels the tip of the spiral pierce her body… her eyes, ears, nostrils, breasts, chest, belly button, everything at once. The pain is unsustainable, and yet freeing. An ecstasy of sorts.

Both officers lunge forward and grab her, perhaps a bit clumsily. Firmly. Her husband, who hasn't noticed her stopping, who has kept going for a while, is running back madly, almost yanking her from the extraneous hands. His face questioning, yet already soaked with despair.

Rage invades the boy's father before a thing is said. He knows without knowing, he knows but doesn't know what.

He isn't hit by guilt or regret, the dad of the boy who passed on the boat for reasons we don't know, but, when found, will appear unreasonable. He doesn't backtrack, crucified by the thought of what he should have done and didn't. He hasn't heard his boy muttering this or that in the car. Mom is the one listening.

He is devastated with rage, angry at the ocean, which has stolen something from him. Angry at the boat, that stolid ferocious whale, swallowing a most precious belonging.

Delicately, the three men have laid down the mother. She is stretched across the pier, rigid, frozen. Eyes wide open, she stares at the darkness above. Her mind has shut down. She is thinking of nothing. A strawberry-colored ache bleeds all over her. A drone rattles her ears. She is relinquishing everything, herself included.

The two officers have walked back to the ferry, now docked. People trickle out in small parties, moving awkwardly, either too fast or too prudently. Talking softly, whispering as if in shame. The air is leaden, heavy, the saltiness sharp and incongruous, as is the lemon quarter of moon, paper lantern indecently probing the sky.

Long Distance

I've made my bed in the workshop, right under the window. The glass panes are coated with a crust of dirt, almost natural, like a moss. Light softly seeps in, muffled, remote, rarefied.

The bed was already in. I only had to push it, ease its feet as they occasionally got stuck between crooked tiles. The iron frame is in good shape, reddened here and there by a touch of rust, like a kiss. The mattress is horsehair filled, crunchy and squeaky. I had forgotten those… you'd think you were in a nunnery. Or in jail. Getting used to it takes a little while, but then it starts feeling like feathers. You can take anything with a bit of drilling. One, two, three, like magic. One, two, three, and even hell becomes heaven.

Since night three, I dive into this bed of thorns like a baby bird in its nest. It has a rustic feel, and quite pleasant.

How should I call this place? Garage? Shed? It's a workshop, I said. A large table, off center, occupies most of it. An electric cord hangs above it, socket at its end. No light bulb. I'll have to find one. There's no rush. It is still summer. At this latitude the sun sets by ten, eleven o'clock. I can call it a day by then, negotiating my rough, prickly couch, an old curtain for a blanket. Before winter (it sounds weirdly remote), I…

I have laid my backpack across two metal chairs,
very close to the bed. I need to keep gathered, collected, my
belongings compact, an island inside this empty space.

It is very crowded, in fact, although surreptitiously. The
shelved walls are an arsenal of undecipherable entities, piles of
randomness, abandoned stuff. An itch runs through my fingers,
through my brain. Unavoidably, I'll start sorting those relics, see
what is what, get them organized as if this were home. God!
When will I tire of starting anew?

But the table is clear. Nothing on it. A smooth, dusty
surface. I am inclined to leave it this way, like a barren field, like
a runway, ready for take off or for landing.

A sink is in a corner, rust, like lipstick, etched around
its hole. I am glad, because my bottled water is gone. Behind a
shade there's a minuscule toilet. It works. I wouldn't mind going
outside, but, especially at night, I prefer not to.

I love nights. I always did, and now more and more. In
this dimness, here, this permanent twilight, I will try smudging
days into nights… one long, unbroken suspension. And I might
succeed.

I dig out of my pack a can and some crackers.
Breakfast, dinner, lunch… meals do not differ. Spoon in hand,
I go sit on the front steps and I watch the landscape, hills
and vales, the peaceful countryside. I know houses are within
walking distance, a few. None of them is visible, hidden by a
mound, a thicket, a turn of the road. Not too far there are a few
cottages, I know, but I hear no noise. I feel safe.

On day two I have found the phone. Do you remember

those? Oh my... Do you still remember old style home phones? They sat on dedicated small tables. They were huge. Kind of rounded in the beginning, kind of bulging and bulky. Very old phones had curves, like the actresses of the same era. Remember those? Funny... Old phones looked human, the squat base like a face, bit dull, openmouthed, the receiver a wig, a hat, a pair of earmuffs.

This one is of an indefinable gray. Once it must have been white or beige. To me it is a teddy bear... I have put it next to the bed, on a stool where I toss things before sleeping, ring, hair tie, stuff out of my pockets (my knife, lighter, and keys). I ran out of cigarettes, but I am not going ballistic. I don't miss them, believe me, more than I miss the rest. But I'll keep the lighter.

I'll get rid of the keys, throw them into the river (there's a creek not too far, I recall. Only, it isn't in view and I can't hear it). Momentarily I'm leaving them on the stool, where the telephone stands like an icon. Like a candle, a framed portrait. A cross.

Yesterday when I woke up it was on my chest, and it tumbled on the side, of course, as soon as I stretched. Oh my, how did it get there? I must have grabbed it. Asleep? I'm not a somnambulist...

Later, though, the dream came to mind. They have such a way to reemerge, like someone whispering in your ear. I recalled... I was on the phone, talking to my uncle. I had called him, or did he call? I was happy. I liked Uncle a lot.

He died young. How was never clear. One night he went to get some fresh air. Such a beautiful night, he said. He was right. Breeze blew from the sea, bringing saltiness to the

nostrils, to the skin. I know the feeling. A sea wind gives you
a natural high of the soft kind, yet pervasive and strangely
intense. The breeze had swept the clouds far away. The sky was
so pure it looked bottomless, its vault electrified by myriads of
stars.

Uncle stopped at the ice-cream parlor. They close at
midnight. He sure was the last customer. Not unusual. They
knew he'd get a small cup of almond sherbet, or jasmine. He
surprised them, they later told the police, when he asked for
rose and mulberry instead, without whipped cream. When they
found him at dawn, car parked at the Vista, doors unlocked,
a dark crimson stain edged his lips. His seat was reclined. He
looked peaceful, relaxed, reports said.

The car wasn't immediately rescued. For a month it
remained parked in front of the strait, as if lingering on its
own before the sumptuous sight. As if it (the car) couldn't
get enough of that openness, that mighty blue wildness, the
two seas, the other coast, the twin town flickering across like a
mirror. And the vanishing shadows, behind.

Every morning the windshield was scattered with
petals, said the passers-by. Why did they recount such trivia,
mulled the cop, typing it for the twelfth time. Who possibly
cared if angels flew around, sprinkling the abandoned vehicle?

Was it true? A local legend? I don't know. Couldn't
check, didn't live there anymore. I heard a rumor. Red roses,
pulled apart, were spread on the windshield night after night. In
the daytime, the sea breeze blew them away.

In my dream, I called Uncle on the phone (the cord,
by the way, has been cut two feet long with a neat, sharp clip.
Seems like all sorts of wires in this residence have been made

superfluous… just relics or so).

His voice! Happy and crystalline. What were we talking about? I remember a word out of nowhere, also severed, useless, unhinged. "I can't…" Nothing sad about it. Uncle was as cheerful as always. "I can't." What?

I am remembering this while I stand in front of a shelf, busy salvaging tools. Tons of them… I have been at this for hours. They are in good shape, though some of them obsolete, some of quite obscure function. Not a problem. I have been cleaning them with a rag, accurately sorting them.

The collection is huge, I said. I have skipped lunch and postponed dinner (for the best… my reserve of cans will not last forever). I am hanging this all on a rack with some handy, perfect metal hooks I have also dug out. Almost sunset… I need to be done before night.

From my bed I can see the rack. Look! Moonbeams seep through narrow slits in the nearby front door. I spot glints of silver. Blades are shining, perhaps the large teeth of numerous saws I have lined up on the right. Yes, toward the exit. Wood saws. For log cutting? I guess. A fire, why not? Cozy, heartwarming in winter, though there's no fireplace in this hangar. In this workshop, and winter is far off.

So is the sea. The strait. The smell of jasmine and roses.

I am dreaming again. I was. I have suddenly awoken. Not entirely. I am half-dreaming. Please, let me resume. Uncle was on the phone… Pray, don't bother me. I have long waited for this chance. Now it is fucked! No matter how hard I try, consciousness has taken hold of me. When it sneaks in, you can't kick it out.

My eyes, blurred by sleep, slowly focus. I am sitting in bed, phone against my chest, tip of its broken cord in my hand. My grip is so strong that my palms, all sweaty, almost hurt. But I don't let go. I shut my eyes once more, savor echoes of our conversation. "I can't," he said, "help…" That's it! I can't help! But it wasn't all.

It is gone now. The dream has dissolved. I sit still, while a sense of vacuity invades me. As if… All is suddenly crumbling on me. Right now.

Then I hear him. Breathe. Him? Don't know. I hear it. Breathe. Pant. An animal? Huge.

It is not an animal, I'm sure. Right outside the door, upon which I've riveted my eyes. My blood freezes. A great weakness lowers into my limbs. I hold my chest, careful not to make a sound, while out there I hear labored inhaling, exhaling. Almost hissing.

My hands cramp around the device I'm crazily clinging to. I should put it down, grab the knife instead, right here, on the stool. Will it be… better than nothing, I guess.

I can't, anyway… leave the phone, ease my deadly grip. My eyes are magnetized by the door, until something makes them shift to my proud range of hammers, pliers, screwdrivers and saws. They are glistening. My gaze swings like a pendulum from the dark wood, thinly parting inside (me) and outside (him, it), to the ominous smile of the blades I have hung in the perfect place. Why did I? I am dead scared.

Is this one of my neighbors? Mad? Just curious? How intentioned? How did he find me (so fast)? Is the shed visible from one of the cottages? From them all? Do they all know? Have I been imprudent?

Do I care if… didn't I come here for… why should it matter how…

I don't want to be attacked. Don't want to be hurt. To be slaughtered, no. I don't want to see b…

Suddenly, I don't know what inhabits me. I just can't stop myself. My finger, ostentatiously stumbling, pushing hard to make the mechanics click and rattle, loud, louder, dials the number. I am letting it ring. Once, twice, thrice. Here we go! Then I start, my voice boisterous, each word an explosion, each phrase a St. Elmo's fire.

"Do you hear me?" " It's me!" " I know it's late…" "What?" "Speak up!"

After all, he is far away, is he?

"Yes! I'm good. Just miss you. What did you say?"

I am talking to my uncle, and I am feeling better. Strength is getting back to my limbs, my blood has resumed its course. I keep yelling, deaf to all but the sound of my own voice. He is answering, of course, I say to myself. I have to believe it, correct? I have to fake it with truthfulness, see what I mean? I have to fool myself in order to make it credible. Anyway, it gives me courage.

He is answering, cheerful as always, though his voice is kind of indistinct. Kind of brittle. Fragile, like shattered glass. Cheerful, still. I can't hear what he exactly says. Wait. "I can't…" Help? Help it? Is it what I heard? Uncle dear, you can't help what? What is it?

This becomes extremely important. What is it he can't help? I need to know. Suddenly, my eyes fill with tears and my voice chokes. Silence.

Silence outside. I don't hear the ominous noise

anymore. True? I don't move. I'm still holding my breath. All is quiet. The shine on the tool rack has dimmed… the moon must be setting. I am still afraid, but too exhausted to think. Should I get up, push some furniture against the front door? Sure. But I am too weary for action.

I put down the phone, grab my knife, squeeze it into my fist till I fall asleep.

It must be late. Not only I have slept. I overslept. I feel confused still.

First, I look at yesterday's job, the tool rack, with a kind of reverence. Painfully, memories of last night's panic emerge. I make it to the front door, push it open, look at the wide expanse of nothingness. Did it happen?

My bare feet feel mushiness where stone steps should be. I am treading on a carpet of petals… a variety of scarlet, crimson, pink, rust.

I almost smile. "I can't help you," he wanted to say. "I can't help you, love. Sorry."

I know. It doesn't matter.

Anthem

Now they let him go out for walks, the man who woke up after surgery speaking Sanskrit. I'm not sure he walks much… Through the bathroom window, I see him sit on a bench. The same, always. Maybe he goes to the bench, sits down and that's all. Then he lies on his side, knees bent towards his chest, so still that he could be sleeping. But I am too far to tell, and too busy.

I only notice him because he is so regular. He shows up every day at five o'clock. And I know who he is because of the incident… They say he chanted in a language unknown, after he came to. A nurse said it, then his feat made the news among staff, patients, visitors. Not for long, as there wasn't much to comment upon. Who cared if he moaned a strange-sounding litany and then suddenly stopped, dozed off, then didn't recall a thing? Not uncommon after GA.

Wait a moment, said the nurse. Something was unusual about it. He looked lucid, aware, eyes wide open. And his voice, loud and clear, arresting, didn't have the slightest trace of a slur. A bit later she performed catheter procedure, she said. As she inserted the thing, she asked, "In which language were you speaking?" in order to distract him, of course. He had no clue. She didn't believe him.

Careful not to look as if she was ridiculing him, she recited the line that had poked a hole in her head (did she like the sounds or was it his tone, deep, metallic, when he spat that particular string of syllables, aba, saba and so forth)? Hey, what did that mean? He stared at her vacuously, either stupefied or indifferent, cramped around the sharp sting of his screaming urethra. He stared at her wearily, as if she were insane.

How did the nurse know it was Sanskrit? Easy to figure out. That night, she typed the sentence (still played on, stuck in her ears like a silly nursery rhyme) on her phone just as she recalled it, without spelling concerns. Then she texted it to her friend who was a crossword champion, go figure. Sanskrit stuff, he answered, all right.

Well, how did she know the man didn't speak it? She couldn't be certain… But as she repeatedly asked, in the following days (she, for one, was curious) he never provided an answer. He kept looking at her with bewildered eyes.

They have dug out a tumor from his left hemisphere, not big, the size of a walnut. They have found it quite early, I got. Damage was contained and mostly reversible, though reeducation will take sort of forever, you know. They will move him from this to another, then another unit, as recovery will slowly proceed. From this to another building, still in the same hospital structure. Same gardens. He will visit the bench under the sycamore for a while, I guess.

Not that I care for it, but somehow he has become familiar, a landmark.

The first image he saw… Wrong, it must be the last. The last image he saw before he came to was the woman with the long scar.

Beautiful. The scar. And the woman, but he only saw her head, neck and shoulders. Just one shoulder, then both, just one, then both from the back as she slowly spun, maybe on a turntable. Yes, on a turntable, because otherwise she was still… like a statue, though a living one and quite so, her skin almost vibrating, translucent. He could see the pores breathe in and out.

But she didn't move on her own. Something, a contraption of sorts, caused her ineluctable orbit. Wait! Not an orbit, no. She twirled on her axis, like our mother…

The planetary association was caused, of course, by her stony calmness. Also, by the impeccably regular shape of her head, her smooth, rounded skull sheathed with short amber curls.

Her eyes somehow eluded him. He did not, could not meet them, mesmerized by the diagonal scar emblazoning one side of her face. A long triangle flaring out on her zygoma, vertex above the ear, base following the lower edge of her mandible.

A fine texture covered that slice of skin, darker than the rest, infused with a coppery hue. First, it seemed just an intricate cobweb, but, as he kept observing, he started deciphering characters. Minuscule, yet the more he looked, the more they came into focus. Neatly traced, they enlarged slightly as the triangle spread through the woman's cheek.

The alphabet was unknown to him, but he felt an itch, an urge to pronounce what his eyes greedily devoured. He improvised, attributing arbitrary vowels and consonants to the small, pretty marks. And the more he spoke, the more his recitation felt natural.

Once, his daughter came by. Oh no, he didn't expect her visit. Like his son, she lived in a distant town. But she had traveled for the occasion. Maybe a spur of remorse, sudden reminiscence of duty? She had always been more compliant than her brother, or just weaker.

She looked preoccupied. So fragile and worn, he felt she might have come to seek help. But she didn't, and she didn't speak of herself if not in the vaguest terms. He had never been able to ask. He noticed that she had cut her hair very short and her head looked childish, denuded, sparrow-like, immensely frail.

Her visit was quick, shy, perfunctory. She left something behind her, a halo of… That gluey thing, that powder of past, like baby talcum… They both said they'd remain in touch.

He needed nothing. All clean. No malignancy. Long stay, covered by his medical insurance. Worry not. Then back home. Fine as always. In touch. She left something unfinished and then she was gone.

He still sits on the bench, the man who chanted in Sanskrit when they scooped him out of the stretcher and tucked him in bed, minty green in his gown, head wrapped in bandages. Well, I didn't see him. I am extrapolating, I know.

He had long hair when he was admitted, said the nurse who clearly had a thing for him from moment one, though there is nothing special about his looks. At least presently, all shaven, regrowth only a shadow.

Very long hair when he came in, she said, darkish though spotted white, long beard, woolen cap. Quite untidy and eccentric, ridiculous, yet eye-catching. Right away, they cleared a

patch for the biopsy, but for surgery they de-brushed the entire
skull. Those long locks, dropping sadly into the wastebasket,
could have filled a small pillow. I haven't seen them. I am
extrapolating.

The scar will be invisible as soon as his hair grows
back. Low, right above the occiput, a delicate spot. At least out
of sight. Not a large cut. Thing the size of a walnut. Talk about
luck. The scar will be unnoticeable. No one will know, as long as
hair… How old is he? Freshly retired, I guess.

How can the nurse be sure he didn't know Sanskrit?
Any retired bloke can study anything when he's left with loads
of time on his hands. Too much time isn't friendly, and it makes
you sick. And what did she say the rhyme (those words that he
sang out loud) meant, already? Either she didn't say or I forgot.
Curiosity tickles me all of a sudden. I will ask her, when I come
back from vacation. In a week. Right.

I watch him through the windowpane as I wipe it.
Actually, I am taking a micro break and some air. After five,
the smell of ammonia makes me feel light-headed, probably
because I have overdosed it all day.

The last restroom. In a minute I'll take off my gloves,
wash my hands before changing into my clothes, before I
even touch them. I glance at myself in the mirror. Tomorrow,
tomorrow I'll get my hair done.

"Eli, eli," said the man who never spoke Sanskrit, "lama
sabachthani." The words… Aramaic, Hebrew… he wouldn't
have known… were engraved on a cross hanging from the
wall right in front of him. To be exact, they inscribed a brass
plate attached at the base of the crucifix. Old style hospital and
forgotten décor. The cross was hung high and the inscription

was small. But he saw it quite clearly, or maybe he did not, his
brain only remembered remote catechisms. His brain, after the
storm, threw that bit of flotsam on sand, then washed it away.

part 7

The Candidate

They were walking on the side of the road, on the sandy slope. Cars rode past them. The sun lit them from behind, cutting sharp the contour of their moving bodies. Yet their faces looked bright and clear, maybe due to their remarkable pallor. They were white as if bloodless, carved in marble. Statuesque. They were white, and glowing.

He had noticed them as he stood backstage in his dark suit, briefly lifting his eyes from the papers he skimmed while, gingerly, his free hand fiddled with the tip of his tie. In the front of the open-air platform, seats were rapidly filling. He was ready, perfectly calm, summoning last minute focus, inhaling, exhaling.

He saw them without seeing. Only minutes later, when he climbed the few steps leading to the podium, the image reached his conscious mind. He hesitated, stopped still, turned back. They were closer. The effect of chiaroscuro was less dramatic by now. The figures more distinct.

He held his breath… The girls were drop dead beautiful. He could not help an instantaneous surge of desire. Tall, and perfectly built. Old-style dresses, black and chaste yet so tight they became provoking, clasped their waists, then flared into full skirts swinging in the breeze. Curled dark hair, shoulder-length, framed their oval faces. Full lips, high cheekbones. Slanted, deep, thick-lashed eyes, tremendously appealing... with a tinge of apprehension, a slight angst mixed in. The girls looked familiar in a way he couldn't pinpoint, and remote at the same time.

They had to be identical twins, although... maybe just an effect of perspective... one seemed smaller and shorter. A bit weaker, perhaps, she couldn't keep pace with her sister. Not quite. They were rushing towards something of extreme importance, no doubt. Fierce, exhilarated, and wild. Were they hurrying to the rally? Where else?

He turned towards the stairs, trying to shake off the interference. He should not...

Why were they dressed that way? Please. It didn't matter. They might have run out of a movie set in full costume, in order not to miss... Or they were members of some sect whose name he could not... Didn't they dress like that?

The boy came to his mind afterwards, at the restaurant.

He was feeling great, also tired. The campaign was almost wrapped up. Tonight's speech was the last before the elections. He was toasting to his hard-won, well-deserved, unavoidable glory.

His hand, holding the glass, stopped in midair. He saw a flash, a reflection... the shade of the wine caught his eye, made him think of... A carnation was pinned on the boy's lapel, like a large spot of blood. Yes, a red carnation. Nothing could be more common. They must have come from a wedding, baptism or such. They, for sure, belonged to some sect... Those who dress as they did in the nineteenth century, how do they call themselves? How come he couldn't remember?

The boy must have been the brother. He walked slightly ahead. He was thin, a bit bent. The hat… The tailcoat, too large. The boy was emaciated, perhaps underfed. How come he had noticed it all in so brief a glance, then forgotten? Now he vividly recalled.

He had a hooked nose, not inelegant, almond eyes, long hair pouring out of the old-fashioned hat like liquid, like tears. Purple lips, a flowery shade, unhealthy. His expression was tense and fragile at the same time. Something weird about him, a tinge of discomfort. Still, the girls were amazing.

And where did they go? He had forgotten about them, of course, as soon as he had walked on stage, before even reaching the mike. But they weren't among the crowd afterwards. He would have recognized them.

At the hospital he sat at her side, as usual.

He had brought carnations. A nurse was trying to fit the vase on her bed stand, fiddling with crumpled tissues and bottles of pills. The nurse was blond, appetizing. He couldn't help assessing her as she obliviously moved around. As if he weren't there.

He always brought carnations. Cheap stuff, but why waste money? She still wouldn't open her eyes. He knew she recognized him. Her hand reacted to his touch with a slight caress of her fingers. Her mouth curled a bit.

She had stopped verbally communicating just a few months before, when the campaign started. Irrational as it might sound, he believed she had done it on purpose, as if wanting to attract… perhaps divert his attention, making things harder for him, why not? He had initially felt that way, then the rush had begun and the rest, all the rest, had become irrelevant.

He still came, of course, once a week, and he talked to her like they said he should. About the campaign, the elections. He told her he would win. Then that he was winning. Not sure she would care, assuming she understood. She had always been kind of… distracted.

Now her hand had lost tonus, then gone totally limp. He looked at her face. Her lips were slightly crisped, corners lifted in a quasi-Gioconda-smile. But her fingers had become mushy. He felt his own growing numb. "Mother? Mother," he muttered.

He thought about the twins. Well, about their chests, stretching the fabric of their vintage dresses. Were there any buttons? He hadn't had time to notice. They were there though, for sure, buttons about to burst. Their chests, lifted by their fast breathing as they walked, almost ran, breasts thrust forwards, ribs tapering down to incredibly narrow waists… The memory gave him a shiver of lust. Two of them. Two of the same. Together.

The boy marched ahead. Slightly askew, yes, his hand, he recalled, pushed against his hip and tense, like a bird's claw. Bird of prey. He recalled the boy's hooked nose. Then, again, the hand pressed to his side, maybe against his pants pocket hidden by the tailcoat. Cramped long fingers. He remembered the red carnation, like a shot of blood in the eye.

"Talk to him. Keep talking," they said to the wife. She sat there, wrapped in a tailored suit fitting her like a glove. She had kicked her high-heeled shoes under the bed, slipped her stockinged feet out of view. Exhausted, she needed some slack.

"Talk to him," they had insisted. Only, she didn't know what to say. Really.

"You have nearly won," perhaps? He wouldn't have liked it.

He would make it, they had said. She hadn't doubted it for a second. This was just a bad scare. Then, things always worked out. Luck never let him down, that is why she had married him. He would not disappoint her.

"Darling," she sighed. Her nails brushed his fingertips while her jaw loosened in an unwanted yawn. She tried stopping it, but she was swamped, faded, spent, washed out. "Darling?" His lips seemed to contract in a sort of smile. His hand didn't move.

The young intern (broad, handsome and manly, she couldn't help noticing) bent over one of the machines surrounding the bed, studied it for a second or two while she kept on him her queasy, questioning eyes.

"Good news. He has been dreaming."

Drift

The last president of the United States is about to perform. It will be a kind of happening in the style of the late twentieth century. Something physical yet conceptual, symbolic or just nonsensical. Something boisterous, eye-catching, yet suggesting a deeper truth to be pondered.

The last president of the United States… you get which… the tall, young, athletic and slim, head as oval as the room where he pondered options and came to conclusions. Those Arthurian days of confabulation are gone. The last president has been home for a while, his mandate exhausted. Still, his fame persists. His public appearances draw a remarkable crowd.

The performance will be mediatized. I see lots of machinery and a plethora of professionals, pacing, intent, mostly wearing raincoats, yellow, orange. It does not look like rain. I hear the booming voice of an anchorman, as distinct (diffused, omnipresent) as the voice of god might well be.

"The last president," he shouts, "has always been fond of dismantling cages… he would not miss the occasion of taking one such apart." Is the statement ironic? Hard to say, when it comes to journalistic eloquence.

He has arrived unnoticed, unseen, hopping casually upon the floating platform that will serve as a stage. A small boat, now docked on the side, must have brought him (did he actually row?) Mountains are in the background, hazy, blurred, nondescript… Perhaps they are just hills, nameless, happy to play no role. On the platform (offshore but not far, a dull slab of concrete chained to the sea bottom) is an ancient building, empty and obsolete, which for unknown reasons needs to be promptly abated. By hand? What a feat, what bravura.

Suddenly, we understand the event is a ritual of sorts, a reenactment of Hercules' twelve… at least one of them. Will our man tackle this on his own? There are helpers.

First, the woman. She looks like an astronaut. Not because of her clothes. She wears sensible gear, as the president does. Sneakers, T-shirt, comfortable slacks, working gloves, all white for some reason. Her hair sticks to her well-shaped skull… maybe it's short, maybe it's tied. Such details are lost in the distance. A few monitors installed for our perusal haven't graced us with any close-ups.

We can't make out her features, no way, though she must be under forty. Very fit, like an astronaut… I mean, something in her body (posture, or rather motion) is aerodynamic and weightless. Energy in her case reigns over matter. Substance constantly transmutes into action.

You can tell by the quality of her gestures how determined she is, what passion she is pouring into the demolishing act. Is she an overachiever? Competitor? Champion? Is she ambitious or just very well paid? Is she real?

Robot? Clone? As I said, the camera hasn't graced us with close-ups.

She harmoniously interacts with the ex-president. Their two bodies intersect, cross and juxtapose as if all had been previously choreographed. Nothing was, I am sure. They must be improvising. And I could swear the lady and the chief never met before.

What about the young man? He must be in his twenties, perhaps thirties, though he's so very slight… Pale, pale, pale, and not because of white garments. But his thinness is such, you ask yourself (assuming the lady is a clone) if he could be a hologram. A projection of something extinct. A flickering shadow.

Clearly the least authoritative, he is agile, quick, nimble no less. I can tell from my vantage point that he works as fast as the others. He tears down, rolls away, pulls and pushes the same amount of stuff in the same quantity of time. Only, his moves are endowed with no initiative. They echo, mimic, repeat those of the other two. He complies rather mindlessly, while his masters/superiors display authentic enthusiasm.

The trio is marvelous in its efficiency, in spite of the giant task. How can they handle pillars, columns, capitals with such ease? True, those pieces are split, cut in portions… after all, when this all was constructed, long ago, people carried the same building blocks on frail vessels, hoisted them with rope, fit them thanks to muscular effort. The assembling joints they employed to fasten the structure must have loosened up, crumbled away.

This ridiculous mausoleum holds by miracle… that is

why it needs furious undoing. It's a hazard bound to precipitate any moment. A mere form, a pretense, façade, simulacrum. Clearing it is a civic action of merit, besides obviously a fabulous exercise, an athletic triumph, awe inspiring.

They are making it happen. Thanks to a few boards inclined at an angle, they (woman, youth, president) slide each piece into a crate momentarily hooked to the concrete platform. A huge wooden container, surreal in proportions, so well wrought you can't help wondering why the storing of debris (essentially garbage) would demand such fine labor. You suspect this thing we are bombastically taking apart has some kind of value… only, with a negative sign. It needs sheltering in a time capsule (right?), going down into history to be then rediscovered, deciphered… It needs sealing as if it were atomic residual, lethal poison. Not at random. It now becomes evident that ex-president, woman, youth, having lowered themselves inside the receiving vessel, are disposing each piece (pillars, columns, capitals) following an intended design. Are they improvising instead? If yes, how very skillfully! Everything is puzzled out so perfectly that the whole (compact, tight, not an inch of allowance left) occupies a trifle of room. Therefore, lots of space in the mega casket is open, free, unutilized. Also, weight is unevenly distributed. On purpose. I am sure you have guessed… When the crate, soon, will be released, when the floaters holding it up will be cut, it will sink because of its load but won't rest at the bottom. It will be carried away. Here the river is deep, and downstream is deeper. Currents are very strong. Have you seen the rapids, a mile south? But these natural data aren't all. Look! The stacking itself

is dynamic, meant for instability. (The mechanics must have
been carefully studied. Or are they worked out on the spot? If
yes, with such ability…) The whole cargo is unbalanced, bound
to fall, roll, engender momentum. From the inside, it will help
the progress as if it were alive.

Just watch. You can see it happen on screen, your TV,
your laptop if you're sitting at home, on your phone, wherever
you are. You can see it quite distinctly, though the camera insists
on a wide shot, privileging a neutral remoteness.

You can now realize the ex-president, woman, boy, are
going along for the ride. They'll stay in, lead the boat, make
sure they'll give those dead rocks a shove in the right direction,
when needed, in order to grant a smooth journey, a nice, regular
flow… and, of course, the success of the entire procedure.
What would all this ado be for, without thorough follow up?

The box is almost closed. We ignore what devices
have been planned for aeration… something fancy, unheard
of, sophisticated. Food supplies? Freshwater? Light is quickly
dimming. As the last of the lid is pulled down (the trio is
shutting it from below… they are still sprite, unscathed, and
perfectly autonomous) darkness suddenly fills the monitors. Is
this over? For the audience it is.

For the vessel and its heroic dwellers the journey
has started. Oh, they will succeed… Some are born for
achievement. They'll reach their destination (the open sea)
without a single doubt. We will be informed at some point.
Presently, we have lost interest.

The crew is wrapping up, closing down, breaking
camp. The mountains (now exposed, quite modest in size) look
hopelessly plain… so to speak. The platform where the ruin

stood is a stump, maimed, pathetic and sad.

And what was the thing, after all? We have seen it for years, for decades, since we have memory, yet we have never known, never inquired. Did the journalist say the ex-president liked to dismantle cages? Was the building a prison? Or a convent, perhaps. A reformatory? Perhaps an aviary. Church? Academy? Factory? Fishery? I give up.

Whatever tiles, marble, stucco, iron curlicues, awnings, flags or insignia enrobed its walls, giving it significance, had long disappeared. Only a washed out skeleton of stone pretended uprightness.

These things must be removed, though with proper caution, savoir-faire, celebration.

Listen, please. It is crucial. These things must be removed.

TRILOGY

1.

His hands rest on the wheel. Lightly, and casually so.
From the passenger seat I'm supposed to stretch my left leg
across, press the gas when needed. Or the brakes. He asked me
to and I obeyed. I don't know why he can't do it by himself, but
I don't feel like arguing. Not now. I can tell he's half drunk, and
I've heard he's done time since I last saw him. Why do I trust
him to drive? Because I don't have a choice.

I have trouble with handling (so to speak) the pedals.
I don't know if it's a matter of strength or position, but to get
a proper response (which of course is crucial) I have to push
with my entire body, tensing every muscle I have. Still, I don't
gather enough momentum and timing is imperfect, delayed…
We didn't crash yet, but our progress is bumpy at best. Crash we
will.

My partner shows a mild discontent. Embarrassed, I
wish he could use his own feet (more conveniently situated) to
get the truck going or stopping. I'm about to suggest it, when a
sudden afterthought seals my mouth. Better this inconvenient
(and illegal) teamwork than to wholly surrender control, having
him completely in charge. After all, my strain is the modest
price for my share of power. I won't give it up yet.

2.

Suddenly, I think of his wives. Such an idle thought. I've met them all over the years, noticing what they had in common, how much they looked alike. Almond eyes, olive skin, curly dark hair, as if they belonged to a same lineage… That caused a reassuring feeling, somehow. The aesthetic continuity seemed to mend the fracture, the repeated failure… if divorce can be so defined, which I do not know.

Now I briskly picture the girls in terms of mere bodies, devoid not just of their facial features but of their entire head. I see them decapitated, correct. Nothing gory in the picture, no severed necks… Only, the upper portion is temporarily eluded. Yes, evaded, and limbs, hands, feet, torsos, abdomens (with relative widths, lengths, angles and curves) come alive with shocking precision, as if my brain had painstakingly gathered a whole bunch of data without letting me know… I didn't have a clue, I swear, until this all keenly drew itself before my inner eye. And I was amazed.

Well, body-wise they couldn't have been more different… The wives. Did he realize? Come on. How did he manage? The task seems grotesquely complicated. On the verge of impossible. Superhuman, at least…

I know it isn't true. Anyone can perfectly deal (intimately, I mean) with a variety of human shapes. Weights, textures, proportions. The adjustment is instantaneous and effortless. It can be repeated countless times. Anybody can handle as many bodies as opportunity allows. Why should I be surprised? Why now? I realize our driving has sickened me. I am dizzy, that's all. The world spins around me, uncreated, undone.

3.

Luckily, we stop at a gas station, both needing a break. We are walking into the bar when I notice his weird collection of rings. He has three of them but huge, entirely hiding his knuckles. How can he bend his fingers, if they are braced that way? Maybe he can't.

One piece is clearly made out of his wedding bands, fused together. Quite irregularly… They are different in thickness and shade, some darkened by oxidation, some with a reddish hue (maybe a lower alloy). Such a metameric device gives out a reptile feeling.

As he sees me watch, he smiles. To himself, I believe. "There's no end," he mutters. Again, "there's no end, no beginning, just one love." Something in his tone bothers me, but I can't pinpoint what… sort of an evangelical halo, vague, nondescript.

Two more rings complete the display. Two gold leaves, juxtaposed, identical, as if sprouted by a same hidden branch, wrap his middle finger bottom to top, like a bandaging. In the center of each a gem is cast, shining diamond-like and yet clearly worthless. Is it just opalescent? No. Shining, and risibly small. The stones capture me like the eyes of a snake. I can't stop staring at them.

He's aware and, again, he smiles, now overtly for me. He explains what that double bind signifies in a tone yet more sanctimonious, more… I nod, but I do not listen.

I must call a cab. With some luck I'll be back in town before dark. I know that he will not stop me. I know he won't care.

Post Scriptum

Rest assured, I have been happy.

Why am I saying this? I should cross it out and start over. I should say I have been well… no major calamities. Let you know I survived, that's all.

But I see the innuendo. The subtext was "without you." "Rest assured, I've been happy in spite of your absence." Which is simply untrue.

I have survived.

On the pretext that his last name was misspelled, they have kept him at reception for hours. How inappropriate a term for this antechamber of hell. They have sat him on a bench by the door. Hours have passed, the first one the hardest. For the first hour he can't bear the helplessness. He can't just sit and wait. He stands up, tries to pace. There's no room for pacing. They have him sit again. The-one-behind-the-desk lifts an eyebrow, imperceptibly nods. The-one-by-the-door shoves him down with a steady push on both shoulders. Ten cold fingers dig into his flesh like prongs, nearly piercing holes in his muscles, which are aching with tension and fear.

Don't say fear. He is not afraid yet. Doesn't know he is.

His hand rushes to the breast pocket of his shirt, seeking his cigarettes. They have taken them. And his cellphone. How scary is the darn empty pocket… the entire world has expired.

Don't say scary, I said.

I remember the restaurant.

No, not one of the joints where we used to meet people. Nice folks, sure. Most of them your friends or acquaintances. Mine, sometimes. We both enjoyed conviviality.

But I am recalling the place where we went alone. You probably don't. It was rushed… You were hurrying from somewhere to somewhere when you chanced upon me, in the plaza, and you said, "Let's have a quick bite, I'll treat you."

We didn't stay long. Was it less than an hour? Still the longest we had, you and I, sitting tête-à-tête. Well… now and then you must have stood up, sought your cigarettes, smoked half, crushed the rest, mindlessly reached for your pack again. I must have watched the deepening crease on your brow. Must have guessed your haste.

But I do remember ten minutes of calm. Happiness, or a decent imitation of it. We discussed the menu, opting for an entrée in order to save time. Lots of dips, pita bread. Yes, it would be plenty. No wine. Spicy smells filled the upstairs room. Through the window, gently brushed by green, leafy branches, we could have enjoyed the life of the square… busy strollers and lazy bench-dwellers, young, old, people and pets. We usually indulged in that kind of spectacle, sharp observers with a kin streak of humor.

But that day I turned my back to the window, focusing on your face only. It was rarely well-lit… We used to meet in late afternoon, in the evening, at night. In dark places, at least

dim. There you were now, painted out in full color. I didn't
mind you seeing me as a contour, as a silhouette, a shadow. You
could see the outside world around me, behind me. I thought
you could see through me.

Beirut, I fell in love. I mean with the town. We had had
Lebanese food before, with friends, and you had already shared
memories. But that day Beirut entered the room. It washed in,
and the midday light became golden. Just a flash. Nothing more
was needed. Soon, the gold began to wear out.

It was early for lunch, the joint almost empty. You were
starving, though. I don't dare imagine how long you had gone
without eating, way too busy, forgetting about it. Days? Perhaps.

Service was prompt. You wolfed up the bread, dipping
into generous sauces. Hummus, eggplant puree, tahini, dill
yogurt. You were quickly satiated. I munched slowly and ate
little. We finished at the same time.

In the meanwhile I wrote on a noisy, very old-fashioned
typing machine. In my brain, of course, and you couldn't hear.
I, on the contrary, was deafened by the shrill, mechanical sound,
and entirely missed what you said. I hope you don't mind. Only
the word Beirut emerges, echoes, keeps coming back.

I typed a whole page while we swept those Middle
Eastern entrées, then you paid, with cash, always. A whole page
of the same three words. Numbers. A date I didn't want to
forget. I haven't.

*There is no misspelling of his last name. The accent seemingly
giving them trouble should be there. How could they not know? Don't the
papers match their records? What the fuck is on their records? What is
on the screen to which the-one-behind-the-desk's eyes are constantly glued?
Slightly shifting, perhaps following lines.*

I remember the first night in the apartment. Of course, it wasn't yours. Friends, acquaintances had let you stay. You always lived in the place of others. In others' places, I mean.

I know it was a good night, at least stretches of it. I remember your arms. First, the mention of them, "I'll take you into my arms." Kind of thing you want to hear when you are two, and you have fallen and scratched your knee. Kind of thing a dad would say. You have been climbing the hill, your small hand in his large one. You have been patient and brave but now you are tired. Night is falling. It is past bedtime. Dad has miscalculated. You have missed dinner. By the way, you aren't going home. Where are you going? "I will take you into my arms," you wish Dad would say.

I remember your arms. And a shirt you gave me to wear because it was winter, after I came back from the bathroom. "Would you like to shower?" you had said afterwards. "At this time of night it's delicious." What an odd remark. And how true. Showering is delicious afterwards, at that time of night, in the apartment of someone you don't know, in the place of others.

He was put into something that looked like a kennel. Naked.
The-one-by-the-door had him strip, piece by piece, after the-one-behind-the-desk left the room without turning off the computer. The machine was still flickering. He still couldn't see the screen.
Then the-one-by-the-door said "shirt," briskly, clumsily, with an accent. He didn't react fast enough. "Shirt," the guy repeated with a drier, more exasperated tone, as if barking. He understood, took it off, put it on

the bench the other indicated with his chin. The rest went as if in a silent movie. The guy pointed at his clothes and then at the bench, mute, his face just a slab of stone. But the concept was clear.

Only, he didn't know where to stop.

Then, keep going.

He expected to be given something, a uniform, a pajama, a sack. He was given nothing. The other put his stuff into a duffle bag, crumpling it with contempt. He was wearing a glove. Not rubber, not surgical, just a gardener glove, made of cloth. Kind of dirty. He could not understand the meaning of it… naked stripping, gloved hand, duffle bag.

Then he was escorted out, a weapon (he thought) pushing against the small of his back. He felt it but he couldn't see it, of course. He hadn't noticed the-one-by-the-door was armed. Was he? He had not paid attention. He panicked. How could he have missed such a thing?

Don't say panic.

Outside it was dark. Wasn't it midday when they took him? Midday, bright, although he had just awoken. Gone out for breakfast and papers. Hours had passed, uncountable.

Outside it was drizzling and cold. Few steps, then the escort shoved him on his knees before what looked like a kennel. Pushed him in, after kicking a small door open. Locked the door behind him. He couldn't stand. He could kneel.

Imagine you are on a train. This is a couchette. Squeeze in. Welcome aboard.

This is not a couchette. It's a casket and he has been buried alive. On the dirt floor there's a sort of rug. In a corner of it a crumpled something… a worn, torn, old T-shirt. Grey, smooth. Slimy. Small. He wears it because he is too cold. He would like to lie on his back, but he needs to bunch up like a fetus. How he misses a hot shower.

Discard this thought, will you? It is stupid. Unfair. Don't do this to yourself.

Drift

He remembers the nights in the desert with the Tuareg, years earlier. And the Yemenite scarf the girl gave him. The Tuareg girl. She explained in Lebanese that it was a Yemenite scarf, the cloth thin, yet indestructible. Men kept those for their entire lives, passed them to the next generation. They lasted centuries, the girl said. Men always carried them along. How she got it, she didn't say. Who first owned it, she didn't say. He should keep it. Forever.

The scarf was quite large (but so thin it could be bunched up, pocket size). A man could wrap himself within it during long desert nights. Even two people could. It was green, deep, the color of malachite, of some jade. With Arabian motifs, sort of hieroglyphs. Did they mean anything?

He remembers them, now, crystal clear. The intricate design seeps under his brow as he shuts his eyes, and he focuses. Then he manages to fall asleep.

Alexanderplatz. The bus crosses it, then shifts to another dimension. East Berlin is a lace, like those I used to dig out of Grandma's closet. How I craved such treasures, no matter how yellowed and torn. They looked... I miss words... They looked as if the fairies had made them. Leaves, birds, flowers. Curls, waves, arabesques. All those intricate patterns. How I craved them.

East Berlin is a lace, torn, frayed and crumbled. I love these *maisons délabrées.*

At the farmer market I see tons of flowers, stuck in plastic buckets lined up on the sidewalk. Vendors sit on small stools behind them. They don't need to get up in order to sell, just to stretch their hand, pull a bunch, hold it out. Roses are kind of pale, cappuccino, faded apricot, nothing more sanguine than that. They are plumped up with greenery or else with *kornblumen, gypskraut*... baby breath, dots and dots, an impressionistic daze.

East Berlin is a giant lace. Nothing has been restored, besides Alexanderplatz and a few other pomposities. Most façades are scarred, ripped and pierced, made of fragments improbably holding together. They were beautiful houses. They will be repaired. But they are still lizard skin, maze of stone, gray, beige, bleeding dust.

I have sat the entire afternoon in a park. The tree canopies are thinning. Autumn will be gorgeous in a month or so. Today it is still timid, a promise. An ice cream truck has come with its carillon. God, is this town outdated. Children screech and run. Parents take them by the hand, line them up like soldiers. How orderly, how quiet are the parents. Now the children as well, their eyes big with longing.

The ice cream truck brings in the tail end of summer… I can feel it linger. The-man-with-an-apron hoists a scoop on each cone with steady precision, hands it down with prefabricated motions. There are several tastes and different colors, variations of tenuous pastels. The scoops are very small, yet the children's faces are luminous. Ecstatic. Few adults also indulge. I fancy one of those cones. But it feels indecent.

I haven't reached my destination. The park has sidetracked me. Luckily, the Jewish cemetery hasn't closed. Maybe it never does, the lovely place… kind of eerie, a medieval forest. Tombs look vegetal, like stumps, like trunks of old trees…

They are made of stone, don't be fooled. They are graves, they are people passed. I like reading inscriptions. It soothes me. It's hypnotic, just give it a try. I decipher names, dates, and history comes alive. I read through a wave of people, a compact tide, husbands, wives, children, families at large, a thick tapestry finely wrought. Strange old-fashioned names, common ones as well. The dates overlap…

Then they stop. There's a sharp break, a void, a weird emptiness. In the nineteen thirties they stop, the names, dates, graves, dead. There are few recent ones. In the middle, a gap as if the ground had opened, swallowing a decade or so. A chasm of impressive magnitude, a black hole. I had not foreseen this. I am choking with sadness. Or is it something else.

Was he soothed by the thought of those who cared, outside? By the certainty they wouldn't forget him, they would search for him, find him, they'd never, ever abandon him.

How naïve. How ridiculous. Sorry to disappoint you. He thought of no one. No one even existed, as if the ground had opened, gulping everyone, the entire past.

The only thing he could think of was getting to the next hour without other inmates torturing him. How not to be kicked in the balls or punched in the gut. Beaten, knifed, wounded, maimed. How not to be choked in his sleep. How not to be killed.

He tried not to offend anyone. He let others go ahead and pee before him. He held his pee until his bladder would burst. He let others take his food, snatch his soup and his bread. He let others steal his blankets. He let others call him names and smiled like an idiot. He could think of nothing else than to save his life.

Not because he cared. Not because he liked life, or wanted to do anything with it. Not because he wanted to see those who loved him again.

He had forgotten about those who loved him. See, they were outside. He wasn't sure they existed. He had slipped into another dimension. Please don't try to understand.

I have fallen in love with East Berlin as I had with

Beirut. Not because both towns start with B. I could fall in love with towns A to Z, believe me. They… take me into their arms, so to speak. It is not truly comforting. Can be smothering. Deadly. I have felt a bit dead, recently.

Restless. Aimless. Maybe I needed a vacation, and that's why I came to Budapest. Another B town. Where will this madness end? The ghetto is the culprit. I so wanted to see it before it went down. True, those buildings are full of sad memories. But they are stunningly beautiful.

There is something about Budapest's ghetto… It is like an island, you see, or else a ring stone, clasped in the very middle of town. I remembered it pink, bricks and stucco, the color of flesh. Now it looks redder, more garish, a wound.

The Jewish quarters hug themselves tight, as if in solidarity, though they have been a prison, rat cage, lethal chamber trapped by fences and walls. Overcrowded… illness spread through them like flame over gasoline. Not a soul was able to escape, yet the Budapest Ghetto is beautiful. Was. Most of it has been torn down. I don't know where else I could go to placate this listlessness.

The good thing, when he was released, was not having a place of his own. If he had one, they would have searched it during his absence, and he wouldn't want to return to a violated home. Chaos of open drawers, clothes, books, files scattered over the floor… he couldn't even fathom the scene.

If he had a place of his own, for sure they would have tapped it. They couldn't have tapped all of his friends' flats. Or… He didn't know how far this had gone. Couldn't guess. Did not understand.

He was given the duffle bag at the door. He felt uncomfortable touching it. He should find a launderette, toss the sack and its contents inside a machine. Sit in front of it, watch it spin. That would help him focus. Oh, he wished he could.

> *Cash? He had forgotten about it. He must have had some in his pants pocket, with his keys and ID, when he was taken. Cigarettes and cellphone were in his shirt pocket and were seized right away. He walked more than a mile, though, in a daze, before even thinking of his phone…*

> *Did they toss everything in the bag? He should shake it open. He could not, couldn't put his fingers inside. He felt nauseous.*

I have kept the scarf since.

The day of the restaurant, I mean. You might have forgotten. It's the kind of detail you would obliterate. It came up in the midst of tales about Lebanon, inspired by the food, the décor, the songs in the background.

You always beamed when about to tell a good story. You shone when you said you had a treasure someone gave you, and I should check out. Though you were in a rush, you decided not to postpone. Let's go find it, you said, right now. Weird. Hadn't you idled in my sole company long enough? Didn't…

The flat where you temporarily dwelled was nearby. Even in daytime it was dim. Blinds were shut, curtains drawn. When you turned on the light, the room still looked gloomy. My eyes shifted towards your bed, undone, and I felt ashamed but couldn't keep them away.

To avoid my embarrassment, I sat on it, I mean on your crumpled sheets, and I focused on the duffle bag, navy blue, you were digging in as you kneeled on the floor, randomly tossing out a scatter of clothes. My eyes scanned your personal effects with a kind of aching. I could sense it, and was afraid it would show. I was embarrassed again.

Out finally came bunched-up-something, green, black,

color of wine, with long knotted fringes. Not exactly my style. I like lace, pastels, beads, embroidered flowers. But you were so proud, I needed to express admiration. And it was the first present you gave me.

The only one. I ought to be delighted. I was. I know there's a story connected to this rag. And I apologize, love, I absolutely, immensely do. You explained it while we dipped pita in tahini sauce, and my brain was occupied by a noisy typing machine. I was mesmerized by your face, sharply lit by the midday sun, the tree canopies adding a livid shade.

I was exhilarated, and it made me sick. I haven't heard a word of this cloth's past feats. I have no clue.

Those he met during the in-between week remember him quiet and poised. Way less rushed than usual. Less brilliant, somehow. Those who met him during that week were quite worried. In his calm, he sounded slightly delirious. Someone feared for his mental health.

No doubt, he had gone through some kind of trauma, yet said nothing about it.

The most striking detail was the motion of his right arm, when he sat at the bar. He could not keep it still. Suddenly, the thing jerked, flexed against his stomach, fist in front of his throat. Like a cramp, a twitch, a seizure of sorts. Was he afraid someone would punch him sideways? Was he shielding his chest? His heart? Hiding something?

And he didn't even apologize. Tell a joke. Give an explanation. It was as if he didn't notice. Was he going insane?

I have never entirely forgiven. I mean your disappearing. Not leaving an address. Doing nothing to remain in touch.

Yes, I knew your plans were urgent and vague, though

                    Drift

sometimes I suspected it to be a pose. I knew the agency could dispatch you anywhere, anytime. Did you have a say? Could you negotiate? I wasn't sure.

You were happy that way. You didn't care for stability. You liked brief stays in temporary abodes. You enjoyed change. You had met scores of interesting people, seen endless places.

We had joked about the chances of their sending you to another B town. Bilbao? I'm kidding. Bombay? Very possibly. I wonder if you have found whatever could prompt you to stay, after all. Landed in Bombay. Stranded? I don't think so…

I have not fully forgiven the vanishing, its abruptness. Should I say brutality? But I have been fairly reasonable under the circumstances. I have survived for a few decades. Only, it seems like yesterday.

Though, once out, of course he has identified the facility (on arrival he had not), something about the entire thing is so irregular he almost doubts its reality.

Fool.

He has been released a week after capture, with the same abruptness. Nothing makes sense in the discharge papers. They bear the official stamps, seem authentic, yet the contents are gibberish. Well, he needs a lawyer to… Of course. He hasn't phoned one yet, which is simply absurd. He still inexplicably hesitates.

He knows these things happen, no matter where. Police slurs. Errors. Legal mishaps. He could sue the authorities. The mistake should be denounced and corrected. He has been grossly mistreated. He has been abused. Lawyers can fix this. The abuse should be denounced and fixed.

Something stops him from proceeding. He should call the agency first, let them know.

It occurs to him… how could they not know? He hasn't been

communicating for days. There should be tons of messages by now, tons of emails. Well, of course his phone was tampered with. His email account must have been blocked. Does it justify… Didn't the agency have other…

Dizzy. He feels more in shock than he admits. He can't glue the events in a correct sequence. Can't connect.

His ID was in the duffle bag. He has checked into a small hotel near the airport. He is waiting for something. He has noticed his cell's acting strange at times. He should reach the agency, of course, before phoning a lawyer, but both things should be soon. Sooner.

He hesitates.

Bombay isn't a possibility, though I have been quite obsessed with it. Once the thought grabbed me, I couldn't let it go. I perceive the insanity of these compulsions. See, they are stronger than me. Longing for a place I have never been to? But it becomes real, becomes present or rather I feel absent, far from the very spot where I should be for some crucial reason. Like the story of Samarcanda and Death… It has been this way since you left. I didn't plan to tell you.

But going to Bombay on a whim seems outrageous. While in doubt, I picked Barcelona. Not too far, maybe will do me good.

Well, it is too bright and too lit. Eerie and magic, but still too sprite and too colorful, like a slap in the face. Once again I've come to the flower market. Yellow is everywhere… sunflowers season… Van Gogh would go nuts. I mean, more. But these sunny guys don't combine with hotel rooms. They need a real home. And tomorrow I'll leave.

I remember our last date. I had bought flowers while I strolled downtown, biding time. It was pleasantly drizzling, the

town soaked in soft sadness. I had bought flowers on impulse.
I couldn't resist those small posies they only sell for a week, in
late April. I had been spying on them every day, an *idée fixe*, but
I'm easily obsessed.

They sure sell, momentarily flooding the town, each
year. Daisies are tightly packed into heart-shaped little clumps
wrapped in tissue paper. They are carefully arranged in a
progression of red, flesh to burgundy, a thick, velvety carpet,
very sensual yet corny. I don't think I'd love it so much (though
the tactile appeal is beguiling) if the forget-me-nots were
missing. Here's the genial touch… daisies flecked with strands
of frail, timid blue. Tiny tears.

I bought you one of those. The occasion felt special.
You hadn't called for a week. That wasn't unheard of, but still
long and still painful. Then a message, a date. Why did I get
nervous? A presentiment. Something in the tone of your note?
I guess my usual fear you might be about to drop us, our thing.
The non-thing we had, right. Still drop it. That you might
be about to take leave. They had assigned you somewhere I
couldn't possibly go. You had been sent… where, you would
not tell me.

I waited in the plaza for hours. It had happened before.
Only, you had always arrived at some point, and that night you
didn't. I waited until I knew you would not. Clear enough. Cruel
enough. Calling was embarrassing. I called with no reply.

I remember leaving the darn bunch on my desk, no
vase and no water, as if it were guilty of something. I forgot
about it, in spite of the forget-me-nots. I dropped into bed and
it was a hell of a night.

Shamefully, I called again a week later, still with no
response. Clear enough, and passably cruel. I haven't forgiven yet.

Barcelona got on my nerves. Gaudí's stuff is extreme. Everything hints at happiness, blunt, sharp-edged and loud. Now I need to do something with the evening. A bar, then a tango joint. Alone? Not for long. Sex, please. I need it tonight. Give me a break, please. I need it.

The best thing, they said, is to have him removed. Not demoted. Removed for an undetermined time. No worries, just a matter of prudence. Crucial, though. They are inquiring. They have some notions about what might have occurred. There will be explanations at the appropriate moment. The action to be immediately taken is temporary removal.

Yes… that would be suited, of course. It would be far enough, safe enough. For time undetermined.

And I hate you for this sense of guilt I can't help. This sense of betrayal, each time. How absurd can it be, since you never cared? You were absent, your mind elsewhere. Why should you care now? Still it feels as if you were witnessing, watching. If not blaming me, at least disappointed.

Or, if I gulp down shame, this sense of unreality. I don't like it either. No, I don't. As if whomever I picked were a substitute. As if whatever occurred belonged to another life. The life of another, I mean. Should I wait longer than I did? Course I shouldn't. Yet, whenever I have sex, something is out of place. I mean in the place of something else.

I have taken a shower. That fixes me, sort of. Weirdly, I never use the hotel's towels. I always carry this cloth in my case, then wrap it around myself. It is highly absorbent… you wouldn't tell. And the colors, after so many washes, haven't faded. This thing is indestructible. You wouldn't believe it. I am dead tired.

Tango leads us to Buenos Aires, correct? Argentina next? Kidding.

She could have sworn she had seen him. Obsessions are like that when they turn insane. You see what you are thinking of, what you want to see, don't you? It happened more than once. When she moved closer, each time, she saw she was mistaken.

Yet in Buenos Aires, on the docks, she could have sworn it was him. But then, no. Perhaps… Couldn't he have changed, somehow?

Not that much. And she noticed how weirdly the man smoked. He held his cigarette backward, hidden within his fist. The wind?

He looked achingly familiar. But he was someone else.

GENERAL GATE

1.

The lovemaking found me unprepared. Not saying it
wasn't predictable. True… at the airport his welcome was cool,
impersonal. Afterwards (loitering with friends in a bar, before
rescuing the bikes) he still acted aloof. But our link was evident.

After the group dispersed we kept walking along the
canal, leisurely, and yet aiming somewhere. Evening approached.
I sensed, wished, hoped it would bring conclusions. Or at least
be a landing. A truce.

The lovemaking… was relief, in a way, until I found
the studs. I almost gasped. A long row, like a wall, a barrage.
Instinct said I shouldn't open my eyes. Did my hand quiver?
Oh, well. Tremor could have had reasons other than surprise.
But I knew I should conceal my astonishment. His anatomy
had to be familiar, no doubt. As I lingered in a casual caress, I
deciphered the rise. The scar, yes, spiked with metal teeth like
a crenelated tower. Why am I mentioning it? I don't usually
expose intimate stuff.

"Usual" doesn't apply. And this isn't my intimacy. I am
not Alicia.

Did I look like her? Must have. Couldn't… Can't tell. I

thought I still looked like myself, though no mirror was in the room and none in the bathroom. Some folks can live without it. They just check themselves on their way to work, in the underground, the elevator…

Whatever. I was pretty sure my body, my hair were unchanged. My face felt the same to my touch, and I had caught glimpses of it as we walked, in shop windows. Just to… just in case.

The clothes weren't mine, neither the winter coat nor the boots. They felt comfy, as if I had long worn them, yet I had had them for only a few hours. They felt mine, but they weren't.

No. No. It wasn't a case of amnesia. I knew who I was, just as I was aware of my appearance. Let me hammer it down. I hadn't changed. The world had, at least its slice comprehending me. I understood… if the process couldn't be reversed… if there was no way back…

I was worried about my forced impersonation, of course. Can one slip into another skin without prompting? How come no one had noticed? Well, I hadn't done much. Not said much, especially. I had made myself inconspicuous. Was it like her? Was she this unobtrusive? Alicia?

Where was she?

And I had just fucked her guy.

Rephrase. I was on a single bed (thin mattress, thin blanket, not real cozy but sufficiently clean) coping with an absurd situation as best as I… Wait. Why was he pierced… Wait.

Oh, was I sick of questions? I had listened to the same a million times. Couldn't tell for how long, really. After giving up

my cellphone and watch (ring, belt, necklace, jacket and shoes)
I had stepped forth with body-and-soul only, so to speak. Isn't
it what defines a human being? Body and soul make a human
being, correct. Undefined.

In my top, skirt (and underwear) I duly presented my
passport to the officer. He snatched it, and he didn't return it.

Xavier lifted the notebook from his desk (a board on
a pair of trestles) and he handed it to me. Nothing else was on
the table, so bare it looked like an altar. The pad had an odd
size, as if custom made. Spiral bound, quite large, lined with
thick brown paper. Xavier opened it to the last written page
with no comment, as if going through a familiar routine.

I stared at the words and felt faint, seeing a language
unknown. All had been speaking English, no exception, and I
had detected no accent. But if we (he, our friends, I) belonged
to an ethnic minority, a linguistic enclave, was I supposed
to… Breathe! The opposite page contained a translation. I
nonchalantly backed up a little. Everything was translated, side
by side.

Then his penmanship attracted my attention. God,
could he shape letters! He must have used a fountain pen,
delivering an irregular, malleable, animated ink flow. Did he
study calligraphy? Unless he was an artist. The text was…
illuminated? Not in medieval fashion… Floral style? Sinuous
shapes (stems, leaves, trees, roots, birds) surrounded the writing,
binding left and right sides within a same frame, as if they were
a painting, a window, a stage. The exquisite drawing enchanted
me, almost made me forget…

I read a few sentences. Oh my. Were these politics?
Rather philosophy, some obscure form of speculation. Could

Drift

Alicia appreciate it? I guess. Debate? I hoped not. Slowly, I put down the pad, then turned the lamp off. A glare filtered through the window. Streetlights, cold, greenish, sour.

They have computers. Their gaze glued to the screen, they don't make eye contact. They hide their face, in fact, behind their large monitors, blocking all but their disembodied hands of which anxiously you try to decode the motions. Words are few or missing altogether. In the absence of verbal cues, you seek mood indicators. You spy the hormonal changes peering through their skin, so to speak, like a pet does with its master. Those shifts can't be entirely concealed. They escape conscious control.

So, what hits your receptors? Anger? Doubt? Meanness? Pity? Are you an enemy? A victim? The distinction is formal. When power is unevenly assigned, the two definitions collude.

Strange, how they always murmur the question, sucking air instead of exhaling. They cast a short phrase like a lasso meant to ensnare you, then to reel you in. First, you don't understand. Well, of course. You are supposed to hesitate, feel confused. You lean forward. I am sorry, please, could you repeat? You are already at fault, testing your interlocutor's patience.

Where were you on this day, month, and year? I felt dizzy, realizing how small is a day in the ocean of time. They were asking about a decade earlier. I thought I had my life straightened up, but now it seemed all muddy. My reaction was visceral. Home! Then a chill ran through me, and I doubted.

Was I traveling instead? I didn't remember. Had I just lied? If yes, would consequences ensue? Should I manifest my uncertainty, or would that cause more trouble? Should I stand by my first reply at all costs?

Meanwhile, where did my passport go? The officer was typing, quietly scanning the screen, nothing on his desk but the keyboard. Oh my, I recalled another man taking my papers, a few seconds before, still walking away. I had seen him, of course, but I had not… My identity leaving the premises sent a jolt of pain down my spine. Now I was no one I could claim to be.

The lovemaking was brief. Not perfunctory and yet not quite sensitive. The discovery stage was long gone, I could tell, between Alicia and X. So was passion. Then what? I had more serious stuff to mull over. How could someone else's ardor, or lack thereof, affect me?

I had refrained from pronouncing his name. Anonymity seemed to dispel embarrassment.

My last name was spelled out whenever a new… clerk, attendant, agent? Officer must be the correct definition, though no office to speak of was visible. Only the diminutive counter I stood by, in the middle of the gigantic hall.

My name was declaimed each time a new lad showed up, exhibited my document, shook it between his thumb and forefinger while conferring with the guy-behind-the-desk (the one who had called this entire drama into being, the initiator, the demiurge).

Though I tried to match their composure (their cool, self-possessed airs), I was quivering like the exiguous booklet they had stolen from me. That thing letting me circulate, cross the gap between my folks in Motherland and my child and mate,

Drift

here… That thing letting me fill the chasm between distant worlds… was mine! It had been released. No one said it could be made captive again.

By the way, was I captive, since I had been dispossessed of my proof of identity? Well, I figured I was. I could go nowhere if my papers weren't returned. Without need for restraint, I was chained. The internal tremor became harder to contain. I had no way to guess the import of whatever was happening, the proportions it might take. I only knew a worrisome stretch of time had gone by. Several steel-faced fellows had played with my ID, first abducting it, then bringing it back with somber looks on their faces.

I was told nothing. Instinct said I shouldn't ask questions. I was asked again and again the same one. Where was I on that particular date, ten years earlier? *Home*, I stubbornly affirmed. Home, the only word I had the strength to produce, to think of.

What was scraping me inside, drawing blood out of me, was fear they would let me neither reunite with my child and mate, nor go back to my folks. Such a prospect of limbo terrified me. Panic sent me into withdrawal mode, a survival mechanism blotting out my surroundings, memories, feelings. Everything faded out, or maybe it was myself paling, diminishing. The effect was equivalent, a bit like hibernating, vital functions reduced to the minimum. Just inhale, exhale. Quiet. Quieter.

The epilogue was rather a precipice. I couldn't have foreseen it, but then I had expected nothing, had I? Two more uniformed agents signaled me to follow them. My heart raced. I lost nerve. I dared asking the man behind the desk, "Why?

What happened?" My voice was shrill and shaky, with a teary undertone. I felt ashamed and I stopped, realizing the jerk wouldn't answer.

But he pointed his chin towards those who were leading me away, meaning, "They are in charge. They will let you know." They won't, asshole. They are my transit team, only vectors. They'll ensure I'll get from where I am abducted to wherever in hell I shall end.

My passport, gone again, hadn't returned. My passport (my passport!) hadn't come to my rescue. It had preceded me, bound for an obscure destination, probably not the same as mine. Someone help me. If only I weren't alone. Isn't it the worst? Having no witness, being unable to whisper, "Here's the number, tell my child, my father…"

Somehow that was the worst, the dire loneliness, my dear ones not knowing… though I'm not sure I would have wanted them to see me, right then.

The bike helped, because I had to push it hard.

I can ride a bicycle, but that one (supposed to be mine?) might have been unfit. I might have looked clumsy and aroused suspicions. Would it have been perfect instead? Custom made, like these boots and coat. I did not wish to know.

I decided to push. It was heavy and that helped. Holding it required consistent effort. Had I let myself slouch, I would have lost balance, the thing would have collapsed and I would have followed. I squeezed the bar as if it were a buoy in stormy waters and my life depended on it. So tight, both my wrists got sore.

And yet nothing around was threatening, truly. Gloomy… towns can be that way. Sad? I couldn't tell, didn't have the needed objectivity. *I* was sad beyond description, so deeply, I no longer felt it. I missed… I feared I would not… not anytime soon.

After a small eternity we let go of the canal, deepening through narrow streets squeezed by tenement blocks. I didn't notice store windows, only a couple of bars and a shoe repair. Then a florist, of all things, hastily closing shop. A few bunches (all wrapped up, blooms invisible) were pressed into a plastic container, other ones carelessly tossed into a garbage bin. They would not see tomorrow. Clearly, they had outlived their chance. The smell was penetrating, intense, rotten, mournful.

A long queue spilled out of a building entrance. Xavier briskly stopped walking and we joined the line. "Since it is on our way," he muttered, "I think we should try." I acquiesced, not quite sure of what the deal was… I would figure it out. The queue originated at the other end of a courtyard, where a small door was lit. Otherwise, darkness was thick, punctuated by crimson dots of lonely cigarettes.

Xavier handed his ID to the weary fellow who had been processing, I bet, too many interviews like the present one. I had a peek, I confess. That's how I learned his name. Earlier on, among pals, no one had pronounced it. "Boss" they had called him, but lightly, nonchalantly. Fine with me. I wasn't curious, not really. But a name would be useful. Sure.

After an intent study of X's document, as if scanning for some coded clues behind the data (or just checking authenticity, based on details invisible to the common eye, small traces the detection of which caused that grave, ponderous, almost mystical attitude)… After such meditative pause, the man pushed forth a couple of forms X started to fill.

I stole askew glimpses, being able to read some of the printed matter. Therefore, I understood he was applying for a janitor's job. We were. I saw a box next to the words "and spouse," and he checked it. If he were to be hired, I'd also live on the premises, sharing some of his tasks.

I got nervous, fearful my turn would come to produce my papers. I had none, as you know. My mouth was very dry, my eyes burned, my breath became shallow. But, absurd as it sounds, nothing was requested of me. Because we were married? Were we? The lovemaking by then should have been predictable. Still, it found me unprepared.

Did anxiety keep me from noticing his handwriting? Was it the same beauty I'd later admire? Did he pull a fountain pen out of his pocket? My memory blanks.

Light barely peered in. It must have been early morning. Cautiously, he pushed the blankets away, then turned on his side, motionless for a while, as if pondering the following course of action. I had awoken when the room was still dark, then lain down in a state of lucid awareness.

I had awoken in a typical after-catastrophe mood. Let me brief you. Something acrid, like poisonous fumes, grabs your throat and makes breathing unpleasant. You feel as if your limbs were weighted with stones. As if someone, during your sleep, buried you in concrete. Now the concrete has crumbled… Daylight and consciousness did it. But those fractured slabs adhere to your skin, hindering your simplest gestures. Dust is lifted whenever you move, further burdening your respiration. All you see is well defined yet rigorously black and white. A gray scale, poor in contrast. No, not like a hangover. Not like depression. Multiply, multiply, add, then

Drift

multiply again.

I was pulling myself together when he abruptly sat
up. Then it all went fast. He had a cellphone. I hadn't noticed
anybody using one such. Seen the oddity of the situation, seen
the bikes, the handwriting, the fountain pen (I know I'm not
making sense, hang on), seen the overall absurdity, and because
my device had been removed since what seemed like forever,
I had assumed cellphones were no more (or not yet) in use.
Maybe I had just forgotten about them.

He had a cellphone and he read a message. He was
sitting on the edge of the bed, his feet on the tiled floor, and
I was contemplating his back. I saw it stiffen. Then he turned
towards me and put his hand on my waist. He started shaking
me. "Hurry, please!" Anguish was in his voice. I detected
emergency. Didn't change lots to me... the nightmare kept
going. Couldn't worsen, in fact.

As he picked his clothes from the floor, wearing them
at the speed of light, I grabbed mine. Though his frenzy made
my heart race, I couldn't help noticing how well everything fit.
The neat flowery dress, mid-calf, the boots and the coat. Even
stockings and bra? For god's sake. Their coziness hit me like
a blow in the stomach. How possibly... Hurry, please. X was
getting feverish.

At the door, I spotted two rectangular cases. Both
were black, buckled, with rigid handles. Made of cardboard,
I guessed, covered in fake leather. X grabbed the largest one.
I hesitated. He stared at me impatiently. "The accordion!" he
muttered with a tone of surprise. What was I waiting for? I felt
weak. Perhaps I was hungry.

I sucked in my abdominals, ready to lift something as

heavy as a cadaver, and equally useless. I was no musician. Alicia must be. I grabbed the smaller case, still too large. As I picked it up, my heart sank. It was light as a feather.

Our train was about to leave, and Xavier started running. I marched on, accordion in hand. The rail station confused me, a twilit, anachronistic cathedral, so contrasting with the airports I had grown accustomed to. When had I last… No time for futilities. Our train was taking off, luckily in the stilted way typical of such means of locomotion, one small forward jolt, a pause of undetermined length, three jolts back.

That it was our train I wouldn't have known. No idea of where we were headed and why. Xavier clutched my wrist, catapulting us after the wagons. I understood he had intended to jump on whatever would leave town first.

The train we had taken (were my hypothesis right, chanced upon) was old style like the station, with compartments of six. We entered the closest one. It was empty. Hastily, X locked it behind us, then he hoisted our cases onto the luggage net. Only after he slumped on a seat I relaxed, melting into the opposite one.

I hadn't paid attention to his features so far. I mean Xavier's. I had registered them, of course. I had formed an accurate mental image of this main role impromptu propelled on stage. I could have recognized him, I'm sure, at a distance, in a crowd, should we… But my brain hadn't linked my perception to attributes, good, bad, pleasant, unpleasant. I hadn't made any judgment, numbed by other priorities: keeping panic on hold, delaying grief, swallowing a desperate need for my kin, eluding pure madness.

The only thing distracting me had been… no, not sex but the notebook, for a minute. The illuminated double pages. The black ink so thick here, like tears of petroleum. So sheer there, like a veil of smoke. The elongated shapes, those oblongs, those spirals, a whole universe I had glimpsed, and it soothed me.

"You…" The interruption cut short my inner musing, which was getting coherent at last. It had almost resumed… personality?… since I had started considering Xavier's face. I had scanned the depth of his eyes, perused twists and bends of his lips, noted how they pressed against one another, then relaxed for no apparent reason.

My eyes lingered on his hands, peering out of the cuffs of a long-sleeved shirt. They were larger than his size implied… he hadn't reached his full genetic potential. Poor upbringing? War, I heard myself think. Which? When? Obsessively, I detailed each tendon, vein, wrinkle, scratch on his skin. Hands don't stay still for long. As soon as a finger shifted, I restarted my catalog. I was studying his hands when he placed them over my knees, so abruptly, it took my breath away.

"You need to understand." His voice sounded different. His tone was deeper, grainier. Did I hear it? He had the slightest of accents.

They furiously knocked at the door. They also shouted, but the glass muffled their words. Xavier's hands went limp. His jaw slackened. His neck turned to face them so briskly, I feared it would break. His eyes seemed to sink deeper, as if they had fallen in, fallen back.

I was not panic-stricken. A strange weariness soaked me, my cells wavering like a blob of gelatin. Only later I started rattling as if I were running a fever, while a wave of adrenaline sent my heartbeat beyond the allowed speed limit. As my cardiac muscle went nuts, my brain trod through cotton, mollified by the minute. It was anger in its initial stage, when, having found yet no goal or strategy, it bites at the first available morsel. Yourself.

X stood up. He advanced towards the doors in slow motion, no doubt planning to unlock them. He didn't have to. They had a pass and were bursting in. Legs apart, they tried to firm their stance in spite of the swing, grabbing what support they could find. Still, they kept a free hand for gesticulating and pointing. A third man peered behind them. He leaned against the doorframe for stability, his bulk blocking the way.

They went straight for the instrument cases. Did they know, or else was it that simple? They barely gazed at the rucksack X had hastily filled. It was lying on the floor. Having nothing, I had brought nothing. Would it look weird? I feverishly sought an excuse. We were going… I was planning… we were headed… I'd find… My brain ran on automatic pilot, trying to fabricate lies as if circumstances were normal. I mean, as if I were I.

I was I… As if my world hadn't shifted, wiping off all parameters of reality, which if skillfully manipulated make lies possible. Now, admitted I had needed it, I had proof of what underscores deception… having a truth to conceal. Presently, I had none, or too many.

My anxiety, as I found no explanation for traveling luggage-less, was just meant to avoid deeper fright. I was sure they wouldn't open the sack. One of them had already lowered the cases. As he grabbed them, I saw a grin on his face, both

outraged and satisfied, his lips stretched to the sides, his mouth
a thin cut.

Right. The cases were locked. They did not ask for
keys. Before I realized, one of them had produced a jackknife
and slid it across, making the bolts pop open. He took time
returning the weapon to his pocket, careful, ceremonious,
absurd.

The suitcases were empty. Why had I expected drugs?
The usual baggies, maybe pinned to the velvet lining I looked
at, mesmerized, because it was splendid. Xavier's, peacock blue,
slightly worn. Mine (Alicia's), light purple, wisteria. Not unusual.
Most instrument cases have such gorgeous padding. Tears were
filling my eyes… where did they possibly come from? Why did
they surface now?

The guys had paused for a second, time for me to get
sidetracked, emotional. X? I hadn't turned his way since… Wait.
Was he saying I should understand… something, now slipped
into the irrelevant side of reality, retrograded from the galaxy of
revelation to the black hole of obsolescence.

He hadn't made a sound after the men's entrance. I
could barely hear him breathe, but I could decode his silence.
He had given in to a catatonic despair, so dark it didn't allow
chiaroscuro, a state of ferocious tranquility, somehow somberly
charming. He had fallen in such a zone as soon as the knocks
were heard. I suspected he had purposely entered it, then shut
himself in.

The third man was cutting the velvet with an x-acto
blade. Not the knife they had just used. A more banal tool,
yet fit for the task. He was slicing the lining along the edges,
carefully lifting it off the cardboard, as if it were mandatory

to keep the fabric intact. He worked slowly and accurately, a surgeon.

The other two had slouched face to face by the sliding doors. The in-between pair of seats was empty. Suddenly, the geometry struck me. I saw a dice. Four dots at the corners (us and them) plus number five in the center, the man gingerly peeling the cases as if skinning freshly killed game. Or, with just a shift in proportions, shelling boiled eggs. Something in the realm of food preparation, prequel to a banquet to come. A ritual. A sacrifice. With my index finger and thumb, I brushed the top button of my coat. It was open. I closed it.

The two sitting folks smoke, steel-faced, yet with relaxed bodies. Time didn't seem to matter. Or did it. Maybe there was plenty of it and it needed filling. I was slowly simmering, my brains progressively fried, a sweet madness. Xavier (I avoided looking at him) was already charred.

Nothing between the pink brocade and the cardboard. The azure plush concealed a layer of tracts. They were photocopies, but I recognized the drawing, the inked arabesques framing the text. As I stared at the pages spread over the floor, I mindlessly started to read, silently pronouncing the words my eyes were deciphering. They belonged to the unknown idiom I had spotted in the notebook. No translation. I couldn't understand. Didn't try.

Simultaneously, the two smokers pulled handcuffs out of their pockets. What a polished script. They led us neither kindly nor brutally… Most impassibly, they led us through the sliding doors, then opposite ways. I didn't turn towards Xavier. We did not say goodbye.

I turned back on exiting the compartment. I was last… the rule must have been "gentlemen first." I looked at the scatter of fliers, all stepped over. Dirty soles had stamped upon them a sad, messy cobweb. Some were crumpled, some torn. Again, tears engorged my eyes.

The van stopped next to a small metal door. I was pulled out then pushed in so quickly, I had no time for looking around. All was going too damn fast. Was I in transit again? Although I could do nothing, I was desperate for a sign, a trace, a direction. Where from? Where to?

Sometimes things run in circles. Nightmares do. Reality as well. Were they bringing me back to the very point of expulsion? Closer to my passport? Were they reconnecting my passport and me, perhaps for re-examination? I didn't hope for a solution, not yet. Some reconsidering? Maybe a chance at…

In the split second left between the van and the building, my eyes rose as if contrived by an invisible power. The sky, the least informative item, was all covered with clouds, amorphous and useless. But I knew. Non-visual clues were enough. Noises, smells. An airport, again. Which meant nowhere and wherever, of course.

My guard hurried me towards a gate. He removed my handcuffs and pocketed them. A quick nod to his mate-behind-the-desk and he went, without saying a word, while a frightening sense of levity chilled me, made me vacillate. I was cold, though I still wore the winter coat.

Let me tell you how I had gained possession of this garment, plus dress, boots, and stockings. I have to back up a day, day and a half. It feels like a century.

The uniformed pair who seized me at the counter, ripping me from the usual course of my existence, guided me through a metal door. Clearly an embarking point, but no signage was visible. While we walked, I registered small markings etched on random pieces of equipment. They said "General Gate." I wondered who the General was, if Gate was his name. I repeated the words many times in their insignificance, storing them for later, perhaps.

In the waiting area a dozen people were seated. Nothing strange about them at first sight, yet a chill emanated from the scene. I was beyond scared or surprised… I had plunged, I said, into withdrawal mode. My burst of despair on removal, when I pleaded for an explanation, had been quickly reabsorbed (its uselessness as clear as day). Still, the vision of the waiting assembly made me cringe, as if someone had given a squeeze to a screw twisted into my guts.

None of the seated fellows were talking. None were interacting. Sure enough, a bunch of loners were gathered, all extraneous to each other. Yet, in such cases, sooner or later someone introduces herself, sparks a conversation, especially if the waiting time is protracted. Here no one spoke.

No one did a thing, read a paper, listened to music, played with an electronic device. The obvious reason being no luggage was there, no purse, bag, briefcase. Postures and expressions were varied, though a kind of distress was evenly spread, not unlike what happens, for instance, in a hospital lounge. Some had their eyes closed, some stared at a window, others rested their cheek on their hand and seemed pensive. Someone's eyes scanned around, listless, worried, others wandered without object, pursuing invisible targets, as you might observe in the hall of a Motor Vehicle Department before driving exams.

By their clothes, hairstyle, make-up, countenance,

people were of different ages and social extraction. Such a combo should have been reassuring… Look harder. No child was there. No elders either. All wore coats, though we were in summer. The oddity of it slowly surfaced, though it might have already subconsciously affected me. I would have expected light jackets, those you bring in view of the air conditioning, the unavoidable draft, but not winter coats. They were wearing them, some with hands in their pockets, as if holding a small, precious, secret belonging.

I had my skirt and top on, right? The rest had disappeared on a tray. I hadn't paid attention to temperature so far. Now the AC felt glacial, I shivered, and that kept me occupied. I sat where my guides had sent me with a thrust of their chins, in the last row like a tardy student, a late spectator slipping in after the movie has started. A nurse came around in minutes. She tapped lightly on my shoulder. All right, I should follow her. My legs had gone mushy, but I promptly stood up.
Did I say nurse? She didn't wear white. Not too sure which color… How could I have forgotten? Her straight skirt, her collared shirt were a shade of green, not quite that of surgery scrubs, yet it must have rung the medical bell. Also, she had the kind of square cap you see in old Red Cross imagery. Lastly, her face was stripped of make-up, which you wouldn't expect from airline personnel.
She led me through a corridor to a niche in the wall, closed by a wooden door reaching neither floor nor ceiling, like for a bathroom stall. Then she spoke, for a change, so softly I had to focus in order to hear, and the effort squeezed out my last drops of sap. "You can leave your clothes here." She pointed at a bench by the wall. "You must wear the gown with

the opening in the front…"

I shook with alarm. Someone help me. "What for?"
I was able to exhale. She spoke louder as if to reassure me.
"Routine check before boarding. Chest X-ray." "A new
regulation?" I asked for the sake of it, knowing I had sunk into
a totally irregular domain. She was holding the door, polite but
impatient. "Just," she hasted, "for few destinations. Always been
done. First time?" As I nodded, I started unzipping my skirt, to
indicate her answers had been satisfying.

She came back shortly, then led me to a room furnished
with what seemed like X-ray equipment, plus a small desk, of
course a computer screen. The procedure was obvious. I had
had chest scans done. She positioned me, ordered me not to
move and told me when to inhale, hold my breath, exhale. We
repeated the routine to capture different angles. Obviously, no
comment was made.

Could I have asked her for help? Could I have said I
had been deprived of my papers, retained, practically arrested?
Come on. How could she not… If she was where she was and
did what she did, she couldn't be an ally. I knew better.

She walked me to the door. "All set. You can get
dressed." I was lost for a minute, then I saw the niche, wrapped
the gown tightly around my body, stepped forth. I heard a lock
click behind me. It didn't strike me as strange.

On the bench, neatly folded, I found stockings, dress,
coat, which weren't mine. I rushed out, holding the paper gown.
I felt naked and vulnerable. I knocked at the room's door to no
answer. Louder. "Please? Please?" Dead silence.

The clothes that weren't mine weren't new. They were
clean, with a smell of soap. I wore them, then I wandered

through the corridor trying to retrace my way. I pushed a metal door that led into the waiting room, where all was unchanged.

I sat down, feeling weak, longing for unconsciousness. God. I wanted to pass out. Maybe I would if I'd just let go, just let myself drift, stop resisting. It shouldn't be hard, but I couldn't. I am not sure how long I sat in that mute, ghostly fellowship. After all, not being alone was a comfort. And so was the silence, in spite of its ominous halo of shocked fear.

Had this happened yesterday?

Now, in spite of the coat, I felt icy. My chest, mainly, and my toes. My hands, which I thrust inside my pockets. Cold. Cold.

The note was all crumpled up… When was it delivered? How come I hadn't found it? Those pockets were uncannily deep. If I stood, my fingertips didn't reach the bottom. A note? It could have been anything. Old receipt. Expired coupon. Completed to-do list.

The awareness of the thing being a message, perhaps of importance, tensed me, suggesting caution. I should postpone reading, of course, to a more private setting.

Meanwhile, another nurse approached me, this one rough, chubby, masculine, harboring a hint of a mustache. Her face was pearled with sweat. Was I the only one freezing? She shared the plain looks, devoid of make-up, of her colleague from… yesterday? And she wore the same kind of garb, dull green near to gray. "Will you please," she said with unexpected formality. A nod would have been more suitable. I had already stood up. Moving, hopefully, would warm up my bones.

Then a thought paralyzed me. She had started off, but I

didn't follow her, as I visualized the entire string of actions that would certainly ensue. Just like… yesterday, I'd shed my coat in a dressing room (right?) and I'd never see it again. Then, for god's sake, I shouldn't leave the note in my pocket. I could leave it…

Nowhere. Put it in my mouth? Only if I meant to swallow it, but I still hadn't read it. Read it while I changed? Swinging door unlocked, my guard standing outside, it wouldn't be safe. My vagina? I had never done it and I wasn't sure I could manage. Despair pierced me between sternum and waist.

She had stopped, turned around, aware I wasn't behind her. Her eyes hardened slightly. I rejoined her. "I need the bathroom," I whispered. She seemed cross, but she nodded affirmatively. As we single filed through the corridor, she pointed at a door. Then she leaned against the wall, gingerly producing a cigarette.

I almost sighed, having feared she would come inside. As I sat on the stool, the keyhole caught my eye. I was tempted to stuff it with toilet paper, but if she was peeking that would have been tale telling, indeed. I peed while still pondering options. My urine first didn't come out, then it burned. Thirst briskly overwhelmed me. I hadn't eaten or drunk… I'd think of it later.

Stroke of luck (the random positioning of the toilets), the note was on the hidden side of my body. Moving with studied calm, I sneaked it out of my pocket. I removed my coat and tossed it over my arm, shielding my closed fist, then I reached the sink, where I stood with my back turned towards the door. I released my fist at the bottom of the bowl… no mirror was there. Carefully, I distended the scrap, then opened the faucet.

Drift

I proceeded to wash my hands and the note. The ink started to fade immediately. In a minute I'd dry my palms with a paper towel, then I'd toss everything into the waste… Wait! No! A fit of pain pierced my guts and again I sat on the toilets, coat across my knees, hands under the coat. Was she watching through the keyhole? Was I on camera? If yes, where would the camera be? I squeezed out a drop of pee in order to look convincing, as I let the note go. I flushed. She knocked at the door.

It was the same handwriting, but miniature. The same fountain pen. I enjoyed the sight of ink smudging, for some reason, washed away under the faucet. Though he must have hurried, all letters were impeccably traced.

"I know who you are. Rather aren't. I know it isn't" The sentence was left unfinished. Below, another began, "Beware of" That's all. Below, an X, so bent to the right it looked like a crooked cross.

When did he slip the thing inside my coat pocket? Why did he deliver a maimed scrap, which didn't make sense? Unless he believed it would. Unless he trusted that I could complete the last sentence. What wouldn't one do under the spell of emergency? Had I forgotten how I felt when the guards abducted me? How I longed for a witness, wished I could cry for help, leave a trace.

X had managed it, and I should try to follow his lead no matter how vague. Later. Now I was too fragile, too worn.

I was given a sundress. Sleeveless, with shoulder straps. Colors (orange and rust) were gaudy, too brash. Not that I cared.

I had understood the routine. Here's a word I had never considered in its true meaning. Understand… support, bear, submit. A new task had been imposed on me, I was sure. It sort of seeped through the dress, but I wasn't interested, besides the kind of cold curiosity brains can squeeze even out of misery. With the tunic, I had found an inconsistent windbreaker. Same color.

On the airplane they gave us a meal. Had they fed us on yesterday's flight? Couldn't tell. Didn't register. I… Now I was present, though still buried in pain, and I munched with a sort of fury, as if biting my enemies, whoever they were. While I untangled green beans from nondescript meat, the thought of my child grew unbearable. Food was doing it… the habit of cutting small bites… My child… a horrifying longing for him, for life in general, grabbed me. Life attached. Life grounded. Life mine.

Paradoxically, longing left behind a hint of determination, like those reverse impressions of color you get when you close your eyes, after staring at something too bright. Those green patches bursting under your eyelids after watching a crimson beach parasol, a red dress displayed in a window. Those wide yellow fields, when you blink after contemplating the ocean.

On its tail end, my sorrow spawned a seed of willpower, a sort of tenacity, a wish to defend at all costs my present non-life, in hope… Hope was too big of a word.

I was not heading back but away, bound to another… mission? The preparatory routine left no doubt. Apparently, a long route (no inflight information, wait, isn't that obvious), and who cared? Boredom was none of my worries. I was long

Drift

past the mental zone where such irritation occurs. Again, I had shrunk to my smallest. My windbreaker zipped up, insufficiently warm (no blanket had been provided) I tried to doze off.

Xavier's note crossed my mind, and I visualized his handwritten sentences, black on white, a hieroglyph I should try to unravel. As when I had perused the notebook, I found solace in the very shape of the letters, their flow… as if my heartbeat, my breathing, my brain could tune into those harmonious patterns.

Had I been instrumental to Xavier's arrest? The question formulated itself, not expressed by hazy, blurred me but by a calmer presence perched above me, light, sheer and yet firm. Had I eased his capture? I must have, though the mechanism of the operation remained obscure. Let's say…

Blank.

Try again, love. Insist.

Let's say Alicia was aware of (or accomplice to) any tract-related activity of Xavier's. Let's say she had traveled for reasons connected to whatever conspiracy, riot, you name it, they were planning. She had been arrested, but had not revealed X's whereabouts. Of course, she could have been used as bait. She'd go back, they'd reunite, and he'd be done for. Unless those who captured her doubted their ability to control her. Unless they feared she'd manage to alert him and allow him to escape, uncaring of personal risk.

Could she match such a Mata-Harish profile? Why not? The above was a sensible reconstruction. So they had kept Alicia, then found a true doppelganger. Just a puppet, subdued, frightened, tame.

I had heard somewhere we all have a double. A few, in

fact. Computers come in handy. Browsing zillions of pictures takes no time at all. Make your pick, locate your victim, get hold of her. Put her on Alicia's return flight.

Maybe not. Put her on a special flight where no IDs are needed. Small airplanes, circulating incognito. A quiet network of sly migratory birds, tiny predators. Dedicated personnel, unobtrusive embarking points.

On and off a light slumber (cold prevented me from deeper rest) I was hatching a nonsense scenario, sounding plausible because I needed a chain of causes and consequences, or else I'd go insane.

Now, even if I were Alicia's clone, please, how could her man buy it? Bear their circumstances in mind. The two of them might be used to altering their looks, slightly or even considerably. Deception must have had a share in their life. Perhaps the feeling "I almost don't recognize her/him" was familiar. Yet they were both lovers and partners in crime… they must have a way of verification.

They sure did. The note ratified it. X had known since he had seen me at the airport. Why did he play along? It is obvious. If Alicia was missing, her placeholder was the very clue to her vanishing, the only lead he had at reach. He grabbed it. Did he sense a trap? No imagination required. Cards were turned up. He'd take whatever risk was implied. For the love of Alicia? Maybe of something she carried, she knew.

The sun shone on my face, too much and too bright. We had landed quite far from the gates… No terminal was even in view, but we had disembarked. Now we waited at the foot of the metal stairs, lightly clothed, unburdened by luggage, looking lost.

Yesterday (was it?) we had been directly poured through the crowd of the arrivals hall. Today the situation was odder, I mean, being singled out. For a second I feared something would happen. A bomb would explode. Someone from behind, from the airplane, would shoot us. But no. Some of us were ushered in a range-rover. Other vehicles drove up from various directions, lifting dust. Again, everything went fast.

They came towards me, unhesitant yet unexpressive, without making eye contact. The old woman hugged me stiffly, her bones pocking mine, a strange, stilted, unnatural welcome. The man was much younger. He drove. They had arrived in a battered pick-up truck. I thought he might be a neighbor providing a lift, then I changed my mind. He must be my something. But he hadn't greeted me at all.

The landscape was ocher and barren. All signs were in Spanish, which I luckily spoke. I imagined my two somehow-relatives also did. They hadn't yet, not a single word. Each of us seemed to concentrate on the road, as if it only counted.

The flat was on the second floor, above a gas station. The room had a single bed. A poster covered a wall, the huge black and white picture of a nineteen seventies star. Judging by the fading and tears, it must have been there for decades.

My mom (yes, I was sure) and the man hadn't commented about my lack of baggage. Neither had Xavier, but he already knew I wasn't I, I mean Alicia, and something was wrong. Had they guessed? They must. Did my mother… High cheekbones, sunken eyes. Who was this woman? None of my business.

Here, another thin mattress. Flimsy blanket. Déjà-

vu. This time I would not… Rage started simmering in my
guts, immediately smothered. It required energy I didn't have,
couldn't summon. Hadn't I felt some gumption, a spark of
resilience on the plane, when a loved memory had sneaked up
on me? Correct, and that ember was alive. Only, I had no use
for it now.

Another thin mattress, all right. I lay down and looked
at the ceiling, with its landscape of stains. I should read them as
if they were grounds of coffee, or a Rorschach test. Sometimes
truth is nowhere and right in your face.

Did I think those thoughts? I started, tried to, then
I melted into a sort of dream, tinted purple. Yes, the color
was what I remembered on waking. It throbbed, all-pervasive,
soaking me like cheap bubble soap. Nice, a cloud I could wrap
myself in, a shield, a protection.

Purple was under my lids when the knocks awoke
me. How long had I been out? The light in the room seemed
unchanged, not too bright, though no curtain was there. The
exposure must have been northwest. Was it morning? Why did I
assume so? My cell…

Did someone have a cellphone? My thoughts kept self-
thinking for no reason, just to pass the time. But I must get up.
The knocks… A sink was in a corner. I should wash my face.
Where was the mirror? Oh my. Definitely, a common thread.

As I turned on the faucet, water splashed all over
the place. Why had I expected a trickle? First I jumped back,
surprised by the impromptu shower, then I greedily reached
forward and drank. After gulping a few mouthfuls in haste,
I let the flow brush my lips, like a finger. A great weakness
invaded me, as it seemed to intermittently occur since it all had

started… waves of paralysis drowning me. When I finally lifted my head, I was drenched. I shut the faucet, and I recalled the note.

My dress glued to my torso, I was shivering. A chest drawer, pushed against a wall, contained a few things, neatly arranged. T-shirts at the top, trousers, sweatshirts, all light colored, tan or beige. The size… they would fit approximately. But then they would fit many. Should I…

I remembered the knocks. I smelled cooking. I heard clinks of kitchenware right across the corridor. The door in front of mine was ajar. I peeked in and saw a table, covered pot in the middle, Mother sat in a slumped pose, empty chair beside her, Brother nervously crumbling bread… Brother?

Neither had said a word, during or after our drive. I realized I didn't yet know my name. Frankly, I didn't care. Did I look like her? Really. How could they be so dumb? Suddenly, I wanted to stare at them in the eyes, long and steady, but I looked at the pot instead. Mother caught my gaze. As if she had been waiting, she ladled a bunch of veggies into my dish. Green beans, a heap, a small pyramid.

She served Bro, then herself. They started eating gingerly, slowly. Was there something wrong? Mother put down the fork. Her hands, bony and wide, rested to the sides of her bowl, a pair of dead birds. She stared at me boldly. I waited for a catastrophe, or deliverance. Both. I waited, yes, for a conclusion of sorts. Actually I *couldn't* wait. "Porque te lo cortaste?" she finally, painfully spat, as if every word hurt her palate. "Y cuando?" Bro whispered, munching on.

The room served as dinner and living. A few trinkets showed off on the shelves of a dark cupboard. A small sofa, an

armchair, a coffee table crowded the same corner. Stuff was on
the coffee table as well, photo frames of dark metal. Oxidized
silver, pewter. Leaving my beans untouched, I reached for the
armchair and I collapsed on it. Again, that exhaustion, like ten
minutes ago. I cradled in, then peeked at the pictures. I knew
what I would find. There, a bunch of strangers in pose, all in
black and white. And myself. Yes, we looked identical. My head
buzzed with a sense of unreality, the same wish for vanishing I
had felt sitting at the gate.

Her hair was much longer, let loose. An imposing
mass of dark curls rippled down her shoulders, cut by the
silver frame. Did they reach the small of her back? Mine
didn't. Mesmerized, I kept watching until a detail struck me...
the embroidery on her dress, where the shoulder strap joined
the neckline. As I stared and stared, it clicked in. She was
wearing the same thing I had on. Grayish, of course, in the
reproduction... the orange sundress. I still didn't know my
name.

Three dolls occupied one of the cupboard shelves,
leaned against the back panel. Casually bunched up, one newer,
one older, one pretty worn out. Heads were painted papier-
mâché, oddly perched on limbs of stuffed fabric dressed
in colorful rags, almost coming apart. The toys caught my
attention. They resembled me, a thrice-repeated caricature.
Not quite daring to pick them up, I went to brush my finger
over their legs, sticking out of the shelf. They were filled with
something else than cotton, finer, more compact. Sawdust.
Sand.

Bro was hastily shaking my shoulder, his hand clamping
my bones. I had a hard time coordinating myself, past and

present. My sleep must have been thick, with no dreams, or
the brisk awakening erased them. Nothing lingered, not even
a color, a mood. As I understood the wind shaking me was a
man's arm, once more it was déjà-vu. Xavier's name came to my
lips but didn't go further. In the meantime I made out the room,
unlit as it was. I had dozed off on the armchair.

"Hola chica, levantate." Sure. "Y vestite." I was dressed
already. Did he mean I should change? I recalled the plain
t-shirts, pants, sweatshirts, suited for whatever travel or flight
was beginning. Wearing those would take a couple of minutes.

I came out of the room empty-handed. Without
luggage, should I have packed... Bro didn't seem to notice. At
the door (I was sheepishly following him) he gave me a brisk
look. "Las muñecas!"

I grabbed them.

The road wound through the countryside. No village,
not even sparse houses or farms were in view. Gradually, the
landscape got greener, cooler, more forested. I must have slept
enough, because I was rested. As I cracked the window open,
scents of unknown vegetation peered in, almost comforting...
as if, paradoxically, no man's land had become the new familiar.
So soon?

The dolls sat between my thighs. I looked at their
painted heads, ugly. Why were we carrying them? Suddenly, I
feared we might be visiting relatives. I mean reuniting. I mean
our... Why had I made him into my brother? How if we were
together? Nonsense. No sign of affection had been... but
then things weren't normal, whatever it meant. Maybe we were
together. After a stop at Mom's we were journeying home, to
rejoin our...

Daughters? The idea was unsettling. I didn't look
forward to exploring it. On the contrary, the mere thought of it
choked me. Also, if he was my husband I wouldn't… this time I
should not… I was ogling the dolls without really looking, as if
they could read my mind, as if they could rat on me. The road
made a sharp turn, or maybe the truck did. Of course beltless, I
lost my balance. Instinctively, I grabbed the toys as if they were
infants, clamped their dead bodies tight, my nails digging into
them. When I released my grip, I understood.

We stopped near a thick grove. Was it the outer edge
of a forest? I heard sounds… nocturnal birds, insects, and they
soothed me like music. I realized that my companion, unlike me,
hadn't napped in the daytime. First, he laid down a blanket in
the back of the truck, then himself on it. He made no inviting
gesture, which was good and bad. What should I do? Stay
seated? Get out, breathe the night air? Walk away while he slept?
If yes, where to? I took a tiny stroll, uncertain and listless, then
I felt overwhelmed not sure by what. Later, I found myself lying
beside him, not sure how I got there.

When dawn broke, we resumed the road. I had a sense
of where we were aimed… I foresaw a border. Not too soon.
After dusk, tonight or tomorrow. Meanwhile, I was starving.
The word "hambre" spontaneously formed itself,
round, clear, confident, then it died in my throat. The long
route, so quiet, the afternoon naps, the night rest… all of it had
piled up, building a veneer of composure and a kind of lucidity,
both impassive and feverish. Therefore, while the impulse
traveled from my brain to my mouth (in that fraction of time)
I realized I hadn't spoken so far. Easy enough, considering the

surrounding muteness. All my mother had uttered was, "porque te lo cortaste." As for him, "y cuando," "levantate, chica," "vestite," "las muñecas." All the rest had been a silent movie, fancy accelerations included.

Would my voice give me away? How could it not?

Xavier? I had said a few things. Hushed, murmured. But Xavier knew since the beginning. Hadn't I concluded so?

The long drive, I said (which should have horrified me, as it led me further away) was grounding me instead. I subconsciously trusted (I know it sounds crazy) it would bring me to a place where I could perhaps get oriented, find help, make a call… Hope? Why did I? My brain, having squeezed its entire capacity of anguish, poured endorphins into my blood for lack of other juices. Oh, survival.

As the sun got higher in the sky, the air scorching, the landscape turned desert again, a desolate mesa. No signs had been in view for several hours. The gas station popped out of the blue, a two-story building so similar to the one we had left, I thought we had gone full circle. In the outside restrooms an antediluvian mirror, so scratched it was foggy, topped the sink. My face almost disturbed me, just the same, unchanged… Of course. Yet. Even my hair, identical, neither tousled nor misshaped… My hair, so well disciplined.

Why did the vision that should have reassured me make me cringe? She (my face?) felt like an unwanted witness, someone who knew too much. Someone to whom I should respond if she asked. Someone I had to carry, and she was burdensome. My face filled me with shame.

My mate brought back two sandwiches. One for me,

bread, lettuce and fish. He ate and drove. Eyes glued to the road, my mind started speeding up. It went faster and faster, but kept turning around.

Had they shadowed me and X from the airport to the plaza, to the house, to the train? Would I have noticed? No. Proper trailing through towns isn't difficult. Had they followed us to the gas station, this time around? Very unlikely. Since we had rushed away, we had crossed wilderness. Positive. No one could be tracking us. I was there for a reason, though, but unless I had a chip… I didn't. Could I have been… The X-ray rooms? I believed the ritual was meant to get me out of my clothes, into a new disguise. Could the X-ray machine have made an implant? Too complex. Could the new/old garments contain… But I wasn't wearing them. I had tossed the orange sundress on top of the drawer chest. It was miles and miles away.

Nothing made sense entirely. Only bits and pieces did, as it occurs in nightmares.

I guessed where we were directed. We would pass a border, no matter from which country to which, carrying the impressive load stuffed inside the muñecas. They would stop us. They were waiting for us. That is what I had become, a mousetrap, a snare. They would grab the dolls, rip them with an x-acto knife. All the snow I had pictured under the lining of the accordion cases would spill out of those ridiculous limbs. They wouldn't arrest me, but him. I mean, they would arrest me, carry me to the next station of this mad globetrotting.

Everyone, I have read, has a doppelganger. Rather a few. How many did I have? Once the stock was exhausted, would they restore me to my former life? I would be a hazard,

Drift

of course. How could I not sq… I wouldn't, I'd swear. Never, ever, for Christ's sake. They must know. They must have done studies. They would count on their (how should I call my like? suckers?) to be harmless. Paralyzed. Mute. Brain-dead. Memory-impaired. Sealed. Zombie-like. I would be a leakless tank. They must have done studies.

The beach… I had not seen it come. For some reason I thought we were directed inland. I had closed my eyes without sleeping, my thoughts tangling in endless loops. I hadn't noticed a change in the air, a faint marine breeze.

The beach (a narrow strip) ran parallel to the road, at the foot of a vertiginous cliff. The ocean (which one?) was gray and indistinct. Seeing it thrilled me in a most irrational way. I had the impulse to open the truck door, jump into the water. As if it were possible from so high. Also, as if I could get somewhere by swimming.

Where was I, besides as far as hell? Hours and hours of flight away from home, no idea in which direction. They had managed to shake me up, disorient me like before hide-and-seek. Still, the sea looked amicable.

It was dusk, and we had made it to no border. I had suspected it would be a long way. We would have to stop for gas sooner or later. But we abruptly left the main road and borrowed a dirt path, tumbling downhill toward the shore.

There were lights, a few shacks, and the sound of music. People. Normal. When had I last… The group of Xavier's friends came to mind, those with whom we had lingered at the bar, then walked while I pushed the bike. Normal people, were they? Not sure. I was so stunned, so shocked

I wouldn't have known. It had happened in a daze, or so I remembered it. Then the line in the courtyard, for the janitor's job… had I dreamed about it? Weren't those folks too quiet? In my present flashback they looked unreal. And the passengers of my last flights for sure weren't normal. I have described them a bit. Like me, they were trapped. Into unreality, I mean. Those folks… why hadn't we exchanged a glance? How was it possible?

Here, now, people were dancing. A few couples did. Others drank, sitting at the tables of what looked like a very small tavern, on the beach.

They danced to radio songs. A few square feet of floor were squeezed between rows of tables and a narrow platform (perhaps two feet large, six feet long). Over such a risible stage were two chairs, a dark jacket tossed across one of them while the other was empty, and the seat shone. At least, a glossy shimmer caught my eye, as if the wood were wet, freshly varnished. Don't know why it felt vaguely obscene. To the left, leaning against the chair, an accordion. My breathing went shallow. Maybe it was the stuffiness of the air, the damp, crowded room. I looked for the instrument case, which was nowhere in view. The accordion itself looked ominous, his keys grinning like teeth. Then it suddenly seemed forlorn, naked, a mollusk without carapace, a snail without shell. *I* felt forlorn, naked, abandoned. My eyes riveted to the scrawny stage, I walked like an automaton, as my brother (was he?) pushed me past it, through a side door, perhaps to the bathroom.

I found myself in a miniature storage area, stinky with the mixed smell of food, cleaning products, and rot. A ledge stuck out of a wall, under which a stool was ensconced. A mirror was above, cracked and stained. Fairly large, though randomly obstructed by pictures. Real ones? And magazine cuttings. Perhaps. I am reconstructing. At that moment my impression was quick, vague and sharp at the same time. More than all, nightmarish. A detail grabbed my attention, freezing me on the spot. It kept happening, did it? A sussultorial motion of consciousness, as if treading in the mud, then suddenly getting pricked by a thorn, stubbing a toe against a rock, an emerging root. Yes, the trivia catching my eye sent all of my sirens spinning, lighting them bloody red.

She sure was no beauty, and her diva poses, with or without squeezebox, were shy. Frankly, kind of pathetic. So was the gauche handwriting smudged over the pics, all signed to the same person, the joint's owner, I guessed. She was wearing the dress I… over and over, yes, thin shoulder straps, deep cleavage. Here a necklace, there a silk rose. Her hair was damn long. In one of the pics she stood on a terrace, leaned against a rail, sporting a swimsuit. Quite a small bikini and I saw the stubs, a straight line from her navel to her pubic bone, where the briefs perpendicularly cut them. They gleamed. Ominously. Two things landed on me that didn't go together. That's why I was paralyzed. First, the awareness of our identity struck me in the face. There I was, inside *and* over the mirror… No doubt about what was expected of me in a few minutes. Simultaneously, my not being her was forever proved, should I have entertained uncertainty, as the skin between my belly button and my Mons of Venus was clear, unbroken, intact.

He had left me in the greenroom without comments (none were needed, the routine must be obvious). He had dumped a rucksack of his, I assumed, in a corner of the ledge, which was crowded with miscellaneous trash. The bag was half open, letting a dash of orange in view... my crumpled sundress. God. The thing had come along, then. I shivered. A comb was beneath it. And a tiny, sad beauty case. Why did I take it out? Why did I unzip it?

I was no musician. Let's sit for a minute. I pulled out the stool from under the ledge. It offered little comfort. I sat anyway, propped my elbows, my head rested in my hands. Drama queenish, but I couldn't see myself at the moment. I was at the end of my wits, that's all. Nothing crucial. I have said it before. The nightmare could only go on, not worsen, not really. Still, I was at the end of my wits. What should I do, where could I...

Mindlessly, I passed my fingers through my hair. It felt less pristine, though it still looked ok in the mirror. Short, of course, if compared to the mane of Alicia-the-entertainer, the star. Now I could understand my mother's bitterness, my brother's (lover, manager?) discontent.

I needed the restroom. I stepped through the main room, gathering a few quick glances, askew. Brother was at the bar, working on a beer. I deliberately slowed down, trying not to look afraid or uncomfortable. A bead curtain led into the kitchen. Wait. The baño must be certainly outside.

A lantern at the front door, a dim neon sign didn't quite break the darkness. There's something about a beach at night, though. It casts its own light. I made out the silhouette of a shed that must be the toilets, headed there, got in, fumbled with the wobbling hook meant to lock it. A large vent in the roof let a glare in, the stars, the moon maybe? The walls must have

Drift

been recently white-washed. They looked eerily luminous. I kept
staring at them while I sat. My urine wouldn't come out. Was I
even trying?

As I had pulled my pants down, I had felt something at
the bottom of a pocket. How come I hadn't noticed it before?
Well, those tough khaki trousers had a bunch of zippers, all
over the legs, in the strangest places. I hadn't opened them. I
hadn't paid attention. In a low pocket, hanging dumbly at mid-
thigh, something lingered. A small pocket knife, and I clicked it
open. From what I could discern it was fairly new, razor sharp.

Then I am not quite sure. I knew where I came to
and it was several places, all blurred now. In the toilets, stool
towering over my face, walls squeezing me tight. At the front
door, or was it the kitchen curtain? Had to be, because beads
kept swinging. They made noise, a rattle, like rain, making
me sick again. Did I vomit? Wait, I came to once more. I
was in the greenroom. I recall the orange dress, a corner of
it hanging close to my mouth. Someone lifted my head from
behind, pushed something against my lip. A plastic cup. Water.
I recall a horrible strain in my neck, and me trying to press
down against whatever lifted it. How I wanted for my head to
fall back, away from my torso. Leave my head alone, please.
I remember a distant throb (my palm?). I think I remember
blood. Faces, known/unknown. Unknown. Was my brother
there? Afterwards, I thought he might have been taken already.
The next time I came to, I was in the van.

"How is your father?" he asked. He had stared at
me in silence, various feelings compressed in his gaze. I had
not expected him. My eyes shifted immediately to his side.

My child's name escaped me, and my voice seemed too loud.
I hushed myself, I, I meant not… I think he understood. "A
play date. He'll be home when we will arrive." His tone and
expression had softened. He leaned forward with an indecisive
smile, kissed my cheek. "You look ghastly." I grasped his
arm and squeezed it, trying to convey something. Affection?
Presence, making up for my exasperating laconism. I am not
sure if he saw the bandage. Didn't ask about suitcases.

My father? I hung by that shred of information, the
end of a ball of yarn I should… unravel? Rather follow through
the labyrinth. I hadn't answered his question. I couldn't. Could
hide underneath it, using it as an umbrella while I tried to fill
the holes. Obviously, he had been informed of my arrival,
given an excuse (concerning my relatives) to explain the delay.
He had seldom met my folks, didn't have a number for them,
didn't speak their language. He would have found a way to reach
them, of course, if he had been too worried. They must have
contacted him in a timely manner. *Who* did? I mean, *who* did
they say they were?

A delay. A short one. Was it? Two days, three? Today
was… Oh, god. How was my father? What had they said? "Not
bad," I muttered, which could mean lots of things. That I was
worried indeed, or in shock. That I'd rather not talk (and I'd
rather not). That I was exhausted (I was).

Dear lord, how screwed was this? I couldn't tell the
truth. Now my own life didn't fit me. It had been poked. It
leaked. It was pierced in the middle, torn by those missing days,
badly stitched over with lies.

In the car I didn't say a word. I shrank myself in a fist,
waiting to see my child, soon, please, sooner. Then I'd land.
Then, little by little, I guessed things would fall into place. I'd

                                        Drift

know how to deal with what had happened, patch and fix.
Would I? I would find counsel if needed, private, confidential.
Just let me get home.

True. Not only my child mattered. Home did too.

My passport came back two months later. I had
reported the (theft, loss?) and a brand new document was on its
way. I had no presentiment as I picked up the envelope, only a
slight curiosity, a puzzlement slowing me down. I lingered, not
quite daring to open it. I had no idea who could have sent it. My
address was handwritten in a nondescript calligraphy, ringing
no bell. A return address was missing, which should have halted
delivery, but apparently hadn't. The print on the stamp was
readable… the thing had been mailed from the local airport,
thirty miles away. A post office was there. Mailboxes as well,
where one could drop an already stamped missive. Red. The
boxes. I visualized one of them shining in the sharp, rarefied
light.

I didn't want to think of it but I did, wildly,
compulsively. I pictured myself sitting on a bench, witnessing
the moment. Calmly observing whoever lifted his hand (hers?
Was it one of the nurses?) and then dropped her load into the
slant. Just my passport was inside the envelope. I was about
to receive the replacement… I would keep both. Should I
say I had recouped the lost one? By instinct, I sensed such a
statement would complicate things. Or not, but I was scared.
Also fascinated. Obsessed. Thinking of the instant when my
papers were mailed made me ache for stopping it. Stop the
instant, freeze time. I must find the person who did it, I felt, as
if my life depended…

It occurred to me, whoever sent the thing back might

have been extraneous. To the whole deal, just a passerby who accidentally found my ID under a seat. Inconceivable… Wouldn't they have either destroyed or recycled it, certainly not… Of course. But things hadn't been logical lately.

Then I wondered about how those studs felt. The two sets, I mean. If they indented like the halves of a zipper. If they touched at all, when… Must have. Did they mean anything? Who had them punched in first? He had a scar. She didn't, from what I could tell. I had just glanced at her picture.

So that's why he had cooled off, that night. Not because he didn't care for Alicia. The hell he did. Because *I* was un-studded. But hadn't he guessed me out since the airport? My fakeness… Maybe he was still in doubt until… or he wouldn't have started. Why didn't he stop?

His distraction, his tepidness, didn't regard Alicia.

But why, why would someone else's ardor, or lack thereof, affect me?

2.

As I park, I'm comforted by the sight of a car pulling to the curb, right behind me, just when I'm shutting the engine down.

I must walk a block to my destination. Not far, but the street is dark and the night chilly. It has rained until an hour ago. It probably won't again. Still, the damp makes me shiver. Most irrationally, I feel as if the car parked next to mine will shorten the distance I will have to walk back. Of course, it will not. It will make it look shorter, perhaps, as I'll come uphill, and I'll see it a second or two before spotting mine. Will that soothe my anxiety (a mild symptom of Post Traumatic Stress Disorder)?

In fact, the last thing I should look for while parking at night in an unfamiliar neighborhood, most deserted, unlit, is someone parking unnecessarily close. My reflexes are kind of screwed-up, since, kind of the-other-way-around.

Those thoughts cross my mind while I get myself organized. As I lock my door, turn around and take the first step, the case almost trips me. It stands on the concrete beside my back door, partially blocking the sidewalk. Shadowed by the semi-obscurity, yet familiar. Of course, I recognize it. My brain spins a wild carrousel. I try to line up memories stubbornly refusing to segue. And I try to do it fast, but velocity only adds to the incongruity. What's my accordion case doing here? Who pulled it out of my back seat? Did I? When? I didn't. Wait! Was it on my back seat at all? It wasn't. Instinct makes me look up, frantically scanning the car that just parked, sensing the solution *must* be there.

The driver's door is cracked open, and the window rolled down. The man sticks out his elbow, then his hand. He is smoking a cigarette. A long face. Do I know him? He is looking at me, seemingly enjoying my confusion, as if he had expected it indeed. He points at the case with his fag. "Yesterday you forgot it," he says. At the joint where I played, he means. Was he there? Did he rescue it for me? Sure, but how did he…

"It was in the hall, by the door. You must have left in a hurry. When I made it to the parking lot…" I have stopped listening. Yes, I do forget things especially when, like after a gig, I am swamped. I forget more and more. It is also a mild symptom of… Christ, not my accordion. And how could I, once home… Was I drunk? I don't think so. How bad…

"Thank you. Thank you!" And how did he find me, I should ask, but I don't feel like it. I know he's headed to the joint where I'm headed. He'll be listening to the band I'm going to listen to. It's a small world. Maybe he thought I would come. Someone, yesterday, told him that's where I'd likely be. He had the thing in his car, he parks and he sees me. Ours is a small world.

As I pick up the case… here's the pain in my side, the cramp I know well. On the right side, don't worry. A bother, that's all. Is the thing too darn heavy? Too light. I click it open, and it is half full of crumpled papers. I have slid onto my knees without noticing. Now I'm bent in front of the case, as if lost in prayer. Doom has grabbed my neck and I feel oppressed. Where's my instrument, and what it this stuff? Balled-up dailies, some more yellowed than others, old, with black and white pictures. Who stuffed this crap in, what's this practical joke?

His voice gets to me, soft and velvety. "Something wrong?" "My accordion…" I mutter. "Not there?" Perspicacious, is he? He walks out of the car. I register a tall dark shape. He is wearing an evening suit, old style… Well, it doesn't matter. As he bends towards me, though, I can't help watching. Yes, something about him is…

"I'm sorry." But he knew, right? Didn't he lift the case? "Do not worry. You forgot to put it back in. It's at the joint, for sure. Do you think they wouldn't keep it?" Well, of course. I have to go back and get it. Now. Give them a call? Just go.

"By the way, yesterday you played divinely, Alicia." He is smiling. He looks ecstatic, in fact. Have I heard this before? "You played divinely, Alicia." I know. I know.

E_{xit}

-2 (Title)

You have it wrong. It was "Edit," I am sure.
It has changed.
Why? The idea was to go back and fix things, was it?
Correct whatever went wrong, redress the crooked narratives.
The first thought isn't always the best. That one crossed
your mind early in the morning, in a moment of unconsidered
optimism. And it was pretentious, of course. Truly, you have
got no chance to redress a comma, and you don't care. You are
looking for a way out. That is all.

-1 (The Road)

Afterwards, she can't remember where she was
directed. Not a clue. It happens. Traumatic amnesia is a classic.
She perfectly recalls how she felt, yes, the determination, the
confidence. The velocity (not reckless, always in control, always
mastered). She was going because she had and she wanted to.
Only, where has become impossible to dig out.
Would a calendar, a schedule book solve the issue? If
she doesn't recall, she might be capable of reconstructing. What

was the day's plan? That's the point. She had no written plans for that Sunday. It was a blessed truce, duty-free, so to speak. She could follow her whim, whatever… What was that she impromptu embraced with such impetus?

Sunday morning, and the freeway was clear. One of those magic moments when no friction is there, nothing stands between your goal and your intention. Both, though (goal and intention) have vanished from her mind.

Why would they matter? Why are we even pretending to care? What could her objective have been? These are details, trivia. Not what we are here to ponder, for sure.

Then, with uncanny briskness, she knew she had to get back. Circumstances imposed it with crystalline evidence. You mean, out of the blue? She was driving, alone on an empty freeway. What happened? A phone call? Did she hear something on the radio? Again, she doesn't know. She suggests no external input caused her decision. Circumstances irreversibly shifted, she believes, due to her thoughts, unleashed by the linearity of the ride. Velocity does it.

Her thoughts must have wandered, as usual, until they found a garden path and acquired momentum, finally coalescing into an epiphany of sorts. Revelation. Nothing strange with it, besides perhaps the mandatoriness of the action implied. No delay was possible.

She saw a ramp on the right, she later said. Out of nowhere, as if her brain itself had designed it, magically fulfilling her wish. No sign. Weird… Well, not really. The sign must have been there seconds earlier and she had not paid attention, as by then she had no need to modify her route. Where did the ramp lead? Should she borrow it without the slightest notion? It cut at a right angle, almost, and she was driving fast, bit too much for such a sharp turn.

At a glance, she saw a ribbon of cars running parallel, going the opposite way. So the ramp must draw a loop, allowing a U turn. Quite a large one, because the oncoming vehicles appeared distant and small, though clearly discernible. That was how she could reverse directions, for sure. She started giving the wheel a good yank.

She froze in midgesture. No ramp was there. A break in the guardrail, then nothing. How… Like I'm saying, a chasm, a steep precipice. A sheer void, no roadside… Was she upon a bridge? Look, a road ran parallel to the one she was about to leave. And she spotted a flow of tiny cars, though they seemed far, on another plane. Other planet? On another level, she meant. Lower.

Hundreds of feet below. How could she have not… Was there something wrong with her eyes? True, the light… the sky had turned dark. Gray, like on a Good Friday. Like before a storm, clouds blocking the sun. Was her sight the problem? Had she lost her perception of depth? She felt a kind of vertigo, yielding, failure of sorts. In her chest. Her heart seemed to slip down. Her hands squeezed the wheel as if it were the branch of a tree, hanging above a ravine.

Correct. She had stopped barely on time, car crooked, on a diagonal. Luckily, no one was behind her. Clear road. Empty Sunday. All of this she neatly recalls, and the aftermath. How the fear left as rapidly as it had come upon her. How calmly, how meticulously she redressed the car, backing it the tiniest of bits. How she squeezed it as close as possible to the guardrail, occupying a slight widening of the lane, a turnout-but-not-quite… an anomaly, a niche, the ambiguous feature she

had taken for an off-ramp, a fork, an entrance to…
    An exit, you mean.
    A way in, leading to…
    A way out.

    None of that was true, they explained over and over.
What wasn't? Yes, she parked on the side thanks to a slight
enlargement of the lane, an anomaly. Yes, she cut the engine,
then reclined her seat and leaned back, staring at the darkening
sky through the clear roof. No sun bothered her, she recalls.
The sight was very calming, and she fell asleep in a state of
profound serenity, knowing she only needed to wait. They
would rescue her. Asleep is how the Highway Patrol found her.
    What wasn't true, they affirmed, is that she saw,
imagined, hallucinated a ramp. Even less a cut in the guardrail,
which was obviously intact. A false memory she forged a
posteriori, sewn up by her brain to bridge over the hole. Not
the rip in the fence, no. That's not what they intended. No.
The hole in her consciousness. She has been sick, that's all. Her
heart? Or a microscopic seizure. They will find out.
    She is sure, though, of the distinctive feeling getting
hold of her as she drove, hindering her momentum, diverting
her course. Yes, she bears the mark of that fulguration.
Circumstances had shifted, bringing clarity to her mind, hence
she needed to retrace her steps, come back no matter how. And
that other, later commandment, equally undisputed, pristine in
its pithiness, that she should quietly wait for someone to rescue
her, bring her home.

    0 (Them)

Mom and Dad? What happened to them?

Please, don't call them that way. They wouldn't allow it. Have allowed it. They are no more around.

Retired?

Sort of.

Gone on a vacation?

Rather a conference.

Everlasting?

Repetitive. Kind of serial. Their stays home between commitments became shorter over time. They preferred to go from location to location, sending the occasional postcard. And the kids had grown up, indeed.

Weren't they in their forties the last time we…

Don't know. Sort of ageless. And they never celebrated birthdays.

Not much of a traditional family.

It depends. Quite conventional under certain accounts. Anyway, rumors say…

Rumors are ridiculous, especially local ones.

But they spread. They become legends. Rumors say the old folks truly went nowhere, just kept to their rooms. His and hers, separated. They were complete suites with bathroom, studio, boudoir, private balcony. Mini apartments. Fair-sized.

Did they take their meals in their quarters?

Rigorously. And they received visitors. They made no more public appearances until…

Their fate dives into mythology, does it?

Yes, it's murky at best. They are told to have concertedly committed suicide, been cremated afterwards, their cinders dispersed from a plane. Or they are told to have been hibernated. There are fancier stories, imbibed with religious overtones.

Ascension? Transfiguration?

Maybe less explicit.

Were they simply buried in the garden? If they were still alive, how old…

I don't know. To me they seemed immortal.

1 (Prometheus)

Our last talk was about meta-something. Meta-literature, I guess.

Why such an abstruseness?

It came up during the conversation. He asked some questions and then…

Were you on the phone?

We had this habit of calling every night.

What for? Summarize the day? What could he have to say? Not a lot to report…

Stop the sarcasm.

Meta-literature! What did he know about it?

Nothing. But the sound of it struck him, and maybe he got curious.

It sounded weird. Sounded like methamphetamine or meth crystals. Of course, it rang a bell. And, you know, the contents of our conversations didn't matter at all. I just liked to check if you were awake, how late you'd stay up waiting. I was playing a game. Seeing if the phone one night would keep ringing, no one picking it up. Then I would have known.

Did it happen? Did the phone ever ring in vain?

No. Therefore I never knew.

Was he found on the rock?

Sure. He never climbed down. The slope was too slippery, he used to say tongue in cheek. The stairs. Three hundred and sixty-five steps, too many, no doubt. You can do the thing once, but never again.

For how long did he live up there?

I've lost track.

Did you call the police?

I did when he didn't pick up the phone. It was lifted by helicopter.

It?

The corpse. It stank.

Who said that?

I do. When I went for identification it still stank like hell. It reminded me of the Oo.

What is it?

I had forgotten about it. When he was a child (small, he barely talked) he had a fascination with him. A beggar. Large and tall, and so covered with rags he looked like a mountain.

Like a rock?

Kind of. Scary, I guess. They called him "The Wolf."

So, that is what "Oo" meant.

Yes, but the vocalic sound is more beautiful. I hadn't thought about it since, but it comes to mind now. It looked just like the Oo when I saw it at the morgue.

Saw it?

The corpse. And it stank just like him.

2 (Antigone)

Sitting in the cemetery all night.

Pacing. She always brings a bottle of wine along.

Must be something stronger.

It is wine. You know, from her father's cellar. He had quite a collection. There are hundreds of gallons in there, good stuff.

You mean her uncle's cellar.

Formerly her dad's.

Does her uncle drink it?

Of course.

That must piss her off. Must be why she steals a bottle per night. Maybe more than one.

Then she knows how to hold it because at dawn, regularly, she walks all the way back to the palace.

On foot?

How do you think? Four miles. And a bit of a climb... Still cool, at that hour.

With nothing in her guts! Two bottles of wine...

We don't know. Perhaps one.

What does she do besides drinking?

I have no idea. I think she writes something.

Does she know how?

I'm guessing.

I learn how to read. This is called an abecedarium, and I love the pictures. They are fading. Not only is the thing old. It has been rained upon. It has both images and letters. One big character is associated with each drawing, one per page, huge, a kind of mighty building. It's not hard to guess that the pattern on the right is the first letter of whatever's shown on the left. Alpha stands for agora (is this a town square?), Pi for peplum. They are out of order, which makes it more fun.

As I wander around, tomb by tomb, a lamp dangling from my wrist, I decipher the inscriptions. It still takes me forever, but I will get faster. Do I want to? I have all the time in the world.

I spill wine over my brother's grave.

He does not have a grave. His body was left unburied. That is why I am here.

Listen up. Every night I steal a bottle of red from dad's (now uncle's) cellar and I come spill it over my brother's grave. Slowly. It looks like blood. I greedily brush it with my fingertips. Then I lick them. Always a different shade of bitterness. Always a different grave.

3 (Ariadne)

To die tangled.

Minotaur, our father. See him shrink. Remember the time when he forgot the keys of the gate.

Wait, officially he didn't. Nothing ever happened by his fault, and we sure understood, as it was a matter of dignity. He was angry because someone had made a mistake and we were at the gate and we, he was, locked out.

Of his own palace?

When an incident, when a mishap occurred, he did not leave the coach but kept seated, newspaper in hand, intermittently inhaling from a fat cigar, his brow knitted, his cheeks ever redder. He shouted orders intertwined with mumbled reproaches, increasingly frantic but comfortably cocooned in velvet and shade.

Locked out? I couldn't believe he dismounted, marched straight to the bars, grabbed two of them, to the left and right

of the poor irresponsive latch. He hooked those frigid poles
with ten chubby fingers. From the back, his dark suit set against
the majestic entrance of his glorious abode, he looked tiny yet
compact. Solid. Fiery.

And he shook, and he shook the bars, wordless yet
emitting a weird animal sound. A rumble. Someone would
have feared an imminent heart attack. Being young and naïve,
I didn't, not then. But I saw the pillar on the left side, there, in
front of me, quiver. A small crack, a very thin line, drew itself
below the pinnacled ball garnishing the top. Was I the only one
who noticed?

Now he is locked in, but he doesn't know. He is aware
of nothing. Believe me, that isn't the worst. The worst is his
fragility, his frame shrinking and shrinking. The worst is his
boniness, his sparrow-like brittleness. And the tubes plugged all
over. The bruises where the needles come in, getting wider.

Still, at times he has an uncanny gesture of revolt
or just plain impatience, so much like him. He occasionally
pulls things off, bandages and such, alas, with bits of himself
attached. But he doesn't react. I don't think he feels pain. If
he does, he cannot express it, except by the slightest wrinkling
of his once fierce forehead. No more than the grimace of
discomfort rippling the small face of a sleeping newborn.

Poor Dad. To die tangled.

As I am, because I can't leave his side. Don't want to.
Have nowhere to go. Should I try, I'd get irredeemably lost,
unable, I swear, to ever find the front door.

4 (Sisyphus)

I liked hiding in silence into recesses, dusty corners and

spots of the servant quarters where they'd never set foot. I liked carrying things in those temporary abodes, the pockets of my checkered smock filled with treasures.

Mostly fruit. Nuts, which I had no idea what to do with, as I never brought a nutcracker. My small paws were still unable to crush them one against another. Truly, I never developed that strength. I have remained a weakling into my adult age. Which doesn't go without advantages.

But this is off topic. My adult age, I mean. Now I am recalling those quiet stations in the shadow. I never turned the light on, secrecy being the gist of those wondrous moments. I was not scared of twilight or darkness, in spite of my reputation of cowardice. Based upon? Who knows? Local rumors.

Aren't they all local?

Some spread wider than others, but honestly I don't care. A presumption of fearfulness, again, can be convenient, as it saves you from many a responsibility. For example, I'd never end on a rock like my older brother, blatantly spat out of society, pointed at, marginalized. Does he think his fate brighter than mine?

Well, I know my remark is unfortunate. He doesn't think at all. First, his brain (quite brilliant, I admit) dissolved in smoke by his own doing. Then he passed away in solitude. I can't say I didn't have feelings for him, at least when I was young. Now I don't miss him.

I would never have ended like him or like my sis Antigone, the nutcase.

Speaking of which. Those wooden balls in my pockets. How I treasured, palmed them, how the solid feeling they delivered filled me... With?

I haven't figured it out.

Epilogue (The Room In The Attic)

was the room of the prodigal son.
Daughter?
Gender doesn't matter.
Androgynous?
It isn't the point. In the closet…
Wasn't it half empty?
Yes, and I can't tell you the sadness emanating from the
dark alcove, especially from the smell of old wood, swell with
dampness. A sort of sweet helplessness, lacerating, grabbing
them by their guts.
What are you trying to say?
Inside were a navy blue sweater and a pair of jeans
so very stiff they couldn't be straightened. They zigzagged,
accordion like. A pale pink dress, absurdly thin-waisted, hung
from a bar so high they had to crane their neck…
What? Are? You?
Something forlorn squeezed their throat as they
dared pulling the mirrored door, half-stuck, noisy. A kind of
suffocation, an engorgement of tears. More than all, guilt, as if
those they spotted (the dress, the pants and sweater) were not
clothes but
Spoils? Who lived there?
No one did. A guest room, I said. That is where the
prodigal children spent the night on their visits.
Rare?
No. They constantly alternated. From the garden I saw
shadows move behind the light curtains. I heard music. They
turned on the radio in the morning, while they packed their
suitcases, I guess.

They…

alternated in no particular order. But they never stayed more than one night. That's the rule of prodigality, of course… extreme brevity. They were totally welcome as long as they kept to the room, and did not overstay the night.

Did anyone try?

Why would they? They were anxious to resume the road. They had things to do of the most various, the most interesting kind. They were fully grown up. But they left a kind note on a pad, each time, dated and duly signed.

Always?

Sisyphus forgot once in a while. Ariadne never did.

The other two?

They signed, rapidly.

So that was the rule of prodigality? Day at a time?

Night. Breakfast wasn't included.

What else was in the room?

Not much. Wait. Three things, but so banal I am tempted to omit them.

Don't. I sense you shouldn't hold back.

Well, there is no secret. A picture hung from the wall. Strange thing, because all the other ones had been removed, leaving an intricate pattern of faded rectangles and squares. But this one was oval.

Subject?

Must have been a landscape. Dampness had eaten it up.

Nothing they could decipher?

Just stains, and the horizon line. Then there was a vase of thick glass, moonish, milkish, iridescent and empty. So chubby they wished they could eat it, especially since no breakfast was served. Then there was a book on the bed stand.

Old, and hand-bound as they don't exist anymore. Those who came with a string for marking the page. A thin ribbon so cheap, it invariably crumbled between their fingers. Either red, gold, or rust. And the absurdity of it, because why would they mark their page if they…

Couldn't they resume when they returned, few days later?

No, they couldn't resume. The books always changed.

One-night stands?

Yes. But please… not casually done. First of all, the titles were chosen with care. A criterion was behind the selection. A presence. Something… dear. Sort of. Obviously, the books were mere decoration as no lamp was provided. The room, truly…

Have you been there?

I haven't. I said those were the prodigal child's assigned quarters. From the gardens I could see the curtains were drawn, in the morning, as the guests changed in front of the smoky closet mirror. I heard music, each time, as they packed their luggage.

Acknowledgments

My gratitude goes to Katia Hage, founder of Elyssar Press, who has believed in these stories and facilitated every step of the journey towards publication; to Stephanie Bou Karam, who has designed the book with exquisite creativity, flexibility and patience; to Linda Johnson and Alex Frankel, who went over the whole manuscript, and gave generous feedback.

FIN